"I guess it's fortur <barcode> S0-AVP-795 d."
Following his lead, she opened the passenger door of the car, and nearly gagged on the stench of stale whiskey and cigars as she slid inside. Still, she forced herself to pull the door closed, shutting out the noise from the street musicians and revelers who'd flocked to New Orleans' French Quarter to celebrate Halloween.

"Fortunate is right, missy. I'm a busy man," he said. "I'll have you know I've got better things to do with my time than wait around for the likes of you."

"Then let's not waste any more of each other's time, Doctor. Did you bring the document?"

"'Course I brought it. But first I want to see the money."

She opened the black tote bag that was filled with $100,000 in cash. Opening it, she angled it so that the light from the street lamp fell on its contents. There was no mistaking the lust in the man's bloodshot eyes. When he reached for the bag, she snapped it closed. "Not so fast, Doctor. First I want the document."

"Sure. Sure." He fumbled inside his coat pocket, drew out an envelope and shoved it at her. "Here."

"You sure this is the only copy?"

"What? Yeah, it's the only one," he muttered, still distracted by all the cash.

She tucked the envelope inside her purse and reached for her gun. "Then I guess this is goodbye, Doctor," she said politely as she pulled the trigger.

METSY HINGLE

FLASH POINT

MIRA

ISBN 1-55166-714-2

FLASH POINT

Copyright © 2003 by Metsy Hingle.

All rights reserved. Except for use in any review, the reproduction or utilization of this work in whole or in part in any form by any electronic, mechanical or other means, now known or hereafter invented, including xerography, photocopying and recording, or in any information storage or retrieval system, is forbidden without the written permission of the publisher, MIRA Books, 225 Duncan Mill Road, Don Mills, Ontario, Canada M3B 3K9.

All characters in this book have no existence outside the imagination of the author and have no relation whatsoever to anyone bearing the same name or names. They are not even distantly inspired by any individual known or unknown to the author, and all incidents are pure invention.

MIRA and the Star Colophon are trademarks used under license and registered in Australia, New Zealand, Philippines, United States Patent and Trademark Office and in other countries.

Visit us at www.mirabooks.com

Printed in U.S.A.

For Valerie Gray, Editor and Friend
With thanks and affection for the guidance,
creative vision and unending support

ACKNOWLEDGMENTS

While I was creating this book, I spent countless hours alone with the characters of this story as I tried to bring them to life. But the finished product would not have been possible without the help of many people who assisted me both technically and emotionally. My heartfelt thanks go to the following people for their help in bringing life to *Flash Point:*

Dianne Moggy, editorial director of MIRA Books, for her trust and support.

Karen Solem, my agent, for her unending support and guidance, and for being my voice of reason.

The amazing MIRA staff, who continue to astound me with their support.

The MIRA art department, which is truly the best in the business.

The MIRA public relations team of Tania Charzewski, Sarah Rundle and Maureen Stead for their support.

The wonderful fans who allow me to entertain them with my books.

Diane Hingle Anding, my sister-in-law and friend, who makes me proud we are family.

Sandra Brown, my dear friend, for her friendship, love and support.

Carly Phillips, friend and fellow writer, for her friendship, support and e-mails.

Dixie Kane and Hailey North, dear friends and fellow writers, for their love and support.

A special thank-you goes to my children and family, whose love and support enable me to spin my tales of love, hope and happily-ever-after.

And, as always, to my husband, Jim, who is my love, my family and all things to me.

Dear Reader,

Thank you so much for picking up a copy of *Flash Point.* I'm both grateful and honored that you've chosen my book when there are so many wonderful books available. If this is the first time you've read my work I do hope it won't be the last. For those of you who are familiar with my books, you won't be surprised to find *Flash Point* is set in my hometown of New Orleans, a city and people that continue to inspire me and make me proud to call them my own. I hope you enjoy reading my latest tale of romance and suspense as much as I enjoyed writing it.

As always, one of the great joys for me as a writer is hearing from readers, and I'd love to hear from you. In fact, as a special thank-you, I've had a commemorative bookmark created just for *Flash Point* and, while supplies last, I'll send one to each reader who writes and requests one.

Happy holidays!

Metsy Hingle
P.O. Box 3224
Covington, LA 70433
U.S.A.

www.metsyhingle.com

Prologue

"It's about damn time you showed up. I've been waiting in this alley for twenty minutes and nearly got mugged twice."

"I was detained," she said coolly, giving no indication of how much she detested having to deal with the sorry creature.

"Well, you're damn lucky I waited," he informed her, his Mississippi drawl even thicker due to the liquor. "Another two minutes and I'd have been gone."

"Then I guess it's fortunate that I showed up when I did." Following his lead, she opened the passenger door of the car and nearly gagged on the stench of whiskey and stale cigars as she slid inside. Still, she forced herself to pull the car door closed, shutting out the noise from the street musicians and revelers who'd flocked to New Orleans' French Quarter to celebrate Halloween.

"Fortunate is right, missy. I'm a busy man," he said, puffing up his chest and straining the buttons on his dated suit coat. "I've got better things to do with my time than to wait around for the likes of you."

Better things like drowning in a bottle of whiskey or slithering into the nearest casino, she thought, even more repulsed by the man now than she'd been when he'd first sought her out six months ago. "Then let's not waste any more of each other's time, Doctor. Did you bring the document?''

''Of course I brought it. But first I want to see the money.''

She retrieved the black tote bag that she'd filled with $100,000 in cash. Opening it, she angled it so that the light from the streetlamp fell on its contents. There was no mistaking the lust in the man's bloodshot brown eyes as he gazed at the money. Like a drug addict about to get his next fix, she thought. But when he reached for the bag, she snapped it closed. ''Not so fast, Doctor. First, I want the birth certificate.''

He fumbled inside his coat pocket, drew out an envelope and hesitated. He narrowed his beady eyes. ''You know, your daddy sure loved that little girl. Used to call her his princess. I imagine he'd have paid a lot of money to find out she didn't die in that fire after all.''

''Unfortunately for you, my father's dead. And I can assure you I don't place the same value on her that he did. My one concern is protecting my family's good name. It's the only reason I agreed to pay you for that birth certificate.''

He tapped the envelope against his palm, gave her a measuring look. ''I imagine your sister would be willing to pay a great deal to learn who her daddy was. Of course, if you was to—''

''I don't have a sister,'' she snapped. Fury caused her vision to blur for a moment before she regained control of herself. More calmly she said, ''And I suggest you quit trying to shake me down for more money, Doctor. Otherwise, I might reconsider whether or not I've made a mistake by not going to the police and telling them about your offer.''

''Now, hang on a second,'' he said, alarm in his voice.

"There's no need to go dragging the police into a little business transaction between friends."

"You and I are not friends, Doctor. And I doubt that the police would see your proposal as a business transaction," she said, toying with him and enjoying the fact that she was making him nervous.

"We had a deal and it's too late for you to try to back out now," he countered, and shoved the envelope at her.

She took the envelope. And while he pounced on the bag of cash and began pawing through the stacks of bills, she withdrew the faded sheet of paper from the envelope. An icy-cold rage whipped through her as she stared at the form, read the names and examined the signatures. For a moment she was eight years old again and listening at the door as her father told her mother he was leaving them. She crushed the paper in her fist. Reaching deep down inside of herself, she channeled her anger, just as she had that night all those years ago, and focused on what had to be done. "You're sure this is the only copy?"

"What?" He glanced up briefly. "Yeah, it's the only one," he muttered and went back to counting the cash.

She tucked the envelope and crumpled paper inside her purse and reached for the gun. "Then I guess this is goodbye, Doctor," she said politely and calmly pulled the trigger.

One

"*No*," *Kelly Santos cried out as flames went up all around her. Bright orange tongues of fire licked at the curtains and raced greedily up the walls, devouring the rose-patterned paper. Terrified, Kelly turned in a circle, searching for a means of escape. But everywhere she looked there were more flames shooting up around her.*

Surrounding her.

Trapping her.

She struggled to see past the blaze and to find her way out of the inferno. But the fire was so hot, the smoke too thick. Her eyes stung from the heat. Tears streamed down her cheeks. As the smoke filled the room, she began to cough. Her lungs burned, felt as though they would burst in her chest at any moment.

Have to get out. Have to get out.

Scarcely able to breathe now, she tried waving the smoke away from her face so she could get her bearings. And then she saw the door. Her heart leapt in her chest—part relief, part panic—as she noted the burning beam that dangled overhead in the space between her and the door. Terrified that the beam would collapse on top of her, Kelly was afraid to move, yet afraid to stay still.

Suddenly an explosion ripped through another section of the house and, without thinking, she raced toward the door. The moment she reached it, she grabbed the doorknob.

She screamed as the hot metal scorched her fingers, burning her flesh. Sobbing, she fell to the floor, cradling her throbbing hand. As she lay there, the burning beam came crashing down to the floor and landed in the spot where she'd stood only seconds earlier. Kelly screamed again. Petrified and in pain, she crawled over to a corner of the room and pressed her body against the wall. ''Tell Nana where you are! Come to Nana,'' she heard a familiar voice call, first by the door, then by the window. Paralyzed with fear, she said nothing. And as the flames ravaged the room, filling it with smoke and depleting her oxygen, she started to choke.

Coughing violently, Kelly jerked awake. Still unable to breathe, she sat up in bed and continued to struggle for air for several moments longer. Pressing a hand to her chest, she dragged air into her lungs. It was just a bad dream, she told herself as she tried to shake off the vividness of being trapped in the fire, of being overcome by the smoke and the heat. With unsteady fingers, she brushed the hair away from her face, discovered her brow damp with perspiration.

''Just a dream,'' she murmured aloud. Not real. There were no flames, no stench of burning wood and fabric and smoke. There was no fire. Just a dream. Unwilling to delve into what might have triggered the old nightmare this time, Kelly closed her eyes and drew in one breath, then another. She followed the ritual she'd used since childhood to rid herself of the aftereffects of the nightmares and visions that had plagued her most of her life. Continuing to focus on her breathing, Kelly attempted to erase from her mind all traces of the dream by replacing the fire and smoke with the soothing images of blue skies, white sandy beaches and a rolling surf.

As her breathing steadied, she could almost hear the surf rushing to the shore, could smell the saltwater in the air, could feel the cool breeze on her cheek. Finally, Kelly opened her eyes. She blinked once, twice and a third time as she adjusted her eyes to the darkness of the room. Scanning her surroundings, she noted the drawn drapes, could make out the table with her camera equipment atop it, her suitcase just inside the door. A glance at the illuminated clock on the bedside table read a few minutes past ten. Morning or night? she wondered, and then she remembered.

New Orleans.

She was in New Orleans. Suddenly all the events of the past few days came rushing back. Returning from the month-long photo shoot in Europe to find a message on her answering machine from the Mother Superior, telling her that Sister Grace was dead. The message had been more than two weeks old.

Two weeks.

Sinking back against the pillows, Kelly closed her eyes again. Silent tears slid down her cheeks. They'd buried the only person in the world who had ever cared about her and she hadn't even managed to attend the funeral. Silently she cursed herself for the hundredth time for not checking her machine for messages. It didn't matter that the only persons who ever called her were Sister Grace on holidays and her agent who had known where she was. She still should have checked the thing. If she had...if she had, she might at least have made it back in time to see the nun one last time.

A new wave of grief washed over Kelly and she covered her face with her hands. Sobbing, she gave in to the pain and wept aloud. And as she sat in the dark hotel room and cried, she thought about the nun who had been the closest thing to a mother she'd ever known. The tiny nun in her navy-and-white habit had been the one person who had made growing up at St. Ann's Orphanage bearable.

Memories came tumbling back. Sister Grace wiping tears from her six-year-old cheeks when a potential adoptive family had returned her to the home, claiming she was the devil's spawn because of the visions. Sister Grace soothing her eight-year-old heart when she'd realized no one was ever going to want her to be their little girl. Sister Grace comforting her as an unhappy eleven-year-old when the other kids taunted her, whispering that she was a witch. And Sister Grace rescuing her as a lonely thirteen-year-old by giving her her very first camera. That camera had been a lifeline for her. It had opened a window to the world and eventually it had provided her with a means of escape.

And she had escaped, she'd escaped and had never once looked back. After all, with the exception of Sister Grace, New Orleans held no fond memories for her. She'd closed that door to her life more than ten years ago, allocating the unhappy memories of her early years to a sad chapter in her life. It was a chapter she'd never intended to open again. Just as she'd never intended to return to New Orleans again.

Yet she had returned. Only, she'd come back too late, Kelly thought, crying harder. Too late to thank Sister Grace for believing in her all those years, for caring about her when no one else did. Too late to tell Sister Grace how much she'd meant to her, how much she'd loved her.

Startled by the sudden squeal of a police siren, Kelly

looked up. Still sniffling, she wiped her eyes with the sleeve of her pajamas and then climbed out of the bed. She walked over to the window, pushed aside the drapes and looked down at the street below. Traffic had come to a halt and had shifted over to the far right lane. As she watched, two police cars with flashing lights came speeding past the hotel and continued toward the Mississippi River.

Once the police units had gone, traffic started to flow again. She noted that, despite the lateness of the hour, people were out in force. Cars hurried from one red light to the next and pedestrians, mostly in pairs or groups, waited on both sides of the street for the arrows to signal it was safe for them to cross. No doubt tourists or convention-goers, she reasoned, since few residents ever paid heed to the signal lights.

A blur of movement at the far corner of the street caught Kelly's eye. A man, sporting a black cowl with horns and waving a devil's red-tipped pitchfork in his hand, raced up to the crosswalk. Several similarly clad people rushed up behind him. She'd almost forgotten that it was Halloween. The devil led a group of what she suspected were college kids across the busy Canal Street intersection. Evidently they were planning a big night of partying in the French Quarter. Although at twenty-eight she wasn't a great deal older than the college crowd, the idea of partying held little appeal for her. Turning away from the window, she stared over at the rumpled bed and debated whether or not to go back to sleep.

She was still jet-lagged, since she'd barely returned to New York before she'd hopped a plane for New Orleans. And the crying hadn't helped. Yet, recalling the reason she'd awoken in the first place—the old nightmare about being trapped in a fire—she knew going back to sleep would be an exercise in futility. Besides, she reasoned, her body was still on European time and that little catnap had taken the edge off her exhaustion. Deciding that a shower and something to eat would be a better idea, she headed for the bathroom.

When Kelly exited the bathroom a short time later, she felt marginally better. The shower had helped. She suspected the crying had, too, since she'd allowed herself little chance to grieve after learning of Sister Grace's death. She'd simply begun making the necessary arrangements to come to New Orleans. Despite the protests of Wyatt, her agent, at her abrupt departure, she'd been right to come back. She'd needed to come back. Not for Sister Grace, but for herself because she'd needed to say goodbye. Once she had done so, perhaps she'd be able to close that last link to her past and to the girl she had once been.

Kelly's stomach grumbled. Pressing a hand to her middle, she acknowledged a hollow ache in her belly that had nothing to do with grief and everything to do with the simple fact that she was famished. When in the world had she eaten last? she wondered. And since she couldn't remember ingesting anything besides coffee since the return flight from Paris, she decided it probably had been much too long.

After slipping into her favorite pair of DKNY black jeans, she pulled on a black-and-ivory cashmere turtleneck and the designer boots she'd picked up for a song while shooting in Italy. She ran a brush through her blond hair, scanned her appearance in the mirror and frowned at how pale she looked. Digging through the cosmetic samples one of the makeup artists had given her, she chose a soft pink blush and rubbed some on her cheeks to give her face some color. Then she swiped the rose-colored lipstick on her mouth. Satisfied with the results, she walked over to the table and picked up the hotel room key. She slipped it into her jeans pocket, grabbed her camera bag, which also functioned as her purse, and headed out the door in search of something to eat.

She found just what she wanted in one of the dozen or so hole-in-the-wall restaurants located in the French Quarter. What the place lacked in decor it more than made up for in great-tasting food—a fact that Kelly discovered after biting into the shrimp po'boy sandwich she'd ordered. In no time at all she had polished off the crisply fried shrimp served on half a loaf of French bread, topped with lettuce, tomatoes, pickles and mayonnaise. She'd even washed down the monster-size sandwich with a bottle of ice-cold beer. Feeling stuffed from her meal, Kelly exited the restaurant, positive she wouldn't be able to eat or drink a thing for at least a week.

But by the time she'd made her way down to Jackson Square and checked out the renovations under way at the historic Saint Louis Cathedral, she was already craving a cup of café au lait and beignets. Cutting across the Square, Kelly headed for the Café du Monde.

The place was packed—not an uncommon sight given that the sidewalk café, famous for its coffee and sugar-covered doughnuts, remained open twenty-four hours a day, seven days a week. The fact that it was Halloween and people were in a party mood only added to the frenzied pace. Spying a table in the far corner that looked out over the sidewalk, Kelly quickly wound her way through the tight spaces to claim it. She flopped down in the seat. Within minutes a tired-looking young man dressed in a plain white apron and matching hat appeared before her. He stacked the used cups, saucers, spoons and paper napkins on his tray and swiped the tabletop with a damp cloth that Kelly suspected had been white at one time, but was now a dingy gray.

"What can I get for you, ma'am?" he asked in a drawl that hinted at northern Louisiana roots.

"Café au lait and an order of beignets."

"Decaf or regular?"

"Better make it decaf," she replied, deciding she'd have a difficult enough time sleeping without the added caffeine.

"Be back in a sec," he told her as he took off in the direction of the kitchen.

There had been a time when she would never have even attempted to sit like this in a crowded café, Kelly admitted. Fear that she would find herself in a crush of people and that touching someone might set off a vision about a person's past or future had made her avoid crowds when she'd been growing up. But the years of living in New York and her frequent travels had helped her. She'd learned to control her reactions far better as an adult than she had as a young girl or teenager.

While she waited for her order to arrive, Kelly did what she always did. She picked up her camera and looked out at the world through the viewfinder. Using the telephoto lens, she panned the scene across the street in front of Jackson Square. Named after Andrew Jackson, the onetime president and war hero who had been immortalized in the statue of him astride his horse, the Square had once been the heart of the city. But even as the city's boundaries expanded and sprawled far beyond the French Quarter, the area remained the center of activity for the city, and a major destination spot for both

locals and tourists alike. She scanned the area to the right
where a string of fortune-tellers had set up tables along
the side of the Square and were attempting to entice
passing pedestrians to have their fortunes told. Kelly
clicked off shots of one gypsy-clad woman as she drew
her finger down the length of a man's palm. Judging
from the fellow's expression, he seemed more concerned
with the woman's cleavage than her predictions of his
future.

Shifting her focus to the left, she noted only two artists working—one doing a portrait in chalk of a woman
dressed like Elvira, Mistress of the Dark, and the other
doing a charcoal sketch of a middle-aged couple. She
clicked off several shots, then scanned the length of the
block in search of more of the artists who supported
themselves by using their skill with a pencil or brush.
But she spied only one. Far fewer than there had been
when she'd left the city after graduating high school, she
thought, and lowered her camera in disappointment.

But the moment the horse-drawn carriage pulled into
view, she lifted her camera once more. The driver no
sooner emptied the vehicle of passengers before he began loading new patrons into the carriage. As long as
she could remember, the old-style carriages had been a
fixture in the Quarter, and she began clicking off shots.
This one was painted in black and white and was hitched
to a chocolate-colored mule that sported a hat with flowers and an orange-and-black ribbon attached to its swish-
ing tail. She adjusted her lens and focused on the carriage's driver. Judging from the way he doffed his hat
and waved his arms, the man was giving his passengers
their money's worth. She could easily imagine him in
that same spot more than a century ago with a bevy of

southern belles ready to embark on a spin around the city's streets.

Kelly clicked off several shots in succession, then zoomed in on the driver's face. She loved studying a person's face. It was like a road map, she thought, as she noted the man's weathered skin. Skin that she guessed had seen more than a half century of sun, wind and cold. A river of lines bracketed soft brown eyes, and given the smile on his face, she suspected a great many of those wrinkles were the result of laughter. The bushy brows and salt-and-pepper hair gave him a dramatic flair. She'd always heard that the carriage drivers tended to embellish history a bit in order to make the rides more exciting and their tips more hefty. Since it was Halloween, she imagined tonight's passengers were in for some ghoulish retelling of the city's already colorful history. When the driver sat down, flicked the reins and drove away, Kelly recapped the lens of her camera and returned it to her bag.

The place was growing more crowded by the minute, she realized, and a flicker of uneasiness went through her. For a moment, she debated leaving. Just as quickly, Kelly nixed the idea. She was being ridiculous. She could handle this, she assured herself. It wasn't as though she was trapped in a crowd with no means of escape. No one was bothering her. Everyone was wrapped up in their own little dramas. And although she didn't want to eavesdrop, the close proximity of the tables made it impossible for her not to overhear bits and pieces of the conversations going on around her.

"Come on, Joey," the tallest of a trio of boys at the table to her left began. "We put on these monster masks and that dude at the door ain't gonna be asking us for no IDs."

While at the next table, a petite brunette declared, "I swear, Sara Beth. I must have been out of my mind to let you talk me into going on that ghost tour with you. I'm not going to be able to close my eyes tonight."

"You're drunk, Mark," the woman at the table directly behind her snapped. "You made an ass of yourself at the party. Now, drink the damn coffee so we can go home."

Trying her best to ignore them, Kelly drummed her fingers on the tabletop and cast an anxious glance in the direction of the kitchen. Unable to see past the steady stream of patrons and waiters, she sighed and focused her attention on her own table once more. She was about to pick up her camera again when she noted the newspaper lying on the chair next to her. It had been days since she'd even looked at a newspaper or listened to the news. Picking it up, Kelly gasped as the vision hit her.

"It's about damn time you showed up. I've been waiting in this alley for twenty minutes and nearly got mugged twice."

"I was detained," she told him.

"Well, you're damn lucky I waited. Another two minutes and I'd have been gone."

"Then I guess it's fortunate that I showed up when I did."

Smart-mouthed, stuck-up bitch, just like her mother, he thought as he climbed into the car. Too bad he needed the money, because he'd like nothing better than to tell her he'd changed his mind and watch the bitch stew.

"Then let's not waste any more of each other's time, Doctor. Did you bring the document?"

"Of course I brought it. But first I want to see the money."

She opened the bag and his mouth watered at the sight of all that cash. To hell with the casinos on the Gulf Coast, he'd rent himself a suite at that fancy new hotel they'd just opened and try his luck at Harrah's. Maybe he'd even find himself a lady or two. Already anticipating the night ahead, he reached for the cash.

"Not so fast, Doctor," she said, snapping the bag shut. *"First, I want the birth certificate."*

He hesitated a moment, wondered whether he should have asked for more money for the damn thing. *"You know, your daddy sure loved that little girl. Used to call her his princess. I imagine he'd have paid a lot of money to find out she didn't die in that fire after all."*

"Unfortunately for you, my father's dead. And I can assure you I don't place the same value on her that he did. My one concern is protecting my family's good name. It's the only reason I agreed to pay you for that birth certificate."

He tapped the envelope against his palm, gave her a measuring look. *"I imagine your sister would be willing to pay a great deal to learn who her daddy was. Of course, if you was to—"*

"I don't have a sister," she snapped. *"And I suggest you quit trying to shake me down for more money, Doctor. Otherwise, I might reconsider whether or not I've made a mistake by not going to the police and telling them about your offer."*

"Now, hang on a second. There's no need to go dragging the police into a little business transaction between friends."

"You and I are not friends, Doctor. And I doubt that

the police would see your proposal as a simple business transaction.''

''We had a deal and it's too late for you to try to back out now,'' he said, and shoved the envelope at her.

While he dug through the bag of cash, she stared at the paper a moment before crushing it in her fist. ''You're sure this is the only copy?''

''What? Yeah, it's the only one,'' he lied. *The bitch would find out soon enough that he'd kept another copy, he thought. Eager to get to the casino, he began stuffing the money back into the bag.*

''Then I guess this is goodbye, Doctor.''

Something in her voice—a cold amusement—alerted him. He looked up and saw the gun. But it was too late. Before he could say a word, she pulled the trigger.

"Lady? Lady, are you all right?"

Kelly dropped the newspaper and came spinning back from the dark alley to the table in the Café du Monde. Her heart still racing, she looked up at the worried face of her waiter.

"Ma'am, are you okay?" he asked again.

"I…yes," she told him, although it wasn't true.

"You sure? You look kind of…strange."

"I'm all right," she assured him.

Looking skeptical, he placed her beignets and coffee in front of her. "That'll be $4.75."

Still reeling from the vision, Kelly grabbed her camera bag and dug out her wallet. She retrieved a five-dollar bill and one-dollar bill and slapped them on the table. "There was a man who was sitting at this table earlier, the one who left that newspaper. Do you happen to know who he was?"

The waiter shrugged. "Beats me. When I came on duty at ten o'clock, the paper was already there. Figured

I'd leave it in case somebody wanted to read it. But if it's in your way, I can toss it.''

"That's all right," she said, while in truth she wished to God she'd never touched the thing. She didn't want to get involved. All she wanted was to see the Mother Superior at the convent and satisfy herself that Sister Grace's death had been a peaceful one, sign any paperwork the attorneys had for her regarding the nun's bequest and go back to New York. But how could she ignore what she'd just seen in the vision? What if the murder hadn't happened yet? If she did nothing, that man was going to be killed.

And what if he's already dead? Do you really want to be the butt of all those jokes and whispers again?

Oh, God, she didn't want to get involved. But what choice did she have? As unpleasant as it would be to open herself to the speculation and talk, she couldn't honestly live with herself if he died because she'd done nothing. She had to do it. She had to go to the police.

"Ma'am, are you sure you're all right?"

"Yes," she replied, already feeling the weight of her decision settle upon her. She pushed the six dollars across the table at the waiter. "Keep the change."

"Thanks," he said, and shoved the money into his pocket.

When he started to leave, she said, "One more thing. The police station, is it still on North Rampart Street?"

He shrugged. "No idea. I've only been in town a couple of months."

"It's still there," a scruffy-looking fellow nursing a coffee at the next table told her.

"Thanks," Kelly told him. Using a napkin, she picked up the newspaper and shoved it into her camera bag. She stood and slid the strap of the bag onto her shoulder.

"Ain't you going to eat those doughnuts?" the old guy asked.

"No. My stomach's not feeling all that well," she said honestly. "But it would be a sin to let them go to waste. Maybe you'd do me a favor and eat them?"

"Well, seeing as how it's a favor, I guess I could do that," the fellow said, his eyes lighting up as she placed the plate of beignets in front of him. "And no point in letting that coffee go to waste, either."

"You're right." After setting her untouched coffee on the guy's table, she hurried out of the café and prayed she wouldn't be too late.

Two

Police Sergeant Max Russo did his best to ignore the chaos surrounding him in the precinct. Eying the clock on his desk, he willed the next twenty minutes to pass quickly so that his shift would finally be over and he could head home.

"Yo, Guthrie, this is a police station—not a dog pound," Detective Sal Nuccio called out when an officer came through the precinct doors with a six-footer wearing a bedraggled brown fur costume and a pair of handcuffs.

"You're a real funny guy, Nuccio," Guthrie fired back.

"I's a werewolf," the culprit replied, his speech slurred from too much hootch or drugs or both.

"And I'm Little Red Riding Hood," Guthrie replied. "Come on."

"It's true," the shaggy fellow insisted. And as though to prove his point, he began to howl like a wolf.

"Knock it off," Guthrie commanded, and smacked the fellow on the back of the head while the rest of the station laughed.

Max shook his head. Halloween certainly brought out the weirdos, he thought as the new rookie, Palmisano, marched in with three dames wearing black leather and carrying whips. Make that two dames, he amended when he noted the tall blonde had an Adam's apple.

"Officer, you're making a terrible mistake. I told you that we were only trick-or-treating. There's no law against trick-or-treating in New Orleans, is there?" the flashy brunette asked.

"No, ma'am. But there is a law against offering to do the kind of tricks you were suggesting in exchange for money."

The wolfman howled again.

"I told you to knock that shit off," Guthrie ordered.

"Maybe you ought to get him a leash, Guthrie," Nuccio chided.

"Up yours, Nuccio. Come on, wolfman. Let's go get those paws of yours printed."

The wolfman shuffled a few steps, then stopped dead in his tracks. "Say, man, I's not feeling so good."

Max looked at the man's face, recognized the shade of green. "Guthrie, if I were you, I'd get him to the can first. And I'd be quick about it."

"The can? But what—" Guthrie swore. "Listen to me, you dirtbag. You puke on me and your ass is going to rot in this jail," the officer promised as he hauled his collar down the hall.

Max chuckled, as did the rest of the precinct, when moments later they heard Guthrie let loose with a string of four-letter words. He sure was glad he was behind a desk now and no longer walking a beat. Max stole another glance at the clock. Another fifteen minutes and he'd be heading home to his Rosie. He could already see himself kicking back in his favorite chair to watch that Indianapolis Colts game he'd set to tape before leaving home this afternoon. While he remained a die-hard Saints football fan he had a soft spot for that Peyton

Manning, since the kid was from New Orleans. 'Course, he'd also watched the boy's daddy quarterback the Saints a couple decades ago. Yep, he thought. Having Rosie serve him an ice-cold one with some of that gumbo that she'd had simmering on the stove while he watched the game was the perfect way to end this crazy day.

Whatever you do, Lord. Don't let me get stuck with some pain-in-the-ass case that's going to make me work late.

But Max no sooner sent up the silent prayer when he saw her walk in. A fresh-faced blonde dressed all in black and white, lugging a bag on one shoulder that was almost as big as she was. Nuccio, who thought himself a ladies' man, wasted no time in making a beeline over to her. Not that he blamed the guy, Max admitted. The lady was a looker, even if she was a bit young for the likes of an old geezer like him. For a minute Max wrote her off as one of them college kids, then he got a better look at her face as she brushed off Nuccio and headed toward him.

Nope. The lady might be young, but those eyes were way too serious to belong to some wet-behind-the-ears kid, he decided. And he didn't imagine any college girl would ignore the scuffle going on only a few feet from her the way she did. Nor did he suspect any college kid would appear so unconcerned by the four-letter words coming from the foul-mouthed drunk, or the way the half-naked perp was leering at her. A cool one, Max thought as she approached the desk.

"Are you the person in charge?" she asked.

"I'm the desk sergeant on duty. Max Russo. What can I do for you, ma'am?"

"I'm here to report a murder."

It was the last thing he'd expected her to say, Max admitted silently. "Why don't you have a seat, Miss…?"

"Santos," she replied as she sat down. "Kelly Santos."

"All right, Miss Santos. Now, why don't we start by you telling me who it is that was murdered and your relationship to the victim."

"I don't know who he is. I mean, I never met him. And I don't know his name. But I saw…I saw him sitting inside of a car and he…he was shot."

Max looked up from the pad he was writing on and asked, "Do you know who shot him?"

Kelly shook her head. "No. But it was a woman."

"All right." He jotted down the shooter was a female. "And where did you see this shooting take place?"

"I don't know. Not exactly. It was dark and I didn't recognize the area. The car was parked at the end of an alley. Somewhere in the French Quarter, I think, because I could hear musicians playing nearby."

Max paused. He looked up from the paper on which he had been scribbling notes. "I'm afraid that somewhere in the French Quarter with musicians covers a lot of territory. I take it you're not from around here?"

"Yes. No." She let out a breath. "I was born in New Orleans, but I've lived away for a long time. I came back…I came back to take care of some personal business. I only arrived from New York late this afternoon."

"Well, the city hasn't changed all that much. Maybe if you tell me what street you were walking on when you saw the shooting, we'll be able to narrow it down a bit."

The lady hesitated. A strange look crossed her face. "Miss Santos?"

"I wasn't out walking when I saw the shooting. I was sitting in the Café du Monde waiting for coffee when I picked up a newspaper." She unzipped her camera bag, and using a paper napkin, she retrieved the newspaper and placed it on the desk in front of him. "This newspaper. It belonged to the man I saw get shot."

Max glanced down at the folded newspaper and then lifted his gaze back up to meet hers. "I'm afraid you've lost me, Miss Santos. What does this newspaper have to do with the shooting?"

"Everything."

Max arched his brows. "Come again?"

She took a deep breath, released it. "Sometimes when I touch a person or a thing, I...I can see what's happened or what's going to happen to that person. Tonight when I touched that newspaper," she said, pointing to the item, "I saw the man who'd left it behind. He was sitting in a car in a dark alley with a woman. She was paying him for some document, a birth certificate. Only, once he gave it to her, she pulled out a gun and shot him. What I don't know is if he's already dead. That's why I came here. On the chance that you can stop her if she hasn't already killed him."

Max put down his pen and sat back in his chair. He'd heard some winners, but never one quite like this, he thought. "I see." And what he saw was that the lady was either on something or a nutcase.

"Trust me, I know this all sounds crazy, Sergeant. It sounds crazy to me, too. But I'm telling you the truth. I have this...this ability to see things. Visions from the past or the future."

"Uh-huh. And tonight when you touched this here newspaper," he said, tapping it with his index finger, "you had one of them visions of a man being murdered?"

"Yes."

Max rubbed a hand along his jaw. The lady was loony tunes if she thought he was going to buy this story. "Miss Santos, when was it you said you arrived in town?"

"This afternoon. I flew in from New York."

"New York? That's a mighty big place. That where you live?"

"Yes. I'm a photographer."

Did those photographer types fiddle around with drugs? he wondered. "That bag there must be for your camera, then," he said, indicating the bag she'd set on the floor beside her and wondering if a search of the thing would reveal whatever she'd been using.

"Yes, it is."

"You mind if I take a look?" he asked.

"Be my guest," she said, and handed him the camera bag. "But I can save you the trouble of looking for drugs. There aren't any."

He hesitated a moment at her response, then told himself the conclusion was a reasonable one and had nothing to do with her being able to know what he'd been thinking. But to satisfy himself, he checked out the bag, anyway. Other than the camera and film, it contained only her wallet and a lipstick. "That's a mighty fancy piece of equipment. You here on business?"

"No. As I told you, I'm here on a personal matter."

"So you did." He slid the camera bag across the desk to her. "Never been to New York myself. My wife, Rosie, has though. She went with her sister a few years ago. I seem to recall her saying it was about a five-hour flight."

"More like three and a half," she informed him.

He ran a hand through his hair, aware that the now-salt-and-pepper strands seemed to be growing thinner on the top with each passing day. "Funny thing about flying. My Rosie, she doesn't bat an eye when a hurricane's coming or the streets are flooding, but put the woman on a plane and she's a nervous wreck. But usually a glass of wine or a cocktail on the plane helps to calm her down. You one of them nervous flyers, Miss Santos?"

"No, Sergeant. I'm not a nervous flyer. And I didn't have anything other than water to drink on the flight."

"And what about at dinner? We've got a lot of good restaurants in New Orleans, probably lots of new ones since you was last here. Nothing more relaxing than to sit down to a fine meal with a glass of wine," he said in what he hoped was a friendly, good-old-boy tone that would put her at ease. The way he figured, if the lady just fessed up to having a few cocktails and making up the story, he'd send her on her way and he could head home to Rosie, a beer and a cup of gumbo, and enjoy the game he'd taped. "You had yourself a glass of wine or two with your dinner tonight, Miss Santos?"

Kelly leaned forward, met his gaze evenly. "I'm not drunk, Sergeant Russo. And I'm not on drugs, either. What I am is wondering why you're sitting here asking about my eating and drinking habits when I've told you that there's a man out there somewhere," she said, pointing to the street, "and if he isn't already dead, he soon will be unless you do something."

"And what is it you want me to do, Miss Santos?"

"I want you to try to find him."

"And just how am I supposed to do that? You said yourself that you don't know the man or even where he is."

She remained silent, but an expression crossed her face. Sadness? Frustration? Max couldn't quite read it or her.

"Miss Santos?"

Her brown eyes returned to his face. "What if I describe him and the location to you?"

Max sighed. This simply wasn't his day, he decided as he watched the clock click within minutes of the end of his shift. May as well let her get it off her chest. "Go ahead."

"He's in his late sixties, a heavyset man with thinning gray hair and brown eyes." She closed her eyes a moment and he wondered if she was going to go into one of her supposed trances. But then she continued. "He's wearing a dark suit coat that's too small for him, and he has a gold ring with a ruby stone on his pinkie finger. And he's in a dark car—black or maybe dark gray. It's a big car, four doors with a tan leather interior. Not new, an older model. It's parked at the end of an alley next to a building with ferns hanging on the balcony." She opened her eyes, looked at him. "He's not from here, so the car might have out-of-state plates. Maybe from someplace along the Gulf Coast."

"That's quite a description."

"I told you. I saw him when I picked up the newspaper. In fact, his prints are probably on it. Maybe if you run it through your system, you can find out who he is and get a better description of the car."

He gave her his most indulgent smile. "I'm afraid it only works that fast on TV and in the movies. It takes a bit longer to check for prints, and if he's not in the system, we have little hope of getting a match."

"Then take what I've given you and use it. If you

radio the police officers out on the street, they might be able to find him in case...in case he isn't dead yet."

"You honestly expect me to issue an APB on some unknown man based on what you *think* you saw in some sort of a vision?"

Some of his co-workers shot looks in her direction. If she noticed, she gave no indication. "I know it sounds crazy," she told him, frustration lacing her voice. "But I'm telling you the truth, Sergeant. If that man isn't already dead, he will be unless you do something. Please, you've got to believe me."

"I do believe you," he assured her in an attempt to settle her down. "You see, I've got myself this aunt, a real sweet little lady in her eighties, who likes to read those books by Anne Rice. And every time she finishes one of them books, it's like clockwork. She's on the phone to me in the middle of the night swearing she's seen one of them vampires lurking around her place. But the truth is my aunt's an impressionable woman and sometimes those vampire stories she reads...well they sort of get all mixed up in her dreams. It's late and it's Halloween. You've been traveling and I'm betting you're tired. Maybe you had yourself one of those waking dreams a body has when they've had an extra-rough day."

"I didn't dream that a man got shot, Sergeant Russo. I saw him."

"I'm sure it seemed real enough, Miss Santos. Just like my aunt's dreams about those vampires seem real to her. But that doesn't mean it was real." Deciding to put an end to the nonsense, he stood. He was more than ready to get home to his Rosie, kick back in his chair with a brewsky and a bowl of gumbo to watch the game. "Maybe what you need is a good night's sleep. If you'd like, I can have an officer escort you back to your hotel.''

She stood. "I don't need an escort to my hotel, Sergeant," she snapped, and there was nothing remotely girlish about the look she slanted at him. But the last thing he expected was for the lady to reach over and grab his arm.

"What the hell—"

"What I need is for you to stop wasting time thinking about kicking back in your easy chair, eating gumbo and drinking beer while you watch some dumb football game and try to find that man before it's too late."

Max jerked his arm free. He could feel the color drain from his face. He dropped back down to his chair. "How in the hell did you know that stuff?" he demanded, his voice a harsh whisper.

"I told you. I can see things, sense things."

Sweet mother of God, he thought, shaken by her response. No, it couldn't be, he reasoned. There had to be an explanation.

"Hey, Max. Everything okay over there?" Nuccio asked.

"Yeah. Everything's fine," he muttered before turning his attention back to the woman. He narrowed his eyes. "You had me going there for a minute. That stuff you just said about the gumbo and beer and the game, you were guessing, right?"

"No."

"Then you must have heard me say something to one of the guys earlier," he offered, wanting, needing to believe that's what had just happened, even though for the life of him he couldn't recall saying a thing about the gumbo to a soul.

"We both know I didn't overhear you saying anything to anyone."

"Then how…"

Kelly resumed her seat across from his desk. She clasped her hands together in that ladylike way women did and met his gaze evenly. "I tried to explain, Sergeant Russo," she began, a weariness in her voice that matched her expression. "Sometimes when I touch a person or an object, I can see things."

He looked down at his shirtsleeve where she had grabbed him only a few moments ago, then back up at her. "And when you touched me, you read my mind?"

"Not quite. It was more a case of reading what you were imagining. In this case, you were seeing yourself sitting in a big brown leather easy chair with your feet kicked up. The room had gold shag carpet and there was a small round table next to the chair with a bottle of beer on it. You were watching a football game on TV and you hit the pause button when a woman came into the room," she told him. "She had red hair and she brought you a tray with a steaming bowl on it. She said the gumbo was hot, but that she didn't want you using that as an excuse to have another beer."

Max swallowed hard and tried to digest the fact that the woman had just described his living room and his wife. "That's my wife, Rosie." And Rosie was never going to believe him when he told her this story. After a moment, he pulled out a fresh sheet of paper and started over. "Why don't you describe that car for me again."

Jack Callaghan ambled over to his police locker the next morning and the first person he saw was Sal Nuccio. Just what he didn't need, Jack thought. After tossing and turning most of the night and feeling like shit over how he'd handled things with Alicia the previous evening, the last person he wanted to deal with this morning was Nuccio. The guy had been a pain in the ass since they were kids. And ever since he'd beaten Nuccio for the starting quarterback position in high school, the man never missed a chance to try to one-up him at everything from the type of car he drove to the women he dated, and now to see which one of them made detective second grade first. At thirty-three, the adolescent games had long lost any appeal for him. Unfortunately, Nuccio couldn't say the same.

"Hey, Callaghan. You hear about all the excitement here last night?" Nuccio asked him.

"No," Jack replied. Not bothering to even look at the guy and hoping he would just go away, Jack worked the combination on his police locker.

"Well, you missed it. Yes sirree, we had ourselves quite a show here at the station last night."

Jack yanked open his locker. "I'll take your word for it."

"You don't need to take my word for it. Ask some of the guys who were here busting their asses last night and pulling extra shifts while you and your partner got the night off."

Irritated, Jack slid his gaze over to where Nuccio was leaning against the wall, nursing a cup of coffee. The guy fit the caricature of a lazy cop, Jack thought, from the beefy jowls and beer belly to the straining buttons on his jacket and the sloppy look of his clothes. "If you've got something to say, Nuccio, why don't you just spit it out."

"Just making an observation. That's all." He tossed

his foam cup into the overflowing trash can and shoved away from the wall.

Determined not to let the guy get to him, Jack stowed his running shoes in his locker and made no comment. He'd learned from experience that there was no reasoning with Nuccio. What would be the point in telling the prick that the reason he and his partner had scored two days off was because they'd worked fourteen days straight and had cracked a three-year-old homicide case? Nuccio would only argue that it had been the Callaghan family name currying favor for him. Which was what he'd claimed to be the reason they were both competing for promotion to detective second grade, even though Nuccio had put in two years more on the force than Jack had. The truth was, his name being Callaghan hadn't helped him one iota—a fact that the captain had made sure he understood the day he'd joined the force as a rookie.

"Besides, the way I see it, you and Vicious might have wrangled the night off, but you also missed out on all of the fun around here."

Jack clipped his shield on his belt, then slammed the locker door shut. "If you say so."

"It's true," Nuccio insisted, obviously irritated by his response. "Things were really hopping here last night and you missed it."

"Hear that, Leon?" Jack called over to his partner, homicide detective Napoleon Jerevicious, affectionately known among his fellow officers as Vicious, the nickname he'd earned on the college and pro football fields. "Nuccio says we missed all the fun last night."

Leon slammed his own locker shut. The former pro football running back, who had been both his partner and friend for the past two years, walked over to join him. "I don't know about that. I had me a pretty good time last night. Tessa and I took the kids trick-or-treating. And after we put them to bed, we did some trick-or-treating of our own, if you get my drift."

"Talk about lame," Nuccio declared with a snort. "I'd have thought a hotshot former jock like you could find something better to do than chase after a couple of snot-nosed kids and bang your old lady."

"Hey man, don't knock it until you've tried it," Leon advised him, unfazed by the other man's derisive tone.

"No way," Nuccio replied. "I've got better things to do with my time. But anytime you get tired of palling around with Callaghan and want to have some *real* fun, you just let old Sal here know. And I'll introduce you to a few of my ladies, make sure they show you a good time."

"That's real nice of you, Sal," Leon said in that low, easygoing voice of his that still held a trace of his Arkansas roots despite the years he'd spent in New York playing football for the Jets.

"Anytime." Nuccio puffed up his chest. "Just say the word and I'll make a few calls, set something up for you."

"I appreciate that," Leon told him. "I really do. But the thing is, I'm afraid having you set me up with your ladies would be a problem."

"Say, if you're worried your old lady's going to find out, don't sweat it. These gals are discreet."

"I'm sure they are, but that's not the problem," Leon explained.

Nuccio frowned a moment, then his eyes widened. "Holy shit! Don't tell me you've never screwed around on your wife?"

"Come to think of it, no. I haven't."

"Hot damn, if that don't beat all." Nuccio let out a hoot. He slapped his leg. "Instead of calling you Vicious, they should call you Choirboy. What in the hell's wrong with you, man? Here I am offering to cut you in on my female turf and you're turning me down because you're married?"

"Actually, that's only one of the reasons I'm turning you down. The other reason is I don't pay women for sex."

Jack muffled a laugh. But the other guys hanging around the lockers didn't. And as the whoops of laughter rumbled around the locker room, Nuccio's face grew beet red. Jack almost felt sorry for him. Almost but not quite, since the jerk had been riding him for months now—ever since Jack had gotten a citation for his efforts in solving an eight-year-old murder that had languished in the cold-case files. A case to which Nuccio had once been assigned.

Nuccio glared up at the much taller Leon. "Up yours, pal."

"No thanks," Leon said, and flashed his pearly white teeth.

"Some sports hero you are. The only woman you're making it with is your own wife."

Leon's smile widened. It was the smile of a man who was content with his life and with himself. A man who wasn't going to be rattled by the barbs of some sorry-ass jerk like Sal Nuccio. "Like I said, don't knock it till you try it."

"Or maybe you don't have any choice, because the chicks aren't impressed with washed-up football stars. Hell, it wouldn't surprise me to find out that you never were a babe magnet—not even during your playing days," Nuccio continued with a laugh. "No wonder the chicks ignore you now."

"Nuccio, my man, you've been reading way too many groupie magazines," Leon said patiently. "The truth is, the ladies don't ignore Napoleon the Vicious. But when I tell them I'm married, they naturally put the moves on my pal Jackson here." Leon slung his arm around Jack's shoulder, dwarfing his six-foot-two, one-hundred-ninety-pound frame. "Ain't that right, Jackson?"

"Sure," Jack responded.

"Yeah, right," Nuccio told him.

Leon released him and drew himself up to his six-foot-six height. "It's the truth. Jackson here is a real player. Why, just last night he was at some fancy party at the Royal Sonesta, and the man had to practically fight the ladies off with a stick. Ain't that so, Jackson?"

"Sure is," Jack said, going along with his partner's story but wondering how Leon knew about the fund-raiser he'd attended since he hadn't mentioned it to him.

"In your dreams," Nuccio countered. "Maybe the chicks give Mr. Ex-Football Star here a second look because he used to be somebody, but no way do they notice your sorry ass."

"According to Tessa's friend Milly, they were noticing a lot more than his ass last night," Leon informed him.

"No shit! That true, Callaghan?" a first-year rookie named Doug called out. "You really have women crawling all over you last night?"

"I don't know if 'crawling' is the right word. But there were about a hundred women at the party," Jack said, doing his best to keep a straight face as he referred to the fund-raiser his mother had guilted him in to attending. "And by the time the night was over, I'd say that at least half of them had hit on me."

"Aw, man," came a comment from behind.

"Some guys have all the luck," someone else grumbled.

Nuccio narrowed his eyes. "You expect us to believe you had fifty women trying to jump your bones last night?"

"Actually it wasn't my bones they were after," Jack confessed. Although, in truth, Alicia Van Owen had made it clear to him that she was more than willing to resume the steamy affair that he'd put the brakes on two months ago. "It was my checkbook. Most of the ladies were members of the Junior League or friends of my mother's or both. And they were hitting me up all evening for donations."

Leon roared with laughter. So did the other guys gathered around who'd been listening to the exchange. The only one who didn't seem to find the story amusing was Sal Nuccio.

"You're a real comedian," Nuccio told him.

"Thank you," Jack said, and took a bow.

"Maybe you ought to turn in your badge and try using that smart mouth of yours to earn a living. Oh, wait a minute," Nuccio continued, a hard look in his eyes. "That's right. You don't actually have to worry about earning a living like the rest of us 'cause your daddy left you a shit load of money. All you gotta do is have your mama make a phone call and wave her checkbook. And the next thing you know you got yourself a citation and the press makes you out to be some kind of hero."

Jack sobered instantly. "I *earned* that citation, Nuccio. And as far as the press is concerned, I don't have any control over what they write and neither does my mother.''

"Uh-huh. And we're all supposed to believe that the Callaghan bucks didn't influence any of it."

"They didn't."

"Yeah, try telling it to somebody who doesn't know any better. The truth is, that if it weren't for your family's money you'd still be a beat cop."

Jack shook his head. And that was the crux of Nuccio's problem with him, the same problem the guy had had since they were kids—even before he'd shared the quarterback slot in high school. His family had had money and Nuccio's didn't. "It still burns your ass that my family has money, doesn't it, Sal?"

"The only thing that burns my ass is the way you get special treatment because of it," Nuccio told him.

When Jack started for him, Leon clamped a hand down on his shoulder. "If I were you, Nuccio, I'd go crawl back under that rock where you live before I set Jackson here loose and he turns you into the city's latest homicide.''

"You think I'm afraid of him? Of either of you?"

"You should be," Jack told him, his voice deadly soft in contrast to the anger racing through him.

"Why? Because you're gonna sic your big black partner here on me?"

"No. You should be afraid because I'm going to whip your fat white ass."

Nuccio made a show of laughing at the remark, holding his sides and wiping tears of mirth from his eyes. "You hear that, fellows? Callaghan thinks he can whip my ass." When none of the other cops gathered to share his amusement, Nuccio curled his lips in a snarl. "Go ahead and turn him loose. And let's see who whips whose ass. I've yet to meet a rich boy who knew how to handle his fists.''

"This one can," Jack assured him.

"Come on, guys, ya'll are cops. You're supposed to fight the bad guys. Not each other," one of the other police officers pointed out. "Besides, if the captain gets wind that you've been fighting, you're both gonna be in a heap of trouble."

"The kid's right," Leon said. "I'd listen to him if I were you."

Jack said nothing. He simply stood there, temper and adrenaline pumping through his veins.

Leon tightened the hand he had on Jack's shoulder. "Let it go, Jackson. He's not worth it."

His partner was right. Jack knew he was. But the urge to plant his fist in Nuccio's face was so strong, Jack nearly gave in to it. And he would have if the door leading to the lockers hadn't suddenly burst open.

"Callaghan! Jerevicious," the lieutenant called out. "The captain wants you in his office."

"What's up?" Nuccio asked as he followed them through the door.

"Looks like the sarge's psychic lady from last night was right after all. Someone just reported finding a stiff in a parked car with a bullet through his chest."

Three

What a night, Kelly thought as she sat in the parlor of the convent the next morning and waited for the Reverend Mother. After the chaos at the police station the previous night, the quiet serenity of the convent was a welcome contrast. She sighed, wondering if reporting her vision had made any difference.

Had they found the man in time? Or had she opened herself up to all the speculation for nothing?

It was too late now to second-guess her actions, Kelly told herself. She'd done what she'd had to do. Doing her best to forget about what had happened, she focused on her surroundings. The dark heavy drapes that hung from the windows had been pulled open, allowing morning sun into the somber-looking room. She could smell the hint of lemon on the freshly polished furniture, and the tile floor gleamed as though it had just been waxed. Shelves of books lined one entire wall, while another wall was adorned with an oil painting depicting the Blessed Mother's Assumption. Ivory candles and a vase of pink roses with baby's breath rested on a table beneath the portrait.

Wandering about the room, Kelly trailed her fingertips across the open Bible lying atop a table. Her lips twitched as she caught herself remembering Sister Grace's infamous white-glove tests in the rooms at St.

Ann's. Not a smidgen of dust to be found in here, Kelly mused. Which came as no surprise. If there was one thing she'd learned in her years at St. Ann's it was that the nuns truly believed in that old adage, "cleanliness is next to godliness."

"I'm so sorry to have kept you waiting, Ms. Santos."

Kelly swung around at the sound of the nun's voice, surprised that she'd been so lost in her thoughts that she hadn't heard the nun enter the room. "Not at all, Reverend Mother," she told the tall, energetic woman in the flowing blue-and-white habit. "I only arrived a few minutes ago."

"That's good. I'm afraid we had a little problem with the choir practice after mass and it has my whole morning running behind schedule." She held out her hand. "I'm Sister Wilhelmina. I'm supposed to be the one who keeps everything in line here at the Sisters of Mary Convent, although I'm not at all sure I succeed."

"From what Sister Grace told me, you do an excellent job," Kelly said, already liking the woman. She shook her hand. "It's a pleasure to meet you."

"You're most gracious as well as lovely, Ms. Santos. Thank you."

"Please, call me Kelly."

The nun bowed her head. "As you wish. Why don't we have a seat over here," she said, motioning to the settees grouped around a coffee table. "I've asked that tea be brought in for us."

Kelly took the seat indicated. "I appreciate you agreeing to see me on such short notice, Reverend Mother."

"Nonsense," the nun told her as she sat down across from her. "I only wish it could have been under happier circumstances."

"So do I."

"Since I've only been here for a short time, I'm afraid I didn't know Sister Grace very well. But I do know she was devoted to 'her girls,' as she called her former charges from St. Ann's. She was particularly proud of you and your success as a photographer."

Kelly swallowed past the lump in her throat. "Thank you for telling me."

The Reverend Mother dipped her head in acknowledgment. "Ah, here's Bess now with our tea," she said as a plump, rosy-cheeked woman brought in a tray bearing a silver teapot, china cups and serving pieces. She placed it on the table. "Thank you, Bess. I'll pour."

"Yes, Reverend Mother," the woman replied, and quietly exited the room.

As the Reverend Mother served them both tea, Kelly experienced a moment of déjà vu. Suddenly she was ten years old again, seated in the parlor of St. Ann's on Christmas Eve. The other girls had all departed for the weekend to spend the holiday with extended family members while she had remained at St. Ann's because she'd had no place to go, no family to visit. Evidently Sister Grace had picked up on her loneliness, because shortly after the last of the girls had left, she had called her down to the parlor. When she'd arrived, the nun had prepared a pot of tea for them and had served it in the convent's good china cups. It had been the first of many holiday afternoons that she had spent in the nun's company.

"Kelly?"

At the sound of her name, Kelly shook off the memories. "I'm sorry. Did you say something?"

"I asked if you'd like sugar with your tea?"

"No, thank you. Just milk, please."

"You looked as though you were a thousand miles

away just now,'' the nun pointed out as she added milk to Kelly's cup and then to her own.

"I was remembering Sister Grace," Kelly admitted. "She served me my very first cup of tea in a silver pot very much like that one. And we had old-fashioned English scones and lemon curd with it."

"Well, I'm afraid we don't have any scones," the Reverend Mother informed her, a smile in her voice that matched the one in her hazel eyes. "But Bess's chocolate-chip-walnut cookies are excellent. Would you like to try one?"

"Yes, thank you," Kelly replied, and took one of the cookies from the dish and placed it on the plate beside her tea.

The nun placed a cookie on her own plate and sat back. "So tell me about your tea party with Sister Grace. Was it for a special occasion?"

"Actually, it was Christmas Eve," Kelly told her. "It became sort of a ritual, you might say. After that, every year, whether I was at St. Ann's or in a foster home, she and I would still meet to have tea and scones together."

"It sounds like a lovely tradition."

"It was," Kelly replied. And instead of dreading the Christmas season because she had no family to share it with, she'd come to look forward to her time with Sister Grace.

"Were you and Sister Grace able to continue your tradition after you left New Orleans?"

"No," Kelly admitted. "When I left St. Ann's, I left New Orleans." And she'd sworn never to return. Kelly put down her teacup and broke off a piece of the cookie. "This is the first time I've been back since I left ten years ago."

"I see. I seem to recall Sister Grace mentioning how

demanding your job is. She said you traveled a great deal.''

''Yes.'' But her traveling and her job hadn't been her reason for staying away, Kelly admitted silently. ''I should have come back to see her.''

''I'm sure Sister Grace understood about the demands of your career, Kelly. I do know that she was happy that you and some of her other girls stayed in touch with her.''

''I still should have come,'' Kelly replied, unable to take any comfort in the nun's words. She met the other woman's eyes. ''A couple of months ago Sister Grace asked me to come. She said she needed to talk to me about something. But I…I put her off and took an assignment in Europe instead.''

''And now that she's dead, you feel guilty.''

Kelly nodded. She returned the untouched cookie to her plate. ''Wouldn't you?''

''Probably.'' The Reverend Mother put aside her tea and leaned forward. ''But there was no way any of us could have known that she would be taken from us so soon. You have no reason to feel guilty for your decision.''

''I have *every* reason to feel guilty,'' Kelly insisted. ''I could have turned down the assignment and come back like she asked me to do. But I didn't because I didn't want to come back here.''

''Why not?'' the nun asked.

''Because I knew coming here would dredge up unhappy memories,'' Kelly confessed. She clasped her hands. ''Except for Sister Grace, there were few bright spots in my life here. I swore to myself that as soon as I was old enough, I'd leave and start over. Build a new life for myself, a happy life.''

"And did you succeed?"

"I enjoy my work and I'm good at it. And I'm not unhappy," Kelly responded, knowing as she spoke the words that the description of her life left much to be desired. "But I wish...I wish I had known how ill Sister Grace was. If I had, I'd have come." And if she had, maybe she wouldn't be plagued with such a sense of loss.

"I suspect that she didn't want you to know. As I told you on the phone, Sister Grace's heart wasn't strong. She'd been on medication for quite some time."

"But she died so suddenly."

"I know, my child. But that's how heart attacks are," the Reverend Mother told her. "You must try to take solace in knowing that she's with our Lord now in paradise."

Kelly knew the nun was right. Yet it did little to ease the ache in her heart. When the church bells sounded, Kelly stood. "Thank you for your time, Reverend Mother. And for the tea."

"You're most welcome." The Reverend Mother rose and escorted Kelly from the parlor to the entrance door. "Will you be returning to New York now?"

"Probably in a few days. I have to meet with Sister Grace's attorneys first and I want to visit her grave." And just saying those words made her want to weep. She still couldn't imagine never hearing Sister Grace's voice again, never receiving another one of her letters.

The Reverend Mother touched her arm. "Sister Grace is at peace now with our Lord, Kelly. Try not to grieve for her, but be happy for her."

"I'll try," Kelly promised. But even as she left the convent to go visit the nun's grave, she knew that it wasn't for Sister Grace that she grieved, but for herself. Because now she was truly all alone.

Jack surveyed the stripped-down, older-model Lincoln in the alley that contained the city's latest homicide. The car's hubcaps and wheels had been stolen, along with the license plate. He stripped off the disposable gloves he'd put on to check the scene for evidence. "Any ID on him?" Jack asked the cop who had been first on the crime scene, where a man had been found with a gunshot wound to his chest.

"No, sir. His wallet's gone and he's not wearing any jewelry."

"Chances are whoever took the wallet, took the jewelry, too," Jack remarked. "What about registration papers on the car?"

"The glove box was empty, too."

Which meant any papers identifying the car's owner were gone, too. "Get a couple of officers and start canvassing the area within a six-block radius. Maybe some-one saw or heard something," Jack instructed, even though he suspected that with all the Halloween hoopla going on last night, they were likely to get more than a few reports of strange happenings.

"Yes, sir," the young cop replied, and started to head off.

"Officer, one more thing," Jack called out.

"Sir?"

"Check around with some of the shop owners and residents, find out which street musicians usually hang out around here," Jack instructed, recalling the state-ment Sarge had taken from the woman, in which she'd claimed there was music playing on a nearby corner. "Question them, see if anyone remembers seeing or hearing something that seemed odd—even for Halloween.''

"Yes, sir," the police officer said. "Anything else?"

"No, you've got enough to keep you busy for a while. Get back to me or Detective Jerevicious if you find anything."

"Yes, sir."

Once the beat cop was gone, Jack walked over to Leon, who had already questioned the woman who had reported the abandoned car with the body and was now conferring with the crime-scene team. "Find out anything new?"

"Not really. Looks like a robbery-homicide. They're dusting the vehicle for prints now."

"M.E. give a time of death yet?" Jack asked.

"I asked and she nearly bit my head off. Figured I'd let you charm her and see if she'll give you an answer."

Jack strolled over to where the medical examiner was finishing up her preliminary look at the victim. "Nice seeing you last night, Doc. I almost didn't recognize you in that red number you were wearing."

"You didn't look so bad yourself, Callaghan," Dr. Jordan Winston declared as she checked the vic's pupils. She flicked off her penlight and motioned for the body to be loaded into the coroner's van.

"What can you tell me about the vic?" he asked.

"White male, probably late sixties, two gunshot wounds to the heart delivered at close range. Small-caliber weapon, probably a .22. I'll let you know for sure when I get the bullets out."

The doc was good, Jack thought, because he'd already figured the gun was a .22 himself. "Any idea on the time of death?"

"Based on lividity, my best guess is sometime between eleven o'clock and one o'clock this morning. I'll be able to narrow it down once I get him back to the lab and run some tests.''

''Thanks, Doc.''

''By the way, Callaghan, I liked your lady friend. Very classy. And smart.''

''Yes, she is,'' Jack said, deciding there was little point in denying that Alicia had been his date last night since everyone—including his mother and Alicia herself—had placed them together as a couple. With any luck, last night he had finally got the message across, at least to Alicia, that they weren't meant for each other.

''She put me onto a sweet little Victorian that's about to go on the market. If the place is half as good as she says it is, I'll be giving her a call and making an offer on it.''

''I'm sure Alicia will appreciate your business. You'll let me know when you can pinpoint the exact time of death on our John Doe?'' he asked, eager to change the topic.

She gave him a pointed look, as though she knew exactly what he was doing. ''Check with my office this afternoon.''

As Jordan Winston returned to her team, Leon walked over to him. ''Any luck on getting an ETD?''

''Piece of cake. I don't know what your problem is with the lady,'' Jack teased, knowing that it had taken him years to establish an easy relationship with Jordan Winston. The lady took a long time to warm up to people and she was still putting Leon through hoops. ''She couldn't have been more cooperative. Maybe you should try changing your cologne.''

''There's not a damn thing wrong with my cologne. The woman just flat-out doesn't like me,'' Leon fired back, and grumbled something about female doctors who had a thing for blue-eyed men. "So are you going to tell me the time or not?"

"Between 11:00 p.m. and 1:00 a.m."

"Well, what do you know. According to the captain, Sarge's psychic came in around midnight," Leon reminded him.

"Yeah, I know," Jack replied as he recalled the description given of the woman named Kelly Santos who'd come into the station last night. He knew in his gut that it was the same Kelly Santos who had gone to school with his kid sister Meredith—the same teenage girl he had rescued from punks in the park years ago. The same girl who had spooked him when she'd announced that he should ditch law school and become a cop if that was what he wanted to do. Since he'd been wrestling with that dilemma for months and hadn't breathed a word about it to anyone, not even the woman he'd been engaged to marry, he hadn't known what to make of her. Nor had he known what to make of her telling him that she was sorry, but his fiancée wasn't going to stand by him. Only months later did he recall that the girl had been dead right on both counts.

"Kind of weird, don't you think?"

"What's weird?" Jack asked, pulling his thoughts from the past back to the murder scene at hand.

"You know, that woman claiming to have had a vision of a man being murdered in a car and then a stiff meeting her description turning up dead in a car just like she said."

Jack shrugged. "I guess so. Strange things happen sometimes."

"Come on, Jackson. Don't tell me it hasn't crossed your mind that the woman knocked the guy off and then came into the station and fed Sarge that line of bull about having some kind of vision to cover her ass.''

While Leon's comments made perfect sense, the idea of the sad-eyed girl he remembered killing anyone didn't set well with him. "It's a possibility," he conceded. "But if she did kill the man, it seems the smart thing would have been to just keep quiet."

"Like I said," Leon began as they headed down the street toward the car. "Maybe she did it to take suspicion off herself."

"Or maybe she really did see him get offed," Jack offered.

"Don't tell me you believe in this psychic shit."

"I'm trying to keep an open mind," Jack informed his partner.

They both stopped on the corner, waiting for traffic. "Then try opening your mind to the possibility that the lady might have killed the vic, decided to make up all that crap about a vision to cover her tracks, and to drum up some business for herself at the same time."

"What are you talking about?"

"I'm talking about this so-called psychic stuff. Come on, man. You've seen how many of them are lined up around the Square. Imagine how many people would be flocking to this Santos woman if word got out she'd predicted a murder."

"She's not one of those scam artists," Jack defended as they crossed the street.

"Hang on a second," Leon said, catching his arm and stopping them both in the middle of the block. "You telling me you're buying her story? That you think this Santos dame really did have some kind of vision?"

"I'm not saying any such thing." Jack jerked his arm free and resumed walking. "All I know is that we've got a dead body and a witness who says she saw the murder.''

"In a vision," Leon reminded him.

"Vision or not, right now she's the only lead we've got," Jack told him as he unlocked the car. "So I say, let's go interview our witness."

But interviewing their witness proved more difficult than he'd anticipated, Jack conceded later that afternoon. The lady had been out when they'd arrived at the Regent Hotel and had yet to return. Not that he and Leon hadn't been busy. They had. In between calls to the hotel, they had spent the better part of the day chasing down leads in the murder investigation. And so far, they'd come up empty. He told himself it was the reason he was more determined than ever to nail down the interview with Kelly Santos. He hit the redial button on his cell phone.

"Good afternoon, the Regent Hotel."

"Has Ms. Kelly Santos returned to the hotel yet?" Jack asked.

"One moment, sir," the operator said. Seconds later, she came back on the line. "Yes, sir. She has. Would you like me to ring her room for you?"

"No, thanks," Jack said, and ended the call.

"She still out?" Leon asked, some of the frustration they were both feeling echoing in his voice.

"Nope. She's back," he told Leon, and they both climbed back into the car. He started the engine.

Fifteen minutes later, he and Leon entered the hotel lobby and approached the front desk. "Good afternoon. I'm Detective Callaghan. This is my partner, Detective Jerevicious. We need to know what room Ms. Kelly Santos is staying in."

"I'm sorry, sir. I can't give out that information. But

if you'd care to use one of the house phones over there…'' she began, indicating the row of phones on the far wall. ''The operator can connect you to Ms. Santos's room and she can give you her room number.''

As discreetly as he could, Jack showed the woman his badge and her friendly smile faded. ''Actually, it wasn't a request. We need to ask Ms. Santos some questions and would prefer not to announce ourselves. So if you'd just give me that room number, I'd appreciate it.''

''I'm sorry, sir. Officer. Detective,'' she amended. ''But I'll need to get my supervisor.''

And after a brief chat with the clerk's supervisor and Jack's assurance that there was no problem with the hotel's guest, Jack and Leon stood in front of Kelly's hotel room door. Jack knocked on the door and it was opened almost immediately.

''Yes?''

For a moment, Jack thought he'd made a mistake. The woman who stood before him bore little resemblance to the scrawny teenage Kelly Santos whom he'd rescued a decade ago. The ivory sweater and coffee-colored skirt she wore skimmed along enticing female curves. Her hair was still blond, but instead of hanging like a curtain behind which the young Kelly had hidden, this woman's hair was styled in layers that fell to her shoulders. Her skin was smooth and perfect, her cheekbones high and the unsmiling mouth too wide for her narrow face. Then Jack looked into her eyes. There was no mistaking those eyes. Big haunting brown eyes that had seemed too old for a young girl's face. Wary eyes filled with secrets. She was the Kelly Santos from his past. And for the space of a heartbeat, he waited, wondering if she would remember him. But if she did, she gave no indication.

"Ms. Santos? Ms. Kelly Santos?" Leon asked, stepping forward to break the silence.

"Yes."

"I'm Detective Napoleon Jerevicious with the New Orleans Police Department. This is my partner, Detective Callaghan. We'd like to ask you a few questions."

A look of utter hopelessness flickered across her features. "You found him." It was a statement, not a question.

"Him?" Leon prompted, and Jack didn't miss the suspicious note in his partner's voice.

"The man in the car. The one I saw get shot. He's dead, isn't he?"

"Yes, he is," Jack said. "And we need to ask you some questions." When a door opened down the hall and the woman who exited cast a curious glance their way, he suggested, "It might be better if we came inside where it's more private."

"Yes, of course," she replied politely, and opened the door wider, allowing them to enter. Once they were in the room, Kelly directed them to the sitting area. "Please, sit down."

Leon opted for the small sofa, his large frame taking up most of the space, while Jack chose one of the two armchairs that had been grouped with the sofa around a coffee table.

"There's probably some soda or wine in the minibar. Would you like something to drink?"

"No, thanks," Jack said, not bothering to point out that they were on duty.

"Nothing for me, either, ma'am," Leon replied.

"All right." Kelly took a seat in the other chair and clasped her hands together. "You said you had some questions for me."

"We need to go over a few details in the statement you gave to Sergeant Russo last night," Jack began. For a moment, he debated reminding her that they had met before, but decided against it. Best to keep things professional, he reasoned.

They went over the details of her statement again and Kelly related the events of the evening—picking up the newspaper, having a vision of the man in the car with the woman in black, of that woman removing a gun from her bag and shooting him. And given Kelly's stricken expression as she related the incident for them, Jack concluded that whether she'd had a vision of the killing or had seen the thing firsthand, the experience had been real for her.

"And you have no idea who the victim or the alleged woman with the gun were?" Leon asked.

"None at all."

"You have to admit it seems kind of strange that you should know every detail about the man's murder, but not know who he or his killer was."

"Believe me, Detective, I'm aware of how strange it sounds. But it's the truth. I've never laid eyes on either of them before I picked up that newspaper in the café. And even then, I didn't see them in the traditional sense."

"What about a description of the woman?" Jack asked. "Can you tell us what she looked like?"

Kelly shifted her somber brown eyes to his face. "I'm afraid it was dark inside the car and she was wearing some kind of cloak with a hood that shadowed her face. I never got a clear look at her. Only of her gloved hand reaching for the gun, then pulling the trigger."

"You said she called the man 'Doctor,'" Jack pointed out, approaching it from a different slant. "Do you think you'd be able to recognize her voice if you heard it again?''

Kelly paused, seeming to consider his question for a moment. ''I doubt it. She spoke very softly, almost a whisper. And the man, well he was breathing kind of hard, like he was winded or maybe had asthma or something. Plus with the street noise and music, she could be sitting across the table talking to me right now and I don't know that I'd recognize her voice.''

''What about—''

Leon's cell phone rang. ''Excuse me,'' he said, and answered the phone. ''Jerevicious. Yeah? Hang on a second.'' He stood. ''I'm going to need to take this call.''

''If you want some privacy, you're welcome to go into the bedroom,'' Kelly offered.

''Thanks,'' he told her, and disappeared into the adjoining room.

When they were alone, Kelly said, ''I see you decided to follow your dream after all.''

''I didn't think you remembered me,'' Jack told her, unable to mask his surprise.

Kelly gave him a slow smile. ''I was an impressionable teenager the last time I saw you. It's not likely that I'd forget the man who saved my most valuable possession.''

Jack swallowed, taken aback by her candor. He also worried that the event had traumatized her more than he'd ever suspected. ''Actually, I don't think those punks would have really *done* anything to you. At heart, they were cowards who got their kicks out of scaring young girls. I doubt they'd have taken things any further.''

The smile turned into a chuckle. ''I wasn't referring to my virtue, Detective Callaghan. I was talking about

my camera. I'd worked after school and on weekends
for six months to buy it. *It* was my most valuable possession.''

Jack flushed, felt like an idiot for overreacting.

"I'm afraid I couldn't resist," she said, stifling a grin.
"From your expression, it was obvious that you were
worried I'd been permanently scarred by that incident in
the park. I wasn't.''

"You could have been.''

The smile faded from her lips. "Trust me, Detective.
Benny Farrell and Reed Parker weren't the first ones to
think that, because no one else wanted me, I was fair
game for them to do whatever they pleased to me. I
never lost any sleep because of them. I'm tougher than
that.''

Because she had had to be. Admiration and anger
ripped at him as he thought of what her life must have
been like. "I'm sorry. I never really thought about what
it was like for you growing up at St. Ann's.''

"There was no reason for you to," she informed him
matter-of-factly. "You come from a close-knit family,
but I don't. That's not anyone's fault. It's simply the
way things are. It's certainly not something you should
feel guilty about.''

"I don't. I'm just sorry that your life was so tough.''

"Don't be," she informed him, her voice turning
chilly. She stood, crossed her arms. "I've done just fine
for myself. So you can save your pity, Detective. I don't
need it or want it.''

Jack shot to his feet. "First off, the name's Jack. Since
we share some history, I think we can dispense with the
formalities. Second, you can quit trying to put words in
my mouth. I don't feel guilty because you grew up without a family and I sure as hell don't pity you. I *admire*

you. I did back when you were a kid. And I do now because you obviously *did* make something of yourself."

She opened her mouth then clamped it shut, as though his remark had taken the wind out of her sails. After a moment, she whooshed out a breath. "I'm sorry," she finally managed to say with all the enthusiasm of someone who'd just been poked with a needle.

Jack chuckled. "I get the feeling that you don't do that often. Apologize," he explained.

"I don't."

"Don't make many mistakes, huh?"

"Hardly," she said. "I make tons of them. But I try not to do or say things that I'll regret."

"Guess that explains why you look as though chewing a bucket of nails would have been preferable to telling me you're sorry," he teased.

Streaks of color raced up her pale cheeks. "It would have," she admitted. "I guess I'm a little sensitive about my heritage. Or lack thereof."

"A little sensitive?" he prompted, hoping to get her to smile at him again.

"All right. A lot sensitive," she conceded, and rewarded him with a hint of that smile he'd wanted. "Anyway, I really am sorry for—"

"Jackson, we've got to roll," Leon said, exiting the other room.

The homicide detective in him took charge. "What's up?"

Leon looked from him to Kelly and back again. "The vic's wallet turned up. We've got an ID on the man."

"Who was he?" Kelly asked. When Leon hesitated, she said, "Please, I'd like to know. 'Seeing' things like

I do—it makes me feel somehow connected to the persons involved.''

Leon glanced at him again and Jack nodded. ''His name was Martin Gilbert. He was from Pass Christian, Mississippi.'' Leon paused a moment. ''And until five years ago, he was a doctor.''

''What happened five years ago?'' Kelly asked.

''His license was revoked for performing illegal abortions on minors.''

Four

"Please have a seat, Ms. Santos," the receptionist at the law firm of Callaghan and Associates told Kelly as she was ushered into an office to wait for Peter Callaghan late Monday morning. "Can I offer you anything to drink?"

"No, I'm fine. Thank you."

"Very well. Mr. Callaghan will be with you shortly," the young woman said, and left the room, pulling the door closed behind her.

Still unsettled by her encounter with Jack the previous day and the disturbing vision that had led to it, Kelly looked at her watch. She felt as though she'd been in New Orleans for weeks instead of just a few days. Eager to put those days behind her as quickly as possible so she could return to New York, she stared at her watch. And she waited. When several minutes ticked by and Peter Callaghan still hadn't made an appearance, she tapped her foot, growing more restless by the second.

Patience was not one of her virtues, she admitted. The fact that she was being forced to wait in a lawyer's office only added to her discomfort. One of those psychological hang-ups from her childhood, she guessed. All she knew was that Peter Callaghan's office made her think about those countless offices she'd been in and out of as a kid. Social workers, child psychologists and various state agencies—all insisting on regular evaluations of her. Granted, Peter Callaghan's office was a far cry from the cramped, dreary bureaucratic offices she'd been sent to as a child. But there was still something about the scent of all those law books, about seeing them lined up on the shelves along with the legal documents hanging on the walls, that triggered her old feelings of being trapped and helpless. Just as she'd felt trapped and helpless all those years ago as she'd been shuffled through the state and legal systems.

But you're not a child anymore. They no longer have any power over you.

Kelly drew in a steadying breath, released it. She *wasn't* a child anymore. Nor was she trapped in the system, she reminded herself, echoing the voice in her head. *She* was the one in control of her life now—not some judge who saw only another unwanted child dependent upon the juvenile system. She didn't have to shift in and out of a string of foster homes and St. Ann's any longer. She didn't have to subject herself to any court-appointed psychologist. Nor did she have to allow anyone to poke around in her mind, asking her a bunch of stupid questions and then diagnosing her as a troubled girl who made up stories about visions to get attention.

What am I doing? Why am I even thinking about all of this stuff now?

Because she was back in New Orleans.

Coming back had triggered all those unpleasant memories that she'd left the city in order to escape. And just as soon as she finished her meeting with Peter Callaghan and collected the items that Sister Grace had left her, she'd escape again, she promised herself. She'd take the first flight back to New York and forget all about the past and the last few awful days.

Too restless to sit, Kelly stood and began to wander about the room. It really was a beautiful room, she realized, noting the expensive drapes, the plush rug with an inlaid pattern, the artwork. She paused to admire a group of Calder prints that adorned one wall and the marble sculpture that sat on a stand in the corner. Moving over to the credenza she found herself studying the array of framed photographs. There was one of Peter Callaghan with a beautiful brunette woman taken in a garden lush with spring blooms. Another shot featured the elder Mr. Callaghan with a smiling Peter dressed in his graduation cap and gown, holding up his law school diploma. She moved to the next photograph, which depicted the entire Callaghan family—Mr. and Mrs. Callaghan, Peter, his sister, Meredith, and Jack.

Given how young Meredith looked in the picture, Kelly suspected it had been taken more than a decade ago, probably back when she and Meredith were still in high school together. There was something warm and moving about the picture of them as a family unit, and she couldn't help but wonder what it was like to share such a family bond—to look at another person and see a resemblance of yourself in them, of them in you. To know that you belonged.

After hesitating a moment, she picked up the photograph for a closer look. There wasn't an ugly one in the bunch. Blond-haired and blue-eyed, they had toothpaste-perfect white smiles and elegant bone structure. Every one of them was gorgeous. But Jack, she mused as she traced her fingertip along his face, Jack seemed to have been blessed with an extra dollop of everything. An extra inch or so in height over his father's and brother's six-foot frames. His hair was a darker shade of blond, his eyes a deeper blue. Even his smile was a fraction wider, a touch brighter.

"Ms. Santos, please forgive me for keeping you waiting," Peter Callaghan said as he hurried into the room. "I'm afraid I got tied up in court," he told her as he dumped his briefcase next to his desk and strode over to her with his hand extended. "I'm Peter Callaghan."

Kelly quickly returned the photograph to the credenza and shook his hand. "It's a pleasure to meet you again, Mr. Callaghan."

Surprise flickered in his blue eyes. He arched his brow a fraction. "We've met before?"

"A long time ago and only briefly. I'm not surprised that you don't remember," she said, and already wished she had never mentioned it.

"Well, *I* am. I can't imagine how I'd forget someone as lovely as you. Tell me, was I temporarily blind?"

"No," she said with a chuckle. Another charmer. Just like his brother, she thought, and she couldn't help wondering if it was part of the Callaghan's genetic makeup, since even Meredith, whom she'd always considered a bit self-centered, could be charming when she chose to be. "It was more than ten years ago and I wasn't all that memorable."

"Now, *that* I don't believe."

"Trust me, it's true." While her looks had changed little over the years, her fashion sense had. And if she was at all memorable now it was due in large measure to her learning how to select the right clothes and making sure she wore the clothes instead of vice versa. That alone had been one of the nicer perks about the business of selling beauty, she thought.

"Now you've got me curious. Where was it that we met?"

"At your sister Meredith's high school graduation. I was the scrawny girl with stringy blond hair who gave the valedictory address. Afterward, you were kind enough to compliment me on my speech and wished me good luck. As I said, I wasn't particularly memorable."

"But you were," Peter insisted. "And I *do* remember you now, and the speech you gave. About ending one journey and beginning another, and about family and heritage. I especially remember you saying that genetics determined a person's looks and even the number of brain cells, but it didn't determine who a person was or who they would become. You challenged your classmates to become the person they wanted to be, to forge the future they wanted for themselves."

Kelly flushed, both embarrassed and pleased that he could recall the heart of her speech. "You have a very good memory, Mr. Callaghan."

"Please, it's Peter," he said with a smile. "And in order for me to be a good attorney, I have to have a good memory. But that's not why I remembered your speech. I remembered it because I thought your remarks were quite profound for someone so young."

"Thank you," she murmured.

He nodded. "I assume from the fact that you're working in New York that you followed your own advice. I understand from your conversation with my assistant that you're a photographer now."

"That's right. Mostly magazine layouts, some print work and occasionally some portraits. I have to travel a lot and only returned from Europe a couple of days ago. It's the reason you weren't able to reach me," she said, still regretting that she hadn't been there for Sister Grace.

"It sounds like an exciting job."

"I enjoy it and it pays the bills." And it also kept her too busy to dwell on the fact that she had little in the way of a personal life. But then, after the disastrous mistake she'd made with Garrett, she hadn't exactly opened herself to the possibility of a new relationship because she hadn't trusted her judgment.

"I see you've been checking out my family's rogues' gallery."

"A professional drawback," she said, shoving thoughts about Garrett aside. "I find it hard to pass a photo without checking it out. This one of your family is very nice."

"Thanks. It's one of my favorites. And judging by how young we all look here, we're long past due for another family portrait."

"Oh, I don't know about that," she said, looking from him to the photograph and back again. "It doesn't look to me like you or Jack have changed all that much."

"You've seen my brother recently?"

"Yesterday," she told him, then wished she'd kept her mouth shut. Deciding she should explain, she continued, "I was a witness in a police matter and he was the detective assigned to the case."

"Jack's a homicide detective," Peter pointed out.

"Yes, I know. I saw a man get shot."

Peter winced. "Talk about an unpleasant welcome home. I'm sorry, Kelly."

He didn't know the half of it, she thought. Eager to change the subject, she said, "This really is a nice picture. If you do decide to take another family portrait, I'd recommend using the same photographer."

"All right, I can take a hint. I won't pry."

"Thank you," she murmured, grateful that he hadn't pressed her.

"Unfortunately, the photographer who took that re-located to L.A. about five years ago. I don't suppose you'd be interested in the job?"

"I appreciate the offer, but besides not having my equipment, I don't expect to be here very long. You shouldn't have problems finding someone else though. Even an amateur photographer would have an easy time of it, since you and your family are so photogenic."

Peter groaned. "Whatever you do, don't let Meredith hear you say that," he said, dropping his voice to a conspiratorial whisper. "A few years ago, she was on this kick to become a model and nearly drove all of us crazy."

Kelly saw no point in informing him that she already knew about his sister's modeling aspirations since Meredith had paid her a visit in New York, positive that Kelly had some inside track. Meredith had been a female steamroller, she recalled. And despite the fact that the two of them had been acquaintances and not friends, she had made a few phone calls on Meredith's behalf. But after Meredith had landed a few print ads, she'd disappeared almost as quickly as she'd appeared. "Is she still modeling?"

"Not at the moment. She's all wrapped up in opening a boutique in the French Quarter. But with Meredith, one can never be sure. She's my sister and I love her, but the woman has had nearly as many careers as I've had cases."

"Now, that I don't believe," Kelly informed him.

"All right. Maybe I'm exaggerating. But my sister has a short attention span. I'll let her know you're in town though, because I'm sure she'll want to see you. Where are you staying?"

"The Regent Hotel." But Kelly didn't really expect

Meredith to come by to see her. Why should she? The two of them may have attended the same school, but that was the only thing they'd had in common. Meredith's family had been able to afford the private school tuition. Whereas, she had been there by means of a scholarship. But even without the monetary differences, her living situation and her ability to see things that others couldn't had set her apart from Meredith and the rest of her classmates. She remembered all too well that on those few occasions when she'd let something slip, the other girls had been freaked out.

"I'll make myself a note to give Meredith a call and tell her you're here."

"Actually, Peter, it's probably not worth mentioning. I mean, I don't expect to be here long. In fact, once we're finished our business, I'll be heading back to New York."

"And if I let you leave without telling Meredith you're in town, she'll kill me," he said as he put down his pen and stuck a sticky note to his phone. "Besides, if I know my sister, she'll convince you to extend your visit for a day or two."

She wouldn't count on it, Kelly thought silently.

"But be forewarned. Meredith's like a puppy with a bone where this boutique of hers is concerned. She'll probably drive you nuts talking about it. I know I've learned more than I ever wanted to know about women's fashions and accessories and marketing."

"You don't approve of her opening a boutique?" Kelly asked.

"I'm all for it—if that's what Meredith wants and it makes her happy. It would be nice to have her stick around this time," he said. "But then, that's enough about my sister. I'm sure you want to get this business with Sister Grace's will out of the way. So if you'll have a seat, I'll get a copy and go over the particulars with you.''

As surreal as it seemed to be chatting with Peter Callaghan like he was an old friend, the reminder of why she was in his office in the first place was sobering. Kelly sat down in the chair across from his desk. ''I was surprised to learn that Sister Grace even had a will. I just assumed whatever she had would go to her order or to the church.''

''Most of it did. But Sister Grace came to my father a few years ago and asked him to draw up a will with some specific bequests. As you probably know, my parents were very fond of her,'' Peter began. ''And although I didn't know her as well as they did, l did like her. I'm sure she'll be missed by a great many people.''

''Yes, she will,'' Kelly murmured. And she already missed the nun more than she'd ever dreamed she would miss anyone.

''The terms of her will are pretty straightforward. Sister Grace had very little in the way of assets. She left directions that any personal savings she had at the time of her death be given to the Catholic church and earmarked for use in the education of children.''

Which is what she would have expected of Sister Grace, since the nun had put a great deal of stock in the importance of education. She'd called it the great equalizer.

''With the exception of a few items that she left to other nuns in her order, Sister Grace left the remainder of her personal possessions to you. I'm afraid their value is more of a sentimental nature than a monetary one.''

''I understand.''

Peter opened the file folder on his desk and pulled out

an official-looking document. "I'll dispense with reading the entire will and just skip to the part that pertains to your bequests, if that's all right with you."

"That's fine," she told him.

"To my former student and beloved friend, Kelly Santos, I leave my rosary given to me by my own mother when I took my vows. I also leave to her my watercolor titled *Serenity*, which has brought me much pleasure…"

As though in a daze, Kelly sat in silence while Peter read from the will. The pain and emptiness she'd felt upon learning of Sister Grace's death washed over her anew. Only years of learning to discipline her emotions stopped her from blubbering like a baby in front of the attorney.

"…Finally, I leave to Kelly Santos all my correspondence and journals to do with as she wishes. It is my hope that she will remember me with fondness when she reads them and that through my words she will someday discover the bonds of family that she so richly deserves." Peter put down the document and looked across the desk at her. "You were obviously very special to her."

"She was very special to me, too," Kelly told him.

"I'm sorry for your loss, Kelly."

Not trusting herself to speak, Kelly nodded.

"We have the items she mentioned here and can turn them over to you now if you wish. Or if you'd prefer, I can arrange to have everything shipped to you in New York."

Kelly swallowed past the lump of emotion in her throat. "I'd like to have the rosary now. And if it's not too much trouble, I'd appreciate it if you would just ship the rest of the items to me in New York. I'll reimburse you for any shipping charges involved."

"I'll see to it." He buzzed his assistant, gave her instructions about the shipping and had the rosary brought to his office. "May I?" he asked, indicating the plain satin pouch that contained the rosary.

"Of course."

Peter opened the pouch and emptied the prayer beads into his palm. The clear crystal beads and pewter crucifix glimmered beneath the light of the desk lamp. "Very pretty."

Kelly thought of all the times she'd seen Sister Grace fingering the beads of that rosary. And when Peter started to return it to the pouch, she said, "Please, I'd like to see it."

Peter dropped the rosary into her open palm.

Kelly closed her fingers around the beads. And without warning, the world seemed to spin out from beneath her. Suddenly she was no longer sitting in Peter's law office. Instead, she was in an empty church—no, a chapel—she realized as she looked around at her surroundings.

And then she saw Sister Grace. Kelly's heart stopped as she realized the rosary had connected her to the nun. And there was Sister Grace, kneeling in the pew, her head bowed and her rosary beads in her hands.

"Hail Mary, full of grace, the Lord is with thee. Blessed art thou amongst all women, and blessed art—" Sister Grace stopped mid-prayer and started to turn around.

"No! Don't turn around, Sister," a woman's voice said from behind her.

A flicker of anger raced through her blood. "What are you doing here?" the nun demanded.

"This is a church, Sister. I thought everyone was welcome."

"This is a chapel and the evening services are over," the nun countered. "What do you want?"

"Maybe I want to pray. Since God has seen fit to throw this nasty little surprise at me and mess up my life, I thought maybe if I prayed real hard, He'd make the problem go away. What do you think, Sister? Will God listen to my prayers?"

"God hears all of our prayers."

"Ah, but the question is does He answer them?"

"He answers them. But the answer isn't necessarily the one we want," Sister Grace replied.

"I guess that means you haven't changed your mind about giving me her name."

"I've told you, your information is wrong. I can't help you."

"That's what I thought you'd say. And since I can't risk having you warn her about me, I'm afraid I have no choice but to make sure that you keep quiet."

And before Sister Grace could move, the woman plunged a needle into her neck.

"Kelly? Kelly, are you all right?"

Kelly dropped the rosary. She felt the world spinning beneath her once more. And then someone was gripping her by the shoulders, calling her name. She blinked, tried to regain her balance. Finally when she was able to focus, she saw Peter standing in front of her, a worried expression on his face.

"Are you okay?"

"Yes," she told him. "I'm fine."

"You don't look fine," he informed her. He picked up the rosary, returned it to the pouch and handed it to her. "You want to tell me what happened just now?"

"What do you mean?" she asked, unsure of what she had said, what she had done.

"One minute you were holding that rosary and the next minute you seemed to...to zone out.

"I can't explain it. And you wouldn't believe me if I told you." After stuffing the pouch with the rosary into her bag she stood, eager to leave. "I've taken up enough of your time."

"Kelly, are you sure you're all right? You're as white as a ghost."

"I'm okay. Really," she assured him. "Thank you for everything, Peter," she said, and after shaking his hand, she raced out of the office.

Once she stepped outside into the cool November air, Kelly attempted to hail a taxi while she digested what she had just learned.

Sister Grace hadn't died of a heart attack. Someone had murdered her.

Anger churned in Kelly's stomach as she recalled the nun's last moments and her fear. Somehow, some way, she had to find out who was responsible. She owed Sister Grace that much.

Five .

After being briefed that no arrest had yet been made in connection with the city's latest murder victim, and the police department's only lead was a self-proclaimed psychic, District Attorney Alexander Kusak sighed as he climbed the steps of City Hall. Just what he needed, he thought and wondered for the thousandth time what had ever possessed him to take this job.

But he already knew the answer. Tom Callaghan had been the reason. The man had taken the badass punk, with a chip on his shoulder, under his wing. Mr. Callaghan had made him believe he could be someone who could make a difference. And most of the time, he admitted, he felt that he did make a difference. He just wished that taking the job hadn't come with the price of his privacy and, in particular, revealing his past. A past that included having a drunk and a whore for parents. Although he'd made something of himself and his life that he was proud of, having all that garbage dug up during the campaign last year had opened old wounds. It had also caused him to see himself through other's eyes—through Meredith's eyes. He hadn't liked what he'd seen. It was the reason he had pushed Meredith away. And she'd done what he'd expected—she'd run off. Again. Only now she'd come back and was making noises like she intended to stay.

Alex started down the nearly deserted hallway toward his office. And when he stepped through the doors and spied all the empty desks, he headed for Edna's station. "Where is everybody, Eddie?"

Edna Boudreaux, the stalwart office manager he'd inherited when he'd taken the office last year, glanced up from the reports on her desk. The woman did a hell of a job. She'd run the office for the retired D.A. for more than twenty years. Alex had been only too happy to keep her on since she knew anyone and everyone, and could cut through bureaucratic red tape faster than a hot knife through butter. He'd also never met a more dedicated employee. But damn if he didn't feel like a punk running from the law again whenever she looked up at him with that "what have you been up to" expression on her face.

The way she was looking at him now.

"It's lunchtime, Mr. Kusak. They're at lunch. As am I," she advised him, referring to the sandwich and pickle slices that sat next to the reports. "And I really do wish you would dispense with that ridiculous nickname. My name is Edna or Mrs. Boudreaux. Not Eddie."

Alex sat on the corner of her desk, helped himself to one of her pickle slices. "Come on, Eddie. Didn't the late Mr. Boudreaux ever call you anything but Edna?"

She waited a moment, then said, "He called me Buttercup."

Alex bit back a grin. With her tidy bun, granny glasses and prim suits, he couldn't imagine Mrs. Boudreaux as anyone's Buttercup. "I think I like Eddie better."

"So you've said, Mr. Kusak."

Alex sighed. Even after working side by side for nearly a year, the lady refused to call him by his first name. As she'd informed him when he'd first suggested she do so, she'd never called the former D.A. anything but "Mr. Newman" in the entire twenty years she'd worked for him. She saw no reason to resort to any such familiarity now. And though he doubted she'd admit it, he had a feeling he was growing on her. "You know, Eddie, one of these days you're going to slip and call me 'Alex,' and when that happens our secret's going to be out."

"And what secret would that be, Mr. Kusak?"

"Why that we're madly in love with each other."

"If you're finished talking nonsense, why don't you tell me what it is you wanted."

Alex flashed her a grin. "I need to get a brief typed," he began, and proceeded to explain what was needed. As he spoke, he loosened his tie. Despite eight years in the D.A.'s office, first as an assistant and now as the district attorney, he still hated wearing the things. He might have come a long way from his days on the opposite side of the law, but he'd never gotten used to being trussed up like a turkey with a scrap of cloth choking him. "Do you think you can get it finished for me to take to court in say, forty minutes?"

Mrs. Boudreaux lifted her gaze from his mangled tie and Alex didn't miss the disapproving set of her mouth. Although she said nothing, he was sure she was comparing him to his predecessor, who'd been a dapper dresser known for his bow ties. "I'll have it ready."

"You're a lifesaver, Eddie. I could kiss you."

"I'd suggest you save your kisses for the young lady in your office," she told him dryly.

"Does the lady have a name?"

"Miss Callaghan," she informed him.

His body went on full alert at the mention of Meredith's name. She'd been driving him crazy from the time she'd been in a training bra and he'd been a juvenile delinquent on a fast track to trouble. "Did she say, uh, what she wanted?"

"Since she doesn't know that I saw her sneak in there while I was getting my sandwich from the kitchen, I didn't bother to ask."

"You going soft on me, Eddie?"

She shrugged. "The girl looked so pleased with herself because she thought she'd gotten by me that I didn't have the heart to ruin it for her."

"Well, what do you know? You *are* a buttercup after all."

She straightened her shoulders, gave him that prim look, but Alex thought he saw a bit more color in her cheeks. "Mr. Kusak, if you expect me to get this brief typed, I suggest you let me get to it."

Alex eased off the edge of her desk and started for his office.

"Oh and one more thing, Mr. Kusak."

"Yes?"

"You might want to suggest to Miss Callaghan that the next time she wants to get by someone unnoticed that she'd be wise to leave the red trench coat at home."

"I'll do that," Alex told her, and opened the door to his office. He stepped inside. And there she was—sitting behind his desk wearing that scarlet-red trench coat and a pair of killer black heels that she had propped up on his desk.

"Hello, Mr. District Attorney."

"Hello, Meredith," he said with a calmness he was far from feeling. Some men had a weakness for booze. Others for drugs or gambling or even sex. For him, his weakness had always been Meredith Callaghan. She was like a fever in his blood, impossible to cure and equally fatal. "You want to tell me what you're doing here?"

She gave him a pout and tossed her strawberry-blond hair so that it fell across her shoulders. "I didn't realize I needed a reason to visit an old friend."

They'd been a great deal more than friends and therein lay the problem, Alex thought as he felt his body responding to her already. "I don't have time to chitchat now. I'm due back in court in less than an hour."

"I didn't come by to chitchat," she sniffed. "I came by to remind you about my mother's birthday dinner tonight. She's expecting you."

"Jack already reminded me. I'll be there."

"Good," she said, giving him another one of those slow smiles that tied him up in knots.

When she made no attempt to leave, he said, "Now that you've delivered the message, I'd appreciate it if you'd get your feet off my desk and your pretty little rear end out of my chair. I need to get back to work."

She beamed at him. "You think my rear end's pretty?"

"I think the coat's pretty."

"You should see what I have on underneath it."

Alex bit back a groan, because he knew every damn inch of her body. "No thanks." He managed the words out of a throat that had gone dry with lust. "Now, move it."

"Not until you tell me why you haven't returned any of my calls. I've left you at least a dozen messages over the past two weeks." She'd actually left only three, but he didn't bother correcting her. "And that Simon Legree secretary of yours keeps telling me you're unavailable."

"Because I'm not available. I'm busy," he told her, and began thumbing through the mail stacked in his "in" box.

"Bull! You've been avoiding me, Alex Kusak, and

you know it." She swung her legs off of the desk and came to her feet. "I've been back in town for three months now and we haven't been alone together for five minutes."

"With good reason," he admitted. Giving up any pretense of reading the mail, he dumped the envelopes back into the tray. "You and I both know what happens whenever we're alone together."

She came over to him, draped her arms around his neck, and looking up at him out of those big green eyes, she whispered against his lips, "I know what I want to happen."

Alex could feel himself growing hard as she pressed herself against him. He breathed in her scent, something wild and exotic like her. He wanted her so bad he ached. It had always been that way with Meredith—ever since that first time on her eighteenth birthday. Even now, he couldn't believe he'd fallen for the lame story she'd given him that night about having a problem and needing to talk to him. He'd left the society bash inside her parents' home and gone with her to the gazebo to talk. And then she'd told him the problem—that the one thing she wanted for her birthday only he could give her. She'd wanted him to make love to her. It was wrong. He'd known it was wrong. But he'd found her impossible to resist. They'd been off-and-on lovers for years, and because they hadn't wanted to freak out family and friends, they'd kept the secret between them. She'd matched him sexually in every way, and since neither of them had been looking for a long-term commitment, the relationship had suited them both just fine.

And then a couple of years ago, something had changed. He still wasn't sure if it was he or Meredith. Whatever there was between them had become more than friendship, more than just good sex. He cared about her, maybe too much.

"Want me to tell you what I'd like to do?" she whispered in his ear. She nipped his lobe with her teeth.

Alex felt himself weaken. Then he remembered the way Meredith had looked at him when all that sordid stuff about his parents had come out during the campaign. There had been pain in her eyes. Pain and shame. For him? For herself? It didn't matter, he told himself. He had no intention of starting things up again—no matter how tempted he was. With a strength he hadn't known he possessed, he caught her wrists and pulled them away from his neck. "It isn't going to happen, Meredith."

"Why not?" she demanded.

"Because I said no."

Suddenly her eyes narrowed. "Is there someone else?"

"What if I said there was?"

Temper flared in her green eyes, turning them nearly black. She grabbed his tie, yanked his face close to hers. "Who is she?" When he didn't answer, she repeated, "Who is she, Alex Kusak? Is it that little witch Alicia Van Owen? Has she been trying to sink her claws into you now?"

"Alicia?" he responded, surprised at the mention of the woman who'd been dating his best friend. "I thought she was dating your brother."

"Jack dumped her."

"You sure about that?" He uncurled Meredith's fingers and attempted to smooth his tie. "When I saw Jack at the courthouse earlier, he told me that Alicia would be at the dinner party for your mother tonight."

"That's because she and my mother refuse to get the

message. Both of them are hearing wedding bells. Well, she isn't going to marry my brother. I refuse to have that woman as my sister-in-law.''

''Ah, you don't like her,'' he said.

''No, I don't like Little Miss Perfect.''

The truth was, he didn't care for the woman, either. Maybe because beneath all that polish, he picked up her disapproval of him. She wouldn't be the first person to think the likes of him had no business being friends with someone like Jack Callaghan. For reasons he'd never understood, Jack and his family had felt differently.

''So help me, Alex. If I find out you're sleeping with that woman, I swear to God I'll cut it off and throw it into the Mississippi River.''

Instinct had him lowering his hand to protect his manhood. ''You shouldn't go around threatening the D.A., Meredith.''

''It's not a threat. It's a promise. I mean it, Alex,'' she told him with all the passion with which she did everything. ''If you've been stupid enough to let Alicia get her hooks into you, I'll kill you both.''

Damn if she didn't look adorable when she was mad, he thought. ''Put away your weapons. Alicia's not interested in me, and I'm not interested in her.'' There was little chance he'd ever fall for an ice queen like Alicia Van Owen. How could he when Meredith Callaghan had been keeping him tied up in knots for years? ''And before you start grilling me again, I'm not seeing anyone.''

Her face lit up and she gave him a sultry smile that made the temperature in the room shoot up ten degrees. Moving closer, she speared her fingers through his hair and gazed up at him. ''Well, what do you know? Neither am I. So you see, there's really no reason we can't be together just like old times.''

"No," he informed her.

Ignoring him, she murmured, "I've missed you so much, Alex. Have you missed me, too?"

"No."

She pressed her body closer. When her knee nudged his erection, she laughed, that husky laugh that made a man think of hot sex and sin. "Liar."

She was right. He was lying. But he forced himself not to respond to her.

She traced his lips with her tongue. "Are you going to deny that you want me?"

"No." What would be the point in denying the obvious? he reasoned as he eased her away from him. "But I'm not going to do anything about it. I told you, Meredith, it's over. Accept it."

"I won't accept it. We're good together, Alex. You know we are."

"The sex is good, but we're not," he said gently, the hurt in her eyes ripping at him.

"We could be."

And for a short time, he'd almost convinced himself that they could be together. Then had come the campaign, the nasty publicity and slams at Meredith's reputation, the shame and pain in her eyes. "You need to get on with your life. We both do. We'll always be friends, but the rest of it…it's over."

"I don't believe you."

"Suit yourself. But I'm not going to change my mind."

Her expression hardened. A steely look came into her eyes. "You wanna bet?"

"Meredith—"

"I'll see you tonight, Alex." She pressed a quick kiss to his lips and slid her hand between their bodies.

"Meredith," he warned, then ruined it by groaning as she stroked his shaft.

"Think of me," she whispered against his lips, then dashed from the room in a whiff of perfume.

Alex leaned back against his desk. He had little choice but to think of her, he admitted. In fact, he'd be damn lucky if he'd be able to think of anything else.

Mary Ellen Callaghan stood in the dining room of her family's home later that evening and surveyed the table. She'd ordered that it be set with her fine china, crystal and sterling silver for the small dinner party she'd orchestrated to celebrate her seventieth birthday.

Seventy!

Heavens, such a large number of years. Good years, happy years, even if the last two had been lonely without her beloved Tommy. Feeling melancholy at the thought of her departed husband, Mary Ellen pushed the sad thoughts aside and reminded herself that just last week at her annual physical Dr. St. Pierre had declared her to be in excellent health. The constitution of a woman ten years her junior, he'd said. And she certainly didn't *think* she looked like a woman of seventy. Or at least she hoped that she didn't. Except for a mini eye tuck at sixty, she hadn't had any work done like so many of her friends. And she'd always taken good care of herself and her skin. Besides, she had no intention of joining her Tommy anytime soon—not when she still had so much that remained undone.

Returning her focus to the evening ahead, she studied the table. Her grandmother's lace tablecloth had been the right choice, she decided, noting how the light from the chandelier picked out the delicate fleur-de-lis pattern. As she moved about the table inspecting the place settings, she straightened a silver spoon, adjusted one of the place cards. She caught the scent of the peach roses that she'd clipped from her garden that very afternoon and had arranged in Waterford vases. Satisfied all was ready, she smiled.

It was perfect. Elegant, tasteful. Perhaps even worthy of a page in *Southern Living,* she mused, pleased with the results of her handiwork. Trailing her fingers along the edge of the lace tablecloth, Mary Ellen marveled at its beauty. She sighed as she remembered when she'd inherited it from her grandmother as a young bride. Oh, she'd been so sure that she would have passed it on to her own daughter or to the wife of one of her sons by now. But neither Meredith nor Jackson had married. And Peter...poor Peter's marriage had been brief and had ended tragically.

But soon all that would change, she promised herself. If all went as she hoped it would, she would get her birthday wish and it wouldn't be long before she'd be helping to plan her son Jackson's wedding. He and Alicia made a lovely couple, she thought. Since her little nudges hadn't been working, she'd decided it was time she gave that boy of hers a little push. Surely Jackson would see, as she did, that Alicia was perfect for him. Once he did, he'd ask her to marry him. And then, God willing, the two of them wouldn't waste any time making her a grandmother.

"There you are," Jack said as he entered the room and walked over to her.

"Jackson, darling. I was just thinking about you."

"Were you now? Good thoughts, I hope."

"Yes." And because she was Catholic, she couldn't help thinking her son's appearance now was a sign.

"Happy birthday, Mother," he said, and kissed her cheek.

"Thank you, dear. But I do think this is a first. You're early and you're never early for parties."

"That's because it's your birthday. Besides, you said this wasn't going to be a party, just a simple dinner with family and a few friends." He eyed the table suspiciously. "This doesn't look like a simple dinner to me."

"Of course it is. But we're having cake and champagne, so that makes it a party, too," she explained. She straightened his tie and couldn't help thinking how much he looked like his father. "You looked so handsome at the charity ball on Halloween. And wasn't Alicia just beautiful?"

"Yes, she was."

Disturbed by the lack of enthusiasm in her son's voice, Mary Ellen said, "She's a lovely young woman, Jackson. She's well-bred and talented. And smart, too. Why look how well she's done for herself since she moved here. She picked up that Devereaux house for a song and turn it into a showplace. And according to Phyllis Ladner, Alicia's already among the top real estates associates in her firm."

"As you said, she's talented and smart," Jack replied with that same lack of conviction.

"It still amazes me that any daughter of Abigail Beaumont could be so sweet-natured," Mary Ellen told him, referring to the former debutante she'd had the misfortune of calling a sorority sister at Vanderbilt. The other woman had been the coldest, most calculating female she'd ever met—and she had met quite a few in her seventy years. "I can only think that Alicia must have taken after her father. I only met him once or twice, but Charles Van Owen seemed like a nice man.'' Suddenly ashamed of her uncharitable thoughts about Abigail she said, ''Listen to me. You must think I'm a mean-spirited old biddy, speaking ill of a dead friend that way.''

''You couldn't be mean-spirited if you tried,'' her son informed her. He held her by the shoulders, pressed a kiss to the top of her head and looked at her out of eyes that reminded her so much of her Tommy's. ''And I certainly don't think of you as old or a biddy.''

She patted his cheek. ''You're a charmer, just like your father was,'' she told him, and sighed wistfully.

''You still miss him, don't you?''

Mary Ellen nodded and attempted a smile. ''We were married for more than forty years. I was lucky we had so long together. Not everyone is as lucky,'' she pointed out, thinking of Peter's short marriage and the death of his wife to melanoma. ''When the right person comes along, waiting isn't always the smart thing to do.''

''Mother,'' Jack began.

Deciding to ignore that ''don't go there'' note in his voice, she forged ahead. ''I know that you're too old to have your mother telling you what to do. And you certainly don't need me to tell you how to run your love life.''

''No, I don't,'' he said firmly.

Taken aback by his bluntness, she said, ''Fine. Then all I'm going to say is that Alicia Van Owen is a wonderful young woman who obviously cares a great deal for you. I don't know what that little spat was the two of you had the other night, and I don't want to know.''

''We didn't have a spat, and I don't want to discuss this.''

Irritated with him for being so stubborn, Mary Ellen

poked a finger at his chest and gave him a quelling look. "We're not discussing it. I'm simply telling you that whatever's wrong, I suggest you fix it and fix it fast. Because if you keep dragging your feet and acting like a horse's rear end the way you've been doing, some other man is going to come along and steal her right from under your nose."

Her son said nothing, but judging by the way his mouth had tightened, he was none too pleased with her remarks. Too bad, Mary Ellen thought. But when a rap came at the door, she was grateful for the interruption.

"What?" Jack snapped.

Alexander Kusak stuck his head inside the door. "What's your problem, Callaghan?"

"Oh Alexander, you came," Mary Ellen cried out, genuinely pleased to see the young man who was practically a third son to her.

"Of course I came. Did you really think I would have missed your birthday?"

Pleasure washed through her. "You're such a busy man these days and it's been months since you've come to dinner. I was afraid you might not be able to get away tonight either."

"I'm never too busy for you." He strolled over, kissed her cheek. "Happy Birthday, Mrs. C."

"Thank you, dear."

"Don't believe him," Jack said, losing some of his somberness. "Kusak only came for the food."

"I came for Mrs. C. *and* the food," he amended.

"Right. You'd better check the kitchen, Mother. The last time this guy showed up here for a party, he practically wiped out the fridge."

"I'm a hardworking D.A. who doesn't have time to cook. And your mother and Tilly took pity on me," he explained, referring to the longtime cook who had been with the Callaghan family almost as long as he had. "They allowed me to take home a few leftovers."

"Leftovers my as—"

"Jackson!"

"Excuse me," her son murmured.

She didn't have to have eyes in the back of her head to know that Alex was grinning at her reprimand of his friend. "And you can wipe that smile off your face, Alexander Kusak."

"Yes, ma'am," he said politely as she turned back to him.

The smile was gone, but not the mischievous gleam in his dark eyes as he exchanged looks with her son. Theirs had been an unlikely friendship, she mused as she considered their diverse backgrounds. Alex had been such a wild and angry young man. And with reason, considering that his mother had left him with that drunken excuse of a father when he'd been little more than a baby. He'd practically raised himself and had been in several skirmishes with the law before he was even sixteen. She had worried that he would be a bad influence on her son. But her worries had been unfounded. Alex had never led Jack astray. For a while during his political campaign she'd even thought that he and Meredith might finally pair up. It had been something she'd hoped for for quite some time. But alas, whatever had gone on between them seemed to be over now. Such a shame, too, because the two of them would have been good for each other, and she certainly would have welcomed Alexander as a son-in-law. Some things just weren't meant to be, she supposed. But she was still proud of him. She was proud of all three of her boys.

And by golly, she wanted them married and making grandbabies for her to spoil.

But one thing at a time, Mary Ellen reminded herself. First she'd have to see what she could do to mend whatever this little tiff was between Alicia and Jack. "Shall we see if the others are here yet?"

"By all means," Alex told her, and held out his arm for her.

She rested her hand atop his arm. "I've asked Tilly to prepare some of those mushrooms stuffed with crabmeat that you like so much," she informed him as he escorted her from the room.

Alex groaned. "Mrs. C., you're a woman after my own heart."

Mary Ellen smiled. "Since the way to your heart is obviously through your stomach, perhaps I should introduce you to my friend Emily's daughter Victoria. She's a gourmet chef."

Six

"I know this is a terrible imposition, my coming here during the dinner hour, Reverend Mother. I appreciate you agreeing to see me," Kelly told the nun as she sat across from her in the parlor of the convent.

"You made it sound so urgent on the phone."

"I know. And I'm sorry if I alarmed you. But I have some questions about Sister Grace's death, important questions, and I didn't know who else to ask. I'm hoping that you'll be able to provide me with the answers," Kelly explained, her stomach knotting again as it had in Peter Callaghan's office earlier that day when she'd first held the rosary.

"Well, I'll certainly try," the Reverend Mother told her. She folded her hands in her lap and sat back in her chair. "What is it you want to know?"

Where to begin? How to begin? she wondered for a moment, then breathed deeply in an effort to calm herself. "You said that Sister Grace's death was ruled as a heart attack. Are you sure that's what killed her?"

The nun blinked her hazel eyes. "That's what the doctor said," she replied.

"When...how did it happen?" Kelly asked, making an effort to speak slowly, rationally.

"We found her in the chapel. When she didn't return from evening prayers, one of the sisters went to look for her and discovered her slumped over in the pew where she'd been praying. She wasn't breathing," the Reverend Mother explained. "We tried CPR, but she didn't respond. By then, someone had dialed 911 for an ambulance and had called her doctor, Dr. Fontenot. Both arrived within a few minutes, but it was too late. Dr. Fontenot examined her and said that her heart had finally given out."

"Did the coroner do an autopsy?"

Surprise flitted across the nun's face for a moment. "Dr. Fontenot didn't see a need for an autopsy. Nor did I. As I said, Sister Grace wasn't well, Kelly. She hadn't been for some time. Besides her heart being weak, she'd never fully regained her strength after that bout of pneumonia she suffered last winter."

"I didn't realize she'd had pneumonia," Kelly said. "I mean, I knew she'd been ill, but she'd told me it was just the flu."

"I'm afraid it was much more serious than the flu. She was in the hospital for nearly two weeks. But even when she was released and returned to the convent, she had to continue breathing treatments for more than a month. We were all quite concerned about her."

"I didn't know. She never told me," Kelly said, more to herself than the nun.

The Reverend Mother reached over and patted Kelly's hand. "Don't fret over it, child. Sister Grace hated to have anyone make a fuss over her. She probably didn't tell you because she knew you would worry and she didn't want that."

But she should have known, Kelly told herself as guilt rushed through her. Just as she should have known that something was troubling Sister Grace. She'd sensed it several times during those last few months. And one of the last times they'd spoken, when Sister Grace had asked her if she'd ever thought about pursuing information about her past, alarms should have gone off in her head. That question alone should have alerted her to the fact that something was wrong.

After all, it had been Sister Grace who had discouraged her from searching for the answers about her past all those years ago. She could remember sitting with her and discussing it almost as though it were only yesterday...

"Sister, I've decided to try to find out who my parents were."

"Buy why, child?" Sister Grace asked.

"Because I want to find out why they left me."

A sad expression crossed the nun's face. "Kelly, don't you remember? I explained to you a long time ago that the authorities tried to locate your parents when you first came to us. If they weren't successful back then, think how much more difficult it would be to find them now, after all this time."

"I realize that it won't be easy," Kelly insisted. *"But there's been a lot of new technology since I was a kid. They might have more luck locating them now."*

Sister Grace shook her head. "Oh, Kelly, I'd thought you'd gotten past this. Do you really want to put yourself through that?"

"Yes," she persisted, refusing to have her hopes derailed. *"I want to at least try to find them."*

"And what happens if you're successful?"

Kelly frowned. "What do you mean?"

"I mean, suppose you do locate your parents. What is it you're hoping for? That they will welcome you with open arms? That they will want you in their lives now after all of these years?"

"No," she answered honestly. She was twelve years old, old enough to know that no one wanted half-grown girls—especially ones who saw things that no one else could see. No, if her parents hadn't wanted her as a baby, she was sure they wouldn't want her now, either. "I'm not hoping for anything."

"Then why do this? What purpose would it serve?"

"Because if I find them, then I would finally know who I am."

"But you already know who you are—you're Kelly Santos." Sister Grace's expression softened. "Kelly, who and what you are, the person you become, isn't determined by genetics. It's determined by what's in here and here," she said, touching her head and then her heart. "God has given you many gifts and the potential to do great things with those gifts, both for yourself and for others. Instead of searching for answers to a past that can't be changed, why not concentrate on the future? Why not become the person the Lord meant for you to be? Become the person you want to be."

And she'd tried to do what Sister Grace had suggested. She'd stopped looking for answers, stopped asking herself why her parents hadn't wanted her, stopped wishing she hadn't been born with second sight. She'd used her skill as a photographer to become someone she could be proud of, someone she respected. She'd accepted herself.

Then why when she'd sensed something was troubling Sister Grace hadn't she pressed the nun for answers?

Because she had feared what those answers might be, she admitted.

"I know that you and Sister Grace were close. I'm

sure the last thing she would want is for you to feel guilty because of her," the Reverend Mother assured her.

But she did feel guilty. And ever since Peter Callaghan had put that rosary into her hand, ever since she'd seen the nun's face, heard her words in the chapel, she was sure of one thing. That Sister Grace's death had not been due to a simple heart attack. Someone had killed her. And she intended to prove it. "Reverend Mother, you said that Sister Grace's body was discovered in the chapel after vespers. Was anyone else with her?"

"Hmm, let me think. It's not uncommon for a few of the sisters to remain a little longer to pray. On that evening, I believe Sister Maria and Sister Veronica, one of our novices, stayed behind in the chapel, along with Sister Grace. According to them, Sister was still in prayer when they left her."

"Would it have been possible for someone else... someone who wasn't a member of the order, perhaps a parishioner or a visitor, to have been in the chapel with her?"

"Possible, but not likely. Once Father completes the Saturday vigil mass, most of the parishioners leave. The few who remain only do so for a short time. As sad as it sounds, to protect the sacristy and the religious, the doors to the chapel are no longer left open. They're locked for the night."

"But they're not locked right away, are they?"

"Well, no. Not immediately, but certainly within a short time after the mass has ended. Either Father or the deacon does a check of the chapel, to make sure that it's empty and then they lock the doors for the night. According to Sister Veronica, Father Allen came into the chapel and told them he would be locking the doors shortly. That's when she and Sister Maria left."

"But Sister Grace remained."

"Yes. She often did."

Kelly leaned forward. "Reverend Mother, suppose Sister Grace wasn't really alone? Suppose there was someone else in the chapel who was hiding, maybe in the confessional or behind the altar. Someone that Sister Maria and Sister Veronica and Father didn't see?"

The nun studied her with troubled eyes. "Where are you going with this, Kelly?"

Kelly hesitated, unsure what to tell her, how to explain what she'd seen when she'd held the rosary. Finally, she opted for the truth. "I don't think Sister Grace died because of a heart attack. I think someone killed her."

The Reverend Mother brought a hand to her throat. "Why would you think such a thing?"

"I can't explain it, Reverend Mother. Not so that you'd believe me or even understand. Sometimes even I don't understand." Kelly whooshed out a breath, then met the nun's eyes. "But I know Sister Grace wasn't alone in the chapel the night she died. Someone was with her and that person killed her."

"How do you know that?"

"I just do," Kelly told her.

The nun paused. "But who would want to kill her? She was a nun. What possible enemies could she have had?"

"I don't know," Kelly admitted, frustrated. "I've asked myself that same question over and over and I keep hitting a blank wall."

"Perhaps that's because Sister Grace wasn't murdered," the Reverend Mother offered, her eyes filled with pity. "I know the two of you were close. And you said yourself that you feel guilty because you didn't realize how ill she'd been. But you mustn't blame yourself, Kelly, and you mustn't search for some other reason or person to blame for Sister Grace's death. Our lives and our deaths, they are all a part of God's plan.''

"Her death wasn't part of God's plan. She was murdered,'' Kelly insisted.

"That's grief talking, child. You—''

"It's not grief, it's the truth. I saw Sister Grace in the chapel and she wasn't alone. There was someone with her, someone who injected her with something and killed her.''

"You saw Sister Grace the night she died?'' she asked, her voice unnaturally calm.

"Yes.''

"But how is that possible, when you told me yourself that you were in Europe when she died?''

"Because I…I am able to see things…things that have happened, things that will happen.''

"You're saying you're psychic?''

"That's what some people call it. Others call it second sight. Whatever it is, when I touch a person or an object, I get a flash…images of what's happened to that person or what's going to happen to them.'' Kelly swallowed and pressed on, just wanting to get it out. "When I was at the attorney's office yesterday, he gave me Sister Grace's rosary. When I held it in my hand, I saw her. I saw Sister Grace in the chapel on the night she died and she wasn't alone. There was a woman in the pew behind her and that woman killed her.''

She'd shocked the nun. Kelly read it in the other woman's face, in the stillness of her body. "I don't know what to say.''

"Do you believe me? That I can see things?''

The Reverend Mother met her gaze. "I'm a Catholic and a nun. I believe in the Lord Jesus, the Virgin Mother and miracles. I believe that Our Lady appeared to peasant children in Fatima and Medjugorje, to St. Bernadette in Lourdes. So I believe in things that can't always be explained.''

''Do you believe *me?* Do you believe that I saw Sister Grace murdered?''

''I believe that you *think* you saw something. But whether it was Sister Grace's murder…well, I simply don't know. The doctor found no evidence that there was any foul play involved. He ruled Sister Grace's death due to a heart attack. There's nothing to suggest otherwise.''

''But what if that's not what happened? What if she was murdered and I can prove it?''

''How would you do that?''

''By having her body exhumed, running tests to see if there was something injected into her system that would cause a heart attack.''

''I'm afraid that's impossible,'' the nun told her.

''No it's not, Reverend Mother. Since she had no next of kin, you could order that they exhume the body.''

The Reverend Mother shook her head. ''You don't understand, Kelly. There is no body to exhume. When the church revised its laws about internment, leaving the choice of burial or cremation to the individual, Sister Grace left instructions that her remains be cremated.''

Jack half listened to the conversation at the dinner table, his thoughts still on the Gilbert murder case and Kelly Santos. When his sister fidgeted beside him, he shifted his focus to those gathered to celebrate his mother's birthday. Just family, his mother had claimed, even though not everyone seated at the table fit that description. In addition to himself, his older brother, Peter, and Meredith, she'd invited his oldest friend, Alex. In many ways, Alex was like his brother, he thought, since the friendship that began when they were both fifteen continued even though they were now thirty-three.

His gaze shifted to Margaret "Margee" Jardine, who was two years older than him. Margee's parents had been neighbors to the Callaghans for years, and she'd been a fixture at their house. Except for a two-week period one summer when they'd both been teens, he'd thought of her as a sister. The only other nonrelative was Alicia Van Owen, who had come into their lives a year ago and had been taken under his mother's wing. At thirty-three, Alicia was smart, sexy and beautiful and he hadn't felt anything remotely brotherly toward her—which explained their affair. But as much as he liked her and enjoyed the sex, there had been something missing. He wanted what his partner Leon shared with his wife. Yet he couldn't see himself spending the rest of his life with Alicia, starting a family with her, growing old with her. Once he'd finally realized that, he had broken things off. Only Alicia hadn't wanted to accept it. At least not until the other night when he'd handled things with all the finesse of a gorilla.

Meredith leaned toward him and muttered, "I still don't know why we couldn't have had a *real* party."

"Because it's Mother's birthday and *she* wanted a small, quiet dinner with just family," Jack pointed out, taking care to keep his voice low.

"Then what's little Miss-butter-wouldn't-melt-in-her-mouth Van Owen doing here? She's not family."

He didn't bother pointing out that technically neither was Alex or Margee Jardine. "Mother invited her. Now quit being a brat and be quiet," he told her.

But within moments, Meredith was whispering, "You

do know that Mother's got her heart set on you marrying her, don't you?''

Yes, he'd figured that out, Jack admitted silently. And despite what his mother or Alicia might have their hearts set on, it wasn't going to happen. Which was what he'd told Alicia point blank at the Halloween gala. He winced as he recalled how poorly he'd handled it. He'd felt like a heel when her hazel eyes had filled with tears, but she'd claimed she understood and insisted she still wanted them to see each other as friends. Either he'd been a cop too long or had known enough women to realize when someone was feeding him a line.

''You're not really going to marry her, are you?''

Unable to resist getting a rise out of his baby sister, he replied, ''And what if I said that I was?''

Meredith whispered, ''Then I'd kill you.''

''What's the matter? I thought you always wanted a sister.''

Meredith shuddered. The look she gave him would have charred meat. ''I'd sooner be an orphan than have her for a sister.''

Jack chuckled.

''Jackson, what are you and Meredith whispering about?'' his mother demanded.

''Meredith was just asking me to recommend a good security company for her boutique,'' he said, trying to come up with a plausible cover fast.

''There are several firms that I've worked with,'' Alicia offered politely. ''I'd be happy to give you a list of them.''

''Since my brother's a cop, I think he can advise me on security firms better than someone who sells houses.''

''Meredith Elizabeth Callaghan! That was uncalled

for, young lady,'' their mother chided. ''Apologize to Alicia.''

''Really, Mary Ellen, that's not necessary,'' Alicia said.

''It most certainly is necessary. Meredith,'' she prompted in that ''you're in deep trouble'' voice that Jack remembered hearing all too often growing up.

''I'm sorry,'' Meredith said without an ounce of sincerity. When their mother leveled her eyes on her, his sister continued, ''I didn't mean to sound ungrateful. I appreciate your offer, but Jack has already promised to help me. Right, Jack?''

''Right.''

''No offense taken,'' Alicia accepted demurely. ''I think it's wonderful that you can turn to your brothers for help. You're lucky to have siblings.''

''Trust me, it has its drawbacks,'' Meredith countered. ''Big brothers can be a real pain sometimes.''

''But at least you never have to worry about being alone,'' she replied, and Jack was reminded that Alicia had lost both of her parents suddenly when they'd been killed in a car accident a year ago.

''But you're not alone, dear,'' Mary Ellen Callaghan informed her. ''You have us.''

''That's very kind of you. You have no idea how much that means to me. Thank you.''

''Nonsense. There's no need to thank me for anything,'' his mother told her. ''Why, you're practically family—just like Alexander and Margaret.''

''She means it,'' Margee assured her. ''I was only knee-high when my parents bought the house down the street. I spent so much time over here that Miss Mary Ellen and Mr. Tommy probably could have claimed me on their tax return. The door's been open to me ever since.''

"And it always will be," his mother replied. "I just wish your parents could have joined us tonight."

"So do they, but Daddy's determined to stay in Paris until he can work out the negotiations for the new hotel the family's trying to buy. But they said to send you their love," Margee told her.

"What an interesting business your family's in," Alicia responded. "I'm surprised you didn't decide to follow in their footsteps and get involved with hotels instead of going into law."

"I found the law more exciting."

"Tell her the truth, Margee. You became a lawyer to irritate me," Peter teased. He laughed and continued, "Margee here was always tailing behind me, making a pest of herself, trying to best me when we were growing up. I think she went to law school just to prove to me that she could do it, too."

"Don't flatter yourself, Callaghan. I went to law school for me—not you," Margee countered.

Mary Ellen shook her head and made a tsking sound. "They've been bickering like this practically from the time they were in diapers," she explained. "Now, if you two will behave, Alicia has some good news to share with us. Go ahead, dear."

Alicia blushed prettily. "This is your birthday celebration, Mary Ellen. No one's interested in hearing about my little bit of news."

"Of course we want to hear. Don't we, Jackson?"

"Sure," he said, because it was expected.

"All right, if you're sure," Alicia began. "I was told today that I've hit the platinum level for real estate sales within the company. That means my sales have exceeded five million dollars already this year."

"Congratulations," Jack told her.

"Yes, congratulations," Alex added, and several more congratulations followed.

"So does that mean you get one of those dorky little pins to wear on your jacket?" Meredith asked, making no attempt to hide the fact that she wasn't impressed.

"Actually, I get a platinum-and-diamond pin and a free trip to Europe," Alicia informed her.

"Isn't that simply wonderful news?" his mother asked.

"Yes, it is," Jack replied, and as his mother turned the spotlight on Alicia, insisting she tell everyone about her latest success, Jack tuned them out. His thoughts immediately returned to Kelly, the way she looked, the way she smelled. Damn, why did she have to be connected to his investigation?

A kick beneath the table connected with the left side of his calf and Jack glared at his sister. "Knock it off."

"Then wake up," she whispered. "Big brother's about to make a toast."

Peter stood at the head of the table, tapping a spoon against his wineglass. "If everyone would please raise their glasses, I'd like you to join me in toasting my mother, Mary Ellen Callaghan, a woman whose beauty remains timeless whatever her age. Happy birthday, Mother."

"Happy birthday!" The words echoed around the table.

"Thank you. All of you. And that was a lovely toast, Peter. I may just forgive you for not attending the Halloween gala on Saturday night. You were missed." She turned her gaze upon Alex. "And so were you, Alexander."

"I wanted to go, Mrs. C. I swear I did, but I had a trial to prepare for," Alex offered as his excuse. "You know how it is, a D.A.'s work is never done."

"Neither is an attorney's," Peter added.

"That depends on how good the attorney is," Margee pointed out, earning a hard look from Peter. "Some of us can actually do the job and still have a social life."

"Now, isn't this something," Jack offered, stirring the pot. "I'm the one who's out there chasing down the bad guys and keeping the streets safe while you guys spend the day sitting behind your desks pushing around a bunch of paper. Yet, *I'm* the one who manages to make it to Mother's gala and you don't."

"Not all of us have cushy jobs like yours, little brother. We don't get to clock out at the end of a shift and go home," Peter informed him with that "gotcha" look in his eyes.

Jack acknowledged his brother's score with a grin. "Yeah, I guess you're right. Chasing down killers is a real cushy job."

"Shall I serve the salad now, Mrs. Callaghan?" Tilly's husband, Edward, asked.

"Yes, please." And once the task had been completed, she directed her attention back to Jack. "Really, Jackson," his mother began. She brought a hand to her throat. "You and your brother can make all the jokes you want, but every time I think of the danger you're in, coming face-to-face with some criminal armed with a gun or heavens knows what kind of a weapon, it makes me absolutely ill."

"Mother, I've been trained to handle dangerous situations. It's my job. It's what I do." Wanting to ease her worries, he quipped, "Besides, haven't you heard? Us good guys always come out on top."

"How I wish that were true," she told him with a sniffle. "I can't help but wish you had stayed in law school and become a lawyer like your brother and Alexander and Margaret. Why did you have to become a police officer?"

"You know why, Mother. Law school wasn't right for me," Jack told her, deciding there was no point in rehashing the subject. "I would have made a lousy lawyer."

"He's right," Peter announced after finishing off the better part of his salad. "Jack would be bored silly dealing with normal people. He's much better suited to dealing with psychotics and criminals. He finds it exciting."

"Whereas Peter's idea of exciting is discussing contracts and corporate mergers with stuffy old geezers."

"Not all of my clients are old geezers," Peter advised him. "Just today I met with a beautiful and intriguing young woman."

"Really?" his mother returned. "Do I know her family?"

"Actually, you've met her, Mother. Her name's Kelly Santos. She went to high school with Meredith."

At the mention of Kelly's name, Jack fell silent. He studied Peter, not sure what to make of his brother's description of Kelly. Nor was he sure why the idea that Peter might have been attracted to her disturbing.

"Kelly Santos is in New Orleans?" Meredith asked.

"Yes," Peter confirmed.

"That name sounds so familiar," Mrs. Callaghan said. "But I can't seem to put a face to it."

"You remember her, Mother. The tall, skinny blonde with spooky eyes that lived at St. Ann's," Meredith explained. "Last I heard she was a hotshot photographer working in New York. What's she doing here?"

"She's one of the beneficiaries in Sister Grace's will. I sent her a letter, asking her to get in touch with the firm," Peter explained.

"I didn't realize nuns had wills," Alicia commented, joining in the conversation. Her hazel eyes sparkled with interest. "I mean, I always assumed that they didn't have very much and that what they did have would go to the church or the poor when they died."

"Actually, she didn't have much in the way of assets—or even possessions for that matter. And most of what she did have went to the church or other members of her religious order. But she had a few personal items that she bequeathed to Kelly."

"How fascinating," Alicia remarked. "And this Kelly person is here to collect her inheritance?"

"I'm not sure the items that Sister Grace left her could be classified as an inheritance," Peter commented.

"Well I certainly hope she didn't leave her those dreadful outfits they make the nun's wear," Meredith remarked. She took a sip of her wine. "Not that Kelly would even want them. When I ran into her in New York a couple of years ago, I was positively salivating when I saw the gold mine of clothes she had at her disposal." She focused on Peter. "Speaking of clothes, how did she look?"

"Nice. Really nice," Peter said with a smile.

Meredith visibly perked up. "What did she have on?"

"I don't know. Some kind of skirt outfit."

"Come on, spill it, big brother," she demanded. "Was it a designer label? I bet it was. She's always shooting magazine spreads for the biggies like Karan and Versace and Valentino. She probably gets the stuff for

free," Meredith said. "Oh, why didn't I become a photographer?"

"Because you like being in front of the camera, not
behind it," Peter told her.

"True," Meredith replied, a grin on her face. "So tell
me, did this skirt outfit have a jacket? Were you able to
get a look at the label inside it?"

Peter laughed. "You're kidding, right?"

Alex joined in the laughter. "Come on, Meredith.
What guy knows a Valentino from a paper sack?"

"Ones who are educated," Meredith tossed back.

"Get real," Jack chimed in. "Do you really think we
men pay attention to those things? A guy notices what's
in the clothes, not whose name is on it."

"Jack's right. I didn't notice any labels. But I certainly noticed her legs. She's got really great legs." Peter
paused and very casually, he asked, "Don't you agree,
Jack?"

"What?" Meredith immediately shifted her attention
to him. "You mean *you* saw Kelly, too? When?
Where?"

"Yesterday. I spoke with her about an investigation
I'm working on."

"But you're a homicide detective," Alicia began,
then her eyes widened. Her breath hitched. "Is she involved in a murder?"

"No," Jack said emphatically. "She's a witness."

"Dear heavens," his mother said, and made the sign
of the cross. "Do you mean to tell me that poor girl
actually saw someone get killed?"

Jack hesitated, unsure how to respond. "Not exactly."

"Not exactly?" Meredith repeated from her seat beside him. "Then exactly how is she a witness?"

"You know I can't discuss a case. So why don't we

just change the subject? Besides, we're supposed to be celebrating Mother's birthday.''

"Oh, my God," Meredith said. "She had one of those visions, didn't she?"

"Visions?" Alicia asked.

"What are you talking about, Meredith?" their mother demanded.

"Back in high school there was this rumor that went around about Kelly, that she could see things that had happened or that were going to happen."

"You mean she's psychic?" Alicia asked, her eyes wide.

"That's what I heard. All I know is that Kelly was always a little strange. She had this way of looking at a person and you'd swear she knew exactly what you were thinking. Some of the girls claimed she was a witch."

"Knock it off, Meredith," Jack commanded, irritated to hear his sister speak of Kelly in such a way. He could only imagine what it must have been like for her in school.

"Your brother's right," Mrs. Callaghan said. "You shouldn't say such things. I'm sure Kelly is a lovely young woman."

"I didn't say she wasn't. I'm just telling you what some of the girls said about her. Anyway, *I* never saw her do any weird stuff."

Mrs. Callaghan shook her head. "I can't understand how a fine school like St. Joseph's would allow such a foolish rumor like that to get started."

"I heard it started during our sophomore year," Meredith said. She sat back, took another sip of her wine. "Supposedly Kelly freaked out one of the teachers, insisting the woman had to hurry home because there had been an accident and her house was on fire with her baby trapped inside.''

''Dear Lord,'' Mrs. Callaghan said.

''Was it true?'' Alicia asked.

''Supposedly the teacher arrived home and found her mother lying on the floor unconscious. The baby was crying in the next room and there was a fire in the kitchen. It was one of those old restored homes without any smoke detectors. And if the teacher hadn't arrived when she had, the place would have gone up with both the baby and the grandmother trapped inside.''

''That's quite a story,'' Margee said.

''It certainly is. Look, it gave me goose bumps,'' Alicia said with a shiver. She rubbed her hands up and down her arms. ''Do you think it's true? That this Kelly person *really* can see what's going to happen?''

Meredith shrugged.

''It sounds like a lot of bull, if you ask me,'' Alex commented.

''I don't recall anyone asking you,'' Meredith informed him.

Ignoring the snipe, Alex fingered the stem of his wineglass. ''What do you think, Peter? Both you and Jack met her. You think she's psychic?''

''I don't know. She seemed normal enough to me,'' Peter replied.

''Jack?'' Alex prompted.

How in the devil was he supposed to answer, Jack wondered. Thanks to the large number of so-called psychics who'd set up shop in the city, the term *psychic* ranked right up there with *charlatan.* He didn't know if Kelly was psychic or even if he believed in such things. What he did know is that Kelly Santos had something. Whether that something was ESP or simply good in-stincts, he wasn't sure. He did know that she'd been on the mark ten years ago about him and, so far, she'd been dead right on the details about the murder.

"I knew it," Meredith said, pouncing upon his silence as an admission. "I was right, wasn't I? Kelly *did* have one of those visions, just like I said. That's why you had to talk to her."

"Is Meredith right, Jack?" Alex asked him.

"I told you, I can't discuss my cases," Jack said firmly.

"Fine, then tell me where she's staying," Meredith replied.

Jack narrowed his eyes. "Why?"

"I want to pay her a visit while she's in town."

"Why?" Jack repeated.

"Because she's an old friend."

"Since when?"

"Oh, for pity's sake, just tell me where she's staying," Meredith demanded.

"She's at the Regent," Peter supplied.

"Thank you, Peter," she said sweetly. "Goodness, would you look at that roast," she exclaimed as Edward carried in a platter of sliced beef with all the trimmings, effectively ending all talk of Kelly Santos and the murder investigation. "Doesn't it look absolutely delicious?"

The roast *was* delicious, along with the rest of the meal, a tribute to Tilly's skill in the kitchen. And more than an hour later after finishing the meal, they gathered around to sing happy birthday.

"Happy birthday to you…" Meredith started them in song as seventy candles burned atop a three-tiered cake decorated with butter-cream icing and edible pink roses.

"…Happy birthday to you," they finished in unison.

"Make a wish, Mother, and then blow out the candles," Meredith instructed.

"Oh my, look at all those candles. So many," she said, catching Jack's hand as he stood beside her chair. "Jackson, I think you'd better get the fire extinguisher ready. I'm not sure I can do this."

"Sure you can," he told her, giving her fingers a squeeze. "We'll help you."

But his mother needed little help. She managed to blow out most of the candles on her own and earned herself a round of applause. "Thank you. Thank you all," she said. "Edward, would you tell Tilly that I want to serve the cake with coffee in the den. And I'd like it if the two of you would join us."

"Yes, ma'am," Edward said. He removed the cake from the table and disappeared in the direction of the kitchen.

Peter eased her chair back and helped her to her feet.

"Thank you, dear. Why don't we all move to the den."

As everyone headed out of the room, Jack fell back a step. He caught his sister's arm. "What are you up to, Meredith?"

She batted her green eyes. "Whatever do you mean?"

"I mean, why the sudden interest in Kelly Santos? And don't tell me it's because she's an old friend. We both know that's not true."

"Well if you must know, I'm going to ask her to shoot some ads for Indulgences."

Jack frowned. "I thought Bobby Hillmann had already done the ads."

"He's done most of them."

"Don't tell me you're not happy with them. You said

Hillmann was the best in the city—that's why you went with him.''

"He is the best—in New Orleans—and his ads are...okay. But Kelly's worked in New York, California, Europe. She's photographed campaigns for some of the biggest fashion publications in the business. I've seen her work, Jack. She's good. Better than good. She's fantastic. Even that noncommercial stuff she's done is light-years ahead of anything Hillmann can do. If I can convince her to do some targeted advertising shots, it could make the difference in whether Indulgences succeeds or not.'' She paused, looked up at him out of serious eyes. "I know everyone thinks I'm just an airhead who doesn't know what she wants and keeps flitting from one thing to the next. And maybe I have been. But this time is different. I *want* to make this work. I *need* her to help me, Jack. I *need* this shop to be a success.''

Jack tucked a strand of hair behind Meredith's ear. "Then it'll be a success,'' he assured her.

"You really believe that? Or do you think Mother and Alex are right, that I'll just get bored and drop it like I did the modeling and acting, and take off again?''

"Merry, I think you can succeed at anything you set your mind to. If you want this shop to work, then it will work. But you don't need Kelly Santos or anyone else to make that happen. Only you can do that.''

She kissed his cheek. "Thanks for the vote of confidence, big brother,'' she said with a smile. "I hope that means I can count on you to come in and drop a bundle when the place opens.''

Jack arched his brow. "I thought this was supposed to be a women's store.''

"It is,'' she said, a sassy twinkle in her eyes. "But since Christmas isn't that far away, surely you can think of at least one deserving female you'll want to pick up a little something special for.''

"You mean Alicia?"

She punched his arm. "I meant me. Or Mother."

Laughter from the other room drifted to them. "We'd better get in there before they send out a search party for us."

"You think Mother would notice if I slipped out? I really need to go."

"You know she would." Curious, he asked, "Where is it you have to go?"

"To see Kelly. Indulgences opens its doors in just a few weeks. If I'm going to talk her into doing those ads, I need to get busy."

"Meredith," Jack began with a sigh. "You said yourself that Kelly's a hotshot photographer now. She's probably heading back to New York soon."

"All the more reason for me to go see her now and convince her to stay. Be a dear and tell Mother I wasn't feeling well and had to leave?"

"Forget it. Besides, the chance of Kelly agreeing to this scheme of yours is slim to none. And as persuasive as you can be, little sister, I don't think even you would be able to get Kelly to change her mind."

Meredith smiled at him. "Watch me."

Seven

"Callaghan, where are you and Jerevicious on the Gilbert case?" Big Mike asked.

"We're still working on it, Captain," Jack informed him as they gathered in the station's squad room. And they were getting nowhere fast, he added silently. "So far we haven't been able to turn up any credible witnesses."

"What about the weapon?"

"No sign of one yet," Jack said.

"Damn. You know this doesn't look good for the city—particularly when we've got a big medical convention going on in town."

"I'm aware of that, sir, and we're doing everything we can to find the killer," Jack told him.

"Then I suggest you work faster, because the mayor's been all over my ass about the bad press."

"Yes, sir. In the meantime, we've checked with the convention authorities, and this Dr. Gilbert wasn't among the registered attendees."

"According to the medical association, Gilbert had his license revoked nearly five years ago," Leon added.

"Then what in the hell was he doing in New Orleans? And why did he have to go and get himself knocked off in our city?" the captain demanded.

"We're trying to find that out now, sir," Jack advised

him. "So far all we know is that he was divorced, no kids. We weren't able to find any listing for his ex-wife under the last name Gilbert or her maiden name. He does have a sister who lives in Pascagoula, Mississippi, whom we haven't been able to reach yet. We're hoping that when we do, she can tell us what he was doing here or give us some leads as to who might have killed him."

"I thought this was a robbery-turned-homicide."

"The jury's still out on that, sir," Jack told him.

The captain swore. "You got evidence saying something different?"

"Not yet, sir. Just a gut feeling," Jack confessed.

"Maybe you're psychic, Callaghan," Nuccio remarked, earning a few chuckles in the squad room.

"Very funny, Nuccio," the captain said dryly. There wasn't even a trace of a smile on the man's round face. He stared hard at Jack. "What about that woman who came into the station...the one that Russo was ranting about?"

"Kelly Santos," Jack supplied.

"You checked her out yet?"

"Yes, sir," Jack replied. "She wasn't able to tell us anything more than what she'd already told Sarge."

"You buy her story about having some kind of vision?"

Jack hesitated, aware of the other eyes and ears taking in the exchange. "She did know details that no one else could have known about the murder."

"Except the killer," Leon pointed out.

The captain shifted his gaze from him to Leon and back again, probably already picking up on the fact that he and his partner were at odds on this one. "If she was the killer, I doubt that she'd come in, report she'd seen

the murder and give us all the details,'' Jack reasoned.
''Why make herself a suspect?''

''Could be to throw us off,'' the captain offered.

''Kelly's not the killer.''

The captain eyed Jack closely. ''This woman a friend
of yours, Callaghan?''

Jack cursed himself silently. ''Not really, sir. She went
to school with my sister, and I met her once or twice a
long time ago.''

''You should have said something sooner. I wouldn't
have assigned you to this case if I'd known there was
any problem.''

''I wasn't sure it was the same woman,'' Jack told
him, which was the truth. ''Before Leon and I went to
question her I hadn't set eyes on her in more than ten
years. And since there is no relationship between us, I
don't believe there is a problem with me being on this
case, sir.''

''All right,'' the captain said after a long pause.
''Make sure it doesn't get in the way of you solving this
case.''

''Yes, sir,'' Jack told him. And he meant to do just
that. He had no intention of letting his personal feelings
where Kelly Santos was concerned—whatever those
feelings were—get in the way of him finding Dr. Martin
Gilbert's killer.

The captain gave him a curt nod. ''In the meantime,
I want you and Jerevicious to check out the woman's
story, make sure she has no ties to the vic. If she is
innocent, then I want you to find out who *is* responsible
for the man's death and arrest that person. And I want
it done quickly. The last thing we need is another open
homicide on the books—particularly when the victim is
a doctor. Do I make myself clear, Detectives?''

"Yes, sir."

"Yes, sir," Leon echoed.

After going over the remaining assignments, they were dismissed. Jack immediately returned to his desk. When he spied Nuccio headed toward him, he picked up the phone, punched in the number for the crime-scene unit and turned his chair so that his back was to the other man.

"Dickerson," the phone was answered on the other end.

"This is Callaghan in Homicide. You guys finished going over the car that came in on the Gilbert case?"

"We're still working on it, Detective," the weary-sounding tech informed him. "Check back with me this afternoon and I'll let you know what we've got."

"Thanks." Jack hung up the phone and found Nuccio standing in front of his desk, doing his damned best to read, upside down, the file he had open on his desk. Jack slammed the folder closed. "Something you want, Nuccio?"

"Thought you'd like to know that me and a couple of the guys—we got us a little bet going about this case you're working on."

"I suppose that's a step up from betting on how many cockroaches you can find in your desk because of all the leftover crap you keep in there. But the truth is I'm not interested. So why don't you get lost. I've got work to do."

Nuccio's mouth tightened. There was hatred in his eyes as he said, "Don't be such a dick head, Callaghan. Aren't you the least bit curious about our bet?"

"No."

Nuccio leaned closer, lowered his voice a fraction, but it was obvious others were listening. "Being the nice guy I am, I'm going to tell you, anyway. We're making bets on how long it'll take you to solve this Gilbert case. And I'm saying it'll depend on whether or not you call on your lady psychic friend for help, because you and that washed-up ballplayer partner of yours couldn't find shit on your own.''

Laughter erupted around him. Ignoring them, Jack stood and grabbed his jacket. "You know, Nuccio, for once you actually have a good idea. Thanks.'' Leaving a suspicious-looking Nuccio standing there, he walked over to Leon's desk. "I'll be back in about an hour.''

"Let me get back to you,'' Leon said to whomever was on the other end of the phone, and dropped the receiver on its cradle. "Where you headed?''

"To pay Kelly Santos a visit.''

Leon frowned. "All right. But I'm going with you.''

"I can handle this one on my own. In the meantime, maybe you can get on to those lab guys.''

"The lab guys can wait,'' Leon told him, and snatched up his own jacket. "We're a team, Callaghan. We work together,'' he reminded him, and together they walked toward the exit. Once they were outside in the parking lot, Leon snapped, "Man, what is with you? Didn't you hear what the captain said in there?''

"I heard him. He wants us to find the shooter and close this case. That's what I'm trying to do.''

Leon shot him that steely look that had given more than one defensive tackle pause during the big man's football career. "I'm talking about you and this Santos woman. The captain already thinks you might have a conflict of interest where she's concerned and here you are running off to see her again.''

"She's the only lead we've got. I'm just going to ask

her some more questions, see if maybe she can help us,"
Jack hedged, and headed for his car.

"And you think that's a smart move?"

Jack looked at his friend from over the roof of his car.
"I know what I'm doing."

"You sure about that?"

"What's that supposed to mean?" Jack countered.

"I mean, I'm not stupid, Jackson. I saw the way you
looked at that woman. It wasn't the way a cop looks at
a witness."

"You're off base, Jerevicious."

"Am I?"

"Yes," Jack insisted. "I don't know what you *think*
you saw, but I told you, I met her a long time ago when
she was just a kid. She went to school with my little
sister, for Pete's sake."

"Yeah, well she's not a kid anymore."

"Like I said, you're off base. There's nothing going
on there."

Leon followed his lead and got inside the car. He
looked over at him. "I hope that's true, Jackson, because
from where I'm sitting, things aren't looking so good for
your psychic lady friend."

"What in the hell are you talking about?"

"I'm talking about the fact that the Santos woman
knows too much about the crime scene not to have been
there. I'm thinking that maybe she was the one who
pulled the trigger and killed the doc."

"You're wrong," Jack told him.

"I sure hope I am—for her sake and for yours."

What did she do now?

Kelly asked herself the same question she must have
asked fifty times since the Reverend Mother had told her

that Sister Grace had been cremated. She'd lain awake most of the night, frustrated and unsure about what to do. A trip to the cemetery to visit Sister's grave again that morning and going over everything that had happened had brought her no closer to an answer. So she'd been driving around for hours, retracing old paths from her childhood and searching for answers.

While the Reverend Mother had been kind, the woman clearly hadn't believed that Sister Grace had been murdered. And with no hope of exhuming the body to prove she was telling the truth, who was going to believe her?

The police? Despite the fact that she'd been correct about that man's murder, it had been apparent that they thought she had a screw loose. Even Jack Callaghan, who hadn't dismissed her claims outright, was just as wary as the others.

And could she blame them? Or him?

Hardly. If she were in their shoes, she'd probably feel the same way. Only she wasn't in their shoes. She was in her own shoes, in her own skin. And she had seen Sister Grace murdered. Somehow, she had to find a way to prove it.

Kelly turned the car onto the familiar street that she had traveled so often—the one leading to the now-abandoned orphanage. Although St. Ann's had technically relocated to a new, more modern facility in the suburbs, to her the ancient buildings located in the city would always be St. Ann's.

She stopped her vehicle in front of the gated area. Shutting off the car's engine, she stared up at the place that had been her home for so many years. Within those walls she'd cried enough tears into her pillow at night to fill the Mississippi River. But it was also within those

walls that she had bonded with Sister Grace. Perhaps it
was why she'd come back there now, she reasoned.
She'd come home to search for answers.

Home.

Kelly grabbed her camera and exited the car. Then
she made her way up the sidewalk. The place was
huge—just as she remembered. Focusing her camera,
she clicked off several shots in succession. Built in the
late eighteenth century as a school and home for or-
phaned girls, the three-story white masonry structure and
its grounds took up the entire city block. Slipping her
camera strap over her neck, she unlatched the gate. The
mechanism creaked as she pushed it open and then she
walked onto the grounds.

The grass was overgrown and the gardens neglected,
she noted. So was the playground equipment. Rust covered the jungle gym. The seat on one of the red wooden
seesaws was faded and chipped. She spun the merry-go-
round, heard the squeak of metal from non-use. Moving
over to the swing set, Kelly felt a wave of sadness as
she took in the disrepair. All that was left of one swing
was the dangling chain. Rust covered the chain links of
the others. The seat on another swing hung by its hinges.
Kelly sat on the one swing that remained intact. And as
she set the swing in motion, she remembered all the
times she'd escaped out here on the swings, away from
the singsong whispers of ''Kelly's a witch. Kelly's a
witch.'' It was here that she had kicked her feet high
until she could no longer hear the cruel voices. It was
here that she had allowed herself to dream. And it was
here that she had pretended she was like the princess in
the fairy tale and she would turn into a swan, then fly
away to some magical kingdom where she was loved.

A gust of wind whipped through the air, rustling the

leaves in the giant oak trees. For a moment, Kelly could almost hear the ghostly, taunting voices of the children who had once played there. Shutting off the unhappy memories, she abandoned the swings. After clicking off several shots of the old oak, she walked over to stand in front of the main house. It seemed strange to see St. Ann's like this, she thought. So dark. So empty. So still.

The wind kicked up again, sending leaves dancing around her and causing the old chapel bell to ring out a solitary note. She aimed her camera at the bell tower, fired off several more pictures. When she finished, she hugged her arms about herself and looked up at the second story where the chapel had been. She'd spent many hours praying in that chapel, she recalled, praying for someone to adopt her, for someone to want her.

At the sound of a twig snapping, Kelly whipped around. "Who's there?"

But only the moan of the wind answered.

Suddenly uneasy, Kelly headed back toward the entrance gate. As she reached her car, she paused and looked around her, unable to shake the feeling that someone was watching her. Out of habit, she lifted her camera and took several shots of the house across the street where the two old-maid Williams sisters used to live. The women had always been generous to Annie's girls at Halloween, she recalled with fondness. And for a moment, she debated going over and ringing the bell to find out if they still lived there. But she didn't see any lights on and there was no movement inside the house. Deciding against it, she lifted her camera and clicked off another series of shots.

Watching Kelly Santos lift her camera again, she pressed her back against the wall of the Williams house and tried to blend in with the shadows. She held her breath, waited. Finally, Kelly recapped her camera lens and got into the car.

Releasing her breath, she didn't move for several moments as she waited for Kelly to start her car and buckle her seat belt. When the car pulled away from the curve, she stepped away from the house. Hatred beat hot and fast in her blood as she watched the woman drive away.

She had thought that killing the old nun would be the end of it, never expecting the woman to have a will. She'd even known a moment of panic when she'd discovered that she'd left one and had made bequests to three of her former charges from the orphanage. That was when she'd realized that one of those three girls had to be the one the nun was protecting.

She'd observed two of those girls at the nun's funeral. One she'd ruled out because of her race. The other she'd been undecided about. She'd been about the right age, but her coloring had been darker than she had expected. So she'd begun gathering additional information on her before ruling her out. On the third girl—Kelly Santos— she had come up empty.

Until now.

Rage ripped through her as she remembered. They'd changed her name to Kelly, but she was the same little girl with long blond pigtails who'd been laughing in the pictures with *her* daddy.

Damn you, Kelly Santos. Why didn't you die in that fire with your mother like you were supposed to?

The newspaper had said that she'd died. So had her mama and daddy. And to think, if it hadn't been for that damned blackmailing Gilbert she might have gone on believing the bitch was dead. No matter, she told herself.

Stepping out of the shadows, she stared down the street where Kelly's car had driven away. "You should have stayed dead," she told her. "Because now I'm just going to have to kill you all over again."

Eight

"We're supposed to be a team, man. I put my life in your hands every time we go out on the street," Leon told him as they headed for the Regent Hotel. "If you can't be straight with me, then I've got to rethink whether I can trust you to cover my back."

"What are you saying?" Jack asked.

"I'm saying if I can't trust you, I don't want to work with you. We go back to the station now and you ask the captain to assign you a new partner. It's your call, Jackson. Either we work on this case together, or you work it with another partner. What's it going to be?"

"Shit!" Jack slammed his fist against the steering wheel, furious with himself because Leon was right. "We work it together."

"No more flying solo?"

"No more flying solo," Jack promised. "I'm sorry."

"All right. You keeping any more shit about this woman from me?"

"No," Jack told him. "I swear it. Just go along with me on this for now, all right?"

Leon paused, looked over at him as they sat at a red light. "You really believe this woman has some kind of ESP that's going to help us find the shooter?"

"Yes," Jack told him, and meant it.

"What the hell then. I guess it's worth a shot."

"Thanks," Jack responded, and hit the gas when the light turned green.

After several moments of silence, some of the tension eased. "You saw the way that little prick Nuccio perked up when the captain jumped your shit for not telling him you knew the Santos woman? He thinks he's going to beat you out of that promotion."

"I know he does," Jack told him. And he just might. Keeping silent about his association with Kelly hadn't been the wisest career move he'd made.

"Man, what in the hell were you thinking?"

"I wasn't thinking," Jack admitted as they pulled up in front of the hotel.

"Then it's time you started," Leon told him as they exited the vehicle.

They walked across the hotel lobby and took the elevator up to Kelly's floor in silence. When they reached her hotel room, Jack knocked on the door.

"Who is it?"

"Detectives Callaghan and Jerevicious."

Kelly opened the door. One look at her face and Jack knew she wasn't pleased to see them. Still, her voice was polite as she said, "Detectives, if you're here with more questions about the statement I gave to the police the other night, now is really not a good time."

"We're not here about your statement. May we come in?"

"Like I said, now is *really* not a good time. I'm waiting for a call."

"I promise, this will only take a few minutes." Flashing her what he hoped was a charming smile, Jack held up three fingers and said, "Scout's honor."

Neither the smile nor the promise seemed to have any effect on her, and just when he thought she was going to shut the door in their faces, she stepped back. "All right. But you'll need to make it quick."

"Thanks," he told her, and stepped inside her hotel suite with Leon right behind him.

"So what is it you want to discuss with me?"

The lady didn't waste any time, Jack noted. And judging by her stance—arms crossed, feet planted firmly on the floor and eyes level—she was not one to suffer fools gladly. "We're here to ask for your help."

Her eyes were as skeptical as her voice when she said, "And just how is it you think I can help you?"

Deciding to just spit it out, Jack told her, "We want you to help us find out who murdered Martin Gilbert."

"I'm afraid I've already told both you and your Sergeant Russo everything I can. There's nothing more I can do."

"Actually, there is," he informed her. "You can—"

The phone on the table next to the couch began to ring. Her gaze darted to the ringing telephone and back to him. It was obvious that she was torn between taking the call and getting rid of them.

"Go ahead and answer it. We'll wait." When she hesitated he said, "You'd better get it or it'll go back to the switchboard."

Kelly hurried over to the phone, snatched it up. "Wyatt, I'm here. Yes, I know we were cut off. Either you hit a dead zone or there was some kind of interference with my cell phone in the hotel. This is a better connection."

She paused a moment and her voice was short as she said, "Obviously, I'm still in New Orleans since you're calling me on the hotel phone. And no, I am not leaving for the airport when I hang up. Hold on a minute," she said, and put the phone on hold. "Excuse me, but I've got to take this call. Can I get back with you about this later? I could be a while.''

Jack looked at his partner and Leon said, ''We don't mind waiting until you're finished.''

She sighed. ''Suit yourself. But you'll need to excuse me while I take this in the next room. If you insist on waiting, you might as well help yourself to something to drink.''

''Thanks,'' Jack said to her retreating back.

''Wyatt? Sorry about that. I wanted to switch phones,'' she began after entering the adjoining room.

Because she hadn't shut the door all the way, Jack had no problem picking up her end of the conversation. And though he told himself he was wrong to eavesdrop, he found himself doing just that.

''I hope you're right about this, Jackson.''

''I am,'' Jack insisted. He was sure of it. Walking over to the counter, he snatched up a bottle of water, handed one to Leon.

''I've already told you I can't leave yet. It's personal, something I have to do.'' She paused. ''I don't know. It could be just a couple of days, maybe a week, maybe longer. I'm not sure. I'll have to let you know.''

Jack moved quietly about the living room of the suite, feigning an interest in the paintings when in truth he was focused on Kelly's conversation and wondering who this fellow Wyatt was and what his relationship was to her.

''Try to put them off for a while,'' she said. Another pause followed. ''Then they'll have to find somebody else to do the shoot because I can't promise I'll be back by then.''

Her boss? he wondered.

''Yes, Wyatt. I understand. Of course, I realize what a great opportunity this would be. And I appreciate everything you've done to make it happen. But I simply can't commit to anything right now.'' She paused again and there was no mistaking the stress in her voice as she continued, ''I told you it's something personal that I need to take care of. I'd rather not go into it right now.''

Jack couldn't help wondering what that something personal was that was causing Kelly so much anxiety. Although his knowledge of her was limited to their encounter ten years ago and questioning her about the Gilbert case, she hadn't struck him as high strung or overly emotional. Quite the opposite, he thought as he picked up the camera that was sitting on the table. He remembered Kelly as being cool, collected, almost resigned under what had to have been distressing circumstances for a teenager that long-ago night. She'd been equally unruffled a few days ago when he and Leon had arrived to question her about the homicide. Judging by her agitated state since they'd arrived, she was major stressed about something right now.

''All right. I promise I'll give you a call in a few days and explain everything,'' she said, her voice softening. ''I will. And I love you, too. Bye.''

Her declaration of love to the faceless Wyatt surprised him, Jack admitted. He wasn't sure why. After all, Kelly was a beautiful woman and no doubt she'd had her share of male admirers. Yet for some reason, hearing her say the words to the guy on the phone disturbed him.

''I'm sorry about that,'' she said, exiting the bedroom. Her gaze immediately zeroed in on the camera Jack was holding. ''I don't allow anyone to touch my equipment,'' she informed him.

''Sorry,'' he said, and before he could return the camera to the table, she was there in front of him, reclaiming the fancy piece. As she did so, her fingers brushed his and Jack didn't miss the way she snatched her hand away, as though she'd been burned. Interesting, he thought. That little spark of awareness. "Your boss?" he asked casually.

"My agent," she said, gently depositing the camera on the table.

"Sounded like he had an important project for you."

She glanced up at him and arched her brow imperiously. "I should think you know it's rude to eavesdrop, Detective."

"Jack," he corrected her. "And my apologies. It was difficult not to overhear."

She sat down on the couch and folded her hands primly on her lap. "You said you wanted me to help with your investigation," she prompted, terminating any further inquiries about why she'd passed on what sounded like a plum project.

Jack took the chair adjacent to the couch while Leon remained standing. "First off, you should know that our captain thinks the Gilbert homicide is a robbery that got out of hand and ended up a murder."

"It wasn't."

He sat forward, resting his elbows on his legs. "I don't think so, either."

"And what about you, Detective Jerevicious?" Kelly asked, looking over at Leon, who stood tall and imposing in front of the window. "Do you agree with Detective Callaghan? Or do you think your captain is right?"

"Let's just say I'm waiting to see how the evidence plays out."

Aware of Leon's misgivings, Jack said, "The problem is that with the exception of your statement, everything points to robbery being the motive."

"It wasn't," she assured him. "This Dr. Gilbert knew

his killer. He even arranged to meet her there to make the exchange and he was angry because she was late.''

"How do you know that?" Leon asked her.

She met his gaze. "The same way that I knew she killed him. I saw it.''

"In a vision," Leon added.

"That's right. He was blackmailing her and the minute he gave her the paper, she shot him.''

And as crazy as the story sounded, Jack believed her. "Then help us prove it," Jack urged. "Help us find out who the woman was who shot him.''

"Just how do you propose I do that?''

"Come with us to the crime scene, see if you can see or feel anything else.''

"No," she said, pushing to her feet. She walked over to the counter, opened a bottle of water and poured it into a glass. "Please, I'd like you to leave.''

"You heard the lady, Jackson. Let's go," Leon told him.

Jack stood, met his partner's gaze. "Would you give me a minute alone with her?''

"We're a team, remember?''

"I know. But I still need a minute." He paused. "Please.''

Leon's mouth flattened, but all he said was "Give me the keys. I'll go pull the car around and meet you downstairs. Thanks for the water, Ms. Santos." He stared at Jack. "Five minutes.''

"Thanks," Jack told him. Once his partner was gone, he walked over and stood behind Kelly. "Kelly, I know sometimes you see things…sense things in people," he said, searching for the right words. "You sensed them in me the first time we met.''

"That was different," she said, her hand unsteady as

she gripped the glass. "You helped me that night in the park. And I wanted to repay you for your kindness. I didn't even know this Dr. Gilbert." She put down the glass and turned to face him. "Anyway, he's dead now. There's nothing I can do to change that."

"No. But you might be able to help me find his killer."

"I can't."

"How do you know unless you try? All you have to do is—"

She glared at him. "I know what you want me to do. You want me to put on a…a psychic sideshow for you and your police friends. Well, forget it. I won't do it. I won't."

"Whoa! Hang on a second," Jack said, taken aback by her anger. "Who said anything about a sideshow? I'm asking you to help me find a killer and I resent the hell out of you for thinking otherwise."

"And why should I believe you?"

"Because I'm telling you the truth," he fired back. "Look inside me if you don't believe me."

"No," she said, and started to move away.

Fueled by frustration, he captured her wrist. "Look inside," he insisted, and moved closer, crowding her space. He heard her breath catch, but she didn't back down. Neither did he. Suddenly Jack became aware of just how close they were standing. Of how soft her skin was. Of her scent—something secretive and elusive—like her. He released her wrist and lifted his hand to tuck a strand of blond hair that had come loose from her braid behind her ear. Then he trailed his finger down her cheek. A shiver went through her, into him. Desire, hot and primal, fisted in his gut.

"Kelly," he whispered, and watched her eyes darken

as he lowered his head. He kissed her. Slowly. Thoroughly. Deeply. And when he lifted his head, he was rock hard and aching.

"You shouldn't have done that," she told him, and pressed her fingertips to the lips he'd just kissed.

"Probably not. But if you're expecting an apology, you're out of luck." And because he was tempted to kiss her again, he turned around and walked out the door.

Long after Jack had left, Kelly stood there and continued to stare at the door through which he'd exited. She touched her lips, remembering the heat and weight of his mouth on hers, the hunger she'd tasted in his kiss. At the memory, heat pooled in her belly and the ache inside her that had flowered at his touch started anew. She wanted Jack. And she didn't have to be psychic to know that he wanted her, too. For a moment, she allowed herself to imagine what it would be like to have Jack hold her in his arms, make love to her, with her.

And what do you think will happen when he sees the real you? Have you forgotten what happened with Garrett?

Reality came slamming back, along with the painful memories of the last time she had believed that she might actually be able to have a normal relationship with a man.

Garrett Scott.

He'd been everything she could ever have hoped for in a lover. Handsome. Charming. Intelligent. Sensitive. He had literally swept her off her feet and made her believe, at least for a little while, that he could actually love her. Shame and hurt washed through her as she thought of her own naiveté. Not wanting to dwell on her past mistakes, Kelly turned away and headed for the telephone to call the Reverend Mother again.

When the Reverend Mother came onto the line, she said, "Hello, Kelly. I'm so glad that you phoned. You seemed so distraught when you left here last night, I was worried. Are you all right?"

"I'm fine, Reverend Mother, but thank you for your concern."

"Not at all. I'm just pleased to hear you're feeling better. Now, how can I help you, child?"

"I was wondering if there's any sort of log of visitors or appointment schedule that's kept there at the convent." Although she hadn't signed any such log during her two visits to the convent, both of her appointments had been written in the Reverend Mother's appointment book and marked off by the secretary upon her arrival. "In particular, I was hoping there might be some record of Sister Grace's visitors for…oh, say the last three months."

"We don't have any visitors' log and the only official schedule is the one posted each month with the various events and the list of chores and tasks assigned here at the convent. However, I keep an appointment book with my schedule, as do some of the other sisters."

"Would you happen to know if Sister Grace kept one?" Kelly asked.

"I'm sorry, but I have no idea." She paused. "What, if I may ask, is it you're looking for?"

"I'm hoping that maybe Sister Grace kept some sort of record of her visitors during the past few months. I think whoever was in the chapel with her the night she died had come to see her before." She'd gone over that chapel scene in her head at least a dozen times since she'd left Peter Callaghan's office, and now she was more convinced than ever that the nun had been murdered. She was also fairly sure that the person responsible for Sister Grace's death had visited her on at least one previous occasion.

"Kelly, does this have anything to do with your theory about Sister Grace's death? About it not being due to a heart attack?"

"Yes," she admitted. "I understand if you don't believe me, but—"

"It's not that I don't believe you, child. I think that you truly believe everything you've told me. But surely you must see that this…this theory of yours is…well it's highly unlikely."

"It may seem unlikely, Reverend Mother. But I can assure you that Sister Grace did not die from natural causes. She was murdered by someone who followed her to the chapel that evening."

Kelly didn't have to see the frown creasing the Reverend Mother's brow to know that it was there. "I wonder if you realize the magnitude of what you're suggesting? That someone actually came into the house of our Lord and murdered one of our sisters."

"Believe me, Reverend Mother. I do realize it. But what if I'm right? What if someone *did* kill Sister Grace? What if Sister Grace isn't the only one this person has killed and she decides to kill someone else? How can I just sit by and do nothing?"

A long silence followed, during which time Kelly wondered whether the nun was still on the phone line. Then she heard a sigh. "You can't, child. And neither can I. What can I do to help?"

"Is it possible for you to find out if Sister Grace kept an appointment book?"

"Sister Maria might know. She was the one closest

to Sister Grace and she packed away her things after…after she died. Unfortunately, Sister Maria's out at
the moment. She teaches religion classes at the community center on Tuesdays, Wednesdays and Thursdays.
But I'll ask her when she gets back,'' the Reverend
Mother assured her. ''Is there anything else?''

''I don't suppose the convent has a switchboard that
records incoming calls, does it?''

The Reverend Mother chuckled. ''We don't generate
enough calls to justify one, I'm afraid.''

''What about an answering service?''

''Unfortunately, we can't afford one. We sisters rely
on the diocese and donations to keep the convent running. Since the scandal in the Catholic Church a few
years ago, the monetary support to the church and to us
has decreased substantially. An answering service would
be a luxury and we cannot afford luxuries.''

Not for the first time, Kelly marveled that Sister Grace
and others like her had chosen such a life—one filled
with few rewards that she could see. It made her all the
more determined to repay Sister Grace by finding her
killer. ''Reverend Mother, is there any one in particular
who's responsible for answering the telephone?''

''Not really. The general rule is whoever is nearby
when it rings answers it. Sister Mary Clarence has been
acting as my secretary for the past year or so, and since
the majority of the calls are directed to me, she's often
the one who answers the phone. If no one answers, the
answering machine picks up and Sister Mary Clarence
retrieves the message later.''

''And if you or whichever sister is being called isn't
available, would Sister Mary Clarence take a message?''

''Yes, of course.''

"Does Sister Mary Clarence keep some type of record of those messages?" Kelly asked.

"As a matter of fact, she does," the Reverend Mother told her, a note of excitement in her voice. "She has one of those message pads that they use in offices. The type that makes a copy beneath it. I'll have Sister Mary Clarence get the ones for the past few months for you."

"Thank you, Reverend Mother. I appreciate it."

"Kelly, do you really think this person actually contacted Sister Grace here at the convent?"

"It would certainly make sense. It's what I did whenever I wanted to reach her. Anyway, it's a place to start," Kelly told her. The other place she intended to look was the nun's journals. "I'd also like to speak with Sister Maria. If she was close to Sister Grace, perhaps she said something to her."

"If you'll give me the phone number where you're staying, I'll have her call you when she returns."

Kelly gave her the hotel's phone number, along with her room number. "And if you'll let me know when Sister Mary Clarence has those phone message logs ready, I'll come by the convent to get them."

"I'll get back with you shortly."

"Thank you, Reverend Mother. I appreciate all your help."

"It's the least I can do," the Reverend Mother told her. A lengthy pause followed and then she said, "Kelly?"

"Yes, Reverend Mother?"

"Don't you think you should contact the police and tell them about your suspicions?"

"What would I tell them, Reverend Mother?" Kelly asked. "That I had a vision and saw someone murder Sister Grace? Do you really think they'd listen to me?"

"I listened," she reminded her.

"You're more open-minded than most people. Trust me, if I went to the police, they'd only laugh in my face."

"But if you're right, you could be in danger."

She'd realized already that by searching for Sister Grace's killer she would become a threat to the person who'd believed she'd gotten away with murder. But it was a risk that she had to take. "I'll be careful, Reverend Mother. I promise." And after assuring the nun that she would go to the police the moment she had any real evidence or found herself in danger, she ended the call.

The next thing she needed to do, Kelly decided, was to contact Peter Callaghan. She dug through her camera bag, found his card and telephoned his office. "This is Kelly Santos. I was wondering if Mr. Callaghan is in?"

"I'm sorry, Ms. Santos, he's in court this afternoon. Would you like to leave a message?"

"Actually you might be able to help me." And after explaining to Peter's assistant that she no longer wanted the boxes of journals sent to New York but to her at the hotel, she said, "If you can just let me know whether the boxes have been shipped yet or not, I'd appreciate it."

"I'll check with the mail room and get back to you," the woman assured her. "And in the meantime, I'll let Mr. Callaghan know that you called."

"Oh, there's no reason to bother Peter. I mean, he doesn't have to call me back. You can just let me know the status on the boxes."

"All right. But knowing Mr. Callaghan, he'll probably call you anyway. In the meantime, let me see what I can find out in the mail room and then I'll get back to you."

* * *

It was Peter who got back to her. "The boxes and painting are in our mail room scheduled for shipping in the morning."

"Would it be possible for me to come by and get the boxes with the journals and letters?" she asked.

"How about I have them delivered to you?"

"If you're sure it's no trouble."

"None at all," Peter assured her. "You want me to have the painting sent to you at the hotel, too?"

She thought about it a moment. "You might as well," she answered.

"Consider it done."

"Thanks," Kelly told him and hung up the phone.

While she waited for the boxes to arrive, Kelly roamed about the suite. As she did so, her thoughts kept returning to Jack and that kiss. When she found herself picturing his face for the third time in as many minutes, she plopped down on the couch and grabbed the TV remote. Five minutes later, she turned the noisy thing off and stretched out on the couch. Tired from her restless night and the events of the morning, Kelly closed her eyes, and within moments she was asleep.

And she dreamed…

She dreamed of fire.

Coughing, she sat up in bed and rubbed the sleep from her eyes. The room was dark. Why was it so dark? Mommy knew she didn't like the dark. Why hadn't she put on her lamp? she wondered.

And what was that yucky smell? It made her throat burn and her eyes sting. She coughed again. She wanted a drink of water. But it was so dark. Slipping out of the bed, she hurried over to the chest and pulled out one of the drawers so she could climb up to turn on the light.

She pressed on the switch, but she still couldn't see well. There were clouds in her room, she thought. Only they weren't the pretty clouds like the ones that she and Mommy looked up at in the sky, the ones that sometimes looked like ponies or ships or castles. These clouds were ugly and they smelled like smoke and made her cough.

Suddenly frightened, she started to run to the door. And stopped.

Somebody's there. Somebody's there. Somebody bad's on the other side of the door. Hurry! Hurry! Have to hide before the bad person finds you.

Terrified, she raced back to her bed and climbed underneath it. And clutching her teddy bear tight, she pressed her mouth against his soft fur so as not to cough, and then she watched as the doorknob turned.

"No!"

Kelly came awake with a start. Sweat beaded her brow. Her throat felt as dry as the desert. And her heart was beating like a drum. She sat up. Her eyes automatically went to the door, where she watched in horror as the doorknob began to turn.

Nine

Grabbing the candlestick from the table, Kelly moved quietly across the room. She yanked open the door, poised to strike.

And the woman standing on the other side of the door shrieked. She dropped the little silver bag she was holding and threw up her hands in front of her face as if to ward off a blow. "Kelly, it's me! It's Meredith!"

Kelly lowered the candlestick and stared at the other woman. "Meredith?"

"Jesus Christ!" Meredith Callaghan pressed a hand to her chest. "You nearly scared me half to death."

"What are you doing sneaking around outside my hotel room?" Kelly demanded, more shaken than she cared to admit.

Meredith hiked up her chin indignantly. "I was not sneaking," she informed her. "I heard you were in town and decided to stop by and say hello."

"You were trying to get into my room."

Meredith let out an exasperated breath. "I knocked on the door, but you didn't answer. I was just about to leave when I heard you cry out. I *thought* something had happened, or that you'd fallen or something, so I tried the door."

"I fell asleep and must have been dreaming," Kelly offered by way of explanation.

Meredith arched one perfect brow. "That must have been some dream," she commented as she stared at the candlestick in her hand.

Feeling somewhat foolish, Kelly said, "I thought someone was trying to break into my room."

"A break-in at this hotel? You've got to be kidding," Meredith said as she scooped up the fussy-looking little bag that had fallen. "The Jardines own this place. Believe me, the security here is top of the line."

"Obviously it's not that great, since you had no trouble getting up here or obtaining my room number."

She gave her that megawatt Callaghan smile. "That's because I've got connections. Where are your manners, Kelly Santos? Aren't you going to invite me in?"

For a heartbeat Kelly considered saying no, but those manners drilled into her by the good nuns won out. She opened the door wider and allowed Meredith to enter.

"Oh, what a lovely suite."

"I suppose Jack told you where I was staying."

"Hardly," Meredith informed her huffily as her eyes swept over the room. "You'd have thought I'd asked the man to divulge classified secrets. He wouldn't tell me anything. In fact, if it weren't for Peter mentioning that he'd seen you, I wouldn't have even known you were in the city."

"I'll have to remember to thank Peter," Kelly said dryly, and shut the door.

"He'll like that. Especially since Jack gave us both grief, saying that Peter shouldn't have said anything and that I shouldn't bother you. As if a visit from an old friend would be a bother."

"Perhaps you should have listened to Jack."

"Why, Kelly Santos, what a thing for a southern girl

like you to say. If I didn't know better, I'd think you weren't happy to see me.''

''The truth is, Meredith—''

''Here,'' Meredith said, and shoved the fussy bag at her. ''I brought you a little gift.''

Kelly eyed the bag and Meredith suspiciously. ''Why?''

Meredith rolled her eyes. ''Oh, for pity's sake, just take the thing.''

Kelly took the bag and simply stared at it. Growing up as she had, gifts had been a rare thing, consisting primarily of a toy at the Doll and Toy Fund hosted for underprivileged children at Christmastime, and sometimes a new dress purchased by the Ladies Guild for the girls at St. Ann's for the holidays. She'd been taught to send a proper thank-you for those gifts. But unexpected gifts like this one from Meredith were something with which she'd had little experience.

''Well, aren't you going to open it?''

Kelly pushed aside the gold tissue and drew out a small glass bottle with a fancy-shaped top. ''It's lovely. Thank you.''

''It's perfume,'' Meredith advised her proudly. ''Both the fragrance and bottle were designed exclusively for me. It's the signature scent for the new boutique I'm opening in the French Quarter next month. It's called Indulgences—the same as the boutique. Just wait until you smell it,'' she said, and taking the bottle from her, Meredith removed the cut-glass stopper. ''Give me your wrists.''

Kelly did as instructed and Meredith drew the tip of the stopper along her pulse points.

''Go ahead. Take a sniff.''

Kelly smelled her wrist. She had to admit the soft floral notes were pleasant.

"Well, what do you think? Sinful, isn't it?"

"It's very nice," she said.

"Nice? You think it's nice?"

Meredith's crestfallen expression reminded Kelly of a child being told that there was no Santa Claus—and she felt herself softening. "Actually, it's lovely, Meredith. Heavenly, in fact," Kelly amended. "I don't think I've ever smelled anything quite like it."

Meredith beamed. "Thanks. That's what I thought, too. I'm hoping it will be a big seller in the boutique. Promise you'll come to the grand opening and wear the perfume."

"I'll probably be back in New York by then."

"Then fly back for the opening. After all, that's what planes are for, aren't they?"

"Well, I suppose that's one way to look at it," Kelly said, amazed that Meredith could see life as simply as she did. One big beautiful apple to be savored as she chose. But then, Meredith had lived a life much different from her own.

"So you'll come?"

"I'll try," Kelly hedged. "Well thanks again for the gift," she said, holding up the bag. "And for dropping by."

"Don't tell me you're going to kick me out before we have a chance to chat. Why, we haven't seen each other in years—not since my little modeling stint in New York. We've got so much catching up to do."

"We do?" Kelly remarked.

"Of course. And I was also hoping to discuss a little business with you."

Which was an explanation that made more sense for

this visit, Kelly thought. "Actually, Meredith, now is probably not the best time—"

"Oh, I promise I won't stay but a minute. Why don't we go sit down and get comfy," Meredith suggested, sweeping passed her in a swish of crimson silk and perfume.

Feeling as though she'd been steamrollered, Kelly followed Meredith into the main area of the suite.

"Oh, isn't this just lovely," Meredith exclaimed. "I can't tell you how impressed I was when I found out you'd booked yourself at the Regent. And a suite, no less."

"Don't be too impressed. There's a medical convention in town and it's the only thing I could get," Kelly explained. She'd hated paying the hijacker's rates and certainly didn't need a suite, but she'd had no intention of postponing the trip after learning of Sister Grace's death.

"Well, you certainly got your money's worth. Look at this view."

Kelly placed the perfume and wrappings on the table. Sister Grace's lectures about good manners kicked in once again and she said, "Would you like something from the minibar?"

"Hmm? Oh, no, thanks," Meredith told her as she began to prowl about the room, running her fingers over a table, checking out the artwork on the walls. "The Jardines have such wonderful taste. You can bet that lamp's an antique and not a reproduction," she remarked, referring to the lamp on a corner table.

"I'll have to take your word for it," Kelly told her, since her knowledge of antiques was limited.

Meredith turned around and gave her another of those engaging smiles that Kelly associated with the Callaghans. "This is so nice, Kelly. It does my heart good to see you doing so well. Why, I remember that little cramped place you had in New York. I swear I don't know how you ever lived in that thing."

"Actually, I still live there."

Meredith blinked, her big green eyes filled with disbelief. "But why? I mean, I know New York is expensive and all, but you're one of the best photographers in the business."

"Gee, thanks."

Meredith waved off her remark. "I'm not telling you anything you don't know already. You're very good at what you do and your work is in some of the biggest fashion magazines in the country. I just assumed you were earning a decent salary and could afford a nicer place to live."

"I am earning a decent salary," Kelly assured her. In fact, she was paid well for doing a job she enjoyed. "But I don't see any point in wasting money on a fancy apartment when all I need is a place to sleep and a darkroom to develop my photos. I'm perfectly happy with my apartment."

"But how could you be? I mean, you don't even have a view."

Kelly nearly laughed, unable to help but be amused by the differences between her and Meredith. "You mean the back of another apartment building doesn't count?"

Meredith gave her a withering look.

"I don't need a view, Meredith. I'm hardly ever home, and when I am, I'm in my darkroom."

"What about when you entertain? Or when you have a guest stay over?"

Kelly's smile disappeared. "I'm too busy working to

do much entertaining. As for overnight guests, I don't have much time for them, either.'' The truth was she hadn't had any overnight guests since her relationship with Garrett had ended.

"Sounds to me like you could use some fun in your life. And lucky for you, I know all about having fun. That's the other reason I came by. Mother's having a little cocktail party this Sunday evening, and when she heard you were in town, she insisted that I ask you to come.''

"Your mother's inviting me to a cocktail party?'' Kelly repeated.

"You needn't sound so skeptical.''

"It's kind of hard not to,'' Kelly told her. "Face it, Meredith, you and I weren't exactly pals back in school, and we certainly didn't move in the same social circles.''

"Oh, don't be such a snob, Kelly.''

"Me? A snob?''

"Yes,'' Meredith insisted. "Back in school, you were the one who always went off by yourself, as if you thought you were too smart or too good to sit with the rest of us girls. I thought when you helped me get on with that modeling agent in New York a few years ago you'd finally gotten over it. Obviously, I was wrong.''

Stunned by the accusation, Kelly didn't know what to say at first. Finally, she said, "I was different from the rest of you.''

"Of course you were different. You were always so intense and focused on what you were going to do with your life. And the rest of us, well, we were just worried over whether or not we'd have a date to the prom and if we did, what dress we were going to wear.''

"Those weren't the only differences.''

"You mean what people said about you...about how you could see the future?"

"Yes."

"I'll be honest. I've always wondered whether or not the stories were true."

"What if I said they were?"

"Really?" Meredith replied, her face lighting up.

"Yes."

"Darn! I wish you'd have told me that when we were in high school. I certainly could have used a friend with a crystal ball back then when it came to boys. I was forever picking the wrong guy. Shoot, I still am," she said with a frown. "Any chance I could get you to take a look at my palm or whatever it is you do now?"

"No."

"Oh well, I guess I'll just have to visit Madam Zara down by the Square," Meredith said nonchalantly.

"Meredith, you said you wanted to discuss some business. Why don't you quit dancing around and tell me what it is you really want?"

"Gosh, you are so darned prickly. You need to lighten up."

"The business, Meredith?"

The other woman sighed. "All right. But first off, I really did come here to say hello and invite you to the party. I also wanted to see if I could hire you to do some ads for me for Indulgences."

"No."

If Meredith heard her, she gave no indication, she simply launched into her plea. "I'll pay you whatever you say—even double your rate," she said, and swallowed as though she'd surprised herself with the offer. "The shop is scheduled to open just before the Christmas season kicks off..."

"Meredith—"

"…and I've got to make a go of this. You'd have complete creative license, carte blanche, whatever you need…"

"Meredith," Kelly tried again. To no avail.

"…and if you'll do this for me, I swear on the Bible that I'll be forever grateful to you. Why, I'll even name my firstborn child—boy or girl—after you." She whooshed out a breath. "So what do you say? Will you do it?"

"No."

"No?" Meredith repeated.

Feeling somewhat guilty, Kelly said, "Even if I wanted to help you, I couldn't. I don't have any of my equipment here."

"But you could get it. I could have it flown in for you," she offered.

Kelly shook her head. "I'm not here to work. I'm here on a personal matter," she explained.

"I know. And I meant to tell you how sorry I was about Sister Grace. My whole family was. Despite the fact that she was a nun, she really was an okay lady and I liked her."

"So did I."

"And I bet if Sister Grace were here now she'd be the first one to tell you that when a friend is in dire straits, like I am, that you should help them."

"Meredith, I hardly see you as someone in dire straits."

"Oh, but I am. I've got to make this boutique work. I've got to," she said, a hint of desperation creeping into her voice.

"Meredith—"

"Don't give me an answer now. Just think about it for a bit and we'll talk again later."

Kelly was about to tell the other woman that she didn't need to think about it because she wasn't going to change her mind. But as though Meredith sensed what was coming, she jumped to her feet.

"Oh, goodness, would you look at the time," she said, making a show of glancing at her watch. "I need to scoot. Now, don't forget. Cocktails on Sunday at seven-thirty."

"I'm not sure I can make it," Kelly began.

"Of course you can. My mother simply won't take no for an answer and neither will I." She scooped up her handbag. "Do you need the address?"

"No. I know the address," Kelly told her. Anyone who had ever lived in New Orleans knew the striking mansion on St. Charles Avenue that belonged to the Callaghan family. "But—"

"No buts. I'll see you on Sunday."

And in the same whirlwind manner in which she had swept into the room, Meredith was gone, leaving a confused Kelly in her wake.

"Come on, Bobby. We've already got you on tape hocking the watch and ring," Jack told the guy they had in interrogation. They had tracked down the man when a check of local pawnshops resulted in a watch inscribed to Gilbert and a family ring with a ruby stone. "What we want to know is where you got the stuff?"

"I already told you, man, I didn't steal the stuff. I found it."

"The same way you found that woman's wedding ring and necklace that you were hauled in for this past summer?" Jack countered.

"That was a misunderstanding," Bobby told him.

Leon grabbed the guy's chair and pulled it around. Then he got down in the man's face. "Do we look like morons to you, Bobby?"

Bobby shook his head no, but Jack suspected he sorely wanted to answer affirmatively.

"Then why don't you just cut the crap and tell me and Detective Callaghan here how you ended up with a watch and ring that belonged to a dead man?"

"I keep telling you, I found it," Bobby insisted.

"Before or after you put a bullet through him?" Leon asked.

"No way. I done told you, I never killed nobody," the guy said, a panicked whine in his voice. The man's dark eyes shifted from Jack to Leon and back again, like those of a trapped animal. "You gotta believe, man. I didn't kill him."

"I want to believe you, Bobby. But the only way I can do that is if you tell me who did kill the guy," Jack told him.

"I don't know."

Leon shoved the man's chair back so that it banged against the back of the table. "We're wasting our time with this piece of shit. I say let's book him for murder and have him tossed in a cell. With the three-strikes policy, he won't have a prayer of ever seeing daylight again."

"No," Bobby shouted, visibly trembling now. "It wasn't me, I tell you. It must have been the woman."

"What woman?" Jack asked.

Bobby wiped his mouth with the back of his hand. "Don't know who she was. Never saw her before, but she came by the corner where my buddy Sly and his brothers were finishing up a number. Sly had his guitar case open and people was throwing in money to, you know, show their appreciation for the fine music. Anyways, this tall chick walks by, tosses in a wad of bills and keeps going.''

"That's a real nice story, Bobby," Jack began. "But it still doesn't explain to me how you ended up with the dead man's watch and ring, or why I should believe that some woman you don't know, and never saw before, is the one who killed the guy."

"I was getting to that," Bobby told him, and from the way the fellow's eyes kept darting about, Jack wondered if he was on something or simply scared half out of his wits. "Anyways, like I said, I sees this chick when she turns onto the corner walking kind of fast-like. She hadn't even been there for Sly's number, but she throws a wad of bills into the guitar case, anyway. So, me, I figure something's not right and I decides to go investigate."

"Because you're such a Good Samaritan," Leon remarked.

"Maybe I was trying to be," Bobby argued.

"So what happened, Bobby?" Jack prompted.

"Well, I goes down the street where I seen the chick come from. One of the streetlights is out, so it's pretty dark, but I sees this car sitting at the end of the alley with out-of-state plates. Everybody knows you can't park a car down there 'cause the police will tow it away, so I decided I'd do the guy a favor. I'd tell him he needed to move his car before the cops come."

"Why, can you believe it, Jackson? Old Bobby here is all heart. A regular good guy. Or maybe he's really a lowlife piece of scum who was hoping he'd found himself an easy mark to rob."

"It wasn't like that," Bobby cried out.

"Then how was it?" Jack demanded, his patience wearing thin. "And no more bullshit."

"All right. The thing is, I thought the guy had just made it with a hooker and that maybe he was looking for more action. So I was going to, you know, offer to recommend a couple of working girls I know."

"You pimping now, too, Bobby?" Leon asked.

"No! I don't do that shit. I was just trying to help out a couple of the ladies. The economy's been tough on everybody, you know?"

"So what happened?" Jack asked, directing the man back to the story at hand.

"So's I knocked on the guy's window, see? Only he don't answer. I can see the dude's got white hair, so I'm thinking maybe the old guy's hard of hearing or something. So's I open the car door and the dude nearly fell on top of me. I see there's all this blood and the guy's not breathing, so I shoves him back into the car and I get the hell out of there."

"But not before you helped yourself to his watch and ring," Leon pointed out.

"The dude was dead, man. What did he need them for?"

"You are one sorry son of a bitch," Leon told him.

"Maybe I am, but I'm no killer. I swear on my mama's grave, I'm telling you the truth. I didn't off the old man, that bitch must have done it."

"What makes you so sure the woman killed him?" Jack asked.

"Because I was watching the corner that night, waiting for my girlfriend. She was supposed to be meeting me and we was supposed to go do some partying when she got off of work. Only first she wanted to go change clothes because she said she'd bought this sweet little costume for Halloween that she wanted me to see.''

"Bobby, you want to cut to the chase here?" Jack suggested.

"That's what I'm doing. You see, my girlfriend, she stays with her aunt down that block—the one where I saw the chick coming from that leads to that alley. So I was watching for my girl. And I don't see nobody come from that direction for at least fifteen minutes before I saw that chick. The way I figure it, the guy must have tried to welch on what he owed her, so she whacked him and took the money he owed her.''

"Then how do you explain her dumping a wad of bills in your pal Sly's case?" Jack asked.

Bobby shrugged. "Maybe she just wanted to take what was owed her."

"An honest working girl who kills her johns but doesn't steal," Leon offered sarcastically. "You are one dumb fuck, Bobby."

"This woman you saw, what did she look like?" Jack asked.

"I don't know, man. I couldn't see her face on account of she was wearing one of them long black cape-things that had a hood on it.''

Leon's gaze met his, and Jack knew his partner was remembering Kelly's description of the murderer. "That's it?" Jack asked Bobby. "You give us this song and dance about a mystery woman that you claim murdered a guy and all you can tell us is that she was wearing a black cape?"

Bobby swallowed, obviously nervous again. "She was a tall chick, kind of on the skinny side from what I could see. Oh, and she was definitely white.''

"How do you know that if you couldn't see her face?" Jack asked.

"I saw her wrist when she reached over to toss the dough in Sly's guitar case. She was wearing gloves, but I saw her wrist."

"A tall white chick on the thin side who was wearing a black cape. Sound familiar, Jackson?" Leon asked him when they left the interrogation room and returned to their desks.

"There are probably a couple of hundred women in this city who fit that description," Jack pointed out. "And probably half of them were out Halloween night."

"Yeah. But none of them claimed to have seen the murder."

"That doesn't mean that Kelly did it," Jack told him.

"Hey, Callaghan, I took a message for you," Nuccio called out as they entered the homicide team's room.

Just what he needed, more grief from Nuccio, Jack thought. He stopped in front of Nuccio's desk and waited. After several seconds passed, he asked, "So you planning to give me the message?"

"Maybe he's trying to send it to you by ESP," one of the other guys joked.

Jack ignored the comment and waited. "What's the message, Nuccio?"

"It was from one of the techs going over your vic's car. He said they came up with something for you."

"What did he say?"

"It was real technical-sounding shit, so I wrote it down. Give me a second to find it," Nuccio told him, and dug through the mess on his desk. He salvaged a scrap of paper from beneath a coffee cup. "Here it is.

He says, they found a strand of hair with a follicular tag. He said for you to call him.''

"Thanks," Jack said, and snatched the piece of paper from Nuccio's fingers. He stopped by Leon's desk.

"What's up?" Leon asked.

"The lab techs came up with a strand of hair in the vic's car with a follicular tag, so it looks like we've got DNA to work with."

"You going to the lab?" Leon asked.

"I'm on my way over there now."

"I'm right behind you." As Leon shoved away from his desk and the two of them exited the station house, he said, "It's about damn time we got a break on this case."

Only Jack wasn't at all sure the information would prove to be the break they hoped for as he listened to the crime-scene tech explain what they'd found. "The good news is this strand of hair was pulled out near the root, so we've got a piece of tissue that will give us the owner's DNA."

Jack examined the strand of blond hair under the microscope lens and stepped aside for Leon to do the same. "And the bad news?"

"The bad news is I ran it through the system and didn't get any hits. So if the hair did come from your killer, she doesn't have a record."

"She?" Leon prompted.

"Yes. Thought I told you. The hair definitely belongs to a woman, Caucasian, possibly her early thirties." The man glanced up from the microscope and apparently caught the look that passed between Leon and him. "You got a suspect who fits that description?"

"Maybe," Jack conceded.

"If we bring her in for a DNA test you'd be able to tell us if she's the one that hair belongs to, right?" Leon asked.

"Absolutely," the tech said. "That little strand of hair is as good as a fingerprint. You get me the DNA on your suspect and I'll tell you if we have a match."

"Thanks for your help," Jack said, and left.

Once they were outside, Leon told him, "The Santos woman is a blonde, Jackson, and she's connected to this case. You know as well as I do that we need to ask her for a DNA sample. It's procedure."

"I know. I'll give her a call," Jack told him.

"Maybe it would be better if I made the call," Leon offered. And once he got back to the station, he called Kelly at her hotel. "Ms. Santos, this is Detective Jerevicious."

"Yes, Detective?"

"Ma'am, I need to ask if you'd be willing to come down and give us a DNA sample."

"Is that a request, Detective?" she countered, her voice cool.

"Right now, it's a request. But if necessary, I can get a warrant. If you'd like to consult with an attorney, feel free—"

"I don't need an attorney, Detective. And save yourself and your partner the trouble of getting a warrant. I'll agree to a DNA test. Just tell me when and where."

Ten

"You do realize, Detective Jerevicious, that this is a waste of my time and yours," Kelly Santos informed him when she presented herself to the police station for the DNA test the following day.

"Detective Callaghan said the same thing, ma'am," Leon told the woman who, as far as he was concerned, was the only viable suspect in their investigation.

"Then perhaps you should have listened to him."

"I'd like to have, ma'am. But as I told Detective Callaghan, the quickest and easiest way to rule you out as a suspect is to run a DNA test on you and compare it to the sample we got from Dr. Gilbert's car."

"Where is Detective Callaghan?" she asked.

The lady was cool. But Leon thought he detected some nerves beneath that cool demeanor. "He's with the captain. He should be here in a few minutes. If you'll come this way, I'll take you on back," he instructed, and led her to a room where the lab tech would come for a swab. He opened the door for her to enter.

She stepped inside the drab gray room.

"Could I get you something to drink while you wait? Some water or maybe a soda?" Leon offered.

"A glass of water, if it's not too much trouble."

"No trouble at all. I'll let the technician know you're here," he informed her. "Make yourself comfortable."

After closing the door, he headed down the hall. He knocked on the door and stuck his head inside. "Stuart," he called over to the tech they'd met with yesterday. When the guy looked up from the test tubes he was fiddling with, he said, "The suspect for the Gilbert homicide is here for that DNA test."

"Be right there. Just need to finish this test."

Leon nodded, shut the door and stopped in the break room, where he retrieved a bottled water from the fridge. Then he headed back down to the room where the Santos woman was waiting. He paused outside for a moment and watched her. Rather than make herself comfortable, she paced the small room, reminding him of an animal caught in a pen. As he watched her, he thought of his partner's defense of her and tried to understand it. Despite Jackson's claim that there was nothing personal going on between them, he had seen the way Jack looked at her. Maybe nothing had happened yet, but his partner definitely wanted it to. That in itself surprised him, because this was the first time in the two years they'd been partners that he'd ever seen Callaghan let personal feelings get in the way of his job. He could understand Jackson's attraction to her. The lady was certainly easy on the eyes. But he'd seen the other man with several women who were flat-out gorgeous—and not one of them had ever affected his partner's judgment or interfered with his ability to do his job.

This one did.

Leon frowned, went over his conversation with Callaghan in his head. The man really did believe the woman was innocent. What was more surprising was that Callaghan bought into her claim of being psychic. Being a southern boy and having spent a considerable amount of time in New Orleans, he was no stranger to the superstitions and spiritual bents of the locals. Hell, even his Tessa had thrown away good money for a tarot card reader to fill her head with nonsense. And Lord knows, he'd been spooked himself once when he'd had a voodoo priestess threaten him with a painful death after he'd arrested her man.

But at heart he was a practical man, Leon conceded. A man who believed in God and country and cold, hard facts. And the cold, hard facts said that the lady knew too much about the murder. She'd either done it herself or she'd been there and seen it done firsthand. Either way, she was involved and he intended to prove that to Jackson. What he didn't believe was that the Santos woman could see the future any more than that fortune-teller last year who'd convinced his Tessa that they were going to have a baby.

Anger burned inside him as he thought about that scam artist, building up his Tessa's hopes. They'd been down that route years ago when he was still playing ball. They'd spent a fortune on doctors, procedures and even tried in vitro, but the fact was his sperm count was nearly nonexistent. There he was, the big football stud, and he couldn't give his wife a baby. That's why they'd adopted. Granted, they hadn't gotten the boys as babies, but they were their sons and they were happy with their kids. But it hadn't stopped his Tessa from wanting to have a baby. A maternal thing, she'd claimed, this desire to hold an infant, have it nurse at her breast. It didn't mean she loved their boys any less, she just had never stopped wanting to have a baby. And he felt like a failure because he couldn't make it happen.

He needed to forget about all that and do his job, Leon reminded himself, irritated that he'd allowed the Santos woman to bring back those unhappy memories. He opened the door. "Here's your water."

She turned around. "Thanks," she said, and reached for the bottle of water.

As she took the bottle from him, she froze. Her eyes shot up to his face. There was something in her eyes, a softening, almost compassion. And Leon had the strangest feeling as she stared at him that she had somehow known he'd been thinking of Tessa. "Is something wrong, Ms. Santos?" he asked, his voice more abrupt than he'd intended, but he didn't like the fact that he'd allowed himself, even for a minute, to believe in the hocus-pocus she'd been feeding his partner.

"No. It's just that you—" She paused. "Excuse me." She turned away from him, opened the water bottle and took a sip.

"What were you going to say?"

She looked back at him, hesitated. "She's pregnant. She doesn't know it yet because she hasn't had time to pick up a pregnancy test from the drugstore. The boys have karate today and football tomorrow, and she thinks she's crazy to even get her hopes up again, but—"

"Who are you talking about?" he asked.

"Your wife."

Anger had him balling his hands into fists. "Listen, lady, you want to play your psychic games with Jackson and Sarge, you go right ahead. But don't try messing with me."

"I'm sorry," she said. "It's just that you were feeling so down and beating yourself up about Tessa—"

Leon's head snapped back. He grabbed her by the shoulders. "How did you know my wife's name?"

"It's actually Theresa, but you call her Tessa," she

told him. "And no, I didn't go check you out from when you were playing pro ball."

Leon released his grip on her as though he'd just touched a live wire. "I don't know how in the hell you did that—"

"I'm sorry," she said. "I didn't mean to pry. Honestly. Most of the time, I can block things out. But sometimes if the emotions are as strong as yours were just now, it's harder to do and I...I'm sorry," she murmured, and lowered her gaze.

He wouldn't ask her. He swore to himself he wouldn't ask, yet the question came tumbling from his lips. "What you said...about Tessa being pregnant... Never mind."

"It's true, Detective. She is pregnant."

His mouth and heart hardened. "Do you know how slim the chance is of that happening, lady? The doctors said it was next to impossible."

"But not impossible," she pointed out.

"Give me one good reason why I should believe you?"

"I can't. But buy a pregnancy test on your way home tonight, anyway."

He was about to tell her that whatever her angle was he wasn't buying it, but the door opened and in walked Callaghan.

His partner immediately went over to the Santos woman. "I'm sorry I wasn't here earlier to meet you, but I got tied up with my captain."

"It's all right. Detective Jerevicious explained."

"The lab guys know we're here?" Jack asked.

"Yeah. Stuart over in the lab was finishing up a test. I'll go see what's keeping him," Leon offered, but just then the tech tapped on the door.

Leon studied the guy as he identified himself and was introduced to Kelly. Average height and average-looking, Stuart looked like what he was—a bright guy who spent his days locked in a room filled with test tubes and high-tech equipment examining evidence from crime scenes. The man's scientific ability to untangle the evidence that they gathered had proved crucial in many of their cases. He was counting on the same thing happening now.

"I'm going to do what we call a buccal swab," Stuart explained. He pulled on a pair of disposable gloves and held up a cotton-tipped swab. "All I'm going to do is swipe the inside of your cheek with this swab here to get a sample of your DNA. All right?"

"Yes," she told him.

"Then if you'll open your mouth for me," he instructed. As she did so, he swiped the inside of her cheek. Then he dropped the swab into a plastic bag. "All done."

"That's it?"

"Yes, ma'am," he said.

"Stuart, we're going to need the results ASAP," Jack informed the tech.

"No problem. After that serial killer situation last year, we convinced the big brass to spring for a new machine that lets us process the DNA on-site and twice as fast. I'll be able to give you the results in a few minutes."

Once the tech left the room, Jack asked her, "That wasn't so bad, now, was it?"

"No. But it's a waste of your department's time and resources because I never met Dr. Gilbert and I certainly was never in his car."

"Then you have nothing to worry about," Leon told her.

"No, I don't," she replied politely.

Jack shifted his gaze from her to him, and Leon didn't miss his partner's frown. Still feeling edgy and confused about the stuff she'd said about Tessa, Leon paced the room while Jack made small talk with her.

Finally there was a tap at the door. Stuart stuck his head inside. "Detectives, can I have a word with you?"

Outside in the hall, Jack asked, "So what's the news?"

"The DNA's don't match."

"Thanks, I'll tell Kelly," Jack said, a triumphant note in his voice and his eyes.

"Uh, Detective, you might want to hang on a second."

"What is it?" Leon asked.

"I said the DNA's don't match," Stuart explained. "But they are related."

"What are you talking about?" Jack snapped.

"I'm saying that the person whose hair you recovered from your crime scene and Ms. Santos are blood relatives."

"You're wrong. There has to be some kind of mistake," Kelly insisted as she sat down at the table with Jack, his partner and the lab technician who'd identified himself as Stuart Hennessy.

"DNA doesn't lie, Ms. Santos," Stuart told her.

Still feeling shell-shocked, she argued, "But it can't be right. I don't *have* any family. No parents. No siblings. No one."

"As I said, DNA doesn't lie. You have at least one female blood relative," Hennessy told her, and stood.

"Thanks again, Stuart," Jack told the man.

"Anytime."

Kelly shoved the hair from her face as she tried to absorb what she'd just discovered. After all these years of being alone, of thinking she had no one, she had family. An actual flesh-and-blood relative. A cousin? Maybe even a sister?

And that relative's DNA has been found at a murder scene.

The reminder sent reality crashing back—along with the questions. Who was the woman? What was her connection to Kelly? And, if she were correct and this was the same woman she'd seen in the car with the gun, why had she killed the doctor?

"Ms. Santos...Kelly," Leon amended.

Kelly dragged her attention back to her surroundings. She glanced up at the towering detective. "Yes, Detective?"

"I owe you an apology. I was pretty rough on you earlier."

"No apology needed. You were only doing your job," Kelly told him. Which was the truth, she reasoned. The man had been doing his job and he'd been convinced she was a killer and a fraud.

He nodded and turned his attention to Jack. "I'm going to head back to the station, see if I can clear up some paperwork so I can get home tonight at a decent hour for a change."

"Detective, don't forget to make that stop I mentioned," Kelly said, and didn't miss the cautious look that came into his eyes. While he no longer believed her to be a murderess, Detective Napoleon Jerevicious hadn't quite made up his mind about the fraud part yet, she realized.

"I'll catch you later," Jack told his partner, and once the door had closed behind him and they were alone, he gave Kelly a questioning look. "What was that all about?"

"Nothing really," she responded. She stood. "I need to go."

"Kelly, wait."

She paused.

"I just want to say that I'm sorry I had to put you through this...the DNA test."

"Like I told Detective Jerevicious, you were just doing your job."

"Yeah, but you got a little bit more than you bargained for," he said, his voice gentle. "How do you feel about all this?"

"You mean learning that I have a sister or a cousin that I didn't know existed? Or the fact that she might very well be a murderer?"

"Both."

"I'm not sure. Strange. Confused," she admitted. "All I know is I have a lot of thinking to do. Which is why I need to go." She also had to make some decisions about finding the person responsible for killing Sister Grace.

"Why don't I drive you back to your hotel?"

"Thanks, but I have a rental car," she said, and picked up her camera bag. "And I think...I think I'd like some time alone."

"Then at least let me walk you to your car," he said, and took the bag from her. He opened the door and motioned for her to precede him. "You know, I realize that we men are always accusing you women of carrying everything but the kitchen sink in your purse. But I have to tell you, I think you've got the sink in here, too. This thing weighs a ton.''

''That's because it's not my purse. It's my camera bag. It sort of does double duty for me.''

''Not everyone who's asked to come down to a police station feels that they need to bring a camera with them. It's got me wondering what you planned to take pictures of,'' he teased.

''Don't get all paranoid on me, Detective. Taking my camera with me is a habit. I've been doing it since I was thirteen years old. I automatically grabbed it when I left the hotel to come here.''

At the entrance, he held the door for her and then began walking with her to the parking lot. ''Most women would have grabbed their purse.''

Kelly chuckled. ''I don't even own a purse,'' she informed him, and stopped in front of the blue sedan. ''Here's my car.''

''You should do that more often.''

''Do what?'' she asked as she unlocked the car.

''Laugh,'' he said, his voice going all serious. ''You've got a really nice laugh, Kelly. One that I wouldn't mind hearing a bit more of.''

Kelly glanced up at him, suddenly realized how close he was. She also recognized the look in those Paul Newman blue eyes of his. ''Yes, well,'' she began, clearly remembering that kiss he'd given her, but determined not to allow herself to be drawn into something she would regret with this man. ''You have to admit, there hasn't been a whole lot to laugh about lately, what with Sister Grace's death, this business about that doctor's murder and now the results of the DNA tests.''

''You *have* had a rough go of it lately.''

''I'm glad you agree,'' she told him, and started to

open the car door, but Jack beat her to it. Quickly she
slid into the seat behind the wheel.

He leaned down. ''Tell you what, why don't I see
what I can do to coax a few more laughs out of that
~~pretty~~ mouth of yours?''

Kelly jerked her gaze up to his. She eyed him warily.

''How about I pick you up at your hotel tonight and
take you out somewhere and see if we can find something for you to laugh about.''

''I can't.''

''Why not? I know you're not working, and my guess
is you haven't made any other plans for tonight. And
since that kiss we shared wasn't all one-sided on my
part, I figure you don't fine me repulsive. Or am I
wrong?''

''No, of course not. But…''

He flashed her that grin. ''Then I don't see any problem, so I'll pick you up at seven.''

''Jack, wait!''

''Yes?''

''I…'' She scrambled for a reason why she couldn't
see him and latched onto the obvious. ''Isn't it against
regulations or something, I mean you being a cop investigating a murder where I'm a suspect?''

''I never did consider you a suspect, and thanks to the
DNA test, now no one else does, either.'' The grin
turned into a full-fledged smile that had the nerves dancing in her stomach. ''How do you feel about Chinese
food? Do you like Chinese?''

''I…yes.''

''Good. Then I'll see you at seven.''

''Jack, it's not a good idea.''

''What? You don't like Chinese? What about Creole?''

Kelly let out a breath. "I'm not talking about food. I'm talking about you and me. *We* are not a good idea."

"I think that's debatable," he told her. "So why don't you tell me what it is you're trying to say."

"What I'm saying is that my life has just gone into a tailspin with everything that's happened. I don't know what I'm going to do. I'm not even sure if I'll still be here tomorrow. So a relationship with anyone is the last thing I need or want right now."

"You finished with your little speech?"

"Yes."

"Then I have a question for you. Are you going to eat dinner tonight?"

"I'm not sure," she said warily.

"Let's try again. Did you eat today? And I'm warning you, don't lie, because us cops know when a witness is lying."

"Yes. I had breakfast." She didn't bother telling him that that breakfast consisted of a stale muffin from the minibar.

"That means you need to eat dinner. So do I. All I'm suggesting is that the two of us eat it together. What harm is there in that?"

"Why do I think this is a trick question?"

"Because you have a devious mind," he told her, and leaned in and pressed a kiss to her lips. "I'll see you at seven."

Jack saw Kelly at seven for dinner that evening, and the next two. And by the time he'd shown up at her hotel on Saturday evening, she'd put up little argument as to why they couldn't share a meal together. While he wasn't sure where things were heading between them, he knew where he wanted them to go. And he was fairly sure if he were to tell Kelly, she'd slam the door in his face and bolt it. She was wary of him, wary of most people, he suspected. That's why he'd taken things slow and easy.

He was making progress, Jack told himself as he tipped the valet who'd brought up his car and then opened the door for Kelly. She no longer pulled away when he kissed her. And she didn't tense whenever he touched her anymore. Best of all, she was talking more, telling him about her work, about her life in New York.

"Where are we going?" she asked when he joined her inside the car.

"Since we've had Chinese, Mexican and Creole, I thought maybe we'd try Italian tonight," he informed her as he pulled the car away from the hotel into the traffic. "Sound okay to you?"

"Sounds great. I haven't eaten any Italian since I was in Italy. But I meant what I said, Jack, tonight I pay for dinner."

"Whatever you say, Ms. Santos," he replied, and headed toward uptown. "So why don't you tell me about Italy."

She told him. About the photo shoot she'd done there for some fashion magazine. About the problems they'd run into when the employees working in the hotel industry went on strike. About her own trek through the Italian countryside and the photos she'd taken for her private collection. About how deeply she'd been moved by the sight of the families sitting together in the little church she'd found one Sunday morning.

"I don't guess I have to ask if you'd like to go back," he said as he turned off the main street into a residential area. "Sounds like you loved Italy."

"I did."

"Makes me want to go."

"Oh, you should. Everyone should go to Italy at least once in their life."

"Then I'll book a flight tomorrow—but only if you promise to come with me and act as my guide," he said as he turned onto a tree-lined street of residential homes.

She went all quiet on him for a moment, making him regret the teasing remark. Finally she said, "You'd do better to find someone who speaks the language. I just know enough Italian to get by."

Jack didn't bother telling her that he was fluent in both Italian and French. He simply pulled the car to a stop in front of his house. "We're here," he said as he shut off the engine. "I hope you're hungry."

Kelly jerked her gaze from him to the two-story Greek-revival-style home. "I thought we were going to eat Italian."

"We are. I've cooked dinner for us." He hopped out of the car and walked around to the passenger side and opened the door for her. "Welcome to Ristorante Callaghan."

She sat there for a moment, simply staring at his outstretched hand. Finally she looked up at him with those big, cautious eyes that had been haunting his thoughts of late. "I'm not sure this is a good idea, Jack."

"Having dinner?"

"Please, don't. I'm not very good at male-female games. I never learned how to play them. And as much as I like you, I won't play them with you now. I'd only end up disappointing you and hurting myself."

Anger sparked inside him at her accusation. "I don't play games with people's feelings, Kelly. Especially not with someone I care about, and I care about you." He let out a breath, softened his tone. "I brought you here because I wanted some time alone with you. I didn't want to go sit in another room filled with people, with waiters hovering around us because they want to turn the table, and with me trying to drag out the meal because I didn't want it to be over."

"Then why not just be honest and tell me?"

"Would you have agreed to come if I had?" At her silence, he said, "That's what I thought." He stooped down, took her hands in his and looked into her eyes. "The only thing I'm planning tonight is for the two of us to have dinner and enjoy each other's company. But if the idea makes you uncomfortable, we can leave. I'll see if I can find a restaurant instead. It's up to you, Kelly. You tell me what you want and that's what we'll do."

She hesitated a moment and Jack thought he'd lost, when she said, "I'd like to stay."

Straightening, he took her hand and helped her from the car. "Then prepare yourself for the best Italian food you've ever eaten."

"That's quite a claim," she told him as he unlocked the door to the house and they went inside. "Don't forget I was in Italy just a few weeks ago. It's pretty hard to top authentic Italian cuisine."

"Then be prepared to be impressed, Ms. Santos."

"All right, I admit it. I'm impressed," Kelly told him after they'd cleared away the remains of the meal and finished tidying up the kitchen. "Dinner was wonderful, Jack."

"You sound surprised," he replied as he put away the pasta pot and colander that she'd dried.

"I am. I never thought of you as a cook."

"Why not?" he asked as he added soap to the dishwasher and turned it on.

"It doesn't fit with the image I have of you."

"And what image is that?" he asked.

Kelly tipped her head to one side. "I don't know. When I was younger, I used to think of you as a handsome, rich playboy. But after you helped me that night in the park, I saw a different side to you, a deeper side. I knew you were someone who cared about people."

"And now?" he asked as he took off his apron, folded it and set it aside next to Kelly's.

"Now I see you as a dedicated police detective who doesn't let his personal feelings get in the way of doing the right thing."

"You're referring to the DNA test, aren't you?"

She nodded. "You didn't agree with your captain and you knew it would upset me, but you had me come down and take it, anyway."

"It's my job."

"I know. But you didn't try to lay the blame on anyone else—even when I was furious with you over it. You're a good man, Jack Callaghan. And a terrific cook."

He took a bow. "Why, thank you, ma'am. I aim to please."

"So are you going to tell me how you learned to cook like that?"

He sighed. "I have a confession. Meatballs and spaghetti is the only dish in my repertoire. It's my favorite, and Tilly, our family's cook, was sure I was going to starve when I went off to college, so she made sure I could at least cook that."

"You fraud," she said, laughing. "And here I was berating myself because my Italian cooking isn't half as good."

She started to throw the dish towel at him, but Jack

caught it and her in his arms. The laugh died on her lips. And his. He watched her eyes darken, and when she lowered her gaze to his mouth, he groaned, "Kelly."

And for the very first time, *she* kissed him.

The kiss was soft, gentle, almost shy. And it was over much, much too quickly, he thought as she eased her lips away from his. "It's getting late. I probably should be getting back to the hotel."

Jack could almost see the wheels turning in that complicated head of hers, knew she was dissecting the reason she'd kissed him, deciding it was a mistake. Determined not to let her do that to herself or to them, he kept his tone light and said, "It's not even ten o'clock yet and you still haven't seen the rest of the house. You do want to see it, don't you?"

"Yes, but only if you're sure you don't mind showing it to me."

"Are you kidding? After all the money I've sunk into fixing this place up, I'm seriously considering charging admission. Come on, I'm dying to show it to you."

He showed her the house, and by the time they were heading back downstairs, she was laughing and at ease again. "I can't believe you've only lived here since March. There's such a feeling of…roots…I guess that's the word I'm looking for. It's as though this house and you were made for each other."

"Funny you should say that. It's the same thing that Alicia said."

"Alicia?"

"Alicia Van Owen," Jack responded, and could have kicked himself for bringing the woman's name up. "She's the real estate agent who found the place for me."

178   *Metsy Hingle*

"She must be very good at her job, then, because she certainly did a fine job putting you and this house together."

"I guess so. She has a real knack for striking deals." Which was true, because Alicia really did seem to know just how to hit a sales figure upon which both buyer and seller would agree. "But this is the room that sold me on the place," Jack said as he led her back to the den with its bookcase-covered walls, fireplace and high ceilings. "The mantel over this fireplace is the original."

"It's beautiful." She ran her fingers along the carved woodwork for a second, then stepped back to glance up at the painting over the mantel. "The woman in the portrait has to be one of your ancestors. Who is she?"

"My great-great grandmother. She was the first Callaghan bride to settle in New Orleans."

"She's lovely. I can see the family resemblance," she informed him as she looked from him to the portrait.

"So you're saying I look like a southern belle?" he teased.

"Not quite. Meredith bears a striking resemblance to her, though. Except for the eyes. You definitely have her eyes."

"Ah, yes, the famous Callaghan eyes. That's what my mother calls them. She said that's what attracted her to my dad."

"I can see why."

"I think you just paid me another compliment, Kelly Santos," he teased, and loved seeing the flush in her cheeks.

"I'm sure it's something you're used to."

"Not from you," he told her.

She shifted her gaze from him to the fireplace itself and hugged her arms to herself. "It looks like you're all set for the winter,'' she remarked, obviously referring to the grate already laid out with wood and with extra logs stacked beside it.

"There's nothing like a fire on a cold night. And speaking of cold, it's kind of chilly in here. How about I light us a fire?'' he suggested, and stooped down in front of the hearth to strike a match.

"No!''

Jack jerked his attention back to Kelly. She'd gone deathly pale and her eyes were wide and terrified. He immediately went to her, caught her hands. "You're trembling. What's wrong?''

"I—I don't like fires.''

Suddenly he remembered her asking him to extinguish the candles at the table in the restaurants. He'd thought it was the scent that bothered her, never questioning it could be for another reason.

"I know it's stupid and I'm sorry.''

"There's nothing stupid about it and you have nothing to be sorry about. Come and sit down,'' he said, and led her over to the couch. "I'll get you a brandy.''

"I don't need any brandy. I'm fine now.''

Jack ignored her because she was far from fine. She didn't have a lick of color in her face. Walking over to the bar, he poured her a tumbler of brandy and brought it back to her. "Drink,'' he commanded.

She hesitated a moment, looked into his eyes, then took one sip, then another. "Thank you.''

Jack took the glass from her and set it aside, then gathered her into his arms. He held her close, resting her head on his shoulder, gently running his fingertips along her arms to relax her. He didn't ask any questions, simply waited for her to tell him when she was ready.

"For as far back as I can remember, I've been terrified

of fire,'' she began. ''I have recurring dreams about being trapped in a room with flames shooting up all around me. The shrinks they sent me to when I lived at St. Ann's thought it might have had something to do with whatever happened to me before I came to St. Ann's. But I don't remember.''

''How old were you?''

''They said I was around three when someone left me at the delivery entrance of the orphanage. Or at least that's their best guess of how old I was. I couldn't tell them who I was or how I got there. According to the doctors, I had suffered some kind of shock and to cope with it I blocked out everything about my past.''

''How did you get the name Kelly?''

''The laundry woman who found me was Irish, and since it was a cold night when I'd been left there, she concluded the saints had taken care of me. So I became Kelly Santos.'' She paused, continued. ''I was told I had burn marks on my shoulder and my left hand. So it's a pretty good bet that I was in some kind of fire.''

Jack took her left hand. He noted the no-nonsense short nails without polish, the lack of any rings. He turned it over, studied her palm. It was soft, pretty and perfect, like the rest of her. He brought her hand to his lips and kissed it.

''It didn't leave any scars.''

Not the ones you could see, anyway, Jack thought.

''Over the years they tried therapy and even hypnosis once, hoping to get me to remember who I was and what had happened to me, how I ended up at St. Ann's. But none of it worked. I couldn't remember. Which I guess is kind of ironic when you think about it.''

''Why's that?'' he asked.

''Because I can see and sense things that are going to

happen or have happened to other people, but I can't see anything about my own past."

Jack couldn't help but admire her, how brave she was, what she had done with her life. He couldn't even begin to imagine how difficult her childhood had been—a stark contrast to the comfort and security of his own. It also worried him that there was a blood link between her and a killer. "You know, there's been a lot of technology since you were a kid. You might have more luck now. And my being a cop gives me access to a lot of resources. I could help you."

She lifted her head, looked at him with that wariness creeping back into her eyes. "And while you're helping me, you might also find your killer."

"All right, I'd be lying if I said it didn't cross my mind. It did. But that's not the reason I offered to help. I offered because you've begun to matter to me. You've begun to matter a lot."

"I told you I'm not good at relationships," she said quietly, and he could already sense her pulling back—emotionally, physically. "I come with too many complications. We're both better off not getting involved."

"I've got a news flash for you," he said, annoyed by her dismissal. "We're already involved."

She stood. "Thank you for dinner, but I'd like to go back to my hotel now, please."

That cool politeness swiped at him, sparked his temper. He retrieved her coat. "Just so you know, Kelly, I'm going to find Gilbert's killer—which means I'm probably going to be digging into your past, with or without your approval. If you want me to share what I find with you, I will. If you don't, that's all right, too."

"Is that all, Detective?"

"Not quite," he said as he helped her put on her coat.

Then he moved in close and said, "You should also know that I fully intend for us to get a lot more involved before this whole thing is over. I want you to think about that tonight when you're lying in bed alone."

Eleven

Kelly walked in the direction of the Callaghan mansion. She'd parked her rental car two blocks away, needing time and the cool November air to calm her. She'd had more than a few uneasy hours since that DNA test and it seemed she couldn't close her eyes now without dreaming. And while she knew the answer to her questions and the nightmare were buried somewhere in her past, she was reluctant to open that door. Having Jack inform her that he intended to go digging around in her past had done nothing to ease her anxieties. Nor had his parting comment.

"You should also know, I fully intend for us to get a lot more involved before this whole thing is over. I want you to think about that tonight when you're lying in bed alone."

She wasn't sure which disturbed her the most—the idea of Jack poking around in her past, or knowing that she was a breath away from becoming his lover. Blast you, Jack Callaghan, she thought as his words continued to echo in her head. *He* was not the reason she'd come tonight, she reminded herself as she continued down the sidewalk. She'd come because Mrs. Callaghan had told her that other friends of Sister Grace's would be there, friends whom she was hoping might provide her with a clue that would lead to the nun's killer.

But once she reached the Callaghan estate, apprehension knotted her stomach again. The place was ablaze with lights. Valets raced to park cars for arriving guests. Elegantly dressed men and women strolled up the steps to the doorway. The place was magnificent, just as she remembered it, Kelly thought. The stately columns and galleries. The beveled glass at the entrance door that opened into a foyer where she could see the glow of a chandelier. The lush gardens with roses blooming and the scent of sweet olive. Even in November with a nip in the air, the lawn remained a thick carpet of green. Majestic oaks stood like sentinels about the grounds, their leaves rustling in the night breeze. At the sounds of laughter and music, she glanced toward the rear and could make out twinkling lights that had been strung through the trees. A beautiful, magical place, she mused.

How many times had she walked by here as a girl, caught a glimpse of the family through the windows and imagined what it would be like to be one of them? How many times had she strolled by on a night much like this one, heard the music and laughter coming from inside and wished she was welcome?

Suddenly she recalled the invitation to Meredith's graduation party. Everyone in the class had received one—including her. And while she'd been tempted to attend, had even bought a new dress to wear, she'd ended up declining at the last minute. She hadn't belonged, she reminded herself.

Tonight was different. She wasn't a penniless orphan anymore. She was a successful photographer—thanks in great measure to Sister Grace. And it was for Sister Grace that she had come. Straightening her shoulders, Kelly marched through the gates, determined to find answers. And she ran straight into Jack.

"Whoa! Where's the fire?" he asked, catching her by the arm when she swayed in her high heels.

"Sorry. I wasn't paying attention," she said, cursing herself ten times over for wearing the ridiculous shoes.

"No problem."

She hadn't seen him since he'd dropped her off at her hotel the previous evening. Nor had she responded to the messages he'd left for her since then. While a part of her had known she was being a coward, another part of her had felt it was a matter of self-preservation. She didn't like the feelings Jack had stirred inside her. Feelings that were stirring inside her again now. "You can let go of me now."

He released her arm, but made no attempt to move out of her path. "Why don't I escort you inside."

"I think I can manage on my own."

"Then keep me company," he said, flashing her a smile. "Otherwise, I might fall asleep."

Kelly arched her brow. "You don't strike me as the type who falls asleep at parties."

"Spoken like a woman who's never found herself trapped at some boring society party. Although my mother swore that tonight wasn't going to be one of those stuffy affairs, you never know."

"It doesn't sound stuffy to me," she said honestly. From the laughter and music and number of people milling about, it sounded like a fun party.

"Why don't we go inside and find out?" Cupping her elbow, he steered her in the direction of the house. "We'll pay our respects to my mother, see what Tilly's cooked up for the event and, if we're bored silly, then we'll leave."

He maneuvered her so smoothly that Kelly found herself exchanging greetings and introductions and brushing elbows with several dozen people before she even had a chance to protest. Or perhaps she hadn't protested because deep down inside she had wanted to be with Jack.

"Not exactly the intimate little gathering my mother promised, is it?" he asked.

"No, but it's lovely all the same." And it was lovely, she conceded. Mrs. Callaghan was gracious and welcoming, as were her friends. Everyone had nothing but good things to say about Sister Grace. But after the first hour, she still hadn't come up with anything that might give her a clue as to who had killed the nun.

"When you didn't return my calls, I was worried you wouldn't come tonight. I'm glad you did," Jack said to her later.

"I phoned your mother to say I couldn't make it, but she was so gracious, I didn't know how to refuse her."

Jack chuckled. "That's my mom. She should have run for Congress. She'd have had those hard-nosed politicians eating right out of her hand."

"After watching her tonight, I'd have to agree. She's charming. You're all very lucky to have her for a mother."

"I think so, too. At least most of the time," he remarked, and Kelly didn't miss his unhappy expression as he spied his mother speaking with a striking blonde in a white cocktail dress.

"Who is she?" Kelly asked.

"Who?"

"The woman with your mother."

"Her name's Alicia Van Owen. She's the real estate agent I told you about. The one who found my house. Her mother and my mother were friends in college."

"She's stunning." And Kelly suspected that Alicia

and Jack had been more than acquaintances whose paths had crossed in business.

"So are you. Have I told you how beautiful you look tonight?"

Kelly's pulse jumped at the heat she read in his eyes. He drew his fingertip down her arm, sending a shiver of longing through her. "Jack, don't. I meant what I said last night."

"So did I. You matter to me and I'm not going to go away." And before she could respond, he motioned for the waiter and swiped an hors d'oeuvre from a passing tray. "These are Tilly's crabmeat-stuffed mushrooms. You've got to try one," he said, and held one up to her lips.

As she bit into the tasty tidbit, Jack's eyes darkened, making her stomach quiver. Kelly swallowed. "It's delicious," she said, barely able to get the words past her lips.

"Yes, it is."

In an effort to calm the desire humming in her veins, she reached for the wineglass she'd set on the table and drained it. When she looked at Jack again, she noted the direction of his gaze and spied Meredith disappearing outdoors into the gardens.

"Are you worried about your sister?"

"A little." Jack said, then turned his attention back to her. He finished off the canapé, wiped his fingers on a napkin. "She's put a lot of herself into getting this shop of hers off the ground."

"Yes, she mentioned it. She seems very excited about it."

"She is. She really wants it to work. So do I."

"Don't you think she'll be successful?" Kelly asked.

"God knows I want her to be. But retail is a tough business. Half the shops don't make it."

"And you're worried that if it fails, that Meredith will give up on herself," Kelly said, picking up on his concerns about his sister. Appalled by what she'd just done, she told him, "I'm sorry. I didn't mean to do that."

"Do what?"

"To intrude on your thoughts that way. It was terribly rude of me."

"It's no big deal. Besides, what you said is true. I am worried about her. My sister talks a good game and pretends this is all just a lark. But it isn't. She's got her heart wrapped up in making a go of it. It matters to her. So it matters to me."

As he spoke, Kelly's own heart softened. He loved his younger sister, was protective of her, worried about her happiness. That knowledge made it impossible for her own feelings not to deepen for him.

He looked at the empty glass in his hand. "I'm going to get me another drink. Would you like another glass of wine?"

"Maybe just some water."

"I'll be right back," he told her.

And while Jack got waylaid on his way to the bar, she decided it was time to do some more investigating. So she went in search of her hostess.

Alex told himself he hadn't come outside to look for Meredith. He'd come out onto the veranda for a breath of fresh air. Despite how far he'd come from the roach-infested apartment he'd grown up in and the boy he'd been, he still felt like an outsider at these society shindigs. He'd only come tonight for Mrs. Callaghan and for

Jack. He hadn't come because of Meredith, he assured himself.

Yet as he scanned the gardens, it was for Meredith that he searched. He heard her laughter moments before he saw her. She emerged from the northern corner of the gardens with her arm tucked through the arm of some guy he'd been introduced to as the son of a family friend. When the man leaned closer and said something to her, jealousy ripped through him with the force of a hurricane wind. Something primal and dark and ugly inside him made him want to drag Meredith away from the other man and stake his claim.

Only she wasn't his to claim, he reminded himself. That's why he'd told her it was over between them and had turned her away when she'd come to his office that last time. He'd told her that she needed to move on. And from all indications, she was taking him at his word. She hadn't called him or come by to see him again. She'd barely said two words to him since he'd arrived at the party.

So why in the hell did he feel like punching some-thing?

Turning away from the sight of Meredith with another man, he walked over to the other side of the veranda. He jammed a fist through his hair, struggled to get a grip on his emotions as he heard the click of high heels approach from behind him.

"Looking for me?"

Alex flicked a glance back in Meredith's direction. "Nope. Just wanted to get some air. Where's your friend?"

"Trent?" She joined him by the railing, turned and leaned her back against it. "He went back to the party."

"As cozy as you two looked a few minutes ago, I'm surprised you didn't go with him."

"I thought it might be more fun to annoy you," she teased.

"I'm not in the mood for your games, Meredith."

"You used to like my games," she reminded him.

A flurry of memories of some of the games they'd engaged in over the years made him ache inside. Determined not to give in, he said, "I guess I've outgrown them."

"And me, too?"

At the hurt in her voice, he softened. "You know I care about you. I always will, but—"

"Don't," she said, and held up a hand. "I can do without another lecture on why I need to move on with my life. In case you haven't noticed, Alex, I have moved on."

"That's good," he said, wanting to mean it. But before he could stop himself, he asked, "You moving on with that fellow Trent?"

"Maybe. Not that it's any business of yours."

"You're right, it isn't. Forget I asked."

Anger snapped in her green eyes. "Fine. I'll be sure to send you a wedding invitation."

When she started to move away, he grabbed her by the wrist. "What in the hell is that supposed to mean?"

"It means that I'm through wasting my time waiting for you to ask me to marry you. Just because you don't want me, doesn't mean that someone else doesn't."

Anger pumped through his veins. "So you're going to run off and marry the first guy you come across to get even with me?"

"If I marry Trent or anyone else, it'll be because I

love him and want to spend the rest of my life with him.''

"Is that right? Then how come you tried your damnedest to get me into bed a week ago?"

"As I recall, you weren't interested. Trent, on the other hand, is.''

"I just bet he is. The problem with you, Meredith, is that you're used to getting everything you want. What you need is a man you can't wrap around your little finger.''

She tiptoed those fingers along the sleeve of his jacket, leaned closer. "You mean someone like you, Alex?''

"I wasn't talking about me.''

She winced as though he'd struck her. And because he couldn't bare to see her hurting, he hauled her up against him. "I don't want to hurt you.''

"You've got a funny way of showing it," she murmured against his neck.

After a moment, he eased her from him. Tipping up her chin with his finger, he looked down into her eyes. "Promise me you're not going to go do something stupid like marrying a guy you don't love to spite me.''

Something died in her eyes. "You know, Alex Kusak, for a smart man, sometimes you can be real stupid. Now, if you'll excuse me, I'd like to go back to the party.''

As she walked away from him and disappeared indoors, Alex gripped the railing tightly to keep himself from going after her. He was doing the right thing, the honorable thing by letting her go, he told himself.

But sometimes being honorable really sucked.

"Kelly," Mrs. Callaghan beckoned as Kelly deliberately brought herself into Jack's mother's line of vision. "Come, dear. I'd like you to meet my very dear friend

Mildred St. Amant. Mildred, this lovely creature is Kelly
Santos. She's the young woman I was telling you about.
Kelly used to live at St. Ann's and is now a successful
photographer in New York. Mildred is the chairman of
St. Ann's Guild,'' she explained, naming one of the or-
ganizations devoted to raising funds for the orphanage.

''It's such a pleasure to meet you,'' Mrs. St. Amant
told her. ''I understand from Mary Ellen that you were
at St. Ann's when Sister Grace was still there.''

''Yes, I was,'' Kelly responded, pleased that her in-
stincts had been right to seek out Mrs. Callaghan. ''Did
you know Sister Grace well?''

''Oh, yes. She was such a wonderful person, and for
her to go so suddenly the way she did… I swear, I still
can't believe she's gone. She touched so many lives, did
so many good works.''

''Yes, she did,'' Kelly said. ''I imagine her sudden
death affected a great many people.''

''Absolutely,'' Mrs. St. Amant assured her, and proceeded to name several things that Sister Grace had been
involved with at the time of her death. ''And of course
there's the annual benefit for St. Ann's,'' the woman
continued. ''This year's benefit certainly won't be the
same without her. She was the driving force behind it,
you know.''

''Mildred is right,'' Mrs. Callaghan added. ''Kelly,
dear, this is absolutely horrid of me to ask when you're
a guest in my home, but Jack tells me that you're an
accomplished photographer in your own right and have
a splendid collection of photos.''

''Well, I'm not sure how splendid they are,'' she said,
wondering what had possessed Jack to tell his mother
about her work—especially when all he'd seen were a
few shots that she'd stuck in her bag before she'd left

GET 2

HOW TO GET YOUR
2 FREE BOOKS AND FREE GIFT!

1. Peel off the MIRA® sticker on the front cover. Place it in the space provided at right. This automatically entitles you to receive two free books and an exciting surprise gift.

2. Send back this card and you'll get 2 "The Best of the Best™" books. These books have a combined cover price of $11.98 or more in the U.S. and $13.98 or more in Canada, but they are yours to keep absolutely FREE!

3. There's <u>no</u> catch. You're under <u>no</u> obligation to buy anything. We charge nothing – ZERO – for your first shipment. And you don't have to make any minimum number of purchases – not even one!

4. We call this line "The Best of the Best" because each month you'll receive the best books by some of today's most popular authors. These authors show up time and time again on all the major bestseller lists and their books sell out as soon as they hit the stores. You'll like the convenience of getting them delivered to your home at our special discount prices . . . and you'll love your *Heart to Heart* subscriber newsletter featuring author news, horoscopes, recipes, book reviews and much more!

SPECIAL FREE GIFT!
We'll send you a fabulous surprise gift, absolutely FREE, simply for accepting our no-risk offer!

5. We hope that after receiving your free books you'll want to remain a subscriber. But the choice is yours – to continue or cancel, anytime at all! So why not take us up on our invitation, with no risk of any kind. You'll be glad you did!

6. And remember...we'll send you a surprise gift ABSOLUTELY FREE just for giving THE BEST OF THE BEST a try.

Visit us online at
www.mirabooks.com

® and TM are registered trademar
of Harlequin Enterprises Limited.

BOOKS FREE!

Hurry!

Return this card promptly to GET 2 FREE BOOKS & A FREE GIFT!

YES! Please send me the 2 FREE "The Best of the Best" books and FREE gift for which I qualify. I understand that I am under no obligation to purchase anything further, as explained on the back and on the opposite page.

Affix
peel-off
MIRA
sticker here

385 MDL DRTA   185 MDL DR59

FIRST NAME	LAST NAME

ADDRESS

APT.#	CITY

STATE/PROV.	ZIP/POSTAL CODE

▼ DETACH AND MAIL CARD TODAY! ▼

(P-BB3-03) ©1998 MIRA BOOKS

THE BEST OF THE BEST™ — Here's How it Works:

Accepting your 2 free books and gift places you under no obligation to buy anything. You may keep the books and gift and return the shipping statement marked "cancel." If you do not cancel, about a month later we will send you 4 additional books and bill you just $4.74 each in the U.S., or $5.24 each in Canada, plus 25¢ shipping & handling per book and applicable taxes if any.* That's the complete price and — compared to cover prices starting from $5.99 each in the U.S. and $6.99 each in Canada — it's quite a bargain! You may cancel at any time, but if you choose to continue, every month we'll send you 4 more books, which you may either purchase at the discount price or return to us and cancel your subscription.

*Terms and prices subject to change without notice. Sales tax applicable in N.Y. Canadian residents will be charged applicable provincial taxes and GST. Credit or Debit balances in a customer's account(s) may be offset by any other outstanding balance owed by or to the customer.

If offer card is missing write to: The Best of the Best, 3010 Walden Ave., P.O. Box 1867, Buffalo, NY 14240-1867

BUSINESS REPLY MAIL

FIRST-CLASS MAIL   PERMIT NO. 717-003   BUFFALO, NY

POSTAGE WILL BE PAID BY ADDRESSEE

THE BEST OF THE BEST
3010 WALDEN AVE
PO BOX 1867
BUFFALO NY 14240-9952

NO POSTAGE
NECESSARY
IF MAILED
IN THE
UNITED STATES

New York. "But yes, I've done a series of New York after 9/11 that have been published, as well a few others. My agent's shopping a series of my prints now for a book deal."

Mrs. Callaghan beamed and exchanged a look with the other woman. "Well, Mildred and I are in charge of the silent auction at this year's benefit for St. Ann's. And we were hoping we could persuade you to donate one of your pictures for the auction."

"It would be such a lovely way to showcase the importance of St. Ann's and to be able to use you as an example of one of its success stories," Mrs. St. Amant continued. "Why, maybe you could even attend the benefit and speak to the guests, tell them about growing up at St. Ann's. Think how inspirational that would be."

Kelly balked at the suggestion. "I'll be happy to donate some photographs for the auction, but I'm afraid I won't be able to attend the benefit."

"Of course, having you there would be the ideal situation," Mrs. Callaghan said quickly. "But Mildred and I understand if you have other commitments. We're just very grateful for your generosity. I know Sister Grace would be, too."

For the next several minutes, Kelly chatted with the pair about the benefit. And when Peter Callaghan came over and asked to see her for a moment, Kelly could have wept with joy.

"You looked like you needed rescuing," Peter whispered as he steered her away.

"I could kiss you."

"I've no objections, but something tells me my brother might," he said and before she could comment, he snagged a glass of white wine from a passing tray and handed it to her.

"Thanks," she said, and took a sip of the wine. "Did I really look that desperate to escape?"

"Yes."

Kelly squeezed her eyes shut a moment. "Perhaps I should apologize to your mother."

Peter laughed. "What for? I'm guessing she and that old biddy either talked you into buying some outrageously priced tickets for a charity event or got you to promise to sit on some organization's board. Am I right?"

"Close. I'm donating photos from one of my collections for a silent auction."

"Figures. My mother's a champ fund-raiser for good causes. She goes for the jugular before you even realize it."

"She wasn't that bad," Kelly argued. "And I'm happy to donate the photographs since the money goes to St. Ann's."

"That's nice of you, Kelly," he said, a softness in his voice.

She liked Peter Callaghan. He was handsome, kind, compassionate. She was comfortable with him and he didn't make her heart race when he touched her—not the way his brother did. So if she had to be attracted to a man, why not him? Why Jack?

"You got all the boxes and the painting I sent to your hotel?"

"Yes. Thanks again for having them sent over," she told him.

"Since you had me send those things to you at the hotel, I take it you're planning to stick around New Orleans for a while?"

"Yes," she said. And she'd been so caught up in trying to find out who might have killed Sister Grace that she hadn't given much thought to her living arrangements—or to the fact that she was racking up some serious hotel charges that might go on for some time. While she wasn't a pauper, she certainly didn't believe in throwing away her money. "I don't suppose you know anyone who'd be willing to lease me a place on a short-term basis, would you?"

"How short term?"

"I'm not sure. Maybe a few weeks. Maybe a couple of months." However long it took for her to find the person responsible for Sister Grace's death.

"I can't think of anyone offhand. But there's a woman here at the party, Alicia Van Owen. She's a friend of the family. She's in real estate, both residential and commercial. She might know of something. I'll see if I can hook you up with her before the evening's over."

"There's no hurry," Kelly said, not at all sure how she'd feel about being hooked up with the woman she suspected had been, and might still be, Jack's lover. "I'll just get her number from you later."

"Whatever you say," he replied, and took a sip from his glass. "Jack mentioned you were some kind of witness in one of his cases. I hope that's not the reason you've decided to stay on in New Orleans."

"No. It's something personal." And before he assumed she was referring to his brother, she added, "Something that concerns Sister Grace."

"Nothing related to her will, I hope."

She shook her head. "No. Just some things that I'd like to look into." She waited a moment, then asked, "Did you happen to see her before she died?"

"If you're asking if she came to the office to see me in my capacity as an attorney, the answer's no. But my mother saw her every few weeks or so. Have you spoken to her?''

''Yes.'' Disappointed, Kelly hadn't realized how much she'd been hoping that Sister Grace had gone to see Peter and had confided in him about the woman who had been with her in the chapel.

''Whatever this is, it's really worrying you, isn't it?''

''Yes,'' she admitted.

''Anything I can do to help? I'm a good listener and as you'll recall a brilliant attorney.''

Kelly smiled. ''Thanks, but legal help isn't what I need. I need to find some answers.''

''Answers to what?''

''I'd rather not say yet,'' she said.

Peter grew somber. ''I don't know what this is about, Kelly. But I recommend you don't go poking around on your own. Maybe you should talk to Jack. He is a cop, after all.''

''I don't want the police involved—at least not yet.''

''Then maybe you should consider a private investigator. I can recommend one if you'd like.''

''Yes,'' she said. ''I'd appreciate that.''

''Give me a call at my office tomorrow, then. I'll put you in touch with someone who's good, reliable and won't cost you an arm and a leg.''

''Thank you, Peter. I really appreciate it.''

''Glad to help. Uh-oh,'' he said, his attention shifting to something or someone across the room.

''What is it?''

''Looks like my mother and a couple of her cohorts have got Jack cornered and he's shooting me dirty looks.''

Kelly followed the direction of Peter's gaze. And sure

enough, Jack was indeed surrounded by his mother, Mrs. St. Amant and two other women.

"I'm not sure if he's glaring at me because he's stuck, or if it's because I'm talking to you." Amusement danced in his blue eyes. "I guess I'll be a nice guy and see if I can spring him. Will you excuse me?"

"Of course," she said. And once Peter had left her, Kelly put down her wineglass. Her cheeks ached from all the smiling she'd done that evening. And her feet were absolutely killing her. Sighing, she wiggled her toes inside the high heels and wondered what on earth had possessed her to even buy the things.

"I'm convinced that it must have been a man who invented high heels," a friendly female voice said from behind her, and when Kelly turned she recognized the stunning blonde as Alicia Van Owen. "Only a man would come up with something that would be pure torture to wear."

"You're probably right."

"I've also discovered that the prettier the shoes, the more uncomfortable they are. And since those are absolutely gorgeous, I'm guessing that they're murder on your feet. Am I right?"

"Yes," Kelly admitted.

Alicia leaned closer and whispered conspiratorially, "Between us girls, I think that was the whole idea behind high heels to begin with. My theory is that some man with a foot fetish was looking for a way to get the ladies out of their shoes and came up with high heels. What do you think?"

"I think you could be on to something," Kelly said, and laughed as she suspected she was meant to do.

"We haven't been introduced yet. I'm Alicia Van Owen," she said, and held out her hand.

"Kelly Santos."

"Ah, so *you're* Meredith's friend."

"Yes, I am," Kelly said, somewhat surprised that the woman would know who she was.

As though she could read her thoughts, Alicia laughed again, a charming musical sound, and said, "I had dinner with the Callaghans last week and your name was mentioned. I understand that you and Meredith attended school together."

"That's right."

"Listen, I'll confess. My feet are killing me, too. Why don't we go sit over there for a bit?" she asked, pointing to the settee grouping in the corner.

Although Kelly hadn't relished the idea of making small talk with the woman, she reminded herself that she'd come to the party for information, so she followed Alicia. After all, she reasoned, who better to provide an inside track into people's lives than the person who sold them their homes? She took the seat opposite Alicia. "I understand that you're in real estate," Kelly began.

"Why, yes, I am," Alicia said, a hint of surprise in her voice.

"I mentioned to Peter that I might be staying in New Orleans for a while and he recommended I speak with you."

"I'll have to thank Peter," she said. "So, are you looking to buy or lease?"

"Lease, but short term. Maybe only a couple of weeks, possibly a month or two. But you're not here to discuss business," Kelly said, wanting to change the subject and avoid a hard-sell pitch. Although she didn't seem the hard-sell type, Kelly admitted. No, Alicia Van Owen struck her as one of those golden people for whom everything in life came easy. And the moment the uncharitable thought popped in her head, Kelly regretted it.

"Actually, I hardly consider it work. I love matching people with places."

"You're obviously very good at it. Jack told me that you found him his house," Kelly remarked.

"True. But it was more a case of blind luck. I went to look at the house for another client, but the moment I set eyes on it I knew it would be perfect for Jack. Have you seen it yet?"

The offhand tone and friendly smile might have fooled most people, but it didn't fool Kelly. Alicia Van Owen was fishing for information. So was she. The difference was, Alicia had sized her up as a romantic rival for Jack and wanted information about their relationship, while she was seeking information that could help her find Sister Grace's killer. "Yes as a matter of fact, I have. And you're right, it does suit him." Deciding to dive in, Kelly said, "I imagine you meet a lot of people in your line of work. Why, I bet you could write a book about what goes on in people's homes—the parties, the problems, their lives in general."

"Well, I do care about my clients, but I try not to pry into their personal lives," Alicia said. "Of course, there are special ones like the Callaghans. But then I don't have to tell you how special they are. That's why I was so pleased to be able to help Jack get his place. And he's done such a fabulous job fixing it up. Don't you think?"

Jack again. Kelly bit back a frown. "I'll have to take your word for it since I didn't see the before version."

"Whoops! I've made you uncomfortable talking about Jack, haven't I?" And before Kelly could deny the charge, Alicia reached over, patted her hand.

"There's no need to be, you know. Jack and I ended our relationship a while back."

"That really doesn't concern me. Jack and I…we're not involved that way," she said finally.

"But I thought…when I saw the two of you come in together… Well now, don't I feel like an idiot," she said, and flushed a pretty pink. "I'm sorry."

"It's all right," Kelly assured her. Eager to find out if she was wasting her time questioning the woman, she asked, "Did I detect a trace of a southern accent just now?"

Alicia's eyes widened.

"You're very good. Most people don't notice. And since my parents spent a great deal of money sending me to boarding schools up north, I was sure that I'd manage to lose the accent."

"It's very faint. Alabama?"

"Mississippi," she replied. "It must be nice for you to come home and hook up with old friends like Meredith."

"It's been interesting," Kelly conceded. "What about you? What made you move to New Orleans instead of going back to Mississippi?"

"I lost my parents in an accident last year," Alicia said, some of the animation fading from her expression. "I needed a change, so I moved to New Orleans."

Kelly stared at the hazel-eyed beauty seated across from her now, sensed an overwhelming sadness and wished she'd never started down this path. "I'm sorry about your parents."

"Thank you. We were very close. I miss them a great deal," she said, lowering her gaze a moment. Suddenly she jerked her head up, her eyes wide with dismay. "Oh, how selfish of me. Here I am feeling sorry for myself because I lost my parents while you, you poor thing, you grew up in an orphanage without anyone. Please forgive me.''

"Forget it," she told Alicia. The one thing she'd never been able to tolerate was pity. "I assure you it wasn't nearly as bad as you think."

"Now I've offended you. Believe me, Kelly, that wasn't my intention. Why, when I heard about everything you'd been through—growing up in that girls' home and having to contend with people talking about…'' Suddenly, Alicia fell silent.

"People talking about what?"

"Your gift," she finished. "Someone mentioned at dinner that you were fey."

"Fey?" Kelly repeated, taken aback with the quaint description and annoyed to realize she'd been the subject of dinner table gossip.

"You know, being able to see things. My grandmother Van Owen, my father's mother, she was fey. Or at least that's what Daddy called it. She could sense things about people. She'd know if a person had a good heart or a dark heart just by looking at them. I was only eight when she died, but I still remember her looking at me with those big dark eyes of hers. I swear she'd take one look at me and she'd know if I'd swiped an extra cookie from the kitchen or if I fudged about my practice time on the piano.'' Her expression softened, making her even more lovely. "I've always wished that she had passed that talent on to me. Imagine how well I'd do if I knew what offers to make on a house for my clients right up-front?"

Kelly sensed Jack approach before she saw him. So she wasn't surprised when his voice came from behind her. "Sorry it took me so long," he said, and handed her the glass of water.

"No problem," she said, taken aback by the temper she sensed in him as she took the glass.

"Hello, Alicia," Jack said politely. "I see you've met Kelly."

"Yes. We were just getting acquainted," she said, and gave him a dazzling smile. "How have you been?"

"Fine," he said, an edge in his voice.

Apparently picking up on the same angry vibe that she had, Alicia stood and said, "Well, I think I'll go see if I can find Peter and let him know I found a tenant for that empty space in his office building."

"Be sure to give Kelly one of your business cards, too," Jack said, never taking his eyes from Kelly. "I understand from my brother that she's looking for an apartment."

"Yes, I know. We're going to chat about it next week," Alicia said.

"Is that right?" Jack asked, his mouth pulled into a tight line.

"Yes, it is," Kelly assured him as she came to her feet.

"And just when were you going to let me know about your plans?"

It didn't take psychic ability to realize that he was furious with her—and that that fury stemmed from the fact that she'd confided in his brother about her plans and not him. Tough, she thought. She owed Jack Callaghan nothing. He had no claims on her or had any right to be angry with her. She didn't answer to him or anyone but herself. And it was just her own rotten luck that she was beginning to care for the man. "To be honest, I never gave it much thought one way or the other."

"Maybe you should have," he said, his blue eyes going stormy.

"And maybe you should mind your own business," she said, still annoyed with him and his family for discussing her with Alicia and God knows who else. "Now, if you'll both excuse me, I'd like to say good-night to your mother and then I'm going back to my hotel."

Twelve

She'd simply had to get away from that house and the party, Meredith admitted as she knocked on Kelly's hotel room door. Thanks to Alex she'd been feeling blue and hurt and flat-out miserable when she'd seen Kelly practically run out of the place. And before she'd even gotten a chance to talk to the woman about doing the photos, too.

Only once she'd gotten into her car, she'd realized she had no place to go. In the past when things had gotten to be too much, she'd always gone to Alex's. But not this time. Not ever again, she swore. Suddenly the ache inside her started all over again as she thought of him, of the way he had rejected her. And on the heels of that hurt came anger. Well, he'd never get the chance to hurt her again, she vowed. She'd show him. She'd show everyone that she could do just fine. And then they would be sorry. More determined than ever, she pounded her fist on the door. "Damn it, Kelly. Open the door. It's Meredith."

Moments later locks clicked and the door opened. Kelly stood there wearing a thick white terry-cloth robe, a towel wrapped around her head and a scowl on her face. "What are you doing here?"

"You left the party before we got a chance to talk

about you doing those ads for Indulgences," Meredith informed her. "So I decided to come over."

"It's late, and as you can see I was getting ready for bed."

"It's not *that* late." Exasperated, she said, "Oh for pity's sake, quit scowling at me and let me in. I really do need to talk with you."

The elevator dinged. "Listen, Meredith, now is really not a good time to start badgering me about doing photos for you because I'm in a foul mood and—"

"Then we should get along just fine because so am I," she said, and to prove her point, she barely missed catching Kelly's bare toes with her spike heels as she bulldozed past her and into the hotel suite.

"Come right in and make yourself at home, why don't you," Kelly told her with no small amount of sarcasm.

"Thank you, I will," Meredith replied, feeling just as annoyed as Kelly looked. She walked over and sat down on one of the couches. "And you might as well stop glaring at me. I told you, I'm in a lousy mood, too."

After a moment's hesitation, Kelly walked over to the opposite couch and sat down. "You know, Meredith, in all the years we were at St. Joseph's together and even when you came to New York a few years ago, I don't think I've ever seen you do that before."

"Do what?"

"Walk past a mirror and not check out your own reflection."

"Funny," Meredith told her.

"Will wonders never cease? You still haven't said a word about the tacky robe that I'm wearing."

"You already know it's tacky. You don't need me to tell you," Meredith advised her. "And if that little dig about the mirror was supposed to tick me off so that I'd leave, you'll have to do a lot better than that. I already know that I'm self-centered and spoiled.''

''All right. Then why don't I just tell you flat out that you and I are not buddies. And I'm not interested in discussing you or your shop or in doing any work for you. So I'd appreciate it if you'd leave.''

To her horror, Meredith felt tears prick at the back of her eyes. She got to her feet. ''Fine,'' she said, mortified by the wobble in her voice. She swallowed hard, then tried again. ''If that's how you feel, then I'll go,'' she told her, and started for the door. The last thing she intended to do was to humiliate herself further by crying in front of the likes of Kelly Santos.

''Great! Now I feel like I just kicked a puppy,'' Kelly muttered. ''Meredith, wait!''

Ignoring her, Meredith continued on to the door. ''I refuse to stay where I'm not wanted,'' she sniffed.

''Oh, would you please cut the Sarah Bernhardt act and come back here?''

Meredith reached the door, started to unlock it.

''Meredith, I'm sorry. I'd like you to stay. Please,'' Kelly added.

Meredith hesitated. She sniffed and blinked several times to fight back the tears that still threatened. And because she really didn't want to go back to the house where the party was going on and where she'd run the risk of seeing Alex while she was all weepy, she relented. ''You're sure? Because the last thing I want is to force my company on you if it's not wanted.'' Heaven knows, she'd done that enough with Alex, she thought, which made her feel miserable all over again.

''Will you come sit down before I change my mind?''

And because she didn't trust Kelly not to do just that,

she made her way back over to the couch and sat down. "Thank you."

"Now, do you want to tell me what you're doing here? And please don't insult my intelligence by saying you're here to talk about ads for your shop."

"I needed to get away from the party, and since I happen to live in the house where the party's going on that made it a little difficult."

"So you came here instead?"

"Yes."

"But why? Why not just rent a hotel room somewhere?"

"Because I...I didn't want to be alone, okay?" Meredith countered. "And I...I wanted to talk to someone."

"And you chose me?"

"Obviously," Meredith answered.

"But why not go to one of your friends?"

"Because with my friends, I'd have to pretend and with you I don't, all right?" she shot back, annoyed. "We may not be the best of friends, but at least with you I don't have to watch every word I say and worry if it will make the rounds of gossip tomorrow."

"Thank you. I think."

"Please, Kelly. I don't feel like fighting with you."

"Okay," Kelly told her. "So do you want to tell me what's happened? And what Alex Kusak has to do with it?"

Surprised, Meredith jerked her gaze up to Kelly's. "You really are good."

"Save the flattery. I saw you when you came in from the gardens tonight and then I saw Alex Kusak come in behind you. Judging by the miserable expressions on both of your faces, it didn't take a genius to figure out that something happened out there between you. So why don't you tell me what's wrong?''

"I'm in love with him," Meredith admitted.

"Does he feel the same way?"

"Yes," she replied, because in her heart she believed that Alex did love her.

"Then I don't see the problem."

"The problem is the man's a pigheaded fool." And because her emotions were still raw from his rejection, she pushed to her feet and began to pace. "He loves me," she assured Kelly, and herself. "But he won't admit it to me or to himself. He thinks...he thinks just because his blood isn't blue and he doesn't have a fortune that he and I shouldn't be together. In his mind, I'm some princess with a pretty pedigree who belongs with someone with an equally pretty pedigree so that I can have babies and make even prettier pedigrees," she ranted.

"Is that what he told you?"

"He didn't have to," she said. "I've known Alex since he was a teenager hell-bent on getting in trouble. But he straightened himself out, made something of himself. Only he still can't forget where he came from."

"Why?"

"His home life wasn't exactly ideal when he was a kid. His mother worked on Bourbon Street and he was just a boy when she ran off and left him with that drunken father of his. The man didn't give a damn about Alex. He practically raised himself," she explained, angry with Alex's parents for not valuing their son. "Anyway, Alex has these hang-ups and thinks he's got some kind of defective gene because of them. Which is all so stupid. He's good and honest and caring."

"He's obviously a well-respected member of the community if he was elected D.A."

"That's what I tried to tell him," Meredith said, and sat back down again. "And I thought he'd finally got past all this garbage when he decided to run for the D.A.'s office. We were so happy working on the campaign together. I was so sure we were going to get married."

"What happened?" Kelly asked.

"Near the end of the campaign some idiot dug up stuff about his parents. And this reporter located Alex's mother out of state and she said some horrible things about him. Every time I think of that woman, I swear I could just kill her with my bare hands," Meredith told her, furious again that the woman who had given birth to Alex could hurt him so viciously. "If it hadn't been for Jack, Alex would have pulled out of the race."

"Evidently the negative campaigning didn't hurt him if he won the election."

"Actually, I think it helped him to win. The people in this city aren't dummies and they don't like dirty politics. He's a good D.A., too. He really cares about the people."

"So what happened to the two of you?" Kelly prompted.

"By the time the campaign was over, he'd put this wall up between us. We've been lovers since I was eighteen, but he wouldn't even touch me. He became so cool and distant, I just couldn't take it anymore, so I did what I always do when something isn't going right, I left town."

"But you were miserable without him, so you came back."

Meredith nodded. "A few months ago. I love him and,

believe me, I've tried not to. I've gotten engaged to other men, tried starting all types of careers that would keep me away from him. But I always end up back here because it's Alex I want to be with. I'd hoped that this time, well that maybe if he saw that I intended to stick around, that I was determined to make a go of the shop, then maybe he'd finally believe that I really do know what I'm doing and what I want. And that it's him I want to be with.''

''Did you tell him that?''

''I tried. But he refuses to listen. And…and he keeps pushing me away, saying that he's wrong for me. Why can't he see that it's *who* he is that matters to me, not where he came from or who his parents were?''

''Maybe because those things matter to him,'' Kelly offered. ''While I don't necessarily see things the way Alex does, I can understand some of what he's feeling.''

Meredith looked at Kelly, noted her somber expression. ''What do you mean?''

''Well, unlike Alex, I don't know anything about my background. I don't know who my parents were or why they left me or even if they're still alive. There have always been question marks for me about who I am. Was I an only child? Or do I have siblings somewhere? Do I look like my parents? Why is my hair blond? Why are my eyes brown? Who did I get my height from? Was my mother from here? What kind of person was she? What kind of man was my father?''

Meredith didn't know what to say. She couldn't even imagine what growing up had been like for Kelly. And along with her empathy for her, she felt admiration. It made her ashamed that she had never really tried to be a friend to Kelly when they were younger. ''I'm sorry. I guess I'm even more selfish than I realized because it never occurred to me what it must have been like for you, growing up without anyone.''

"I had Sister Grace,'' Kelly said softly.

"And now you've lost her, too.''

"Yes.''

"I really am sorry, Kelly,'' Meredith told her, and truly meant it.

"Thank you.''

She paused, met Kelly's gaze. "Have you ever thought about trying to find out who your parents were?''

A shadow came into Kelly's eyes and she lowered them. "We're not talking about me, we're talking about Alex and you trying to understand where he's coming from,'' she explained. "You come from a wonderful, respected family that loves you. And you've always known that no matter what happens they'll go on loving you. I'm guessing Alex didn't have that same sense of security. That makes him different. And no matter what he accomplishes, there's always this little voice in the back of his head telling him that he really isn't like you and that sooner or later you're going to discover that.''

"So what are you saying? That just because I had a happy family and Alex didn't that he and I can't be together?''

"No, what I'm saying is that maybe Alex is pushing you away because he's afraid if he lets you get too close that you'll hurt him.''

"But I'd never hurt Alex.''

"You know, I honestly don't think you would. At least not intentionally.''

"Not unintentionally, either,'' Meredith insisted.

"I'm not the one you have to convince. Alex is.''

"But how?''

"That, I'm afraid, is something I can't answer. The truth is, I'm probably the last one you should be asking for advice about relationships."

Curious, she asked, "Have you ever been in love with anyone?"

"I thought I was once. But it didn't work out." Kelly stood and said, "Listen, I don't know how much help I've been, but it's been a long day and I'm really tired."

Meredith realized at once that she'd probably probed a little too deeply. "It helped a lot, just having someone to talk to. Thanks for listening." She slipped her shoes back on and stood.

"I hope things work out for you and Alex," Kelly told her when they reached the door.

"I'll just have to figure a way to make them work," Meredith replied, feeling more hopeful than she had when she arrived and also more determined. "You know, we never did get around to discussing you doing those ads for me."

"Meredith, I—"

"Tell you what, I'll give you a call tomorrow," she said, cutting off Kelly before she had a chance to refuse her. And because she truly was grateful, she reached over and gave Kelly a quick hug. "Thanks again," she said, and hurried off toward the elevator.

Kelly turned off the blow-dryer and brushed out her hair. Not bothering to braid or clip the blond mass with a barrette, she allowed it to fall about her shoulders. Too wired to sleep after Meredith's visit and fearful that if she lay in bed, she would only relive that scene with Jack, she decided to tackle the journals again. She retrieved another stack from the boxes that had been delivered to her by Peter's office.

After grabbing a juice from the minibar, she sat on the couch, curled her feet beneath her and opened one of the journals. She felt a jolt at the sight of the neat, slanted handwriting with its beautiful loops and strokes. Perfect penmanship, she thought fleetingly, probably a product of Sister Grace's own Catholic grade-school teachers when she was a girl. A memory of Sister Grace sitting at a table in the library with her, helping her to form her letters, surfaced, but Kelly clamped down on it. Memories could not help her now, she reasoned. What she needed to do was concentrate on the journals and hope that somewhere within those pages, she would find answers to why someone would kill Sister Grace.

She stared at the date at the top of the page. This one was dated ten years ago, the November following her high school graduation. She began to read....

I spoke with Kelly today. She seems to be settling in at college just fine and is very focused on her studies. She said she loves having four seasons for a change and is looking forward to seeing her first snowfall. She sounded content and, as always, was enthusiastic about her photography. Except for mentioning her professors and answering my questions about her dorm mate, she spoke little about the new people she's met. I had so hoped that when she moved up north that she might come out of her shell, be a normal teenager experiencing the excitement of living on her own and making new friends. Perhaps my expectations were too much, too soon. But I will pray harder, because I know that if Kelly would only give others a chance, they would see what a beautiful, giving person she is. If only...

At the knock on her door, Kelly glanced up. After eleven o'clock, she noted, sticking a slip of paper between the pages. She put the journal down on the coffee table and rose. Another knock sounded, this one more impatient, and Kelly hurried over to the door. She glanced through the peephole and felt a mixture of irritation and apprehension at the sight of Jack standing on the other side. He was still in the dark evening jacket he'd worn to the party. But his tie dangled around his neck and the buttons at the collar of his white shirt had been opened. His hair looked like he'd jammed his fist through it more than once and his mouth was pulled into a tight frown.

When he raised his fist to bang on the door again, Kelly unhooked the safety latch and turned the lock. Only opening the door a fraction, she asked, "Don't you Callaghans have anything better to do than bother me tonight?"

His frown deepened. "What are you talking about?"

"Never mind," she said with a sigh, deciding there was no point in telling him about Meredith's visit. "What do you want, Jack?"

"That's a loaded question," he told her, and lowered his gaze to the open neck of her robe. "You sure you want the answer?"

She flushed and yanked the robe closed. "It's late and I'm not in the mood for juvenile games. So why don't you tell me why you're here."

"We need to talk."

"We have nothing to talk about," she informed him, and started to close the door.

Jack wedged his foot inside. "We're going to talk, Kelly. The question is whether we do it in private or out here in the hall? It's your call."

A part of her wanted to slam the door in his face. Another part of her knew she was being unfair. Saying nothing, she stepped back and allowed him into the hotel suite. "All right, you're inside," she said, still smarting at the knowledge that she'd been fodder for his dinner table conversation. "So why don't you say whatever it is you have to say and leave?"

A muscle ticked angrily in his cheek at her remark. "Why don't we start with you telling me why you ran out of my mother's party in a snit?"

"First off, I didn't 'run out,' I decided to leave. And second, I was not in a 'snit.' I was furious with you and your family," she said, hurt and angry all over again to realize that Jack had discussed her with his family and friends. "How dare you use me and my life as...as entertainment at your dinner parties?"

"What in the hell are you talking about?"

"I'm talking about you telling Alicia Van Owen, your family and God-knows-who-else about my visions."

"Jesus! So that's what this is all about." He drew in a breath, released it. "I don't know what Alicia told you, but I didn't say anything to her or anyone else."

She wanted to believe him, but was afraid to believe him. "Then how did she know?"

"Because when we were at my mother's for her birthday, Peter mentioned to Meredith that you were in town. He also told her that I'd seen you because *you* had mentioned it to him. One thing led to another and when I explained that I'd seen you in conjunction with work, Meredith put two and two together and came up with you being a witness in a murder investigation. I refused to discuss it, but Meredith remembered the rumors in school about you having visions and figured out what had happened. When my mother didn't understand, she explained it to her," he said. "I did my best to end the discussion and little else was said about it. But apparently Alicia remembered. I'm sorry, Kelly."

Discovering that Jack hadn't made her the subject of dinner table gossip eased the sting of betrayal she'd felt since her conversation with Alicia. Because she was feeling vulnerable, she walked over to the window and looked out. Folding her arms, she said, "I left here ten years ago because I wanted to get away from the talk, away from the stares. I should never have gone to the police station that night. All I accomplished by going was to stir up the stories again."

"It also brought you back into my life."

"I'm not in your life, Jack."

"Yes, you are," he said, moving behind her. He turned her around so that she faced him. "And I'm in your life, Kelly. That's why I don't understand why you would go to Peter for help instead of coming to me."

She had hurt him. She sensed it, read it in his eyes, felt it in his touch. He deserved an honest answer, she reasoned. "Because if I'd come to you, things would have become complicated. I don't like complications."

"No, you like everything neat and tidy, don't you?" he countered, a hint of that temper surfacing again.

"Yes," she admitted, and walked over to the table where she'd left her juice glass. She picked it up and carried it to the counter by the bar.

Jack followed. "You know what I think?"

"No, but I'm sure you're going to tell me," she said, unwilling to allow him to intimidate her.

"I think the reason that you've always got your face stuck behind that camera is because you don't want people to notice you. In fact, I think that's what you were counting on happening with me. Only it didn't work because I *did* notice you. I noticed you ten years ago when you were still a kid, and I noticed you again the minute I came through that door more than a week ago," he said, jabbing a finger toward the entryway. He moved closer, boxed her in at the counter by placing his arms on either side of her. "I also think that I scared the hell out of you Saturday night when I told you I had feelings for you."

"You're wrong," she told him, even though her heart pounded in her chest. He was close, so close she could smell him—the scent of woods and pine and outdoors.

"Am I?"

"Yes," she insisted, barely recognizing the breathy sound of her own voice.

Jack lowered his head a fraction until his mouth was poised just inches above her own. "Liar," he whispered, his breath warm and moist against her lips.

The blood simmered in her veins as she anticipated the feel of his mouth. Only he didn't kiss her. He waited. Watched and waited. He wasn't going to seduce her or make the first move, she realized. Jack wanted her, but he wanted the decision to be hers. "Jack." She said his name like a prayer, felt a trembling in her knees.

"Don't be afraid, Kelly."

She wasn't afraid. She was terrified. But what terrified her most was that he might walk out and she would never have known even once what it would be like to be with him.

"I won't hurt you," he promised.

Oh, but he would hurt her. Kelly was sure that he would. Yet she was so tired of being alone, of trying to play it safe. Just this once, she promised herself. Just this once she would take for herself, give him what little she had in her to give. So it was she who closed the distance between them. It was she who lifted her mouth and kissed him.

Jack groaned. Or maybe it was her. She could never

be sure. All she knew was that his mouth was hot and wet and thrilling. She could drown in his kisses, she thought, and hadn't realized she'd said the words aloud until Jack chuckled.

"No drowning allowed. Not when there is so much I want to do to you, with you." He reached for the belt of her robe, untied it. Kelly's breath hitched as he parted the folds of her robe, found her naked beneath. His eyes darkened to steel. She quivered as his hands skimmed her bare shoulders, down her arms, then sent the robe into a heap at her feet. "Tell me what you want."

"You." She managed to get out the word from a throat that had gone desert dry. "I want to feel your hands on me."

"That's good," he told her as he scooped her up into his arms and headed for the bedroom. "Because I want my hands on you." He placed her on the bed and, never taking his eyes off of hers, pulled off his jacket, tossed it to the floor. His shirt and tie followed. "And I want your hands on me."

And she wanted her hands on him, too, she admitted as he kicked off his shoes and joined her on the bed. He pressed a kiss to the corner of her mouth, the tip of her chin, her lips. When he nipped her lower lip, she opened to him and he took the kiss deeper. The blood hummed in her veins as his fingers skimmed the side of her ribs. She tore her mouth free, nearly cried out when he closed his palms over her breasts. His hands were rough and calloused against her softer skin. And Kelly thought she might die from the pleasure.

Her head was still swimming and her body pulsing beneath his touch when he began to kiss his way down her neck, along the slope of her shoulder. Changing direction, he made his way to the base of her throat and moved lower. "You're so beautiful, so perfect," Jack murmured, and laved first one nipple, then the other with his tongue. When he closed his mouth over the tip of her breast, Kelly arched her back and forgot to breathe.

"Jack," she panted.

Lost in the sensation of his mouth on her body, Kelly reached for him. She smoothed her palms over his shoulders, thrilled at the ripple of muscles and corded sinew beneath her fingertips. He wanted her with a fierceness that should have frightened her, but excited her instead. With her defenses down, there was no blocking out what he was feeling.

He wanted her.

Jack's desire for her flooded Kelly's senses, fed the need building inside her. But it was the tenderness, along with his violent need, that disarmed her completely. She closed her eyes, gave in to the pleasure of having his hands and mouth on her body. It had been years since a man had touched her like this, wanted her like this.

Not since Garrett had she dared to allow herself to be with a man. But not even for Garrett, a man whom she had believed herself in love with, had she ever felt an ache like this, a passion so powerful.

And what happens when he's repulsed by you as Garrett was?

Suddenly that disastrous last meeting with Garrett when she'd confronted him with his lies came flooding back.

Frigid. Freak.

Garrett's words punched through her desire-riddled senses. She couldn't bare to see that revulsion in Jack's eyes. To have him see her that way, to have him shrink from her touch.

As though he could read her thoughts, Jack caught her

chin. "Open your eyes and look at me, Kelly." When she did as he commanded, there was no mistaking the seriousness in those blue eyes. "There's no room in this bed for ghosts. I want you more than I want my next breath. But I won't share you. So if you don't feel the same way, tell me now."

"I do feel the same way. And there's no one else. It's just that I'm not very good at this. I don't want to disappoint you."

Jack caught her hand, brought her fingers to his lips. "The only way you could disappoint me is if you let fear make you push me away. Do you want me to stop?"

"No," she whispered, and it was the truth.

"Then tell me what you want."

"You. I want you," she said, and reached for his belt.

Heat flashed in his eyes. Quickly he helped her finish disposing of his slacks and briefs. And when he joined her on the bed again, he linked his fingers with hers. He kissed her. Slowly. Gently. Stringing one kiss into another and another still. Each kiss just a little deeper, just a little bit hungrier.

He nipped at her jaw, her breasts, drew a line with his tongue to her belly, setting off a thousand explosions of heat with his mouth. He made her want. He made her ache. Need became a painful beast gnawing at her belly. She reached for him, wanting him to fill her and put an end to this terrible craving.

"No, not yet," he growled. "I want you to take. And when you've taken everything and think you couldn't possibly take more, then you'll take again—with me."

She reached for him, but he was already moving down her body, and before she could protest, his fingers were parting her. At the touch of his mouth, she lifted her hips and cried out, "Jack!"

She struggled to resist, to hold back a piece of herself, a piece of her soul, fearful of ever allowing anyone to touch her that way again. But with each flick of his tongue, each scrape of his teeth, she felt herself losing the battle. Suddenly the first orgasm took her, spinning her world out of control. Stars exploded around her, in her, as he took her up again. And again. And again.

"Take it, Kelly," he urged her.

She took. Tears streamed down her cheeks. Tears of amazement. Of pleasure. Of embarrassment at her greed. And with the tremors still shuddering through her, she reached for him. "Jack, please."

His eyes went nearly black. And this time when he took her mouth, he ravaged it. She could taste herself, taste him. His scent filled her head, overpowered her senses. She gripped the covers in her fists and arched her hips, pleaded with him with her body.

When he tore his mouth free and moved between her thighs, his voice was whiskey-rough as he said, "Look at me, Kelly."

Kelly looked at him. She read the questions in his eyes, felt them swimming in the savage need that had him in its grip. No room for ghosts, he'd told her. He wanted no one in the bed with them. Only her and him.

"Only you, Jack. Only you," she said, letting him know it was only him she was thinking of, that no one had ever made her feel the things he'd made her feel.

"Only me," he repeated, and entered her in one swift thrust.

Kelly gasped as he filled her. He linked their hands once more. His eyes, so blue, so brilliant, remained locked with hers. And then all she could do was feel. The weight of him. The heat of him. The strength and tenderness of him. She moved with him, marveled at this dance they'd engaged in together.

And as the tempo quickened, as she felt the pressure begin to build inside her once more, the last small vestige of resistance begin to slip. Only instead of fighting that loss of control and protecting herself, this time Kelly let it go. She opened herself to Jack completely. She matched him stroke for stroke, moved in rhythm as one until she felt the world tremble beneath them before bursting into a thousand pieces.

And as Kelly felt herself being consumed by the brilliant flashes, she heard Jack shout her name before following her into the sea of exploding lights.

Thirteen

Jack lay in the bed with Kelly still in his arms, her head resting on his shoulder, her legs tangled with his. A fantasy come true, he thought with a smile. He pressed a kiss to her head. "I've imagined you here like this at least a dozen times," he confessed.

"I know," she murmured sleepily.

"Guess I wasn't too subtle, huh?"

"Not really," she said, and yawned.

She looked so beautiful, he thought as he gazed at her. In the dim light of the room, her pale hair shimmered like gold silk across his shoulder and down her arm. Even her skin seemed to have a glow, and those legs that he'd fantasized about were even longer than he'd dreamed. A smile curved his lips as he imagined several ways he'd like to see those long, lean legs wrapped around him when they made love again.

"I don't think that's anatomically possible."

He chuckled at her remark. "Go to sleep," he told her, gently planting another kiss to her temple. She needed to rest, he reasoned, and Jack contented himself just to hold her. But now that his body was sated by their lovemaking, he became aware of other needs—namely his stomach. He'd skipped dinner and had only munched on cocktail party food earlier in the evening, and as a result, he was now starving. A glance at the bedside clock revealed it was well past midnight. Was there anything in the minibar worth raiding? he wondered.

"Just some stale crackers and cheese," she mumbled.

"What?"

Kelly went stiff beside him. She scrambled to sit up. "I'm sorry."

"For what?" he asked, confused.

"I didn't mean to do that. I swear I didn't," she told him, fumbling to hold the sheet up around her. Her eyes were wide with horror and looked huge in her pale face.

Jack sat up, and when she tried to put more distance between them, he caught her by the arms, held her in place. "Damn it, Kelly. You're not making any sense. Now, tell me what's wrong."

"I looked inside you. I picked up on your thoughts," she said, shame coloring her voice. "I never meant to. I swear I didn't, but I was feeling relaxed and was half asleep and…and it just happened."

"Okay," he said, easing his grip on her but not allowing her to pull away from him. "So if the minibar's no good, how do you feel about me ordering room service?" He thought about the town gossips, knew they'd have a field day if they got wind of him being there with Kelly. He didn't care for himself, but she was another matter. "If it would embarrass you to have the hotel staff discover me here, I could go out and pick up something for us and take the service elevator back up."

She gave him a baffled look. "Aren't you angry?"

"Why? Because you took a peek inside my brain?"

"That's not exactly what happened, but yes. Don't you mind?"

"No. Why would I?"

"Because it's not right to go nosing around into someone else's thoughts that way."

"Says who?"

She didn't answer.

But Jack knew from her expression that she was thinking of *him* again—the guy whose ghost had intruded earlier before they'd made love. The realization didn't please him at all and made him more determined to chase all thoughts of any man but him from her thoughts for good. "I'm not him, Kelly."

Her eyes shot to his. "Who?"

"Whoever the jerk is that did such a number on you."

"I've made you angry. I'm sorry."

"Quit apologizing, dammit." Irritated with himself for losing his cool, he tried to rein in his temper. "You're right. I am angry with you—but not because you happened to take a look inside me and read what I was thinking. I'm angry with you for confusing me with the asshole who hurt you and made you think what you did was wrong. I'm not him, Kelly."

"I know that."

"And from now on anytime you want to take a peek inside me, you go right ahead."

She stared at him, wide-eyed and wary. She shook her head.

"Why not? I can think of several advantages to having you know what I'm thinking."

She looked at him as though he'd lost his mind.

"In fact, the more I think about it, the better I like the idea. So why don't you come over here and take a look inside me right now, then you can let me know how you feel about trying what I'm thinking the two of us could do," he suggested. Tugging the sheet from her fingers, he pulled her back down onto the bed and leaned over her.

"Jack," she began, that same wariness in her voice that was in her eyes.

Because he wanted to erase all traces of that wariness away he took her mouth. He kissed her—deep, hard, hungrily, wanting to wipe everything and everyone from her thoughts but him. When he lifted his head, he was breathing hard. So was she. Her eyes fluttered open.

"This is insane," she whispered. But the fear was gone from her eyes now and her body was slick and hot with need. "*You're* insane," she accused, even as she arched her hips against his hand as he readied her.

"Only about you," he said before driving himself into her heat.

And as he began to move inside her, she clung to him, made those little whimpering sounds that fed his own hunger. When she bit his shoulder, he groaned. She met him, stride for stride. And when he increased the pace, she wrapped her legs around him, took him in even deeper—just as he had fantasized. Then he couldn't think at all as he took them both over the edge.

"Want some more milk?" Jack asked her.

"No thanks," she said, still unable to believe she was sitting in her hotel room at four o'clock in the morning eating pizza with Jack Callaghan after making love half the night. Kelly's heart kicked at the sight of him. Bare-chested, wearing the black slacks he'd arrived in earlier that evening and nothing else, he stood by the counter pouring himself a glass of milk. God, but the man looked liked Brad Pitt with a Tom Cruise smile, she thought. Realizing that she was practically drooling, Kelly dragged her gaze away from him and stared at the pizza on her plate.

"So what did you think of Mother's party?"

"It was nice," she told him, although she'd felt out of place there. She also couldn't help measuring herself against Alicia Van Owen. The woman was everything she was not—beautiful, sophisticated, accomplished. She was much more suitable for Jack than she was.

Jack placed his glass of milk on the coffee table and returned to his seat on the floor adjacent to her. "In other words, you were bored out of your mind."

"No," Kelly assured him. "Really, I wasn't. Your mother was a very gracious hostess. I liked her."

"She liked you, too," he said as he reached for the last slice of pizza. "But be forewarned, she's going to hit you up for a donation to one of her charities."

"She already did." At his surprise, she explained, "Apparently you mentioned my photos to her, so I'm donating some pieces for a benefit for St. Ann's."

He winced. "Do you mind?"

"Not really. I'm glad I can help. After all, it was my home for a long time."

He scooped up a dollop of the tomato sauce off the plate with his finger. "Peter said you asked him to recommend a private detective. Does it have anything to do with that DNA test and you being related to Gilbert's killer?"

"Not exactly."

"I don't suppose you're going to tell me what exactly it is about, are you?"

"No, at least not yet. Not until I'm sure."

He paused a moment, then said, "All right—for now."

"Jack—"

"You going to eat the rest of that?"

Caught off guard that he didn't press her, Kelly looked down at the half-eaten slice of room service pizza on the plate in front of her. "No, I'm stuffed."

"In that case," he began, and snatched the gooey cheese-and-pepperoni slice from her plate.

He grinned, that devastating grin that made her stomach dip each time he aimed it in her direction. "My mother always said it was a sin to let good food go to waste," he claimed and proceeded to polish it off.

"Somehow I doubt that your mother had hotel pizza in mind when she issued that particular rule."

"True," he conceded with a laugh. "She laid down that particular law when I was ten and turned up my nose to the caviar she'd put on my plate at a party."

"Picky, weren't you?" she teased.

"Definitely. Especially when it comes to something that's important to me."

"Like your stomach."

He nodded. "And the woman I make love with," he advised her, and Kelly's pulse started skipping again at the hungry way he watched her. He reached for his glass of milk, drained it. "Besides being particular, I'm also real big on rules."

"Like not letting good food go to waste," she said, trying to lighten the conversation. She wasn't any good at this sort of stuff, never had been, and was at a loss what to do with Jack.

"Yes. You gonna finish that milk?"

She shook her head, handed him her glass. "Thanks," he said, and finished off her milk. He set the glass down, looked directly at her with those piercing blue eyes. "I also have rules about casual sex. I don't engage in it."

Kelly flushed. "If you're worried that I...that we..."

He leaned over the table, caught her chin, kissed her. "I'm not asking for a health report. I'm simply giving you fair warning. Tonight meant something to me. *You* mean something to me and I'm not going to let you push me away. So get used to the idea."

"Jack," she began, but he silenced her with another quick kiss.

"Quit trying to analyze what's happening between us, Kelly, and accept it. I have."

"You make it sound so easy."

"It's only complicated if you make it complicated. I don't know what he did to make you so afraid to trust, but I keep telling you that I'm not him."

"I know that." And never in a million years could she mistake Jack for Garrett. "His name was Garrett Scott," she told him. "I met him when I was working out on the West Coast. He was a struggling author, working on a book with a photographer as a main character. He came to one of the shoots I was doing for research for his book."

He slid over onto the floor beside her, held her close. "What happened?"

"He was movie-star handsome, like so many of the men on the West Coast. But unlike most of them, he wasn't at all self-centered. He was kind and sensitive and generous. And he seemed really interested in my work and me. We became friends, started spending a lot of time together. I showed him some of my noncommercial work and gradually told him more and more about myself. I expected him to withdraw once I told him about...about the psychic thing. But he didn't. Instead he made me believe that it wasn't a bad thing, that it made me special somehow," she said, her voice cracking as she thought back now to what a fool she'd been, to not have listened to the things he didn't say.

"You don't have to explain," Jack told her.

Kelly shook her head. "I want to. So that you'll understand." After a moment, she continued, "We became lovers. And I began to believe that Garrett was right. That maybe it really was a gift instead of a burden. I admitted that unconsciously it probably even helped me with my work. I'd learned to control and compartmentalize my own emotions. And I guess, as a result, I'd become good at reading other people's moods without...without poking around inside their heads and it carried over into my work. Even with the most temperamental models and actors, I'd be able to judge their moods, knew just what to look for in a shot to make it good, to make the emotion come through."

"I'm sure that's why you're so good at your job."

"Maybe. Anyway, Garrett was always asking me questions about my work, about me, about what I felt, what I saw when I looked through the camera's lens. I was naive enough to believe it was because he cared about me, because he wanted us to be closer. I actually thought he loved me."

"Kelly, baby, don't," he said, brushing the tears of humiliation from her cheeks.

"I need to," she said, because she wanted him to know, wanted him to understand. "I thought it was strange that Garrett never shared anything with me about his own work. But he claimed he was superstitious and that he never discussed his work before it was published. Deep inside, I think I knew he was lying, but I ignored all the little signals that something wasn't quite right and convinced myself that because I loved him my inner radar was off."

Jack said nothing, simply held her close and waited for her to continue.

"By this time, I'd given him a key to my apartment. I was doing pretty well, making good money, so I'd splurged and gotten myself a nice place to live. Your sister would have been proud of me. It was bright and airy and had lots of windows," she said, recalling Meredith's description of her New York flat.

"It sounds like something Meredith would like."

"Garrett loved it." Oh, how he'd loved it, she thought, recalling how he'd wanted to move in with her. And even though she'd allowed him in her bed, all those years in Catholic school and knowing that Sister Grace would disapprove had made her refuse. Shaking off the hypocrisy of her actions, she continued, "Since Garrett shared a small apartment with two roommates, he said it made it difficult for him to write, so he started spending a lot of time at my place working on his laptop when I was out on a shoot."

"What happened?"

"One day I came home from a shoot early. I'd just been offered a plum assignment and wanted to celebrate. I bought champagne and a new dress. When I got home, Garrett was in the shower, but his laptop was sitting there, still on with the section he'd been working on up on the screen." Kelly swallowed. "It was about me, the fast-rising photographer who was making a name for herself by using her psychic powers to capture her subjects when they were most vulnerable. He claimed I invaded their souls, searched out their secrets. It wasn't true, none of it was true," she said, furious over the lies and distortions.

"I know it wasn't," he whispered, holding her even closer.

"When he came out of the shower and saw that I'd read the lies he'd written, he said he was doing it for us, for our future, that he wanted to surprise me with the news that he had an offer for the book. But I knew he was lying and I told him so. I told him just what he was thinking, all the anger he was feeling and that he didn't have any offer on the book, that he'd been turned downed by every publisher he'd approached."

Determined to finish, she said, "It was the wrong thing to say because he went ballistic. All that ugliness I had refused to allow myself to see came out then. He told me what a freak I was, that he was glad everything was out in the open now because he wasn't sure how much longer he could have gone on pretending to love a frigid, messed-up bitch like me."

"I'd like to wring the son of a bitch's neck with my bare hands," Jack grumbled.

She smiled, warmed by his gallant streak. Jack was right. He wasn't Garrett. Nor was he anything like him. Jack was an honorable man, the type of man she could fall in love with if she wasn't careful. But that was one mistake she had vowed never to make again. She'd survived losing Garrett, survived his betrayal, and had managed to rebuild her life. But she wasn't sure she could survive having Jack look at her with revulsion someday as Garrett had. And he would. It was only a matter of time before he would, she reasoned. So she would simply keep things in perspective. She'd accept and enjoy the physical relationship between them while it lasted, and once she found the answers surrounding Sister Grace's death, she would see justice done and then leave New Orleans for good. But she would take with her the memories of Jack.

"Are you still in love with him?"

"No," she answered honestly. "I moved to New York when it was over and after a while I realized I was more ashamed and angry with myself than hurt by Garrett's betrayal, because I had fooled myself into believing that I was someone I wasn't." She turned in his arms, cupped his jaw. "I'm not like other women, Jack."

He caught her hand, planted a kiss in her palm. "I know that."

But he didn't believe her. And because she wanted a little more time with him, she didn't fight it.

"I'm going to have to leave soon and I'll be gone most of the day."

"You're going out of town?"

Jack hesitated, then said, "To Mississippi. We located Gilbert's ex-wife and Leon and I are driving over to interview her this morning."

She sobered at the mention of the dead doctor. "Do you think she's involved in his death?"

"She sounded bitter enough on the phone to want him dead, but she was nowhere near here when he was shot. I'm hoping she'll be able to give us a lead on who might have wanted him dead. We're going to find the killer, Kelly."

She didn't doubt him. And when he found the killer, he would also find a link to her. The realization had her stomach pitching again. "Whoever she is, she's my flesh and blood," she said aloud.

"She's related to you by blood. That's all," he insisted. "And since I've got two whole hours before I have to pick up Leon, I'm not going to let you spend it worrying about some woman you don't even know."

She knew he was trying to ease her worries. Trying

to follow his lead, she asked, "Then how do you propose
we spend those two hours, Detective?"

"I'll give you two guesses."

"Watch a movie."

"Nope," he said and began to kiss her neck.

"Play cards?" she suggested in a voice that had
grown breathless as his tongue traced the shell of her
ear.

"Wrong again. Why don't I just show you?" he told
her, and reached for the belt of her robe.

"As I told you on the phone, Detectives…what were
your names again?"

"Callaghan and Jerevicious." Jack supplied his and
Leon's last names to the former Eugenia Gilbert, now
Eugenia Phillips. After more than a week, they'd finally
been able to connect with the woman and had driven to
the small Mississippi town to see her.

She poured them each a cup of hot tea. "Milk?" she
asked in that thick, lazy drawl so common in Mississippi
natives.

"No thanks," Jack said.

"No thank you, ma'am," Leon replied.

She added milk to her own tea, stirred it and picked
up the cup. She sat back in her chair. "Well, as I told
you on the telephone, I was sorry to hear that Martin is
dead, but I'm not surprised. What does surprise me is
that someone didn't kill him before now. The man was
absolutely no good."

Spoken like a bitter ex-wife, Jack thought. "I take it
your divorce wasn't an amicable one."

"No, it wasn't," she said, her lips thinning. "The man
humiliated me so badly that I left Pass Christian. That

was more than fifteen years ago and I've never set foot in that town since.''

"I'm sorry to have to dredge up bad memories, Mrs. Phillips," Jack told her as she dabbed at her eyes with a lace handkerchief. "But anything you can tell us about your ex-husband might help us to catch his killer."

She tucked the handkerchief back into the sleeve at her wrist. "What is it you want to know?"

"When was the last time you saw your ex-husband?"

"In the Hines County courtroom at the time of our divorce."

"Have you spoken to him recently?" Leon asked.

"Actually, I did," she told them. "He called me out of the blue about a month ago, wanting to borrow $5,000. As if I would lend him a dime."

"Mrs. Phillips, did he say what he wanted the money for?"

"No, but if I had to guess I would say it was for gambling debts. He always had a problem with that. I imagine with the casinos on the Gulf Coast now, he'd have managed to get himself into quite a bit of trouble."

"Did he say how he intended to pay you back?" Jack asked, going on the assumption that Kelly had been right. That Gilbert had been killed when some type of deal went wrong.

"He claimed he was expecting a large amount of cash in a few weeks and swore that if I'd lend him the money, he would pay me back with interest."

Jack exchanged a look with Leon as he remembered Kelly's description of Gilbert meeting with someone who had a bag of money. "Did he say where he was supposed to be getting the money from?"

"Oh, he gave me some nonsense about collecting money due him from the family of a former patient."

"Did he happen to tell you the name of that patient?" Leon asked.

"No. And I didn't ask him either. I told him not to call me again and hung up the phone."

"Mrs. Phillips, can you think of anyone who would want to kill your ex-husband?" Jack asked.

"Probably more people than you have space to list in that little book you've been scribbling in," she told him. She took a sip of her tea, then set the cup down on the saucer. "Detective Callaghan, if you'd asked me that question fifteen years ago, I'd have told you. I hated Martin when we divorced and I'd have been only too happy to put poison in his tea."

Leon stopped with the cup midway to his mouth and set it down on its saucer.

"And now?" Jack asked.

"Now I'm married to a good man, an honest man who doesn't put his shoes under anyone's bed but mine. So I don't waste my time thinking of ways to get even with Martin anymore." She blotted her lips with the linen napkin and set it aside. "But from what I've heard over the years, Martin collected enemies like most people collect postage stamps. There was a new one every few weeks."

"Any idea who some of those enemies were?" Jack asked.

"Take your pick. Business associates whom he swindled, people he owed money to, angry patients and their families. Martin was a charmer, always working an angle, looking to make the big money quick. He could have been a great doctor, made a good living. Instead he was into shortcuts, living too fast and too high, taking too many risks."

"Is that why he started performing illegal abortions?" Leon asked.

"So you know about that," Eugenia said. "Yes. Although I didn't know it at the time, I found out later he'd been performing them on underage girls for some time and eventually it cost him his license. I understand there were a lot of angry parents, and one girl's parents threatened to make him pay. You might want to check out some of them."

"We will." But they'd already checked out several of the complaints filed against Gilbert. So far, the people's alibis checked out. "We noted your ex-husband had quite a number of lawsuits filed against him, but only one actually went to trial. According to court records, the other cases were dropped. Do you have any idea why?" Jack asked because this had bothered him from the moment he began investigating the doctor's past.

"I suspect it had something to do with his 'good friend' in high places," Eugenia Phillips replied. "But apparently not even his 'friend' was able to bail him out of that last mess he got himself into."

"His good friend in high places?" Jack prompted.

"That's what Martin used to call him. Or her. I was never sure if it was a man or a woman because Martin wouldn't tell me who it was. It was one of his little secrets," she said, a grimace crossing her face. "Martin was a very ambitious man, especially when he was younger. He'd go out of his way to curry favor with people he thought might be able to help him someday."

"What kind of favors?" Jack asked, although he suspected he knew.

"I never asked. And he never told me. But he was always fawning over the rich folks and politicians in town, ingratiating himself. If someone called in the middle of the night because they had a problem or needed a prescription, he was only too happy to help.''

''Can you remember the names of any of those people?''

She gave them a few names of politicians and others she claimed were society types. ''Apparently all of his kowtowing paid off because the first time he got in trouble, his 'friend' took care of the problem for him.''

''When was that?''

''Oh, I guess it was about twenty-five years ago. You have no idea how terrified I was when he came home nervous as a cat in a tub of water. He'd performed an abortion on a fifteen-year-old. The poor girl had started hemorrhaging and had to be taken to the hospital. I was appalled and worried sick. I was sure he was going to lose his practice and that we'd be sued. He left the house and didn't come back all night,'' she said. ''The next morning when he finally came home and I asked about the girl, he told me to forget he'd said anything. The problem was taken care of and I was never to mention it again.''

''No charges were filed against him?'' Leon asked.

''Not as far as I know. After that, he never said anything about his work to me. I only learned about the lawsuits filed against him around the time of the divorce.''

''Mrs. Phillips, do you have any idea who that friend of his was?'' Leon asked.

''Not really. But because of the way that thing with the girl was hushed up, I assumed it was someone political and that he or she was pretty high up the ladder.''

''Why's that?'' Jack asked.

''Because I don't think the local sheriff could have

kept it out of the newspapers.'' She glanced at her watch and stood. ''I don't want to be rude, Detectives, but my husband, Conrad, is due home shortly from his golf game. And I'd prefer it if you weren't here when he arrives.''

Jack stood. So did Leon. ''Of course. You've been most helpful, Mrs. Phillips. Thank you for speaking with us.''

''Yes, ma'am, thank you,'' Leon echoed.

After she showed them to the door, Jack turned and asked, ''Mrs. Phillips, one more question if I may.''

She nodded.

''We haven't had any success in locating the records for your former husband's practice. Do you have any idea what might have happened to them?''

She shook her head. ''If anyone knows it would probably be Eve.''

''Eve?'' Jack repeated.

''Eve Tompkins. She was Martin's office nurse,'' she said with a scowl. ''Or at least that was her official title. The little trollop was always after him. I was against him hiring her from the start. But Martin insisted she was good with the patients and that she needed the job. What she needed was a man of her own, if you ask me. I divorced him when I came to his office one afternoon and found her...servicing him. If there was anyone who knew Martin's secrets, Eve would.''

''Do you know where we can find this Ms. Tompkins?'' Jack asked.

''Last I heard, she tried to kill herself when Martin took up with some other woman. I was told she'd spent some time in a mental hospital, the Good Shepherd. If you ask me, she never was right in the head to begin with.''

"Thank you again," Jack said, and he and Leon exited the house. As they walked over to his car, Jack
commented, "Sounds like the not-so-good doctor's ex
wouldn't have minded killing him herself."

"Yeah, but the lady and her saintly new husband were
on a cruise at the time, and unless she hopped off the
ship in Miami, swam here and back, she's in the clear,"
Leon pointed out.

"I suppose this Eve character could be a possibility.
She had motive. But seeing how she'd have to be in her
sixties now, I don't see her offing the guy," Jack said.
"So that leaves us with the woman whose family
brought Gilbert to trial."

"Except that she took the settlement money from him
just like the others did."

"Her parents took the money. Not her," Jack pointed
out. "And let's not forget that Gilbert's the reason she
can't have kids now. To some women that's a really big
thing."

"So you think she might be our shooter?"

Jack fastened his seat belt, then started the car. "No,"
he admitted. "I think our killer is the blonde whose hair
we found in Gilbert's car. The woman he was blackmailing."

"You still think that this is about blackmail?"

"Yeah, I do. Gilbert had to get the money to pay off
all those people from somewhere. And it certainly
wasn't coming from his medical practice."

"But who? If your theory's right, he's been blackmailing someone a long time, and according to the DNA
on that hair sample, the mystery blonde is in her late
twenties or early thirties. She'd have to have been a baby
when the blackmail started."

"Maybe she was acting on behalf of the blackmailer," Jack suggested as he pulled his car away from the curb.

"And maybe this has nothing to do with blackmail."

Jack cut a glance over at his partner. "How can you say that? You heard what Kelly said. She saw a woman giving Gilbert a bag of money in exchange for a document before she killed him. Are you telling me you still don't believe her?"

"I don't know what to believe, Jackson. This psychic shit is all new to me. I mean, I'm still trying to wrap my brain around the fact that she knew my Tessa was pregnant. How in the hell could she have known that? Even Tessa wasn't sure until I brought home that pregnancy test kit. I don't understand it."

Jack braked at the stop sign before continuing across the intersection. "I don't understand it, either, but I know it's real. She's the real thing."

"You don't find it suspicious that the DNA tests show her and this mystery woman are related?"

"No," Jack told him, irritated that Leon still harbored doubts about Kelly's innocence. "In case you've forgotten, she's an orphan. She doesn't know anything about her family."

"So you're saying it's just a coincidence that our only witness to Gilbert's murder is a psychic with no history of her biological family, but whose DNA links her as a blood relative to our killer?"

"I'm saying that I believe Kelly," he told him.

"You speaking as a cop or as a man who's sleeping with her?"

Jack tightened his grip on the steering wheel. "You got something to say, pal, say it."

"I'm saying that I think you might be too close to this one."

"Why? Because I happen to believe she's innocent?"

"No. Because the Jackson Callaghan I know always told me there's no such thing as a coincidence. Yet these coincidences keep piling up and they all lead back to Kelly Santos."

And it was those coincidences leading back to Kelly that had been troubling him. Because while Kelly may not know who Gilbert's killer was, the killer might know about Kelly. If she did, Kelly could be in danger. Somehow, he had to find the connection, and every instinct told him he had better do it soon.

Fourteen

"Thank you so much for your help, Sister Mary Clarence," Kelly said to the nun who led her into the convent's library and directed her to a table stacked neatly with the phone message pads she'd asked to review.

"I was happy to be of service," the cherub-faced nun told her. "I'm just sorry it took me so long to go through those phone records. With the Advent season approaching, we've just been so busy here at the convent and the chapel that I didn't have time to get to them before now."

"I understand, Sister, and I really do appreciate you getting these for me," Kelly assured her.

The nun's dark blue veil moved as she bowed her head. "As the Reverend Mother explained, the original messages taken were given to the appropriate individuals. But we do keep the pads with the carbon copies for a time. She said you only asked for the past few months, but I went ahead and pulled out the ones for the first part of the year, too, since that's how I had them stored."

"That's fine."

"I also highlighted all the calls that came in to Sister Grace for you."

"Sister Mary Clarence, you didn't have to do that. I would have gone through them myself," Kelly told her, hating that the nun had gone to the extra work on her behalf.

"I know, dear, but my handwriting is not what it used to be and sometimes if I'm rushed, I use my own form of shorthand, which makes no sense to anyone but me. So I thought it would be easier if I just went through the messages myself and marked them. As you'll see, Sister Grace had lots of friends. And your name showed up many times. It was good of you to keep in touch with her as you did."

"She was very special to me," Kelly told the nun. And she owed it to Sister Grace to find out who was responsible for her death. "And, I appreciate you going to all this trouble for me."

"It was really no trouble." She paused. "The Reverend Mother says that you have some concerns about Sister Grace's death, that you think it may have been caused by something besides her bad heart."

Kelly wasn't sure what to say. "It was just very sudden," she finally told her. "I'd like to assure myself that there wasn't..." She hesitated, and instead of saying "someone," she said, "something else that contributed to her death."

"Accepting the loss of someone we cared deeply for is never easy," Sister Mary Clarence replied, her voice sympathetic.

But accepting the murder of someone she cared for was impossible, Kelly thought. "Sister, those last few weeks before Sister Grace died, did you happen to notice if she seemed...I don't know...different, like something was bothering her?"

Sister Mary Clarence tapped her finger against her chin. A frown creased the brow just below the wimple of her veil. "Actually, she was quite distracted that last month or so. She forgot to light the candles in the chapel twice and she was late for vespers several times—which wasn't at all like her. Sister was a stickler for punctuality.''

''Yes, I know,'' Kelly replied. ''But she didn't seem worried or nervous to you?''

''Well, no, not nervous. Maybe a little anxious.''

''Anxious? Do you know why?''

The nun shook her head. ''Her health wasn't good. And illness can be very stressful. Perhaps Sister knew her time here on earth was nearing its end.''

Or perhaps someone was threatening to make it come to an end, Kelly answered silently and was all the more determined to find out who that someone was. She just hoped she could find some answers among the people who'd called the nun during those last months of her life. ''Thank you, Sister. I'll go through these and get out of your way as quickly as I can.''

''Take your time, dear,'' Sister Mary Clarence told her. ''If you have any problem reading my writing or need anything else, just let me know. I'll be right down the hall in the Reverend Mother's office.''

''I will. And thank you again, Sister.''

Even before the nun had closed the door, leaving her alone in the library with the stack of books, Kelly began poring over the yellow-colored pages. Deciding to go through the incoming calls in chronological order, Kelly began with the message book marked January of that year. Each page contained three messages. Some pages were merely recopied messages that had been written in what Sister Mary Clarence had called her shorthand.

There were quite a number of good wishes for the New Year, including her own, among those in early January. She went through month after month, skimming

the messages highlighted. She saw a number of calls that
came from her, several from Mrs. Callaghan. Three from
Mildred St. Amant, referring to the St. Ann Guild's benefit that winter. More calls from her physician's and den-
tist's offices, reminding her of appointments. She wrote
down the names and numbers of several people that she
didn't recognize, making a note of the date they'd called
and any message they'd left. At the end of the calls for
June, she spied the name Dr. Gilbert.

A chill went through Kelly at the sight of the man's
name. What possible connection could he have had to
Sister Grace? She wrote down the number listed, noting
the Mississippi area code. Her heart beating fast now,
she attacked the next group of books and found three
more calls from the doctor during July and August. She
was halfway through the list of September's calls when
she saw a message from Margee Jardine. She recognized
the Jardine name, recalling that their prominence in New
Orleans rivaled that of the Callaghans'. She also recalled
being introduced to the pretty young woman at Mrs. Callaghan's party and being told she was a lawyer. She
copied Margee's phone number and the message saying
she needed to discuss something personal with Sister
Grace.

She flipped through the next two pages and saw another message highlighted that had been for Sister Grace.
This one read, "Lianne called. Says she's an old student
and wants to see you. She'll call back."

Two similar messages from Lianne came the following week, and a third message said she'd meet Sister
Grace at the shrine of Our Lady of Perpetual Help the
following day and gave the time. In October there was
another message from Margee Jardine, saying she
needed to speak with Sister Grace and the word *impor-*

tant was underlined. There were also several more calls from Lianne, one coming the day before Sister Grace's death.

Who was Lianne? And what was it that was important for Margee Jardine to discuss with Sister Grace? And how did Sister Grace know Dr. Gilbert? From what little Jack had told her, the man had practiced in Mississippi and had lost his medical license years ago.

Questions. Pieces of a larger puzzle, Kelly mused, and all those pieces somehow linking back to Sister Grace. Sitting at the table in the library, she attempted to make sense of what she'd discovered. Was she wrong in thinking that there was some connection to Sister Grace's death and the murder of Dr. Gilbert? And what about the calls from Margee Jardine and this Lianne person? She was still mulling over the questions when Sister Mary Clarence returned.

"I'm going to run some errands for the Reverend Mother and I thought I'd check to see how you were doing before I left," the nun told her.

"Fine, Sister. Actually, I was just finishing up." She stuffed the notes she'd made about the messages and phone numbers into her camera bag. Then she stacked the last message book atop the others and stood.

"Did you find what you were looking for?" Sister Mary Clarence asked.

"Maybe. I'm not sure," Kelly answered honestly. "Sister, do you remember a Dr. Gilbert calling for Sister Grace a couple of times during the summer?"

The nun creased her dark brown brows together. "Not really. A great many of our sisters are getting up in age now, so we have a lot of doctors' offices calling here usually to remind them about an appointment or a test, or just to check on them if one of them's been ill. And unfortunately, after she turned seventy, Sister Grace had an increasing number of health problems, so she was under the care of several physicians. As I'm sure you saw, she had doctors' offices calling nearly every other week.''

She had noticed the number of reminder calls from the internist, the cardiologist and the diabetes specialist. But why would an OB-GYN from Mississippi be calling a seventy-one-year-old nun? ''This wasn't someone from Dr. Gilbert's office, but the doctor himself who called.''

The nun shook her head. ''I'm sorry, but I don't remember him.''

''What about someone named Lianne?''

''Lianne,'' the nun repeated.

''She didn't give a last name or phone number, but she called for Sister Grace several times during September and October and left messages. One of them said she was a former student.'' Kelly had sensed the moment she'd seen that last message that it was important, that this Lianne person was important. This Lianne could be the link she'd been looking for.

''Oh, yes. I remember her now. Very polite, lovely voice. She said she was one of Sister Grace's girls when she was at St. Ann's. She was visiting New Orleans and wanted to see Sister. I believe Sister Grace met with her several times during her visit.''

''Sister Mary Clarence,'' Kelly began calmly while adrenaline flashed through her system. ''Did Sister Grace say anything or act differently after you gave her that message?''

The nun frowned again. ''Well now that you mention it, she wasn't all smiles like she usually was when one of her girls called. In fact, when I first relayed the mes-

sage, she went white as a ghost and asked me to re-
peat it.''

"Did you see this Lianne?" Kelly asked.

"No. They didn't meet here at the convent. But I do
remember asking how her former charge was doing, and
Sister Grace said she was not doing well. She said the
woman was troubled, that she had some serious problems. Grace said that she needed to pray to Our Lady
for guidance so that she would know how to help her. I
told her that I'd keep them both in my prayers.'' She
shook her head as though shaking off the memory. ''Was
this Lianne at St. Ann's when you were there?''

"Not that I recall." But she intended to find out. And
to do that, she might have to ask Jack for his help.

Jack sat across the table from Kelly in the restaurant
that evening, pleased it hadn't taken him much convinc-
ing to get her to join him. For a Monday night, the place
was packed, and while he would have preferred a less-
crowded place to talk, he'd hoped the homey atmosphere
would put her at ease. There were no candles on the
tables, no frilly linens, just your basic restaurant with
good food and good service.

"So let me get this straight," Jack began once they'd
ordered. "You're saying that Sister Grace didn't die of
a heart attack, but that someone came into the chapel
where she was praying and murdered her?"

"Yes."

"And you're just now telling me? Why didn't you
say something sooner?"

"Because you would have wanted me to go to the
police."

"You're right, I would have. Because catching mur-
derers is police business. Hell, it's what I do. You have

no business playing detective, Kelly.'' And if she was right, she damned well could have put herself in serious danger. Furious that she had taken such a chance, he spoke sharply, ''You should have told me. I'd have gone to the police with you.''

''What was I supposed to say, 'Oh, by the way, Sister Grace didn't really die of a heart attack. She was murdered.' And when your police sergeant asked me how I knew that and I told him that when I held her rosary, I saw a woman sitting behind her in the chapel stab her in the neck with a needle and kill her, what do you think he would have said? Do you honestly think anyone would have believed me? I have no proof. And you saw what I've had to go through since I told them about seeing that Dr. Gilbert murdered.'' She shook her head. ''I'm not putting myself through that again.''

She had a point, Jack conceded. But it didn't erase the fact that she'd kept this from him. ''You could have come to me, Kelly. You know that I would have believed you.'' Jack reached across the table for the hand she had bundled into a fist. He covered it with his own. ''So why didn't you?''

''Because I knew if I asked for your help, we would end up getting involved.''

''And, of course, you didn't want that, did you?'' he fired back, and wished he could have five minutes alone with that jerk Scott who had scarred her so badly.

''I've made you angry.''

''No,'' Jack said, shaking off the temper, because he knew she would sense it whether he wanted her to or not. ''I'm not angry—at least not with you. I just wish you would trust me, Kelly.''

''I trust you more than I've ever trusted anyone in my life.''

"But…?" he prompted, because he knew there was a *but*.

"But you want more from me than I have in me to give." She pulled her fingers free.

"I don't believe that for a minute. And I won't accept it, either. There is so much more to you than your being able to see what's going on inside other people's heads. But I think you don't want anyone to know that. That's why you push everyone away. It's why you keep pushing me away. Because you're afraid if you let anyone get too close to you that they'll hurt you again. That they'll leave you again—the same way your parents left you."

"Thanks for the psychoanalysis, Dr. Callaghan. But I'm afraid that you're off base. I came to terms with who and what I am a long time ago."

But she hadn't, not really, Jack thought as he watched her trying to erect those barriers between them again. "It's not going to work this time, Kelly."

She eyed him warily. "What isn't going to work?"

"You trying to shut me out. You see, you messed up last night. You messed up big time. You let your guard down and I saw the real Kelly Santos. I made love with her, ate pizza with her in the middle of the night and I slept with her in my arms. And now that I've seen the real you, I have no intention of letting you hide her from me again."

"We had sex, Jack. Very, very good sex, I'll admit. And I suppose it was unrealistic of me not to think it would happen because of the physical attraction between us. But sex is all that it was. Please don't read any more into it."

"Look at me, Kelly," he commanded, and she lifted those big brown eyes to his. "We both know there was a great deal more than sex going on between us last night. I love you.''

"You're wrong," she said, shaking her head in denial.

"No, I'm not," he told her, but because he could see she was upset, he decided not to press her further. At least for now. "But we'll deal with that later. Right now, I want you to tell me everything you've found out about Sister Grace's death."

She told him, beginning with the troubling messages on her machine from Sister Grace before her death. She told him about her subsequent visits to the convent and conversations with the other nuns, about her slow progression through Sister Grace's journals. And she told him about the telephone calls that Sister Grace had received from Dr. Gilbert, Margee Jardine and someone named Lianne. Finally she told him about her conversation with Sister Mary Clarence, who had claimed that Sister Grace had been anxious shortly before her death.

"I keep going over it all in my head, trying to come up with some logical reason why Dr. Gilbert would have contacted her, but I can't."

"Maybe that's because there is no logical reason," Jack offered. He couldn't help thinking of his conversation earlier with Leon. What were the odds of Gilbert's murderer being related to Kelly, a woman who had predicted his murder? And here he was faced with another coincidence. Gilbert contacting Sister Grace and, within weeks, both of them ending up dead.

"Do you think I'm making too much of this? That it's all just a coincidence?"

"No," Jack told her. "I don't believe in coincidences."

"But where's the connection?"

"You."

"Me?" she returned.

"Think about it, Kelly. You're the one link between both Gilbert and Sister Grace's deaths. And if I'm right, you could be in danger."

"I'm not going to back away from this, Jack."

He didn't expect that she would. "Then I want you to let me check out those leads for you."

"But—"

"No buts, Kelly. You'll need to trust me on this."

"Two Monday night specials," the waitress announced as she placed a steaming plate of red beans and rice with sausage in front of each of them. "Want refills on those teas?"

"Yes, please," Kelly said politely.

Jack nodded.

By the time their tea glasses had been topped off a second time and they'd put a dent into their meals, Kelly had relented somewhat. "I copied all the phone messages that were logged in for Sister Grace at the convent during this past year," she told him. Pulling out several sheets of paper from her camera bag, she handed them to him.

Jack scanned the half-dozen sheets of neatly written names with the dates, phone numbers and messages on them. "Sister Grace was a popular lady."

"Apparently. I called the number listed for Dr. Gilbert, hoping maybe I could reach someone who could tell me why he was calling Sister Grace."

Jack didn't bother telling her that she had no business doing that and it was a police matter because he knew that, as headstrong as Kelly was, it would likely fall on deaf ears. "Any luck?"

"No. The number was disconnected."

"I recognize some of these names—including my mother's—I'll check out the ones that I don't."

"I already have," she informed him.

"And?"

"Most were people from the parish, former students or friends. The only two that I didn't contact was this Lianne person and Margee Jardin, because there was no number for either of them." She paused. "I met Margee at your mother's party. She's an attorney, right?"

"Yes." He speared another bite of sausage from his plate, ate it while he considered Margee's calls. Her message had said she needed to discuss something important.

"How well do you know her?"

"Almost as well as I know Meredith. She and her family lived down the street from us, and she hung around our house a lot when we were growing up. She's sort of like an honorary sister. Why?"

"I just wondered. Does she work at your brother's firm?"

Jack smiled and put down his fork. "Hardly. She and Peter are always at each other's throats. They've been that way since we were kids. Margee used to be with the D.A.'s office, and a couple of years ago she took an offer from a big criminal firm here in the city."

"I guess she could have been one of Sister Grace's students, but I don't remember her being at St. Joseph's with Meredith and me."

"That's because she's my age. She was already in college when you were just starting high school. Besides, Margee didn't go to St. Joseph's. She went to Ursuline

Academy,'' he told her, referring to the city's oldest Catholic school for girls.

''Maybe she was calling on behalf of a client,'' Kelly suggested.

''It's possible,'' Jack answered. ''But instead of speculating, why don't I give Margee a call tomorrow and ask her about the calls?''

''I'd appreciate it,'' Kelly said.

Jack caught the note of relief in her voice, wondered at it. ''Did you think I'd refuse?''

She shrugged. ''I wasn't sure how you'd feel about it since she's a friend of your family's. I don't want to cause you any problems.''

''It won't be a problem.'' And he hoped that it wouldn't. ''Then that leaves this Lianne person. You said she claimed to have been at St. Ann's?''

''Yes,'' Kelly told him. ''At least that's what she told Sister Mary Clarence. But I don't remember anyone with that name when I lived there, and except for a few stints in foster care, I was there until I turned eighteen.''

Jack felt that ache in his chest again as he thought of Kelly's early life. How lonely she must have been. Somehow, someway, he would make sure that she never felt alone again.

''I guess it's possible she lived there before me or even after me. I mean, Sister Grace was a nun for more than fifty years and half of those were spent at St. Ann's.''

''But the name Lianne isn't all that common. Maybe someone who's working at St. Ann's now will remember her. I'll stop by and see what I can find out, maybe we can get a last name on her.''

"Actually, I've already tried," she confessed. "I went by after I left the convent."

No surprise there, Jack thought. "Did you find out anything?"

"Not much. No one at the new location remembers anyone by that name, but Miss Sally, she's the cook who's been there forever, she remembers a girl named Lianne who lived there a long, long time ago. She said it was at least thirty or thirty-five years ago."

"Then I doubt it's the same woman," Jack told her. "You said Sister Mary Clarence described the woman on the phone as a polite, lovely *young* woman. The Lianne the cook remembers would have to be close to fifty. There has to be another Lianne."

"I guess you're right. But I don't know who she is or how to find her. I've already asked the Mother Superior running St. Ann's now if I could go through the records to try to locate this Lianne person, but she refused. She said information on the girls who lived there is confidential. And since I didn't feel I could go into the reasons why I needed the information, I didn't press it."

"Maybe I'll have better luck. If they still say no, I'll ask Alex to issue a search warrant and force them to give us the records," Jack told her as he reached for his glass of tea. He took a swallow, continuing to watch Kelly over the rim of the glass.

"I don't think that's a good idea."

"Why not?" Jack asked.

"It probably wouldn't be good for you careerwise."

Jack set the glass aside. "What's that supposed to mean?"

"It means that I'm sure you're already getting some flack for your relationship with me because of the Gilbert case. What is your captain going to say when you tell him I had another vision about Sister Grace's death? And Alex Kusak may be your friend, but no district attorney in his right mind is going to issue a search warrant based on a psychic's visions."

Although he hated to admit it, Kelly had a point. But the truth was, he needed a look at those records, anyway. And he'd already started the wheels rolling. To find the killer, he would need to open the doors to Kelly's past—something that he knew she was reluctant to do.

"Tomorrow I'm going to go to the Our Lady of Perpetual Help Shrine and see if, by chance, anyone remembers Sister Grace meeting with someone there last month, and tonight I'm going to try to go through some more of Sister Grace's journals," Kelly said.

"I think I just might know of a way for us to get a look at those records at St. Ann's."

"How?"

"My mother. She's on the board of St. Ann's Guild," Jack explained. "She could say she's doing a tribute in honor of Sister Grace and say that she needs to get in touch with the girls who lived at St. Ann's during her years there," he continued as the idea took shape in his mind.

"Jack, I can't ask your mother to lie for me."

"Who says she'd be lying? She'll think doing the tribute is a great idea. She'll probably thank us for thinking of it."

She gave him a wry look. "I'm not sure about that, but it might help us find out who Lianne is."

Deciding he had to tell her the rest of it, he reached over and took her hand. "There's another reason I need to go through those records, Kelly."

"Me," she said, her voice barely a whisper. "You need to find out who I really am, what my connection is to Gilbert's killer."

"Yes. I'm sorry. I know you'd rather I didn't go poking around in your past, but I don't see where I have a lot of options. The DNA link to you is the only solid lead we have. It may be our only shot at finding the killer."

"I understand. You have a job to do. It's just…it's just that I've deliberately kept that door closed all these years."

"Is there any particular reason why?" The question had gnawed at him for some time now.

"Remember the dream I told you I have about the fire?"

"Yes."

"I think my mother died in that fire. And I think the reason I don't remember and have always had those horrid dreams is because the person who killed her was my father. I think he meant to kill me, too. I think the reason I never pressed to find out about my birth parents is because I didn't want to find out the truth. Somehow, not knowing for sure seemed easier to live with."

Jack squeezed the fingers he was holding tighter and wished he could wipe out that haunted look in her brown eyes. Instead he was sticking his nose into a past that would probably cause her more pain. But what choice did he have? "I'm sorry."

"So how are you folks doing? Ready for some dessert

and coffee?'' the waitress asked as she returned to the table and began clearing away the remains of their dinners. ''We've got hot apple pie, chocolate mousse cake, bread pudding and lemon torte. What can I get you?''

''Nothing for me,'' Kelly told her, and pulled her fingers free from Jack's. She folded her hands in her lap.

''Just a check,'' Jack said. And when they were alone again, he said, ''Kelly, you know, there might be another way for us to find Gilbert's killer without me poking into your past.''

''How?''

''Let me take you to see Gilbert's car, the one his body was found in,'' he suggested. ''You saw the man's murder when you picked up the newspaper he'd been reading. Maybe if you see or touch the car he died in, you'll be able to see who the murderer is.''

Sitting in the bar at the far end of the restaurant, she dipped her head so that the red hair from the wig shaded her face. She ignored the come-on looks from the cowboy three stools over. She lifted her martini glass to her lips and watched in the mirror over the bar as the police detective whispered something to Kelly Santos before standing to pull back her chair for her. Then picking up her camera bag, he motioned toward the exit.

The rage that she'd lived with for the past year threatened to consume her as the pair made their way to the door. What she wouldn't have given to know what she'd told him that had his face going all serious. The little bitch had wrapped him around her little finger. She'd seen right through her act. The way she had encouraged him to touch her, to hold her hand. Sweet, delicate, sad little Sarah, conning people with those big, sad brown eyes.

Damn her!

All these years, she'd thought she'd gotten rid of her, had even forgotten she'd ever existed. Only to have her come back now using the name Kelly Santos and threatening to ruin her life.

Well, she simply wouldn't have it. She'd killed her once and gotten away with it. She'd simply have to kill her again. And this time, she'd make sure she stayed dead.

Fifteen

"I expected there to be a lot more people here," Kelly told Jack and Leon as they led her to the police department garage section where evidence from vehicles in crime scenes was analyzed.

"There usually are," Jack informed her. "But I asked them to take a break. I thought it would be easier for you without an audience."

"Thank you," she said, moved by his sensitivity. She shouldn't be surprised, she told herself. Hadn't Jack been sensitive to her feelings ten years ago when she'd been a pathetic teenager? Now here she was, embroiled in a passionate affair with him while she was trying to find out who killed Sister Grace. Only the more time she spent with him, the harder it was becoming for her to keep her emotions separate, to not allow herself to be lulled into believing that she could actually have a future with him.

You know what happens when you let your emotions interfere with your judgment, Kelly. Don't you remember what happened with Garrett?

"The car they found Gilbert in is that dark gray Lincoln in the third bay over there on your left," Leon said, motioning to the car.

Leon's words brought Kelly back to the task at hand. The November chill in the air outside permeated the concrete garage, yet her palms felt damp as she stared over at the vehicle. Its two front doors were open, reminding her of a hawk with its wings spread in flight as it prepared to swoop down on its hapless prey. She shivered at the analogy.

As though sensing her apprehension, Jack asked, "You okay?"

Kelly nodded and continued toward the car. She stopped a few feet away from what Jack had called the bay, that section she'd seen in commercial service stations where they lifted a car up on a rack to look beneath its underbelly. Only no mechanics raced around it. There were no noisy whooshes of air or straining metal sounds, no radios blaring. The car simply sat there in the concrete square. Waiting. Waiting for her to come and search out its secrets.

God, she didn't want to do this. She didn't want to see what had happened in that car again, feel Dr. Gilbert's shock, then fear as the life drained from his body. But she had to do it.

Take control of your emotions, Kelly. Remove yourself from the equation. Do what you did when you were at St. Ann's. Pretend it's not real, it's not happening to you. Pretend you're reading a sad story. Pretend you're watching a frightening movie.

Jack cupped her chin, tilted her head upward. "I know I pressured you to do this, but if you're not up to it, it's okay. Just say the word and we'll leave."

"No. I can do it. I *need* to do it."

"All right, then. Just take your time. The car's already been dusted for prints, so you don't have to worry about touching it. Okay?"

"Okay," Kelly told him, and turned her full attention to the car. In her vision she'd only glimpsed the car beneath the light of a streetlamp. She'd attributed her impressions of shabbiness to the poor lighting in the alley. But here in the well-lit crime investigation sector, the car looked just as shabby. She suspected the dark gray color was actually black that had faded with age and exposure to the elements. The interior upholstery that at one time had been a rich tan leather was now a sickly hue that fell somewhere between beige and dirt. The leather was cracked in several places. A strip of silver tape had been used over what she suspected was a large gash in the seat. Two cigarette burns were visible on the driver's armrest. The leather casing on the steering wheel was torn. But it was the dark stains on the driver's seat and the mat beneath the steering wheel that made her stomach pitch. Blood. Dr. Gilbert's blood.

Bracing herself, Kelly reached out and touched the passenger's seat. Immediately she felt herself spinning, as though whirling about like a leaf in the eye of a storm, until suddenly, she was back to that night…back in the French Quarter alley with street musicians and Halloween revelers celebrating in the distance…

"It's about damn time you showed up. I've been waiting in this alley for twenty minutes and nearly got mugged twice."

"I was detained," she said cooly, and wished the muggers had taken care of him for her. It certainly would have saved her the trouble of having to sneak away from the party and come here to deal with him. But at least tonight she would finally be free of him.

"Well, you're damn lucky I waited," he informed her, his Mississippi drawl even thicker due to the liquor. "Another two minutes and I'd have been gone."

"Then I guess it's fortunate that I showed up when I did." Following his lead, she opened the passenger door

of the car and nearly gagged on the stench of whiskey and stale cigars as she slid inside. Furious that she had been forced to deal with such a cretin, she made herself pull the car door closed, shutting out the noise from the street musicians and revelers who'd flocked to New Orleans' French Quarter to celebrate Halloween.

"Fortunate is right, missy. I'm a busy man," he said, puffing up his chest and straining the buttons on his dated suit coat. "I'll have you know, I've got better things to do with my time than to wait around for the likes of you."

Better things like drowning in a bottle of whiskey or slithering into the nearest casino, she thought, even more repulsed by the man now than she'd been when he'd first sought her out six months ago. "Then let's not waste any more of each other's time, Doctor. Did you bring the document?"

"Of course I brought it. But first I want to see the money."

She retrieved the black tote bag that she'd filled with cash. Opening it, she angled it so that the light from the streetlamp fell on its contents. And there was no mistaking the lust in the man's bloodshot brown eyes as he gazed at it. Like a drug addict about to get his next fix, she thought. But when he reached for the bag, she snapped it closed. "Not so fast, Doctor. First, I want the birth certificate."

He fumbled inside his coat pocket, drew out an envelope and shoved it at her.

While he pounced on the bag and began pawing through the stacks of bills, she was grateful to be wearing gloves as she opened the envelope and withdrew the faded sheet of paper. Rage whipped through her as she stared at the birth certificate. Sarah Tompkins. Or at least that had been her name before those stupid nuns had changed it to Kelly Santos because the girl had been too young and stupid to remember who she was.

She skipped past the name of the mother and focused her attention on the father's name. Seeing her own father's name there was like a slap in the face, filling her with a black hatred. Reaching deep down inside herself, she channeled her anger just as she had done so often as a child until she was able to focus again. She would not allow Kelly to ruin her perfect life. She would destroy her, just as she should have been destroyed the first time. But first, first she needed to take care of business. "You're sure this is the only copy?"

"What? Yeah, it's the only one," he muttered, distracted by all the cash.

She tucked the envelope inside her purse and reached for the gun. "Then I guess this is goodbye, Doctor," she said politely, and pulled the trigger.

Kelly heard the doctor's cry of surprise. Then suddenly she felt the sharp pain in his chest, the warm, sticky feel of blood on his fingers, smelled the sickening scent of his blood. Panic raced through him, through her, as he felt the life flowing from him. Suddenly Kelly's legs started to buckle beneath her, then she felt arms going around her and heard the sound of Jack's voice.

"Kelly! Kelly, come out of it, baby!"

"Is she all right?" she heard Leon ask.

Her head still spinning and her heart racing, Kelly blinked and suddenly she was in Jack's arms. His face was pale, his blue eyes filled with worry as he stared at her.

"I'm going to call a doctor," Leon said.

"No," Kelly cried out. "No doctor."

"Hang on," Jack told his partner. "Are you all right?" he asked her, his voice anxious.

"Yes. I think so." She clutched at his shirt. "Jack, he was blackmailing her."

"Yeah, I figured that out from what you were saying. Something to do with a birth certificate."

"Yes," she said, her head still reeling, her body still trembling from the aftermath of the murder. "She thinks she has the only one, but she doesn't. He made a copy of the birth certificate."

"Where is it?"

"I don't know. I don't know," she repeated with a shake of her head.

"Do you know who the woman is?" Leon asked.

She shook her head. "I couldn't get a fix on her, or see her face or feel who she was. There was just all this darkness in her, darkness and rage when she saw the name on the birth certificate."

"Whose name was on the birth certificate?" Leon asked.

She looked over at Jack's partner. "Sarah. Sarah Tompkins."

Leon frowned. He glanced over at Jack. "Did you tell her?"

"No."

"Tell me what?" Kelly asked.

"Gilbert's office nurse, the woman we're trying to find, her name is Tompkins. Eve Tompkins."

"Could be Eve Tompkins is this Sarah's mother," Leon suggested. "Maybe Sarah Tompkins is our shooter."

"Sarah Tompkins didn't kill him," Kelly informed them.

Leon narrowed his eyes. "How do you know?"

"Because I'm Sarah Tompkins. Or at least that's who I was before I was left at St. Ann's."

"Holy shit," Leon exclaimed.

Jack held her by the shoulders, watched her closely. "You're sure about this?"

"Yes. And there's something else you should know."

"What?" Jack asked.

"The woman who killed Gilbert is the same woman who killed Sister Grace. And she intends to kill me."

"Just set them down over here," Meredith instructed the deliverymen who carted in the shipments of evening clothes that she'd ordered for the shop. When her cell phone rang, she moved behind the counter to retrieve it from her purse. "Be careful you don't take out any of my glass shelves," she warned the burly fellows who were edging dangerously close to her display case of baubles.

"Relax, lady. We ain't gonna mess up your stuff," the beefier of the duo told her.

If he valued his life he had better not, she thought, because she had a small fortune tied up in the expensive crystal-and-jewel trinkets. Eyeing the two men carefully, she snatched the still-ringing phone from her bag. "What?"

"Meredith?"

"Hang on a second, Jack." When the delivery team actually managed to unload the last of the boxes without doing anything more than causing a vase to wobble, she breathed a sigh of relief. After signing the ticket and seeing them out the door, she turned her attention to her brother. "Sorry about that. My delivery of evening wear for the shop finally arrived."

"That's good, then. I guess," he said, not sounding the least bit impressed.

"Yes, it is a *very* good thing," she told him. "The store opening is less than two weeks away." And she'd been worried sick that the gowns wouldn't arrive on time. Now that they had, she was just itching to rip into those boxes and check out her purchases.

"Meredith, you still there?"

"Sorry," she said, and turned away from the boxes. "So what's up, big brother?"

"I need a favor."

"If that favor includes allowing you to bail out on me for the preview party this weekend, forget it. I expect you and Peter both to come and spend obscene amounts of money. And the fact that you don't have a current lady friend is not an acceptable excuse. You can buy something for your sister for Christmas."

"You own the shop, Meredith," he pointed out dryly.

"Exactly. So you can be sure that whatever you buy me, I'll love it." Which made perfect sense to her.

"I'll keep that in mind. But I wasn't calling to bail out on your party. I need you to do me a favor."

He sounded so serious, Meredith thought. "All right. What's the favor?"

"I need you to stay with Kelly today and let her think it's your idea."

"Kelly Santos?"

"Yeah. I'm worried about her and don't want her to be alone. But Leon and I have to go to the Gulf Coast. So I'd like you to stay with her until I get back this evening."

Her brother and Kelly?

Meredith sank down in one of the cushy lounging chairs she'd had grouped around a glass table, hardly noticing the crystal vase of flowers she'd taken such pains in arranging.

"Meredith, did you hear me?" Jack asked, his voice sharp.

"Yes. Yes, I heard you." She thought back to her mother's cocktail party, and vaguely remembered Jack talking to Kelly. But she'd also seen him with Alicia. Her brother and Kelly? The notion boggled her mind. "Jack, are you and Kelly—"

"Yes. You have a problem with that?"

Testy, she thought. "No. No problem. As a matter of fact, I'd rather see you with just about anyone instead of Alicia Van Owen. But my brain's just having a little trouble computing the idea of you and quiet, spooky-eyed Kelly Santos."

"Then I suggest you get used to it," he snapped, and followed with a deep sigh. "Listen, Kelly had a rough time this morning down at the precinct. And I'd feel a lot better if I knew she wasn't alone at that hotel. She could really use a friend."

"I'll give her a call," Meredith told him.

"No. Don't call. She'll tell you not to come. Just go over there."

"And assuming she let's me through the door, just what am I supposed to do once I'm there?" Kelly had turned her down flat when she'd followed up with a phone call wanting to discuss her doing the ad for In-dulgences.

"I don't know. Do whatever it is women do when they get together. Gossip. Talk about men."

"We're talking Kelly Santos here, big brother. She's not exactly the gossip/let's-trash-men type," she reminded him.

"I have faith in you to come up with something."

The "something" she'd come up with was to get Kelly to help her at the shop. Two hours later, she had the woman, who had apparently snagged her brother Jack's attention, in a sea of tissue paper as she unearthed evening dresses, flirty shoes and trinkets from the shipment she'd received earlier.

"This box has more dresses," Kelly announced as she pulled out a strapless emerald-satin evening gown and a black-beaded cocktail suit. "Where do you want these?"

Meredith looked up from where she'd been pairing the silver Jimmy Choo heels with a vintage de la Renta dress on a display mannequin. "Oh, those are the Ralph Laurens. Very classic, don't you think?"

"They're pretty," she offered.

Meredith laughed. "Thank goodness you're not a customer, Kelly. If the rest of the women in this city were as ecstatic as you about the things in the shop, I'd be out of business before I ever began."

Kelly flushed. "I see this kind of stuff all the time, Meredith. It's just not that big a deal to me anymore."

"You've been working in New York too long. It's made you jaded if you can't salivate over a beautiful dress anymore," she informed her. "You can put them over there in that armoire," she said, pointing to one of the pieces she'd brought in because she hadn't wanted to be just another store filled with racks of the same dresses. Every item in her shop was a one of a kind. While she would order different sizes of the same design to fulfill a customer's request, she'd purposely chosen different styles in different sizes, hoping to appeal to the woman who didn't want to see anyone else at a party wearing the same design.

Meredith looked around the shop, felt a sense of pride at the progress she'd made. During the past week she'd been spending practically every waking moment in the place. True, while it helped keep her mind off of Alex, it had also given her a sense of purpose. A sense of accomplishment.

"Are things any better between you and Alex?"

Meredith slid her glance back to Kelly. "If by 'better' you mean has he changed his mind about him and me being together, the answer's no. But then, I decided to let him stew awhile, wondering whether or not I'm going to take off again."

"Are you?" Kelly asked as she slipped the dresses on padded hangers and hung them in the armoire.

"No. I'm through running. I'm staying this time."

"I think that's a good decision," Kelly told her as she unwrapped another dress. "Oh my, this is lovely."

Meredith glanced over to see what had elicited such a response and smiled. "It *is* pretty, isn't it?" she replied at the sight of Kelly holding the strapless pale-gold tulle and beaded dress. "I chose it because it reminded me of the Elie Saab that I saw an actress wear to the Oscars last year. Why don't you try it on?"

"It's not my style. I generally stick with something more simple."

"You mean something safe. There's nothing wrong with the classics, but why not try something a little more daring? Shoot, you've certainly got the body for it, and this will look great with your coloring. And it also happens to be your size."

Kelly frowned. "How do you know what my size is?"

Meredith laughed. "Because it's my business to know. Now, go in the dressing room and try it on. I'll bring you some shoes and accessories."

Blowing off Kelly's protests, Meredith insisted the other woman try on the delicate metallic heels she'd chosen to go with the dress. "You sure you don't need any help with the zipper?"

"No. I've got it."

"The stole goes draped across the front of the bodice."

"The stole?"

Meredith rolled her eyes. "That long, sheer thingy with the sparkles on it." After a few seconds more, she said, "Hurry up. Let me see how it fits."

When Kelly emerged from the dressing room, Meredith was taken aback. "Oh, Kelly." No wonder her brother was smitten with the woman. She looked like a Grecian goddess, tall, golden, regal. And, oh blast it, if she didn't envy her those legs.

"It's a little skimpy on material, don't you think?"

"I think it's perfect. You look beautiful." And Jack wasn't going to know what hit him when he got a load of her in this dress. "Turn around."

She wobbled as she did so. "How on earth am I supposed to walk in these shoes?"

"Carefully. Don't move. I've got the perfect earrings to wear with it." She raced over to the display case and snagged the Fred Leighton knockoff diamond chandeliers from the velvet bed and brought them to Kelly. "Here, put these on."

Kelly did as instructed.

"God, but I'm good," Meredith said, loving the effect. "Now, come sit down over here by the dressing table and let me pin up your hair."

"Really, Meredith, I should take this off before I mess it up—"

"Go," Meredith insisted, and pointed to the dressing table. Within moments, she'd gotten rid of the braid and was fashioning Kelly's thick hair into a French twist.

"Please tell me this color came from a bottle," she said as she brushed the pale blond hair. "God wouldn't be so unfair as to give you those legs and hair like this, too."

Kelly chuckled. "Look at it this way, you got a double helping in the boobs department."

"I did luck out there, didn't I?" Meredith replied, seeing no reason for false modesty. "There, what do you think?"

Kelly stared at her face in the mirror. "I look... different."

"You look gorgeous," Meredith amended. "For the party, we'll put on some pink lipstick, a little blush, and do up your eyes with some gold-and-bronze shadow, a little mascara, and Jack won't know what hit him."

Kelly's eyes darted to her own in the mirror. "But I'm not coming to your party. And even if I was, I certainly wouldn't wear this dress."

"And why aren't you coming to my party? And what do you mean you wouldn't wear this dress? What's wrong with it?"

"First off, I don't like parties. And second, I couldn't wear something like this. It's...it's not my style."

"No offense, Kelly, but maybe it's time you had a style update."

"There's nothing wrong with my style. Besides, I know what these little designer numbers cost and it's not in my budget."

"Fine. Then consider it a gift for letting me cry on your shoulder the other night."

"As I recall, it wasn't much of a shoulder," she said dryly. "And while I appreciate the offer, I can't accept this."

"But you need something to wear to the party. And

don't say you aren't coming. Jack's coming and he'll want you to come with him. So do I.''

Kelly hesitated. "All right. But I'll wear the dress I wore to your mother's party. It's new. I just bought it last week.''

Meredith wrinkled her nose. "It's nice, but you need something with a bit more...flash. You don't want to look like you're attending a funeral, do you?'' Not waiting for an answer, she grabbed Kelly by the hand. "Come here,'' she said, and dragged her over to the trio of mirrors. "Look at yourself. See how it skims your body without hugging it? It was designed for somebody who's long and lean like you are. It even gives a hint of cleavage here in the front, see? And I have some bras, those new miracle ones that are filled with gel, that will make you look like you're a size C cup. Stay here and I'll get one for you—''

"That's okay,'' Kelly said. "I'm perfectly happy with what I've got.''

"Well, even without the bra, you can see the dress is perfect for you.''

"It is pretty. But I don't know,'' she said, but Meredith could see she was weakening. "How much is it?''

"$5,500 for the dress. The shoes and earrings are another three grand.''

"Forget it. I can pick up something just as nice on one of my shoots and get it for half that. If I make their clothes look good, those designers are only to happy to cut the prices.''

"I'll tell you what. I'll make you a deal that not even those hotshot designers can top.''

"What kind of deal?''

"A trade. You do the photo layout for my Christmas brochure and the outfit is yours.''

"Do you have any idea what it would take to put a brochure out in time for this Christmas? You need lead time on that kind of project if you want it to be good."

Meredith mulled over that. "Well, what about doing one for Valentine's Day? That's a few months away. So you'd have time to do a bang-up job and get it out, say, for the first of February."

Kelly narrowed her eyes and met Meredith's gaze in the mirror. "The shoes and earrings are part of the deal, too?"

"The shoes and earrings, too."

"All right. You've got yourself a deal."

Meredith hugged the other woman and beamed. She saw no point in telling Kelly that her dealer's cost was only a fraction of the retail price for the outfit and that she would have gladly paid her twice that figure to get her to do the layout. She almost felt like she was taking advantage of her.

"You're not."

"I'm not what?" Meredith asked.

"Taking advantage of me. Since it looks like I'm going to be in town for a while, anyway, I'd already decided to do an ad layout for you as a favor."

"You did?"

Kelly nodded. "But I liked your offer better," she said with a grin.

Sixteen

"**Y**ou're sure you don't have any record of an Eve Tompkins here?" Jack asked as they hit the last of what had to be twenty nursing homes in the three-county area. Since the woman had been discharged from the Good Shepherd mental facility, she seemed to have disappeared. So he and Leon had tried calling hospitals and nursing homes, hoping to locate Dr. Gilbert's former nurse. When they kept coming up empty with the phone calls, they had decided to drive over to the Gulf Coast and see if they had any better luck in person. So far, they hadn't.

"She used to be a nurse in Pass Christian," Leon explained to the woman at the desk. "She's probably in her late sixties or early seventies now."

"I'm sorry. But we don't have any Eve Tompkins here," the receptionist told him. "Did you check at Magnolia Gardens? Some people get us confused with them."

"We checked," Jack assured her. Just as they had checked every other nursing home and medical facility in the area. "Well, thank you for your time, ma'am," Jack told her.

"It was a longshot, Jackson. Who knows? Maybe Gilbert's ex was wrong and this Eve Tompkins left the state," Leon said as they headed for the exit.

"Just a minute," the receptionist called out.

Jack turned, as did Leon. "Yes, ma'am?"

"Did you say this Eve Tompkins worked for a Dr. Gilbert?" the woman asked.

"That's right. We were told she was his office nurse at one time."

The brunette stared at him from behind her tortoise-shell-framed glasses. "Well, we don't have an Eve Tompkins here, but we do have an Evelyn Gilbert."

"Eve could be short for Evelyn," Leon pointed out.

And if the nurse was as hung up on the now-deceased doctor as the man's ex-wife claimed, it was possible that she'd either convinced the man to marry her or simply decided to take his name. "Is it possible for us to see this Evelyn Gilbert?"

"I don't see why not. Just let me check with my supervisor."

Ten minutes later, the supervisor led them to a large room where at least thirty men and women were engaged in various forms of entertainment—all of which were going on at the same time. "This is our recreational area," the woman told them, raising her voice to be heard over the television set, radio, piano-playing and conversations. "Some of our residents like to gather here in the afternoon before going in to dinner."

"It's only four-thirty," Leon pointed out.

The woman gave him a patient smile. "I know, but our seniors have delicate constitutions. So we think it's best if they have their evening meals early."

And it also meant that they could send the old people off to bed early and be done with them for the night, Jack thought cynically as he looked around the room. Though the sofas and chair groupings were bright and cheery, there was something sad about the sight of all these people—mothers and fathers, aunts and uncles, sisters and brothers—now living under one roof with strangers.

He glanced around the room. Three women and one man were gathered around the television, with the snowy-haired gentleman commandeering the remote and the volume blaring. The ladies stared at the screen as though unaware that the pictures were changing every three seconds and that they were only catching snippets of dialogue.

A quartet of women sat around a table, engaged in a lively game of bridge and sipping iced tea. And they appeared to genuinely be enjoying themselves. A frail-looking gentleman sat in a wheelchair, gazing out the window, not appearing to notice the efforts of his son trying to speak with him. In the far corner a woman in a bright pink dress, with a pink bow in her hair, played a lively old tune on the piano and sang off key.

"Excuse me," the supervisor who'd called herself Mrs. Floyd said. "Let me see if I can get the remote from Mr. Willie and turn the volume on the TV down a bit. Then I'll take you to see Miss Evelyn."

Once she had left them, Leon said, "Man, I feel like we just stepped into the Twilight Zone."

"I know what you mean. Makes me grateful that my mother is still so active and that my dad was playing golf when his time came."

"That's the way to go, all right. Lucky for you, you got good genes."

He was lucky, Jack thought. And he couldn't help thinking about Kelly. He'd taken his genetic history for granted, whereas Kelly had been denied hers. She'd said she hadn't wanted to know. Was that the truth? Or had she simply been afraid of the answers she might find?

"Sorry about that," Mrs. Floyd said. "If you come this way, I'll introduce you to Evelyn. She's the one playing the piano. But as I warned you, she's in the third stage of Alzheimer's. She has good days when she's quite sharp for a little while before the confusion sets in. Unfortunately, those episodes are more frequent and lasting longer now."

"We understand," Jack replied. They stopped beside the piano.

"Evelyn? Evelyn," Mrs. Floyd repeated. She touched the woman's thin shoulder. "You have visitors."

The piano playing stopped. Evelyn pivoted on the piano seat and stared up at him with big brown eyes. She grinned at Jack from pink lips that looked as though they'd been painted on by a child who had been playing with her mother's makeup.

"Hello, Miss Evelyn. My name's Jack Callaghan."

"Did you like my song? Mama says I play it pretty."

"It was lovely," Jack told her, and tried to contend with the fact that this woman might be Kelly's grandmother.

She reached for a framed photo of a young woman holding a baby and showed it to him. "This is my mama and me when I was a baby. Isn't she pretty?"

Since the woman in the photo was wearing a modern dress and had her hair styled in that Farrah Fawcett look from the seventies, Jack doubted she was Evelyn's mother. "Yes, she is," Jack assured her. "This is my partner, Miss Evelyn. His name is Leon."

"He's very tall. Almost as big as my papa."

Since Leon was bigger than most men, he couldn't help but wonder how big the woman's father had been. "We'd like to talk to you for a few minutes if we could. Would that be all right?"

She lowered her head, looked up at him out of shy eyes. "Mama said I mustn't ever talk to men again unless her or papa are with me."

"It's all right for you to talk to these men," Mrs. Floyd told her.

"You promise Mama won't get mad? She was really mad at me for talking to Johnny Connors. She said he was up to no good and that I was a bad girl 'cause I let him kiss me."

Oh, boy, Jack thought, and exchanged a glance with Leon.

"Neither of these gentlemen are going to try to kiss you. And I'll be right here with you, so it's all right to talk to them. I promise," Mrs. Floyd assured her.

She grinned again, the grin of a young girl. "All right. Do you want to sit next to me and I'll teach you to play the piano?"

"Tell you what? Why don't I sit next to you and we'll just talk. Would that be okay?"

After a glance at Mrs. Floyd, who nodded, she said, "Okay. What do you want to talk about?" she asked as she scooted over on the bench to make room for him.

"I wanted to talk to you about Dr. Martin Gilbert. Do you remember Dr. Gilbert, Miss Evelyn?"

She frowned. "Marty?" A confused look came into her eyes. "Did Marty come back?"

"No, Marty isn't here right now. But we need to talk to you about him," Jack told her. "He needs your help, Evelyn. He needs us to get in touch with his good friend. Remember his good friend? The one he used to call when he needed a favor?"

"Mustn't tell. Mustn't ever tell or he'll hurt the baby."

"What baby, Evelyn? Who will hurt the baby? Is it Marty?"

"Do you know how to play 'Jingle Bells'?" she asked. "I know how to play 'Jingle Bells.' Listen, I'll play it for you."

And as she began playing the Christmas tune, Jack knew further conversation now wouldn't yield any results. "Thank you, Evelyn," he said, but she gave no indication she heard him. She simply continued to play.

"As I said, she drifts in and out," Mrs. Floyd told them as she escorted them from the room.

"Does she ever get any visitors?" Jack asked, hoping maybe someone close to her might know something.

Mrs. Floyd shook her head. "I'm afraid not. Her husband—or at least the man she said was her husband—only came a couple of times since she's been here."

"When was the last time?"

"Oh, gee, it must be about a month ago. And the visit was really short, if you ask me. Didn't seem at all concerned about her."

Sounded like Gilbert, Jack thought. "You mentioned she was in stage three of Alzheimer's. Does that mean it's going to get worse?"

"Unfortunately, yes. When a patient reaches stage five, they often become violent. So when that happens we'll have to move her to another facility. But for now, our Evelyn is quite delightful."

"Thank you very much for your time, Mrs. Floyd," Jack told her, and shook hands.

"Yes, thank you," Leon echoed.

"My pleasure. I'm just sorry the visit didn't prove more productive for you. Perhaps you can come back and try another time."

"We'll do that," Jack said, and exited the nursing home with Leon.

And the next time he came, he would bring Kelly, Jack decided. If Evelyn couldn't provide them with the answers they needed, maybe...just maybe...Kelly might be able to help him get them.

"Okay, that's the last of them," Kelly told Meredith as she finished unpacking the boxes of ridiculously priced and incredibly uncomfortable shoes. Although she worked in fashion and had a healthy love of clothes, she wasn't a slave to it. So she didn't understand why any woman would spend a small fortune on strips of gold and silver and colored leather or plastic that would make her calves ache for a week.

"We still have the evening bags to unbox," Meredith told her as she dashed back into the storage room to get an armload of shimmering wraps.

"Forget it. If I have to spend another minute sifting through boxes of tissue and peanut packing, I'll slit my throat."

"Well, I guess we could take a short break," Meredith conceded. "Come on, I have a fridge out back. But just remember, we need to make this quick. We've still got to get those evening bags unpacked before we leave this evening."

"What is this 'we' stuff?" Kelly asked as she followed her to the rear of the shop, past more boxes and racks filled with merchandise to an area that had been set up with a desk, filing cabinet and fax machine. "In case you've forgotten, I'm free labor here. That means I'm working for nothing."

She opened the fridge. "Water or diet cola?"

"Any real cola?"

Meredith gave her a look and handed her a regular Coke and snagged a diet one for herself. She sat down behind the desk. "I'd hardly call being paid with an Elie Saab original nothing."

"I thought you said it looked like an Elie Saab," Kelly corrected her, and moved a stack of fashion magazines from the side chair and sat down. And it was a darned good knockoff, Kelly admitted.

"What I meant to say was that it looked like one of the higher-end designs I'd seen by Elie Saab. But this one was priced to accommodate the everyday woman. That's why I got it for the shop."

Kelly laughed. "Meredith, the everyday woman does not spend five thousand dollars for a dress. The truth is, I can't believe I'm doing it. I must be out of my mind."

"You're not paying for it," Meredith reminded her after taking another sip from her drink. "You're swapping your services as a photographer for it. And don't even think about trying to renege on our deal because I'm holding you to it."

"Don't worry. I'm not going to renege on the deal."

Meredith sat forward, a mischievous gleam in her light eyes. "I don't suppose you'd reconsider and do the brochure for Christmas?"

"No. And unless I get moving and find a place to set up a darkroom, you won't have it for Valentine's Day, either."

"So you're really serious about sticking around New Orleans?"

"Yes," Kelly told her, although her agent had been none too pleased with her about that decision. Yet she had little choice if she was going to find out who killed Sister Grace and why that person wanted her dead.

"How long are you planning to stay?"

"I'm not sure. Maybe a month, maybe two." Or longer, depending on what she was able to find out. "Long enough to do your brochure and take care of some personal business."

"That personal business, does it have anything to do with Jack?"

"What do you mean?" Kelly asked.

Meredith brushed an imaginary piece of lint from her winter-white slacks. "I'm just wondering what your intentions are toward my brother. Are you serious about him?"

"Meredith, I really don't think—"

"That it's any of my business? You're right. It's not. But when has that ever stopped me?" she replied smoothly.

"Probably never."

She ran one beautifully manicured nail down the side of her cola bottle. "Exactly. But the truth is I think Jack's serious about you. And no matter how much I want you to do that brochure for me, you should know that I'll cut your heart out and ship it back to New York in one of my pretty little boxes if you do anything to hurt him." She lifted her gaze to Kelly's and smiled. "I do hope you understand."

"Of course. I just hope you understand that Jack is the last person in the world whom I'd want to hurt." And the person most likely to be hurt was her.

"Well, I'm glad we've got that out of the way," Meredith replied. "So why don't you tell me what you're looking for in the way of a rental?"

"Something with a couple of rooms, preferably at least one without any windows, where the landlord will allow me to install some tanks for developing film," she explained. "I spoke with Peter and he recommended I talk with Alicia Van Owen. I met her at your mother's party and told her I'd call her.''

''Forget about Alicia. The little viper will probably lock you into a long-term lease on something you don't want or need,'' Meredith insisted.

''Both Peter and Jack said she was very good.''

''What do they know? They're men,'' Meredith said with no small amount of disdain. ''Besides, why would you want to waste your time with Miss Butter-just-melts-in-her-mouth Van Owen when I already have the perfect place for you.''

''*You* do?''

''Yes, I do.''

''And just where is this perfect place?'' Kelly asked.

''Upstairs,'' Meredith told her with a grin. ''I've rented the spaces above me for the next two years. The place directly above this one used to be a gift shop, but it's been empty for a while. So I asked that an option to expand Indulgences to the second level be built into my current lease. That way if the shop's a hit, I won't be faced with a major jump in my rent too soon and will only have to handle the build-out.''

''Very clever,'' Kelly said.

''I thought so,'' Meredith said. ''I was planning to use the third floor apartment for storage space. But I don't have to have it.'' She pulled open the desk drawer, snagged a set of keys and said, ''Come take a look and tell me what you think.''

''I think it's perfect,'' Kelly told her fifteen minutes later after she walked through the apartment a second time. Located on the third floor of the building above

Meredith's shop, the place was small with a combination kitchen/living room, a medium-size bedroom and a surprisingly large bath. "I'd need to blacken or board up the windows in this room, but I could set up my developing tubs here and here. And I could have lines running across there for hanging my proofs," she said, more to herself than to Meredith as she envisioned dressing out the room. She turned to Meredith. "How much?"

Meredith told her the figure.

"How long a lease would I need to sign?"

"A year."

"Three months," Kelly countered.

"Six months, and not a day less."

"All right, six months." Compared to what she was paying for her place in New York and the added cost of the hotel suite during peak convention season, the place was a steal. Exiting the bedroom, she scanned the living area. She could also continue searching through Sister Grace's correspondence and journals without worrying about the housekeeping staff seeing any of the nun's personal writings. She'd also feel better knowing that no one else had access to the items. "There should be enough room in here for a sofa sleeper, maybe even a coffee table and a couple of chairs. Don't you think?"

"I suppose so. But why would you want a sofa sleeper in here?"

"To sleep on," Kelly informed her.

Meredith looked appalled. "Kelly Santos, don't tell me you're thinking of living here?"

"Why not? I'd have everything I need, plus a darkroom for my work. And it was obviously designed as living quarters."

"But where would you put your clothes? And what about your dressing table and your makeup and accessories and…and…"

"And what?" Kelly teased, unable to help but be amused by Meredith.

"Essentials," the other woman said, exasperated.

"Meredith, what I consider essentials and what you consider essentials are two different things."

"Obviously." She looked around the small space and shuddered. "You know, we have a huge house with lots of empty rooms. My mother would love to have you stay with us."

"Thanks, but I don't think so."

"What about Jack's place?"

"What about it?" Kelly asked.

"Well, if you and he are…"

"No," Kelly replied. "I like living alone." And she was used to it, she told herself. She'd resigned herself to being alone a long time ago. Just because she and Jack were engaged in an affair was no reason to think things would change.

Meredith shrugged. "Suit yourself. I'll have Peter draw up a lease tomorrow and I'll need a check for the first and last month's rent."

Kelly eyed her curiously, impressed by how smoothly she'd reeled her into the deal.

"What?" Meredith asked.

"I was just remembering you telling me that your brothers were the smart ones and you were just the pretty one, that your looks were all you had going for you."

"So?"

"So you underestimate yourself, Meredith. You're a good businesswoman."

Meredith beamed. "You mean that?"

"I wouldn't have said it if I didn't."

"Well, thanks. And you're not so bad yourself, especially for someone…you know, who's a little strange at times with that mind-reading thing."

"Gee, thanks," Kelly said dryly.

"Come on, don't be that way," she said. "I was paying you a compliment. Now, why don't we go downstairs and you let me see if we can find you some pretty new workday clothes."

"I like my jeans and sweaters just fine."

"But we really need to put you in something with a little more color. And I think I have just the thing."

"Whatever it is, I can't afford it," Kelly informed her.

"Sure you can," Meredith insisted. She hooked her arm through Kelly's and angled her toward the door. "Don't worry. I'll give you a deal."

And that was just what she was afraid of, Kelly thought as she followed the other woman out of the apartment.

"You know, I still can't believe Meredith got you to agree to do those photos for her," Jack said after he'd bought dinner for both his sister and Kelly and was now taking Kelly back to her hotel.

"I can't believe she did it, either. All I know was that one minute I was helping her unpack boxes in her shop and the next minute I was agreeing to do a brochure for her and negotiating a lease on the apartment upstairs."

"Remind me to thank my sister," he said as he turned onto the street leading to the hotel.

"She's a businesswoman," Kelly told him. "I think Meredith has finally found her calling."

"I think you might be right. Maybe I'll buy a few things from her shop to show her my appreciation."

"A word of caution. Leave your credit cards at home or she'll have you maxing them out in no time."

He laughed. "I'll remember that."

"You didn't have to have Meredith baby-sit me, you know."

"I know," Jack replied. He drove the car into the garage of the hotel and began climbing the ramp. "But I've got a bad feeling about this case. The link to Gilbert and Sister Grace is you." He pulled the car into a parking slot, shut off the engine and turned to her. "If we're going to find the killer—" he began, refusing to think of the murderer as Kelly's sister "—we need to find out who your parents were."

"I know."

"I realize that isn't something you wanted, but I don't see where we have much choice."

"I understand," she said, but he could see the shadows in her eyes.

Jack tipped up her chin, leaned across the seat and kissed her gently. "Whatever I find out, it's not going to make any difference in how I feel about you."

"It's getting late," she began, and although she didn't physically pull away from him, he could feel her doing so emotionally. "Maybe it would be better if you didn't come up. I really wanted to read through some more of those journals tonight."

"Then I won't stay long. I'll just make sure that you get to your room safely," he said, frustration gnawing at him. He felt as though each time he took a step forward with Kelly, she took two steps back. But he was a patient man, he reminded himself. He would just have to be patient and prove to her that he wasn't going to disappear the way everyone else in her life had.

"I hardly expect anyone to mug me here at the Regent," she told him as they exited the car and made their way to the elevators.

"Neither do I. But I'll sleep better if I see you to your room myself."

Together they stepped into the elevator and rode to her floor in silence. When they reached her room, Jack held out his hand for the room card. She retrieved it from her bag and handed it to him. Jack inserted the coded card, and when the green light flashed, signaling the door was unlocked, he turned the knob and motioned for Kelly to precede him.

Kelly stepped inside the room and came to a halt. Her entire body went stiff.

Someone was here.

"What's wrong?" he asked as she stood frozen.

"She was here. Sister Grace's killer was in my room."

He pushed her behind him and said, "Stay here." Then he reached for the weapon in the holster at the small of his back, withdrew it and moved farther into the room.

"She's gone," Kelly said from behind him.

"Just stay put," he insisted, and checked out the suite, anyway, first the bedroom, then the bath and back to the main room. But as far as he could see, nothing looked out of place. No drawers had been pulled open. No bed stripped. No closets ransacked. Yet he didn't doubt for a second that Kelly was right. He believed her. Returning his weapon to its holster, he headed toward the phone. He'd have the place dusted for prints and have Security do a check and find out who had access keys to the room. Intent on calling hotel security, he grabbed the telephone receiver.

"They won't find her prints. She wore gloves and she used a maid's key and uniform that she swiped for access."

Jack hung up the phone. Frustration and worry pummeled him.

She walked over to where the boxes of journals and correspondence had been stacked up against one wall. "She was looking for something," Kelly began.

"You're not staying here tonight. You're coming with me to my place," Jack told her. "Go pack a bag."

But Kelly didn't seem to hear him. She stooped down in front of the boxes, a strange expression on her face, as though she saw something that he couldn't see. And then she began to speak.

"It has to be here. It has to be. Where is it? Where is the damn thing? I've got to find it and destroy it before that bitch gets her hands on it. How dare she come back here? How dare she think she can steal what's mine?"

"Kelly," Jack said, afraid for her.

"Where is it? Shit! The maid's at the door to turn down the bed. Have to get out of here before she sees me. Have to try again later. Too bad I can't just get rid

of her now once and for all. But can't do that yet. Not until I find it.''

Alarmed, Jack grabbed her by the arm and pulled her to her feet. "Kelly, come out of it. Come out of it, baby."

Kelly blinked, fell limply against his chest. "There's so much rage, so much hate inside her. She wants me dead. And she intends to kill me. But killing me isn't enough. She needs to...she needs to erase me."

"It's all right," he soothed. "No one's going to hurt you. Let's go pack a bag and you can come home with me."

"No." She lifted her head, gazed up at him. "I have to stay. I have to see if I can find out what it is she's looking for."

"Then I'm staying with you."

Seventeen

Kelly still couldn't believe everything that had happened in the space of a week. Alone in her new apartment, she collapsed atop the sofa bed, which Jack had personally delivered, with the help of Leon, the previous afternoon. She, Jack and everyone around them had moved at a frenetic pace since that night in her hotel room to get her moved into the apartment above Meredith's shop. She didn't even want to think about the arms that had been twisted to get the place painted, the phone line installed and the darkroom conversion done so quickly. But at last the task was complete. While the fumes from the fresh coat of paint were still a bit strong, they were bearable. And while she hadn't wanted to admit it, she'd been as anxious as Jack for the move.

She'd gotten a few pieces of furniture, had allowed Meredith to talk her into springing for some new clothes, and had notified everyone who needed to know of her new address and phone number. The only thing she still needed was her camera equipment—and Wyatt was handling that. She still wasn't at all sure about this turn in her relationship with Jack. She wasn't used to sharing her problems or herself with anyone. Yet, she'd found herself sharing both with him. Probably because she'd been too shaken by first the discovery of who she really was, and then to find that someone had been searching her hotel room, to fight him.

And as unsettling as all of the activity had been over the past week, it had helped to keep her from dwelling on the fact that she was responsible, at least in part, for Sister Grace's death. What it hadn't done was lessen her determination to find the person who had killed the nun. A woman who was her own sister—a woman who wanted her dead, too.

But who was she? And who had Sarah Tompkins belonged to? Jack had told her about Gilbert's nurse with the same last name. Could this Evelyn Tompkins be her mother? And who had been her father? What about the fire that haunted her dreams? And who was her sister— the mystery woman who'd killed Gilbert? What had been their connection to Sister Grace? Her mind swimming with questions, Kelly looked over at the journal she'd left on the coffee table the previous evening. Somewhere within those journals there had to be answers.

Picking up the journal, she began reading the entries again. An hour later, she closed the book and was about to select another one when the telephone rang. Setting aside the journal, she picked up the telephone receiver. "Hello, Wyatt."

After a pause, he quipped, "I do wish you wouldn't do that. It messes with my rhythm—especially when I'm calling to badger you again and plead with you to come to your senses."

Kelly sighed. Sinking back down on the couch, she listened to her agent recount all the reasons she had to come back to New York, how she should forget about this foolish notion to extend her stay in New Orleans and the warning that she would be virtually committing career suicide if she did. After a particularly long rant, during which she'd remained silent, he demanded, "Kelly, have you even heard a word I've said?"

"Of course," she replied. "You said, and I quote, 'It's bad enough that you're committing career suicide for yourself, but you're going to put me in the poorhouse while you do it,' end quote."

"And that doesn't matter to you?" he demanded. "That I'm liable to find myself living on the streets?"

"Wyatt, you and I both know that you represent at least a half-dozen photographers with much higher profiles and earning power than me. As for you living on the street, the truth is you could probably open your own bank branch just to hold all the money you're making."

"But, darling, you know you're my favorite. Why, I've been so distraught over the way you're throwing your career away that I'm seriously considering shutting down the agency."

Kelly laughed. She had to because the statement was so outrageous. "The only way anyone will get you to close that office is when they carry you out in a wooden box for your funeral."

He sighed. "You know me too well, Kelly Santos. That's why I love you. I want you to come home."

"I know you do," she said, feeling a tug of affection for the man who had been her agent and friend for so long. "But I have obligations here that I have to take care of first."

"One of those obligations wouldn't happen to be the gentleman who answered your phone the other morning when I called, would it?"

Kelly squirmed in her seat. "Jack is...he's a good friend," she told him. "But he's not the reason I'm staying." She hadn't let her relationship with Jack play any part in her decisions. And she didn't intend to let that change. She couldn't afford to. If she were to find Sister Grace's killer, her emotions had to stay out of it. "It's a personal matter, Wyatt. I'm sorry, but I can't explain. You'll just have to trust me. I know what I'm doing."

"I hope you do, my darling. I certainly hope you do," he said with another sigh—this one of resignation.

She prayed that she did, too. "What about my equipment?" she asked, feeling the need to change the subject.

"I went over to your place with Gino, and I must say, Kelly darling, I don't know what you've been doing with your money, but it's obvious you haven't been spending it on your living quarters." He made a tsking sound. "Darling, we really must find you a new place when you come home. Why, I have closets bigger than that place."

"It seems everyone does," she said. "Wyatt, the equipment?"

"Oh, yes. Well, I had everything boxed up and shipped off to you. It should be there in a few days."

"Thanks. You're a sweetheart."

"I know," he said proudly. "But you know, Kelly, I've been thinking. If you're truly determined to stay in that heathen place and want to do some work while you're there, I could make a few calls. Now mind you, it won't be the same caliber of work or fees that you're used to getting here, and Lord knows no one down there is going to fly you to Europe for any shoots, but you won't have to resort to snapping photos of tourists on street corners, either."

"Thanks. I appreciate the offer, but I've already lined up a job to do a slick brochure for a high-end boutique here," she told him.

"Tell me you haven't already negotiated your fee."

Kelly smiled. "Yes, I'm afraid I have."

"You really shouldn't have done that, darling. You artists are terrible with the business end of things. Maybe it's not too late for me to fix things. Why don't you fax the contract over to me and I'll take a look at it, see if I can improve the terms."

"I'm sorry, I can't do that. I already took my fee in merchandise."

Wyatt groaned. "This is why you need an agent for these things, Kelly. Don't you see what's happened here? You've let some fast-talking boutique owner hustle you into being paid off in overpriced merchandise. You're liable to end up starving. Now, I want you to promise me that before you sign another contract with anyone that you'll send it to Uncle Wyatt first."

"All right. I promise."

After thanking him again and promising to stay in touch, Kelly hung up the phone and went back to reading the journals. Nearly two hours later, the words had begun to blur so Kelly closed the book and stood. She stretched to ease the muscles in her neck and back, then walked over to the window. She stared out at the rain that had been falling since she'd awakened at daybreak. She smiled, remembering how she'd awakened that morning with the feel of Jack's lips on her bare shoulder.

For someone who had spent most of her nights alone and valued her private space, she'd quickly grown accustomed to having him spend the nights with her, she admitted. Not even Garrett, a man she'd loved with all her heart, had invaded her life so completely the way that Jack Callaghan had. In just a few short weeks, she'd come to anticipate the feel of his body next to hers in the night, the weight of his arm slung across her, the

scent of him on her skin. Even that morning she'd
thrilled at the nip of his teeth on her flesh, his hands
cupping her breasts. And it had been she who had turned
to him in those early hours of the morning, wet and
wanton. It had been she who had reached for him,
guided him inside her. It had been she who had clung
to him, cried out his name as he took them both through
the storm.

Made breathless by the memory, Kelly turned away
from the window. Reminding herself that she couldn't
afford to allow her emotions to cloud her judgment or
deter her from her mission to find Sister Grace's killer,
she went back to the boxes of journals. The answer was
there somewhere within the pages of one of those journals, she told herself. It had to be and she had to find it.
And with that thought in mind, she reached for another
journal—one of the older ones, she guessed by the faded
cover and yellowing pages.

Returning to the sofa, she opened the journal and began to read an entry made nearly thirty years ago.

*I heard from Lianne today. Oh, what a joy it was to
hear her sweet voice again. I have missed her so in these
months since she left us to make her way in the world.
There has been an ache, an emptiness inside me that I
imagine is similar to that of a mother when her little
one leaves the nest. I know that is probably wrong of
me, that I should not feel such an affection for Lianne,
and I will have to pray to the Blessed Mother and our
Savior for forgiveness. For I know we're not supposed
to have favorites among the girls. They're all God's children entrusted to us and each is deserving of our love.
Yet there has always been something special about
Lianne. I've felt it from the time she first came to us as
a child. I know many of the girls here were jealous of*

her because of her physical beauty and I know it is her physical beauty that most people see first. But there is so much more to the girl, an inner beauty that eclipses the outer loveliness.

Kelly's heart raced as she finished the entry. Could there have been two Liannes at St. Ann's? No, not likely, she reasoned. This had to be the Lianne who'd called for Sister Grace. Yet this Lianne would have to be in her late forties by now and Sister Mary Clarence had insisted it was a young woman who had called the convent. Sure that she was on to something, Kelly continued to skim through the pages of the journal, searching for more entries referring to Lianne. She found another one five months later.

Lianne called today. I don't think I've ever heard her so excited. She was like a child on Christmas morning, just bursting with joy. She told me that she had wonderful news—that she had found her birth mother. The woman was living nearby all these years in Mississippi. She claims to have never forgotten the baby girl that had been taken from her. Lianne was so thrilled to learn that she had been wanted, that I didn't have the heart to tell her the truth—that her mother had been little more than a girl herself when her family had sent her to us pregnant with her own father's child.

Kelly gasped as the implication of what she'd read hit her. Lianne had been the result of incest—fathered by her own grandfather. Lianne's mother had borne her own father's child. Poor Lianne, she thought. And Lianne's poor mother. She couldn't even imagine what that must have been like for the woman. With tears in her eyes, Kelly picked up reading where she'd left off....

Lianne finding her mother was the one thing I prayed would not happen. Even when Lianne had first told me that she wanted to find the woman who had given her life, I had tried to discourage her. I so feared what it would do to her were she to learn that she was the result of an incestuous relationship between a father and daughter. That poor girl had paid a toll because of what that evil man had done to her. She'd been unstable, not able to care for herself, let alone a child. If only Lianne hadn't gone to look for her.

Perhaps I should have lied to Lianne, told her the woman who had borne her had died in childbirth. But I feared even more that she would then search for her father, so I remained silent. Now that decision to remain silent has come back to haunt me. I know it is a sin to lie, but surely God would have forgiven me a lie told to protect the innocent. Alas, I can only pray that Lianne will never learn the truth. I will also encourage her to move on with her life and pursue her dream of painting.

Tears streamed down Kelly's cheeks as she finished the entry. Poor Lianne, she thought, feeling an empathy for this girl that Sister Grace had loved so much. She skimmed through several more entries and learned that Lianne had gotten a job, working in a doctor's office and that she had met someone, a fine gentleman from a good family.

A doctor's office in Mississippi? Gilbert had been a doctor in Mississippi. A coincidence? No. Jack had been right. There was no such thing as a coincidence. Had Lianne been the woman in the church who had killed Sister Grace? Had she been the one who'd killed Gilbert? Had Lianne discovered the truth and killed them both to keep the truth about her paternity a secret?

Quickly Kelly flipped through the pages, searching for names, places. She found none, just more reflections of Sister Grace's daily life, the financial problems at St.

Ann's, the nun's own sense of needing to do more. Then she spied Lianne's name again.

Lianne called today. Except for a card and the watercolor she sent me for my birthday, it was the first time I had heard from her in months. I thanked her again for the lovely picture and told her that I'd had it framed and placed in my office at St. Ann's. I was so glad to hear from her that it took me several minutes before I realized that something was wrong. Finally, Lianne broke down in tears and confessed. She had sinned and was too ashamed to tell me. She is pregnant and the fine gentleman whose child she carries in her belly is already married. Although she refused to tell me his name, she did say that he is a prominent figure and his name is one I might recognize. He cannot afford to be touched by the scandal a divorce would cause at this time. She intends to keep the child and when the time is right and he can leave his marriage, they are to be married. Alas, I fear my Lianne is wrong. I tried my best to reason with her, but there was no dissuading her from the course she has chosen. She has asked me to pray for her, for her and her child's father to be together. Though it pained me to deny her, I could not in good conscious condone this match. Nor could I promise to pray for this man to break his vows to his wife so that he can be with Lianne. But I will pray for Lianne nonetheless, and beseech Our Lady to guide her and protect her innocent unborn child.

When she came to the end of the entry, Kelly poured through the rest of the pages but found no further mention of Lianne or her child. Mulling over what she'd just read, she considered the implications. Gilbert had been a physician, an occupation that many would consider prominent. He was also married. Was it possible that

both Lianne and her own mother had been involved with
Gilbert? Had they both borne him children? No. That
couldn't be. The killer had called Gilbert 'doctor,' not
'father.' So who was the father of Lianne's child? Who
was her father? And what had happened to Lianne's
child? Oh, God. Was it possible that Lianne wasn't her
sister, but her mother?

More questions without answers, Kelly thought.
Weary, she set aside the journal and stood. She walked
over to the wall where she had hung the watercolor left
to her by Sister Grace. The picture itself was simple—a
small wooden house painted yellow with white trim.
Two huge magnolia trees sat in the yard beyond the
house and a swing fashioned out of rope and a wooden
seat was suspended from the branches. Kelly leaned
closer to try to read the signature in the lower right-hand
corner. And there it was. In small flowery letters with a
heart dotting the ''i'' was the inscription *Lianne.*

So engrossed was she with the discovery that Kelly
didn't hear the knock at her door, nor did she hear Meredith calling her name until the other woman had used
her key to enter the apartment.

''Jesus, Kelly! I swear, I think I may have bruised my
knuckles I was pounding so hard. Didn't you hear me?''

Kelly blinked and stared at Jack's sister, who was
decked out in a fashionable cranberry suit. ''I'm sorry,
I guess I wasn't paying attention.''

''You look...strange.'' Meredith frowned. ''Are you
all right?''

''Yes,'' she said, and tried to shake off the lingering
worries that she had picked up from Sister Grace's journals. ''Did you need something?''

''A favor. Can you watch the shop for me while I run
to the bank? The idiot computer keeps saying that I have

the wrong access code and I can't get a real person on the phone. So I need to go over there. And before you tell me no…'' Meredith launched into the reasons she needed Kelly to do her this favor. ''So you see, if I'm not here to accept the delivery and it has to be rescheduled, there's a chance I won't have the merchandise in time for the preview party. And if I don't, I may as well just close up the shop before it opens. So will you come downstairs and keep an eye out for the delivery truck for me?''

''Sure.''

Meredith beamed, reached over and gave her a little hug. ''Thanks. You're a lifesaver.''

After grabbing another journal from the box and her camera, Kelly locked up her apartment and followed Meredith downstairs to baby-sit the shop.

Alex didn't notice her until he'd passed the shop a second time. That's when he spied the blonde slouching on a chair next to a jungle of red-and-white poinsettias and a mess of frilly things with her nose buried in a book. Much to his disappointment, she wasn't Meredith.

He looked at the prettily wrapped box he held in his hands that contained the charm bracelet he'd purchased for Meredith. A token gift to wish her good luck with the shop, he'd told himself when he'd picked it out at the jewelers'. Standing there on the sidewalk under the awning while the rain teemed down in the streets only inches away, he felt like an idiot.

Admit it, Kusak. You miss Meredith. You bought the gift and came by to deliver it because you want to see her.

It was the truth, he admitted with a scowl. Since that scene in the gardens at her mother's he hadn't been able to erase the memory of that bruised look in her big green eyes before she'd walked away. He'd felt lower than the belly of a snake and had been in a piss-poor mood ever since. And he was sick of feeling like someone had ripped the heart right out of him.

So he'd come by with the gift and a trumped-up reason to see her.

And hoped for what?

He didn't know. He only knew that there had been no late-night phone calls from Meredith. No surprise visits to his office. No coming home to his apartment to discover her waiting for him on his doorstep with a bottle of wine, a slab of cheese and French bread and wearing nothing beneath her coat but skin.

Obviously Meredith had taken him at his word this time and had accepted the fact that they had no future together. After all, he'd meant it when he'd told her that it was over, that she needed to move on with her life. It was what he'd wanted, what he'd been trying to get her to do, Alex reminded himself. So why in the hell was he so damned miserable?

Deciding he'd made a mistake by coming there, he was about to walk away when the blonde looked up. Her eyes met his through the window. And before he had a chance to take more than three steps out into the rain, she was at the door. "Alex? Alex? It's Kelly. Kelly Santos. If you're looking for Meredith, she's not here right now."

Heedless of the rain pelting him, he made no attempt to get under the awning again. "Oh well, I'll come back then."

"Is that for Meredith?" she asked, indicating the wrapped box in his hand.

"Yes. Just a little something to wish her good luck with the party this weekend. I'll catch her later."

"But you're getting soaked and so is Meredith's gift. Why don't you come inside and dry off?"

"I really should go. I have a ton of work waiting for me back at the office."

"And I'm sure it'll still be there when you get back. Come on," she said, waving for him to come inside. "Meredith just ran to the bank. She'll be back in a few minutes. In the meantime, we can keep each other company."

Seeing no polite way to refuse, he let her urge him inside the store. "Okay, but I've only got a few minutes."

"That's fine," she said as she locked the door behind him.

"Meredith's not going to be too happy with me if she discovers I've dripped all over her floor," he joked.

"Something tells me that she'll forgive you," Kelly said. "Why don't you take off your coat and dry off a bit while I see if I can revive the ribbon on your package?"

"Thanks," he said, and handed her the package. Then he hung up his wet coat on the rack next to the door.

"There are some towels in the bathroom out back. Just go through those doors and you can't miss it," Kelly told him, and motioned him in the direction of the rear of the shop.

When he exited the bathroom a few minutes later, Kelly was in the working area at the back of the shop where a small kitchen had been set up with a refrigerator, tables and chairs and a microwave.

"You look like you could use this," she said, handing him a steaming cup of coffee.

"Thanks."

"Meredith has one of those fancy cappuccino machines, but I'm afraid I don't know how to use it. So you're stuck with my bad coffee."

He took a sip. "Tastes fine to me."

"Glad you approve," she said as she walked over to the countertop and began blotting the red ribbon on the box with a dish towel.

Alex drank his coffee in silence and watched her. He noted, as he had when he'd met her at the party, that she was not much for small talk. Apparently she didn't feel the need to fill the silence. Neither did he, so he sipped the hot brew and regarded the back area of the shop that had so occupied Meredith during the past few months. He noted the tidy desk with fresh flowers atop it, a file cabinet, a computer and fax machine. It was much more businesslike than he'd expected from Meredith. "This is quite a setup Meredith has here."

"You sound surprised."

"I guess I am. I didn't know she was taking this so seriously. When it comes to a career path, Meredith tends to have a short attention span. I'm not saying that to be critical," he offered, not liking the way that sounded. "It's just that she's so talented. She could do just about anything she sets her mind to do and succeed. I guess that's why she keeps switching direction."

"Maybe she keeps switching direction because what she wants hasn't been available to her," Kelly told him as she looked up from her ministrations to the ribbon.

Alex shifted, suspecting she was referring to his and Meredith's relationship. And no way did he intend to discuss that. "Well, I know her family would like to see her stay, so I hope this shop works out for her."

"And what about you, Alex? Do you want her to stay?"

"Sure. I like having Meredith around."

"You should tell her that," Kelly said nonchalantly as she poked at the ribbon.

Deciding to ignore the remark, he said, "Jack said you work in fashion. Do you think this shop of hers has a shot?" The last thing he wanted was for Meredith to be disappointed again.

"Well, I'm a fashion photographer. I'm not in retail, but from what I've seen Meredith's got a real feel for the market, for what's hot and selling. And my personal opinion is that she's going to clean up."

"Really?"

Kelly nodded. "She's a smart, savvy businesswoman. I almost feel sorry for the people who come through the doors once this place opens. Like lambs to slaughter."

"No kidding."

"No kidding. I've seen Meredith in action. She could sell snow to an Eskimo."

Alex laughed for the first time in weeks. He was as proud as could be of Meredith. "Sounds like you're speaking from personal experience."

"I am," she told him. And as she refilled his coffee cup and poured one for herself, she explained how Meredith had conned her into trading her photography services for merchandise.

He wasn't surprised. He'd always known that Meredith was bright. It had simply been a question of whether or not she would stick with something, or grow bored and move on to another venture. The only reason their relationship had probably lasted as long as it had was because she'd never stuck around for very long. Sooner

or later she would move on again, he told himself as he
took another swig of black coffee.

"You're wrong, you know. She's staying this time."

Alex jerked his head up, narrowed his eyes. Suddenly
he remembered the stories at the dinner table a couple
of weeks ago, about how Kelly had this ability to see
things, know things.

"That was very rude of me. I'm sorry. But it's obvious that you love Meredith. What I don't understand
is why you haven't told her."

"Because she deserves better," he confessed, and put
his coffee cup down with a slap.

"You're what she wants. She loves you."

"Meredith only thinks she loves me. She's always had
a wild streak in her, a tendency to want what's not good
for her. In this case, it was me. I'm not going to let her
throw her life away."

"Actually, you don't have a say in the matter," a
familiar voice said from behind him.

Alex jerked his attention over to the doorway, where
Meredith stood looking beautiful and polished in a snug
red jacket, short skirt and matching heels. She also
looked angry as hell.

"I better go back out front and wait for that delivery-
man," Kelly said. She picked up the still-damp box, and
shoved it in his hands. "Nice seeing you again, Alex."
And within moments, she was gone, leaving him alone
with a none-too-happy-looking Meredith.

Meredith removed her jacket and hung it up neatly by
the door. She brushed past him in the tiny kitchen and
went over to the cappuccino machine. As she did so, he
caught a whiff of some exotic floral scent mixed with
rain as she moved by. She measured coffee, fed it into
the fancy machine, then walked past him again, as she

made her way over to her desk. She picked up a stack of mail and began to peruse it. "Was there any particular reason you came by?" she asked.

Alex stared at her, noted the way the red-silk top flowed over her breasts like water. Three shiny ribbons held the edges of fabric together and he found himself hoping for a glimpse of skin.

"Alex?"

Alex snapped his gaze back to her face. "What?"

"Did you come by for a reason?"

He looked down at the package in his hands. "Yes. To bring you a little gift to wish you good luck with the shop," he said, and held up the package in his hands.

"Well, are you going to give it to me?"

He walked over to her and handed her the gift. "Congratulations on the shop, Meredith."

She smiled at him and the twitch of those red lips made him ache. Like a kid at Christmas, she oohed and aahed over the wrapping, and when he would have ripped the thing open, she took her time. By the time she finally got down to the jewelry box, he was almost as anxious as she was. "Oh, Alex, it's lovely," she told him as she removed the charm bracelet from the velvet box. He'd selected three charms—a star, a champagne bottle and a high heel—and had them anchored to a rope of gold. She held out her wrist. "Will you put it on for me?"

He worked the clasp around her delicate wrist, keenly aware of the feel of her soft skin, of her scent. "There you go."

She held it up to the light and laughed in delight. "Oh, it's simply wonderful. Thank you," she said, and kissed him smack on the lips.

"You're welcome," he told her, and forced himself

to ease her away from him. He moved to the opposite side of the desk. "Well, I'd better be going. I've got a lot of work waiting for me. And I'm sure you're busy, too."

Her smile disappeared. So did the light in her green eyes. "So you really did come by just to bring me a gift."

It was a statement, not a question. "To bring the gift and to make sure that you were all right," he confessed. "I was worried about you after that last time we spoke."

"As you can see, I'm fine," she told him, her voice as serious as her eyes. "I didn't fall apart, and obviously I didn't run away like I did the last time you tossed my love back in my face. So if this is a guilt gift, it really wasn't necessary. You have nothing to feel guilty about," she assured him, but there was no mistaking the anger and hurt behind her words.

"Meredith—"

"It was sweet of you to be so concerned about me, Alex. But I already have two brothers to worry about me, I don't need a third."

"I know that," he snapped. "And my concern for you isn't brotherly."

"Then what is it?" she asked innocently as she came to stand directly in front of him. "Was it the concern of a friend? Surely that must be it. I mean, I know we've been sleeping together for years, but you made it clear the last time we spoke that you wanted me to move on to someone else's bed."

"Shut up, Meredith.".

"Why? It's the truth, isn't it? When I said I wanted a real relationship, you told me to count you out. You suggested I look in another direction. So—"

He grabbed her by the shoulders, dragged her against

him. "I said to shut up," he repeated through gritted teeth.

"Make me."

Something inside him snapped. And without thinking of the consequences, he claimed her mouth. He kissed her hard with all the fury and hunger that had been building inside him for weeks. Hell, not weeks, he admitted. Years. Since she'd been a sassy-mouthed kid in braids. When he lifted his head a fraction, he felt a jolt of satisfaction at the dazed look in her eyes. He danced her backward until she came up against the desk, then he angled his mouth and moved in for another taste. Tongues tangled, teeth nipped and he still couldn't get enough.

"Alex," she gasped against his neck. "Please, touch me."

The request ripped away the last thread of his control. He pulled open the dainty bows at the front of her blouse and made short work of the clasp at the front of her bra. He filled his hands with her breasts.

She gasped again as he tweaked the nipples. And suddenly she was tearing at the buttons of his shirt. He heard the fabric give, the sound of buttons flying, and her frenzied response only fed his desire. When her teeth closed over his shoulder, Alex reached behind her, unzipped the skirt and let it fall in a puddle around her ankles. She was wearing a scrap of red lace and a pair of stockings. Real stockings—not panty hose—with lacy edges at the tops that came up to her thighs, designed, he was sure, to tempt a man to sin.

"This is crazy," he warned.

"I know," she said even as she reached for the buckle of his slacks and worked his zipper down.

And it *was* crazy. He was crazy, he told himself as

he pulled off her panties. He swiped his arm across her desk, sent files and paper clips crashing to the floor. Blind with need, he lifted her up on top of the desk. He needed her, wanted her more than he wanted his next breath.

When her fingers encircled him and guided him to her, Alex lost it. Groaning, he drove himself into her. He took her. She took him in a frenzy of heat that had her clinging to him, urging him. When the explosion came, she convulsed around him and cried out his name.

"Meredith," was all he could manage to say before he slammed into her one last time and the world exploded around them.

When the tremors had subsided, Meredith lay limp against him. Horrified by what he had done, Alex zipped his slacks, then picked Meredith up. He carried her over to the small couch and gently laid her down. Grabbing the throw from the arm of the couch, he draped her with it, then knelt down beside her. "Are you all right?"

"I'm a lot better than all right," she told him, a lazy smile curving her lips. She had the look of a kitten that had just finished a bowl of cream. "I love the way we christened my new office. And as soon as I can move again, we'll have to pick a spot in the store next."

"How can you joke about what just happened?"

Her smile faded. "Alex, we made love."

"That wasn't lovemaking. It was…it was brutal. I took you like an animal."

She sat up, heedless of the throw slipping down her shoulder. "There was no taking involved. We were giving to each other, sharing ourselves. That's what two people do when they love each other. I love you, Alex. I thought you loved me. Was I wrong? Have I been kidding myself all these years that you really love me, too?''

He didn't answer her. He couldn't, because if he said the words aloud to himself or to her, he might weaken and never be able to let her go. And he had to let her go. "I don't deserve your love. And you certainly deserve someone better than me, someone who'll treat you the way you deserve to be treated.'' Not the way he'd just treated her, attacking her like some kind of animal in heat. God, he really was no better than his parents.

"What I deserve is a man who isn't a coward. I deserve a man who loves me enough to admit it and to plan a life with me. I want that man to be you, Alex. But if you're not willing to face whatever demons keep making you pull away from me, then I want you to leave.''

She was right, Alex decided. Feeling as though his heart had just been yanked out of his chest, he stood. He walked over by the desk to pick up his tie. Turning back to her, he said, "I'm sorry.''

She looked as though he'd punched her, but she held her chin high like a queen's. No tears for his Meredith, he thought. "If you walk away from me now, Alex Kusak, you walk away from me for good. I'm through running off to lick my wounds and then coming back six months or a year later to let you break my heart again. So if you walk out that door, make sure you don't come back.''

And though it was the hardest thing he'd ever done, he turned away from her and walked out the door.

Eighteen

Jack stopped by his partner's desk at the station house. Shoving aside a stack of files, he sat on the edge of the desk and asked, "You having any luck with those tax returns on Gilbert?"

"I finally tracked down the CPA firm that filed them. The guy who actually did the returns retired and sold the business about ten years ago. The fellow who owns it now said Gilbert wasn't on their client list and they'd never filed any returns for him. But he's going to dig through some of the records they inherited and see what he can find."

"Did he give you a phone number or address where we can contact the former owner?"

Leon held up a slip of paper and flashed him a smile. "The fellow moved to Natchez. I've been trying to call him, but keep getting a busy signal. Guess he didn't want to spring for call-waiting." Leon sat back in his seat. Lowering his voice, he asked, "How about you? Making any progress finding out whether or not Kelly is the Tompkins woman's kid?"

Since Kelly had revealed what she'd learned from the journals, Jack and Leon had pursued the angle that Evelyn Tompkins was the mysterious Lianne's mother. But digging through birth records had proved a daunting task. He'd accessed the New Orleans records but come up empty. There had been no record of Evelyn Tompkins giving birth to a daughter within the two-year period preceding or after what was presumed to be Kelly's birth date. "Nothing in Orleans Parish, so far. I'm just getting started on the surrounding parishes." And he had yet to tackle records from Mississippi.

"Let me see where I get with Gilbert's former CPA, then I'll give you a hand."

"I'd appreciate it. In the meantime, I'm going over to Margee Jardine's office. I think I'll have a better chance of her telling me what she went to see the nun about if I go see her alone."

"No problem," Leon told him. "I'll keep trying to get Gilbert's numbers' man in Natchez."

"Thanks, buddy."

Leon nodded. "Jack," he called out when he started to walk away.

"Yeah?"

"The captain was asking for an update. We're going to have to tell him something, man."

"I know." And he did know. But he was fairly certain that the captain wouldn't approve of the direction in which they were headed—particularly when he learned they were relying on info from a psychic. "Try to stall him. And if you can't, tell him we're running down stuff on the Tompkins woman and her family," he said, which, he reasoned, was the truth.

"All right. But he isn't going to be fooled by that crap for long."

"If we're lucky, we'll be able to hand over the killer to him soon enough." At least that's what he was counting on, Jack told himself as he headed out of the station. Because that warning ache in his neck that he likened to his cop's sixth sense and that had saved his hide on more than one occasion was acting up now. He couldn't shake the feeling that Kelly was right. Whoever Kelly's sister was, she had killed Gilbert and the nun, and was only waiting for an opportunity to take out Kelly. And the closer they got to the truth, the more danger Kelly was in.

He was still thinking about that danger to Kelly when he arrived at Margee Jardine's office thirty minutes later. "Ms. Jardine will see you now," the perky assistant informed him as she ushered him into his old friend's office and closed the door.

"Jack, I'm sorry I kept you waiting, but my conference call ran long," she told him as she came from behind the desk to greet him.

"No problem," he said, and returned the sisterly hug. "Say, this is nice," he told her as his gaze swept over the spacious office. Smart and aggressive, Margee was among the few female attorneys who'd made partner in the law firm.

"Thanks. I'm still trying to get used to having so much space," she told him, her hazel eyes twinkling. "Please have a seat and make yourself comfortable," she said, indicating the chairs positioned in front of the desk.

"Peter seen these new digs yet?"

"No. He claims he's been too busy to come by." Jack thought he detected a note of annoyance in her voice.

"When he does see this place, I have a feeling that Callaghan and Associates is going to be shelling out big bucks for new offices. Especially when I tell him that your office makes his look like a closet."

Margee laughed and the lighthearted sound transformed the sophisticated, all-business attorney sitting across from him into the girl he'd grown up with. "You always did like to stir things up, didn't you?"

"Still do," he told her. "Seriously, you done good, kiddo. I'm proud of you."

"Thanks," she said, and sat back in her chair. "So why don't you tell me what you're doing here? You sounded so serious on the phone."

"I need to talk to you about something personal."

Her smile faltered and her eyes went lawyer serious. "Jack, you're not in any kind of legal trouble, are you?"

"No, no. Nothing like that. This personal thing, it has to do with you, Margee."

"Me?" she replied in surprise.

"Yes. I need to ask you some personal questions."

Her surprise immediately shifted to wariness. "What kind of personal questions?"

Jack took a breath. "Shortly before her death, you made a couple of phone calls to Sister Grace. I need to know what the two of you talked about."

A shield seemed to slide down over her face. "That is none of your business."

"I know it's not, but I need to ask you, anyway." He sat forward. "Margee, I know you called her twice, and the last time you left her a message saying it was important that you speak with her. Please, I need to know what was so important that you had to discuss it with her? It might have something to do with a case I'm working on."

"You're wrong. What she and I discussed was a personal matter between me and Sister Grace."

"Margee—"

"Leave it alone."

"I can't." He could see that he'd upset her and whatever had passed between her and the nun was painful.

He didn't want to add to that pain. Yet with Kelly's life possibly at stake, he couldn't afford not to. "Margee, you know I love you like a sister and the last thing I want to do is upset you. I wouldn't ask if it wasn't important."

"What possible good can come of my telling you something that...that is very painful for me to talk about?" she countered, a hitch in her voice. "No, I won't do it. I promised myself I wouldn't ever talk about this again."

"Would it make a difference if I told you that by doing so you could help me catch a murderer and protect the woman I love?"

Margee's eyes narrowed.

"Kelly Santos," he replied, saving her the trouble of asking. "She thinks Sister Grace was murdered."

"Murdered," Margee repeated, losing some of her defensiveness. "But I thought she had a heart attack."

"That's what someone wanted everybody to think. Kelly believes Sister Grace was injected with some kind of drug that simulated a heart attack."

"And you believe her?"

"Yes, I do," Jack told her.

"Do you have any evidence?"

Jack shook his head. "The body was cremated. But I believe the same person who killed Sister Grace also murdered a doctor from Mississippi a couple of weeks ago. Since the doctor who was killed had also made several calls to Sister Grace, there's a good chance the two murders are connected."

"And this theory of yours, are you basing it on Kelly's psychic impressions?"

Jack's own defenses rose at the skepticism in her tone.

''That and the fact that someone broke into Kelly's hotel room last week. I think she'll go after Kelly next.''

''She? You think the murderer is a woman?''

''The DNA of a hair sample from the crime scene confirms it was a woman in the car with the victim. And we have a witness describing a woman who fits the description.''

Margee scooped her dark blond hair behind her ear. ''Still I don't see how my conversations with Sister Grace has anything to do with your case.''

''It might not. But there were only two people's names that came up that weren't part of her normal circle. Yours and someone named Lianne, who used to live at St. Ann's. So far, I haven't been able to locate this Lianne person. And since Peter's handled any legal matters for Sister Grace since my father passed away, I assume you didn't contact the nun on legal business.''

''As I've already told you, it was personal and I don't see how what we discussed can possibly help you.''

''Why don't you let me be the judge of that.''

She stood and walked over to the sweep of windows that looked out over the busy street. When she turned around, she said, ''All right, I'll tell you, but I want your word it doesn't leave this room.''

''If it impacts this case—''

''Your word, Jack, or I tell you nothing.''

''You have my word. I won't say anything to anyone.''

''That includes Kelly and your partner,'' she insisted.

''I said you have my word,'' he snapped, not liking the fact that she was tying his hands.

''Very well.'' She swallowed. ''I wanted Sister Grace to tell me who my parents were.''

It had been the last thing he'd expected her to tell him. "But Caroline and Robert Jardine—"

"Are not my parents," she said, her voice shaky. "At least they're not my biological parents. I was adopted."

Stunned by the revelation, he said, "I didn't know."

"No one outside of the immediate family knows. I only found out myself by accident a few months ago when my mother had surgery and family members were asked to give blood. My blood type…" She paused, turned away. "Let's just say that I discovered that there was no way that Caroline Jardine could have given birth to me. When Mom came home from the hospital, I confronted her and my father and they told me the truth. They adopted me from St. Ann's when I was an infant. They planned to tell me when I was younger, but didn't know how. After a while, it just didn't seem to matter to them that I had been someone else's child first because I was their child. So they never told me. They never told anyone."

Jack went up behind Margee, squeezed her shoulders. "I'm sorry, kiddo."

"Me, too," she said, and turned around to face him. "It was just such a shock. I feel like someone's ripped the carpet right out from under me."

Jack held her close, patted her back and allowed her to weep. After a few moments, he handed her his handkerchief.

"Thanks," she said, dabbing at her eyes.

"You know this doesn't change anything, don't you? You're still Margee Jardine."

"I keep telling myself that."

"Then believe it. Seriously, Margee. This whole blood thing is overrated. So what if someone else's egg and sperm got you started. All that means is that they're responsible for the color of your hair and your eyes. It doesn't have a thing to do with who you are. You're still Margee Jardine, daughter of Caroline and Robert Jardine, the pain-in-the-ass girl from down the street who was always tagging behind me and Peter.''

She gave him a watery smile. ''In my head I know that you're right, but there's a part of me that feels like a piece of me is missing. I thought if I could find out about my biological parents, I'd feel better. But the records were sealed.''

''Is that why you contacted Sister Grace?''

She nodded. ''I know that she was at St. Ann's for a long time. I thought she might be able to tell me who my real parents were.''

''Did she know who they were?'' Jack asked, not bothering to point out that her real parents were Caroline and Robert Jardine.

She shook her head. ''She wouldn't say. She told me that from the moment she placed me in my mother's arms, I was Caroline and Robert Jardine's daughter.''

''Maybe she was right,'' Jack offered.

''That's what I've been telling myself since Sister Grace died. You know, I saw her that evening in the chapel, probably less than an hour before she died.''

He hadn't known that. ''You were in the chapel with her?''

Margee nodded. ''I went to evening mass and prayed for some sign, some answer that would give me peace. When the service was over and everyone was leaving church, I saw Sister Grace kneeling in a pew alone and I approached her. I pleaded with her for answers about who my mother was.''

''What happened?''

''She said that God had already given me my answer.

That the sealed records were God's way of telling me that Caroline and Robert Jardine were my parents. The next day when I learned that she had died, I finally accepted that she was right. The Jardines are my parents and whoever the woman is who gave birth to me really isn't my mother. Caroline Jardine is.''

"It's true, you know."

"Yes," she said, giving him a weak smile.

"Margee, I need you to think back to that night in the chapel. Do you remember seeing anyone else, another woman hanging around after the service? She might have been in another pew or at the back of the church."

"No," she began, then stopped. "Wait. There was someone. A woman in the confessional with these fabulous black Prada boots." As though recognizing his blank look, she explained, "Great shoe designer and very expensive."

"Margee, the woman," he said, steering her back on track.

"Anyway, I remember thinking at the time that it was odd for her to be waiting in the confessional since Father doesn't normally hear confessions on Sunday."

"Anything else you remember about her?"

She shook her head. "Just the boots. The rest of her was screened by the confessional box. All I saw were her shoes."

"Thanks," he said, and gave her a hug. "I appreciate your being straight with me about the adoption stuff. And for what it's worth, I think Sister Grace gave you good advice. You're Margee Jardine. Nothing's going to change that."

"I know," she said, and hugged him back.

When he started to leave, she said, "Jack?"

"Yeah?"

"Good luck."

"Jack, what are you doing here?" Kelly asked when Jack showed up at her apartment the next day—only a few hours after he'd left her bed that morning to go home. "I thought you said you were going to use your day off to Christmas shop."

"Christmas shopping can wait. My mother called me a few minutes ago. She struck pay dirt. She found a Lianne Tompkins in the archived records at St. Ann's that coincide with the dates on the entries in Sister Grace's journals."

Kelly sat down on the couch, tried to absorb the information. Lianne Tompkins, the woman who was probably her mother, had grown up at St. Ann's just as she had. "She's Evelyn's daughter, then," Kelly said more to herself than to him.

"Leon's still working on trying to find a birth certificate. The only thing they had on the records about her at St. Ann's was that her mother was a sixteen-year-old white female who had been residing at a home for unwed mothers. She gave birth to a healthy eight-pound girl and signed over the infant to St. Ann's so that she could be adopted."

"Only she wasn't adopted," Kelly said, recalling the journal entry where Sister Grace had feared Lianne would discover the truth about her birth. "It was because of the incest. The nuns must have had to reveal that she was the result of incest."

"That could explain it," Jack said. "I did a background search but couldn't find anyone using the name Lianne Tompkins in the current databases. Not even a tax return. What I did find was a piece of property in

Pass Christian, Mississippi, that's owned by Evelyn Tompkins. Guess who owned that property before Evelyn?''

"Lianne Tompkins." She paused, let that sink in for a moment. "But where is she now? Why would she have signed over the property to her mother—assuming we're right and that Evelyn was her mother."

"That's what I'm going to find out. Since I'm off duty, I thought you might like to take a ride with me to Mississippi and meet Evelyn."

Meet the woman who was probably her grandmother. A grandmother, Kelly thought, not quite able to grasp the concept of having any family.

"Kelly, if you'd rather not come, it's all right."

"No. No," she repeated. "I'd like to go with you. Just let me get my camera and jacket," she said. And after locking up, Jack led her downstairs to his car and they headed for the interstate.

Nearly an hour later, they took the interstate exit for the Mississippi Gulf Coast and Jack recounted his conversation with his mother, his own search for Kelly's birth records and Leon's conversation with the retired CPA who'd handled Gilbert's tax returns. "The tax guy told Leon that Gilbert stopped using him for tax work a good five years before he sold the accounting firm and retired, but he did remember that Gilbert's nurse/office assistant was named Evelyn. He didn't remember anyone working there named Lianne, though."

"Jack, I know all of this stuff to do with the investigation is classified. How many rules are you breaking by telling me?"

"A lot."

"And what happens if your captain finds out? What happens if someone learns you took me with you today to see a witness?"

"Let me worry about it," he told her.

She reached across the seat, touched his arm. "I want to know."

"It'll probably cost me my badge."

"Oh, Jack. You shouldn't have put your career at risk because of me."

He glanced at her, his blue eyes serious. "You mean more to me than my shield, Kelly. This is important to you. So it's important to me."

Because she didn't know what to say, she said nothing. She simply listened as Jack ran his theory of the chain of events by her.

"Evelyn Tompkins gives birth to a baby girl, Lianne, and signs her over to St. Ann's so that she can be adopted. And the nun she deals with at St. Ann's is Sister Grace. Sister Grace takes Lianne under her wing. In the meantime Evelyn goes to work for Gilbert and becomes his lover."

"Then Lianne shows up, looking for her mother," Kelly added, following his line of thought. She tried to imagine Lianne doing so, imagined how she herself might have felt searching for her own mother and finding her.

"One of Gilbert's acquaintances falls for Lianne. They have an affair. Lianne gets pregnant, has a baby, but the guy is married and not willing to leave his wife. Lianne tries to make it on her own for a while, but something happens and she decides she can't do it. So she turns to the one person she knows she can count on."

"Sister Grace."

"Yes," Jack said. "It would make sense, Kelly. If you're Lianne's child, she would have taken you to the one place where she thought you'd be safe. She'd have taken you to St. Ann's to Sister Grace."

"But what happened to Lianne?" Was it possible that all these years she'd been wrong in believing that her mother was dead?

"I don't know. Maybe she changed her name, married and made a good life for herself. Then Gilbert finds out where she is, that she has money now or a position to maintain, so he blackmails her, threatens to expose her past unless she pays him."

"So she murders him and Sister Grace to keep them quiet?"

"If she married well, has a family to protect, she might have felt she had no choice," Jack offered.

"Then how do you explain the DNA from the hair? The woman is supposed to be late twenties or early thirties. And what about what I saw?"

"Maybe the DNA test was wrong. Maybe you made a mistake," Jack offered.

It was, Kelly told herself. She'd made mistakes before. It also brought to full circle the connection between Sister Grace and Gilbert, because the man would have known about Evelyn's daughter's ties to the orphanage. Yet it didn't feel right. She remembered the watercolor Lianne had given Sister Grace, the depth of emotion and sensitivity in the painting. And she also recalled Sister Grace's journals, the way she'd described Lianne. Kelly shook her head. "I don't know, Jack. It sounds plausible, but it just doesn't feel right."

"Why?" he asked as he turned off on the exit that led to Pass Christian.

"Because I don't think Lianne's a killer. And even if the DNA test was wrong, I don't think I am."

Jack was silent for several minutes. "Then there's another possibility. If Gilbert's ex is to be believed, the not-so-good doctor liked to ingratiate himself with im-

portant people. If Lianne's married lover was a prominent citizen, Gilbert could have used that information
for his own benefit.''

''That would explain Gilbert being able to skirt all
those lawsuits against him, but why would he contact
Sister Grace? He could hardly blackmail her. She didn't
have any money or influence.''

''But she knew who you were, what your name had
been changed to and where to find you,'' he pointed out.

Kelly went still. She didn't want to believe it, hadn't
wanted to believe it for weeks now, that Sister Grace
had lied to her all these years. Worse, that she had died
in her attempt to protect her.

Jack pulled the car off to the side of the road, shifted
into Park. He touched Kelly's arm. ''Kelly, think about
it. If the father of Lianne's child—your father—was
powerful enough to keep Gilbert out of jail all those
years, he probably couldn't have afforded the scandal of
an affair. He certainly would have tried to keep news
that he had a lovechild quiet. Maybe he convinced
Lianne to give up the baby. And, you said yourself, that
since Lianne herself had been at St. Ann's, it would be
logical for her to bring you there to Sister Grace.''

Was that what had happened to her? Had her father
been ashamed of her and convinced her mother to aban-
don her? Had that memory of a woman singing to her
been just wishful thinking on her part? And what about
the dreams about the fire? The smell of the smoke, the
sound of her mother arguing with a woman, and then a
man's angry voice threatening her. She thought about
the woman in the chapel with Sister Grace and the DNA
link to her. Her father's legitimate daughter? A daughter
who didn't want to be tainted by the scandal of her father's mistake?

"Kelly? Are you all right?"

"Yes." Something hardened inside her. "I want to see Evelyn Tompkins. If you're right and the woman is my grandmother, maybe she can give me some answers." Like who was her father? And where was her mother? And who was responsible for killing Sister Grace?

"All right," Jack told her, and pulled the car back out onto the road.

Twenty minutes later they turned off onto a gravel road lined with magnolia trees. At the end of the road sat a large white stucco house that looked in need of a good coat of paint. As they drew closer, she could see ramps had been added on to accommodate wheelchairs. Several rockers and wheelchairs lined the front gallery and the occupants didn't seem to notice that the sun had dipped behind the clouds.

After clearing things at the front desk, she and Jack were led to Evelyn's room by one of the nursing staff. "She's had a good morning. So she might be of more help to you today, Detective."

"Thank you. We won't be long."

"Ready?" he asked Kelly as they stood outside the room.

Kelly nodded and they stepped into the room. Fueled by anger during the last part of the drive, Kelly hadn't given much thought to how she would feel about meeting her grandmother. But as she stared at the frail-looking woman with her head bent, sitting in a chair knitting a baby's bootee, what she felt was sadness. Sadness and regret.

"Hello, Evelyn. Remember me? Detective Jack Callaghan?"

Evelyn looked up, smiled at Jack. And Kelly's heart

skipped a beat. She recognized that dip in Evelyn's chin as her own.

"Of course I remember you," Evelyn said, and rocked in her chair as she continued to knit. "I was hoping you'd come back to see me."

"I've brought a friend with me." He urged Kelly forward. "This is my friend Kelly Santos."

"Hello, Evelyn," Kelly said, and extended her hand.

"Ladies don't shake hands," she admonished. "Is Jack your beau?"

Caught off guard, Kelly fell silent a moment, but Jack stepped in. "Yes, I'm her beau."

"I have a beau, too. He's very handsome and smart." She leaned closer. "He's a doctor and he and I are going to get married as soon as his wife gives him a divorce."

Kelly's heart ached for this woman who had obviously been lied to and used by Martin Gilbert. "That's a lovely bootee you're knitting, Evelyn," she said, stooping down in front of her. "Who is it for?"

Evelyn looked around, as though searching for prying eyes, then she whispered, "It's a secret. Promise not to tell?"

"I promise."

"My daughter's going to have a baby. But we can't tell anyone yet."

Kelly held her breath a moment, got a grip on her ricocheting emotions. Then she noted the framed photograph in the woman's lap beneath the skein of yarn. "Is that a picture of your daughter, Evelyn?" Kelly asked, pointing to the photo.

"Yes."

"May I see it?"

Evelyn picked up the photograph, clutched it to her breast. She eyed her warily out of faded brown eyes.

"I promise to be careful."

After a moment's hesitation, she handed the picture to Kelly. Kelly held the simple frame, hoping to feel some connection, but the images and impressions were all confused just as Evelyn's mind was confused. She stared at the photograph. The professional photographer in her saw that the photo was poorly centered and a filter should have been used to soften the brightness of the direct sunlight. But the girl in her who had always wondered what her mother looked like took in every detail of the slim, smiling blonde who stood on the porch. She was young, Kelly thought. Her brown eyes looked bright, eager and happy. There was a freshness about her, a joy in her smile that said "I'm happy. My life is beautiful and perfect."

Kelly shifted her gaze to the tow-headed child on the woman's hip whose little fingers she was waving at the camera. Dressed all in pink, the baby had straight pale blond hair like her own, not the caramel-colored waves of her mother. But her eyes were brown—just like the mother's.

Is that child really me?

Struggling to keep her emotions in check, Kelly studied the rest of the picture. The yellow-and-white wood-framed house. Oh, God, the house in the watercolor, she realized, and drank in every detail. The buckets of flowering plants on the porch. The sandbox with a red plastic pail and shovel off to the right of the house. The two huge magnolia trees that sat off to the left of the house with a swing strung up between them. Kelly drew her finger over the face of the woman in the photograph.

Are you Lianne? Are you my mother?

"Kelly?" Jack placed his hand on her shoulder. She stood, showed him the photograph.

"Evelyn? Is this Lianne?"

Evelyn snatched the photograph from him. "It's mine. Can't let anyone know I have it."

Jack looked at Kelly, then back to the older woman. "Evelyn, do you know where Lianne and the baby are now?"

"They're gone," she said, a sadness in her voice.

"Gone where?" Kelly demanded.

"With the angels and saints. Ashes to ashes. Dust to dust," she began, reciting the words from the burial ritual.

"Evelyn, what about Lianne's baby? Do you know what happened to the baby?" Jack asked.

Evelyn stopped the singsong recital, looked up at Jack. "Won't tell. You can't make me tell. I promised never ever to tell."

"Evelyn, who did you promise you wouldn't tell?" Kelly asked.

"Shh. Do you hear her? It's my baby. My baby's crying for me," Evelyn said. "Where's my baby? Sister, do you know where they took my baby girl?"

"It's all right," Kelly told her, and touched her shoulder to comfort her.

But the moment she touched her, she was surrounded by Evelyn's grief. They'd taken her baby from her. She had a flash of a stern-looking man and woman standing over a young girl with tears streaming down her cheeks, of the man cruelly crushing the girl's fingers around a pen and ordering her to sign the papers.

"Kelly. Kelly." Jack reached for her hand, pulled her back from Evelyn and the heart-wrenching memories. As though he understood, he said, "She won't be able to tell us any more today. We should go."

Once he led her outside, he took her in his arms. Kelly

held on to him and explained, "They forced her to sign away her baby, Jack. Her father nearly broke her fingers, he crushed them so hard around that pen. And he forced her to give Lianne away."

"I know," he murmured, and pressed a kiss to the top of her head.

"I'd like to come back again—later."

"We will," he promised, and led her to the car.

"I don't know," she said when they reached the car and he opened the door for her.

"You don't know what?"

"I don't know who Lianne's lover was. Evelyn's thoughts were all jumbled and I couldn't make sense of what was real and what wasn't. But I can tell you that I recognized the house."

"You're going to have to explain that to me."

"It's the house in the watercolor that Lianne sent to Sister Grace, the one that Sister Grace left to me in her will." When he slid into the driver's seat of the car, she turned to him. "Do you have the address on that property that you said belongs to Evelyn?"

"Yes."

"I'd like to go there."

Worry clouded his blue eyes. "Kelly, are you sure you want to do this? You've had a lot to deal with today already. I can check it out another time by myself."

"I need to see it, Jack. I need to find out what happened at that house and why someone was willing to kill two people to keep me from learning the truth."

"All right," he told her, and reached across the seat for her hand. "We'll be there in a few minutes."

Fifteen minutes later, they turned down a small road about a mile from the beaches. The houses were mostly shanties and all were worn, weather-beaten and in need of paint. Every few houses there was an empty, over-grown lot with remnants of what had once been a house. Probably lost in one of the hurricanes that swept through the Gulf Coast and wrecked havoc each year. Many people rebuilt while others gave up the fight and moved on to less hostile turf.

"This is it," Jack said, pulling the car to a stop in front of a lot upon which only a cement slab remained. The pretty little yellow-and-white house was gone. So was the porch with its blooming pots of flowers. The green lawn upon which she'd seen the sandbox had given way to broken tree branches, dirt and weeds. The two big magnolias were still there, but one of them was tilted and the top half of its trunk dangled like a broken arm. "Are you sure you want to do this?" Jack asked.

"I'm sure," she said, and opened the car door.

Jack took her hand and walked with her up the broken and cracked sidewalk to the site of what had once been Lianne's home. Had it been her home, too? she wondered as she approached the slab. The wind whipped across the lot, sending a chill through her. She sensed Jack's apprehension and turned to him. "I'll be all right. But I have to know."

"All right," he said, and when she tugged her fingers free, he released her. Bracing herself, Kelly reached down and pressed her palm against the cold cement slab.

Almost at once, she felt the world tilting beneath her feet, spinning her back. Back to another cold day. To another time. To the past. To a house scented by the smell of burning wood in the fireplace. To the sound of a woman's voice cooing...

"Come on, my precious. You need to lie down for your nap. Daddy's coming to see us this evening and we

don't want to be all cross because we're tired now, do we?''

"I wear princess dress for Daddy?"

The woman laughed, a lovely musical laugh. "That's supposed to be your Christmas dress, Sarah, and Christmas isn't until next week."

"Pwease, Mommy?"

"All right. You can wear the princess dress for Daddy, but only if you take your nap."

"I see it?"

Her mother smiled and her brown eyes twinkled. They always twinkled when Daddy came to visit. She walked over to the closet and took out the dress and hung it at the end of the bed. "Okay, here it is waiting for you. But first you need to close your eyes and sleep for a little bit. Then when you wake up, we'll put it on and surprise Daddy. Okay?"

"'Kay," she said, stretching out on the bed. She hugged her teddy bear close and closed her eyes.

"That's my good baby girl," her mother said, and after pressing a kiss to her forehead and one to Teddy's, she slipped out the door.

She wanted to be a good girl. She wanted to sleep like Mommy asked. But her eyes kept opening and she couldn't stop looking at the dress. It was so pretty, she thought. Blue and silver with shiny stuff on it. A Cinderella dress just like in the movie. Maybe if she put it on, she could go to sleep, she told herself. And wouldn't Mommy be surprised if she were all ready when she came to wake her from her nap?

So she crawled out of bed, pulled off her jammies and put on the princess dress. She twirled around once, stumbled and fell on her bottom. But she didn't cry. She hardly ever cried. She got right back up and twirled around again to show Teddy how pretty it was. Then she climbed back into bed, closed her eyes and dreamed of being a princess in a magical kingdom. In the magical kingdom there were big white horses for her to ride and lots and lots of children for her to play with. And her daddy was always with them, so her mommy was always laughing.

Only she couldn't find her daddy.

And her mommy wasn't laughing anymore. Neither was the lady she was talking to.

"You shouldn't be here," her mommy said in her angry voice.

"I have every right to be here since it's my family's money that paid for this place," the mean-sounding lady said. "Do you really think he's going to walk out on me? Walk out on our family, especially now when he's on the verge of becoming one of this nation's most powerful politicians?"

"He can still have his career," her mother insisted.

"Don't be naive, Lianne. A man in his position couldn't be elected dogcatcher married to someone like you."

"He loves me and we have a child together," her mommy told the woman.

"You're nothing to him. You or that bastard of yours. And I'll never give him a divorce. Never! Do you hear?"

"Fine! Then we'll live in sin because I'm not giving him up," her mommy told her.

"Why you filthy little slut," the woman yelled. "I'll kill you before I let you steal him from me."

A slap followed and her mommy cried out.

"Jesus Christ! What are you doing here? Lianne, what happened?" a man's angry voice demanded.

"She provoked me and I hit her. She tripped and hit her head against the hearth," the mean woman said.

"Christ! She's bleeding. Lianne, darling, are you okay?"

"Yes. Please just get her out of here."

"Have you lost your mind? You could have killed her?" he accused.

"I did it for you," the mean woman said. *"She was threatening to ruin us, to tell the press about your affair."*

"Liar," her mommy said.

"She's the liar. She wants to destroy our family."

"That's enough," the man said. *"I could kill you with my bare hands for what you've done."*

"Please just go. Both of you leave here now."

"Lianne—"

"Please, just leave. I don't want Sarah to wake up and see me like this, to see the two of you."

Sarah huddled beneath the covers and pulled the pillow over her head. Feeling sad, she tried to fill her thoughts with happy things—of the horses and pretty dresses—until she drifted back to sleep.

Somewhere in her dream, she thought she could hear her mommy asking, *"What are you doing here?"* again, and a big crash. But she shoved those sad memories aside, not wanting to let go of her dream.

Until she began to cough.

Pushing the pillow away from her face, Sarah sat up in bed and coughed again. Awake now, she looked around the room. It was dark—and she didn't like the dark. Mommy knew she didn't like the dark. Why hadn't she put on her lamp? And what was that yucky smell? She slipped out of bed and hurried over to the chest where the lamp was. She climbed up on the drawer and *turned it on. Only she couldn't see too good. The room was all smoky. Frightened, she jumped off the chest of drawers, fell and hit her knee. Her knee hurt, but her throat hurt her, too. And she coughed. "Mommy? Mommy, where are you?"*

She coughed again and ran toward the door. And stopped.

Somebody's there. On the other side of the door. Somebody was there waiting for her. Not her mommy. Not Daddy. Somebody angry who wanted to hurt her. Hurry! Hurry! Lock the door and hide before the bad person comes in and finds you.

Terrified she turned the lock on the door and raced back across the room. Climbing underneath the bed, she clutched her teddy bear. And she waited. Sarah could feel the anger, the hatred drawing closer. Could read the mean thoughts, "You can't hide. I've killed your mother and now I'm going to kill you, too."

Fighting to hold in her cough, she watched in terror as the doorknob began to turn.

And Kelly screamed.

She heard Kelly scream. And from her position across the street in the shadows behind the battered shack, she watched as Jack Callaghan shook the sobbing Kelly and held her in his arms.

Had that old witch grandmother of hers told her what had happened? She'd been told the woman had Alzheimer's, but supposedly even Alzheimer's patients had moments of lucidity. Or had Kelly remembered that night all those years ago when she'd snuck out of the car and watched the scene between her mother and that woman Lianne? She'd been worried that her daddy had seen her, but he'd been too busy fussing over that bitch Lianne to notice her. Lianne and that brat of hers.

But she'd fixed them. Lianne hadn't been afraid when she'd seen her come into the house after her parents had gone. So she never saw her pick up the fireplace poker until it was too late. It was then when she saw Lianne's painting of Sarah and the paint supplies that she'd gotten the idea. She was eight years old, old enough to know about flammable liquids. She'd used the paint thinner, splashed it around the room, then used one of the fireplace matches to light it.

"Mommy!"

Hatred filled her heart as she remembered hearing Sarah cry from the other room. She'd gone to the room, used a towel to turn the door handle. But it was locked.

And she'd been so sure the little witch had burned along with her mother that night. Until that blackmailing son of a bitch Gilbert had shown up, claiming Sarah was alive. Well, she'd put an end to his schemes and she'd stopped the meddling old nun from revealing her daddy's shameful little secret, hadn't she? She hadn't worked this hard just to have Kelly Santos come and mess things up now.

Did you really think that after all this time, I'd just let you come back and steal what's mine? I stopped you once. I'll stop you again. But this time, I intend to make sure you stay dead.

Nineteen

After that scene with Kelly at the abandoned house site in Mississippi the previous evening, the last thing Jack wanted to do that morning was to leave her alone—even for a second. But he needed answers and he needed them fast. And the best place to get them was there at the station, he reasoned. So there he was on the phone, barking at some poor clerk, "So where in the hell is the fax you were supposed to send? I've been waiting twenty minutes."

"It should be coming over the machine now, Detective. Yours isn't the only request we have. We process them in order."

"Yeah, thanks," he said, and slammed down the phone, then headed for the fax machine. The cover sheet was spitting out already. He grabbed the grainy sheet that followed, a copy of an article that appeared in the Mississippi newspaper twenty-six years ago, detailing the tragic death of twenty-year-old Lianne Tompkins and her thirty-four-month-old daughter, Sarah, in a fire five days before Christmas. Heading back to his desk, Jack sat down and read the article again.

Tragedy struck in the Magnolia subdivision of Pass Christian only days before Christmas when fire claimed the lives of Lianne Tompkins and her thirty-four-month-old daughter, Sarah. The fire is believed to have origi-

nated in the fireplace and quickly spread through the wood-framed house. No smoke alarms were installed in the house. The remote location, where the small homes were used primarily as summer getaways, caused the fire to go undetected for more than an hour before the fire department was notified. According to the fire chief the house was engulfed with flames upon his arrival. After battling the fire for ninety minutes, the chief and his men were able to recover the mother's badly burned body from the living room, where she was found slumped in front of the fireplace. The nursery was completely gutted by the blaze and it is believed that little Sarah Tompkins's body was destroyed in the blaze.

Only Sarah Tompkins hadn't died. She had escaped and been reborn as Kelly Santos in New Orleans. Had Kelly's father come back to save her? Jack remembered Kelly confessing her fear that her father had killed her mother. Was that what had happened that night? he wondered. And if so, who had saved Kelly? Her father? Gilbert? He didn't think so. The only other person who would have saved the child would have been Evelyn. After all, she was Lianne's mother and Kelly's grandmother.

It was the only answer that made sense, Jack reasoned. If Evelyn feared the person who killed Lianne would come after her granddaughter, she would have wanted to take her someplace where she would be safe. And what place was safer than St. Ann's and the nun to whom she'd entrusted her own daughter as an infant?

Jack glanced over at Leon's desk, where his partner was on the phone. He'd filled Leon in on the events of yesterday when he'd returned last night, so when Leon hung up the phone, Jack walked over to his desk and handed him the fax. "Take a look at this."

"Shit!"

"My sentiments exactly."

"But how did she get out of that fire without anyone knowing?"

"Meet me in the john, I want to run a theory by you."

After he and Leon checked to be sure they had the men's room to themselves, Jack laid out what he thought might have happened and how Evelyn was most likely the one responsible for dropping Kelly off at St. Ann's.

"I think you might be on to something," Leon told him. "And given the Tompkins woman's mental state, she could have let something slip to Gilbert about the baby not dying in the fire. It would explain Gilbert contacting the nun to try to find out where she was now. If her father is some kind of politician, Gilbert could have used that information to blackmail him."

"My guess is he'd been blackmailing the man for years already." He saw no reason to tell Leon that there was the possibility that the man had also killed Lianne and that Gilbert had known.

"The only problem with the theory is that Gilbert's killer was a woman, and according to Kelly, it was the same woman who killed the nun," Leon pointed out. "So whoever this politician is, and no matter what he's done, he's not the killer."

"No. But I think his daughter is. His legitimate daughter," Jack amended. "The one whose DNA matches Kelly's."

"And you think her next target is Kelly."

"Yes," Jack replied.

"You got a plan?" Leon asked.

"Yes. I need you to do some more digging, check out politicians in Mississippi and Louisiana going back thirty years," Jack explained. "In the meantime, I'm going to work it from another angle and see if I can get a look at some adoption records.''

''Adoption records? I thought Kelly was never adopted.''

''She wasn't. But her sister might have been.''

''You want to explain that?'' Leon asked, a puzzled look on his face.

''If I'm right, I swear I'll explain it all to you. But if I'm not, an innocent person could be hurt. So for now, I'm going to ask you to trust me on this one.''

''Just watch your step, Jackson. You're walking a fine line on this one, my friend.''

Leon was right. And he knew it, Jack admitted as he returned to his desk and found the messenger envelope he'd been waiting for sitting on top of his desk. Jack sat down in his chair and ripped open the envelope. And he stared at the copies of Margee Jardine's original birth certificate—the one that he'd broken enough rules to get and could very well cost him his job. He stared at the mother's name, Diana Gray. But it was the father's name that worried him—Robert Jardine. Margee's biological father and his wife had adopted his own daughter, a child, evidently, who was the result of an affair. He wouldn't have pegged Robert as an adulterer. The man had served as a member of the Senate for the state of Mississippi before he'd opted out of public life and moved back to Louisiana to join his family's hotel business.

And it was the man's political past and ties to Mississippi that he couldn't ignore now. If Robert Jardine had strayed once and Margee was the result, was it possible that he'd done so again? Could he have strayed that second time with Lianne Tompkins? Damn, if only he'd been able to locate a copy of Kelly's original birth certificate.

Questions riddled his brain as he tried to compare the facts he had with the people he'd known most of his life. He didn't want to believe that Caroline Jardine was the woman who argued with Lianne. Nor did he want to believe that Robert Jardine was capable of murder. They were good people, people he cared about. So why had they lied about Margee's adoption all these years?

Was it possible that Caroline Jardine didn't know that the child she'd adopted was fathered by her husband? It would make sense, he reasoned. He'd seen Caroline with Margee and the woman truly adored her. Or had she known the truth but had drawn the line at raising a second child from her husband's indiscretions? He didn't know the answers and wouldn't until he could do some investigating. But what he did know, Jack reasoned, was that the Jardine family was powerful. Even without Robert Jardine's years in the Senate, the name Jardine was equated to royalty in New Orleans because of their hotel empire. They were right up there with the Hiltons. Their public image had cracked a little in recent years when news came from the matriarch of the family, Olivia Jardine, that she had an illegitimate granddaughter. Things had since settled down. But twenty-eight years ago such a scandal would not have been made public under any circumstances. All measures would have been taken to keep such a secret under wraps—just as Margee's adoption had been kept a secret all these years. Was Robert Jardine Kelly's father? Even as the nephew of the matriarch of the hotel dynasty, he was a powerful man with strong connections. An ideal target for blackmail.

"Callaghan! Jerevicious! In my office now," Big Mike yelled.

Jack looked across the desk at his partner. Leon gave him a what'd-we-do-now look, to which Jack shrugged. He stuffed the items back into the envelope and put it, along with the article and folder, in his desk drawer. He locked it and pocketed the key.

"Looks like Big Mike's about to bust a gasket," Nuccio pointed out. "I sure wouldn't want to be in your shoes right now, Callaghan."

"Don't sweat it, Nuccio," Jack told him. "You just might get that promotion after all."

"Yeah, by default," Leon added, and the two of them headed into the captain's office.

"Shut the door," Big Mike ordered.

Nuccio was right, Jack decided as he and his partner stood at attention in front of the captain's desk. Big Mike did look like he was ready to blow. His face was red all the way up to his bald spot, and from the way he was chomping down on the unlit cigar in the corner of his mouth, Jack expected steam to start coming out of his ears at any second.

"Is something wrong, sir?" Leon asked.

"You're damned right something's wrong. I want to know why my detectives have been demanding that sealed adoption records be opened, and why they are threatening state employees with jail time if they don't comply?"

"That was me, sir," Jack said, taking a step forward. "Leon had nothing to do with it."

"That's not how I run this precinct and you know it, Callaghan."

"Yes, sir."

"Then you better have a damned good reason for breaking policy or I'm suspending your ass right now."

"I needed the information for a case, sir," Jack told

him. "It's part of my investigation of the Gilbert murder."

"Gilbert?"

"Yes, sir."

"Well what in the hell does his death have to do with sealed adoption records?"

"It's a long story, sir," Jack began, and gave him a brief rundown of all that had transpired, including the suspicions about Sister Grace's death and his own fear for Kelly's safety. What he didn't tell him was that he suspected a member of one of the city's most prominent families could be involved. He couldn't do that to Margee or her parents—not until he'd had a face-to-face with Robert Jardine.

Big Mike removed the cigar from his mouth and ran a hand through his thinning hair. "That's quite a story. I take it you and this psychic woman, Kelly what's her name—"

"Santos," Jack supplied.

"Right. You and this Ms. Santos involved in a personal way?"

"Yes, sir. But that hasn't affected my abilities or my judgment as a cop," Jack assured him.

"Maybe you think it hasn't affected your judgment, Callaghan, but it's kind of hard for it not to when you're sleeping with the woman."

"Sir, if I may?"

Big Mike sat back in his chair, making it squeak. "Go ahead, Jerevicious."

"Sir, I've met the lady. And I'll be the first to admit that I was skeptical. I mean, I don't understand beans about this psychic stuff. But I'm telling you, the lady's got something. She's for real. So I'm with Jackson on this."

Big Mike looked from Jack to Leon and back again. "All right. But I don't want any more rules bent and you follow policy. You bring me evidence that I can take to the D.A.'s office and demand a warrant to open those files and I'll give it to you. Until then, you follow procedure. Understood?"

"Yes, sir," they replied in unison.

"Now go find me that shooter. And do it soon. I want the mayor's office off my ass about the unsolved murders in this city. Now, get out of here. I got work to do."

"Yes, sir," Leon said.

"Yes, sir," Jack echoed. "Thank you, sir."

Big Mike made a grumbling noise that sounded like "yeah." "Callaghan?"

Jack stopped at the door. "Yes, sir?"

"Your sister sent me and my wife an invitation for some private preview party she's having at her store tomorrow night. The woman's all excited about going to the thing."

"Um, that's nice, sir," Jack said, but knew from the captain's face his boss didn't share his wife's enthusiasm.

"How am I supposed to dress for the thing?"

"I'd recommend a coat and tie, sir."

"Damn. I was afraid of that," he muttered. "You and Jerevicious going to be there?"

"I'll be there, sir," Leon told him. "Tessa's excited about being invited, too."

When the captain looked at him, Jack grimaced. "I'll be there, sir. A command performance ordered by my sister. If I don't show, you'll be adding another murder to the city's tally—me."

"Then I guess I'll see you there."

* * *

"Oh, isn't this charming," Mary Ellen Callaghan said as she entered Kelly's apartment, determined to get a feel for just how serious things were between her son and the young woman with whom he'd been spending so much time. "You've done a lovely job fixing this up, Kelly."

"Thank you," Kelly murmured. "You really didn't have to come all the way over here to pick up the photographs, Mrs. Callaghan. I would have been happy to bring them to you."

Mary Ellen waved the idea aside. "Nonsense. I told you, I came by to see if Meredith needed any help before the party, so it was no trouble to come upstairs and get the photos for the guild's auction next week."

"May I offer you something to drink?"

"No thank you, dear. I really can't stay long." Just long enough to find out if her daughter was right—that Jackson might have actually found the woman he wanted to marry. She hadn't expected that woman to be Kelly Santos. Not that she had anything against the girl. She didn't. She was a pretty thing with her blond hair and serious brown eyes and so polite. A genuine lady. But her Jackson needed a woman with passion. And she'd thought that woman was Alicia. It was why she'd been so bitterly disappointed when his relationship with Alicia had ended. Because along with it ended her hopes of becoming a grandmother.

"I'll get the photos for you," Kelly told her, and disappeared into the other room.

While she was gone, Mary Ellen studied the tiny apartment, noted the homey touches—the fresh flowers on the table, the photographs on the walls, and her son's favorite leather jacket hanging on a door hook as though it belonged there.

"Here they are," Kelly said, exiting the other room. "It's a series I did of the French countryside when I was in Europe this fall."

Oh, but the girl was talented, Mary Ellen thought as she stared at the matted photos, noted the vivid color and detail of the French manor house, the people working in a vineyard, a family in prayer at the country chapel. So much emotion in those pictures, she mused. She wouldn't have expected it from a girl who seemed so guarded. Perhaps it was this emotion and passion that her son had seen. Feeling enormously relieved, she smiled.

"I hope they're all right."

"They're perfect, Kelly. Absolutely perfect. Why, I may just have to bid on them myself."

Kelly blushed. "I'd be happy to make you a set—my gift," she added quickly.

Mary Ellen patted her hand. "That's very sweet of you, dear. But I think I'm going to enjoy outbidding Olivia Jardine for these and adding to the till for St. Ann's."

"I'm sure St. Ann's will appreciate it," Kelly offered.

"You and Jackson are coming, aren't you?"

"I…um…we haven't discussed it."

"Well, I'm just going to insist he bring you. Oh, what a lovely picture," she said as she spied the watercolor. "Don't tell me you paint, too?"

"No. It was…Sister Grace left it to me."

She didn't miss the sad note in the girl's voice, in her eyes. "I'm sorry, dear. When I look at you, sometimes it's hard to believe you were an orphan. I know I would have been very proud to have you as my daughter." But with luck and prayer, she might soon be her daughter-in-law.

"That's very kind of you," Kelly said, and Mary Ellen could see that she'd flustered the girl.

"Oh my, look at the time. I'd better run and get these
over to the hotel for the auction." Unable to resist, she
gave Kelly a hug. "I'll see you later at Meredith's party
and I want you to promise me you'll help me pick out
something special for the holidays."

Kelly didn't have time to help Mary Ellen pick out
anything special for the holidays or for anything else this
evening. She was too busy racing around the boutique,
snapping photos and dealing with the press. For some
reason Meredith had gotten it in her head that no one
but Kelly knew what pictures should be taken, what people should be photographed, what items from the shop
should be touted for the local media in attendance.

And to be honest, she was enjoying herself, Kelly admitted as she did her best to move about the rooms discreetly and fire off candid shots of those in attendance.
Even though she hadn't lived in New Orleans for a decade, she knew tonight's guests read like a Who's Who
of New Orleans society.

Busy taking photos, she didn't realize that Alicia was
beside her until the other woman said, "Hello, Kelly.
Alicia Van Owen. We met at the Callaghans' party."

"Yes, I remember," Kelly told her, unable to forget
the gorgeous creature who had been Jack's lover. "It's
nice to see you again."

"My, aren't you stunning. And that dress is breath-
taking. Why, you look like a princess," Alicia told her.

Kelly flushed. "Thank you. Your dress is gorgeous.
Blue's the perfect color for you."

"That's what my daddy used to say, too. He loved
me in blue," Alicia told her, a hint of melancholy in her

voice. "So tell me, did you get that outfit in New York?"

"Actually it's from Meredith's shop. She insisted I had to have it."

"And I was absolutely right to do so," Meredith said, coming over to join them. "Hello, Alicia. Thanks for coming."

"I wouldn't have missed it," the other woman told her.

"Well, I hope you brought your checkbook because I expect you to spend lots and lots of money. Ooh, there's the mayor's wife. Got to run," Meredith said, and dashed across the room, leaving her alone with Alicia.

"Poor woman," Alicia said. "I hope she brought her platinum card."

Kelly laughed. "That's for sure." When she caught Alicia studying her, Kelly looked down at her dress and up again. "Is something wrong?"

"The camera," she said, pointing to the instrument in Kelly's hand.

"What about it?"

"You need to ditch the thing. It doesn't work with your outfit."

"It's like a part of my arm," Kelly advised her. "I'd be lost without it. Besides, I promised Meredith I'd take pictures."

"Forget about Meredith," Alicia insisted. "She'll have plenty of pictures. Why, I think she has more press here than they had for the president's visit to the city last month. Why don't you forget about snapping pictures for a while and let's see what goodies Meredith has for sale?"

"Maybe later," Kelly hedged, still not comfortable with the chummy relationship Alicia seemed to be offering. "The truth is, I'm enjoying myself. I hadn't realized how much I missed working. In fact, why don't you stand over there by the mirror and let me take some photos of you?"

"Tell you what, why don't we get someone to take a shot of you and me together?"

Kelly started to balk at the suggestion, but Alicia had already grabbed a man and asked him to take the picture. Seeing no graceful way to refuse, Kelly set up the shot and showed the gentleman which buttons to push, then she stood with Alicia.

"Say cheese," the guy said, and clicked off the shot. "Here you go," he told Kelly, and while Kelly reset her camera, the man chatted up Alicia.

"Over here," Meredith said as she pushed her way through the people with a newspaper photographer in tow. "This is the famous photographer from New York that I told you about, Kelly Santos."

Meredith made short work of introducing the photographer to her and to Alicia. And Kelly kept a pleasant smile pasted on her face as the man told her how he, too, aspired to work for the fashion magazines in New York.

"Ms. Santos is wearing a design from Indulgences," Meredith pointed out, directing the man's attention back to the shop. "Maybe you can get a shot of her and me together. Oh, and would you take one with Kelly's camera, too?"

"Sure thing, Miss Callaghan."

While Meredith beamed at the camera, Kelly managed to smile. She much preferred being on the other end of the camera.

"Got it. How about I take a few more shots with all of you pretty ladies?" the photographer suggested.

"Sure," Meredith said, and the three of them posed for a series of shots, which he took with both his camera and Kelly's.

"Nice piece of equipment you've got there," he told Kelly when he returned the camera to her.

"Thanks. I like it."

"We're using a lot of the digital stuff now. But if you ask me, it's not half as good as the stuff you get with one of those babies. You develop your own stuff?" he asked.

Kelly spent the next several minutes engaged in a conversation with the cameraman about her darkroom, her preferences in filters and lenses. He was asking her a question about her lenses when Kelly realized that Jack had arrived. She hadn't seen him come in and with the ever-increasing number of people, she didn't have a clear view of the door—despite her added height in the heels. She'd surprised herself at how often she'd found herself looking toward that door, waiting for him to arrive. She'd told herself it was because she'd been on pins and needles while she'd waited to hear what he'd found out about her past, about who her father was, about what had really happened that night of the fire.

But it wasn't the only reason she'd been waiting for him to arrive. She'd been waiting because she'd simply wanted to see him. Needed to see him, to be with him, she admitted.

Because she loved him.

Kelly sucked in a breath, stunned by the realization. Both stunned and frightened because she wasn't at all sure a future with Jack Callaghan was possible. How could she be when she wasn't sure who she was?

"Miss Santos? Are you all right?"

The cameraman's voice finally penetrated. "I'm sorry," she said. "Will you excuse me a moment?"

"Uh, sure thing. It was nice talking to you, ma'am."

But Kelly didn't bother responding. She was already searching for Jack. She needed to talk to him. Trying her best to maneuver the room in the too-high heels that forced her to take small steps instead of her normal stride, she bumped into the back of someone. "Oh, I'm so sorry."

"Don't be. I needed the jolt," the dark blonde in the Audrey Hepburn-inspired cocktail dress told her with a smile. "I was actually toying with spending two hundred dollars on that little purse that couldn't hold more than a lipstick. I'm Margee Jardine. You're Kelly, aren't you? I thought I recognized you when I saw the camera."

"Yes," Kelly told her, impressed. "We met at the Callaghans' party. You're the attorney."

"Now I'm the one who's impressed." Margee picked up the silvery bag. "So what do you think? Is it worth two hundred dollars?"

"It is if you like it," Kelly offered, and glanced past Margee in search of Jack.

"Looking for anyone in particular?" she asked.

"Jack," Kelly told her, then flushed.

Margee laughed. "It's all right, Kelly. I know about the two of you. Jack came to see me, to ask me about my conversations with Sister Grace. I assumed he told you."

"Only that the two of you talked," Kelly said. "I mean, he said that the conversation was personal and that he wasn't able to discuss it with me, that he gave his word."

"Is there a quiet place where we can talk?"

"Meredith keeps an office out back. I don't think the party has spilled into it yet. Come on."

Jack searched every twist and turn and room of the shop. But he couldn't find Kelly anywhere. He'd arrived late, had missed a great many of the early guests and had gotten waylaid by Big Mike and his wife, then Leon and Tessa. By the time he'd broken away, he'd lost sight of Kelly.

Spying his mother, Jack asked, "Have you seen Kelly?"

"Not for a while now. She was taking photos earlier and chatting with one of the reporters," his mother said. "Oh, Jack, the girl is darling. I couldn't be happier with your choice. And before you tell me to mind my own business, I want you to know that I expect you to ask the girl to join us for Thanksgiving—"

"Good idea, Mom. I'll do that—just as soon as I can find her. Catch you later and don't let Meredith talk you out of a discount for that pile of stuff you've got behind the counter."

Jack completed another round of the shop, staked himself outside both fitting rooms and the ladies' room to look for Kelly. There were fewer than a dozen people still in the shop and most of them were either at the register or the door, preparing to exit. His mother was behind the counter with the two sales clerks zipping credit cards through the machine like a pro.

He was just about to give up and go see if Kelly had returned upstairs to the apartment when he saw Meredith duck into the powder room, dabbing at her eyes with a tissue. Torn between finding Kelly and checking on his sister, Jack swore and headed for the powder room.

Meredith looked up from her seat at the dressing table

and met his gaze in the mirror. It was obvious from her red-tipped nose and the mascara smudges under her eyes that she'd been crying. "What's wrong?"

"Nothing," she said with a sniffle, then began repairing the mascara streaks under her eyes. "Just all the excitement. I didn't see you doing any shopping, big brother, and I want you to know that I expect you to spend an obscene amount of money before you leave here tonight," she informed him as she began to dab some concealer under her eyes to make the red disappear.

A part of him wanted to take her at her word, leave and go find Kelly to make sure she was all right. But another part of him knew his sister too well. Something was wrong. Deciding to deal with his sister first, he said, "Cut the act, brat, and tell me what's the matter."

Her shoulders slumped and all the sass and sparkle seemed to flow right out of her. "If you must know, I'm upset with Alex."

"Alex? What did he do?"

"He didn't come tonight," she said.

"Come on, Meredith. The man's got a tough job. He works more hours than I do—and that's saying plenty. When I saw him this morning he looked like hell and said he was coming down with a cold. Cut the guy some slack."

Meredith's eyes flashed in the mirror. She spun around and threw the tube of makeup at him.

Jack batted the tube away. "Hey! Are you nuts? What'd I do?"

"Don't you dare defend Alex Kusak. He's a lousy, heartless jerk. I hope his cold turns into pneumonia, that he's confined to his bed for months and that his stomach muscles turn to flab."

"What in the hell has gotten into you? Alex is practically family. Don't tell me you're still carrying that schoolgirl torch for the guy. I thought you'd gotten over that. I mean the guy's practically like a brother to you."

"Brother? Brother, my ass. He and I have been lovers for years."

Jack froze. Suddenly like the tumblers on a safe, all the cylinders clicked. Alex and Meredith's closeness, the way he always defended her, wanted to include her in their jaunts. The way Alex moped around every time Meredith took off. The way Meredith always asked for him whenever she'd call home. The son of a bitch. "I'm gonna kill him."

"Jack!" Meredith jumped up, ran after him and wrapped herself around his middle.

"Let go of me, Meredith."

"No, not until you listen to me."

Struggling to keep his temper, he spat out, "All right. Make it quick."

"I love him. I always have," she said, and the tears started to flow. "And he loves me, but he doesn't think he's good enough for me. And…and we had a horrible fight the other night. I told him he was a coward and either he had to marry me or we were through."

His best friend and his little sister? The idea still took some getting used to. "What did he say?"

"You don't see him here on bended knee with a ring, do you?"

"He will be when I finish with him," Jack promised.

"No," she said firmly. "I mean it, Jack. I don't want him that way."

Suddenly he took a hard look at his sister. She wasn't a flighty little girl anymore, he realized. She was a woman in love. "I'm sorry, Meredith."

"Me, too."

"I can't believe I'm saying this, because it's going to take me some time to wrap my brain around the image of you and Alex as a couple, but maybe he'll come around."

"Maybe, but I'm not going to hold my breath." She sniffed again, then hiked up her chin. "But I appreciate you wanting to defend my honor."

"Anytime. You know that I'm always here for you, don't you? That I'd cut out the heart of anyone who hurt you?"

"I know." She gave him a hug. "Well, my love life may suck, but at least yours is looking up. Thank God you had the good sense to ditch Alicia for Kelly."

"Come on, Meredith, Alicia wasn't all that bad," he said, but in truth he wondered why the affair had lasted as long as it did.

"Well, she did spend a chunk of money here tonight and as long as you don't make her my sister-in-law, I guess she's all right."

"That's my girl."

"Speaking of making someone my sister-in-law, what did you think of Kelly's outfit? And before you start gushing, you should know that I expect you to thank me for it later."

He chuckled. "I'll do that—as soon as I see it. I caught a glimpse of her when I got here, but then she disappeared. I was just on my way to see if she was in her apartment when I saw you come in here."

"But she didn't leave—at least not before you came in here. I was keeping a close watch at the door, making sure I thanked everyone for coming tonight."

"You must have missed her, then. Because unless

she's hiding in one of those bathroom stalls, she's not in the shop.''

"Did you try my office? I saw her heading in that direction with Margee earlier.''

Jack's blood suddenly ran cold. He didn't bother responding to his sister. With the sound of his own heart pounding in his ears, he flew out the door, racing toward the office and praying he wasn't too late.

Twenty

Jack burst through the door into the office like a man possessed. "Kelly," he shouted while scanning past the piles of cartons and crates.

"Jack? What's wrong?" Kelly asked, an anxious note in her voice as she stepped from around a corner. "Has something happened?"

Relief rushed through him. Barely noticing the shimmering gold dress she wore, he grabbed her and hugged her tight against his chest.

"Where's the fire, Callaghan?" Margee asked as she stepped around the same corner.

Everything inside Jack went cold at the reference to fire. His voice was hard, his heart even harder as he stared at her. "No fire," he said. Not this time, he thought silently, and wondered if Margee knew about the other fire, the one in which Kelly was supposed to have died. She couldn't have, Jack told himself. Margee would have been a kid at the time.

"Well, that was certainly a dramatic entrance," Margee said with a laugh. "For a minute there, I was sure either the building was on fire or Meredith was collecting the scalps of those of us who hadn't bought anything yet."

"No fire. And as far as I know, Meredith hasn't gone scalp-hunting yet," he said, trying to calm his nerves while assessing Margee. Damn it, he wished he'd been able to fly out to San Diego earlier today to see Robert Jardine instead of being forced to take the red-eye tonight. But if he was right and Jardine was Kelly's father, Margee was a murderer.

"Shame on you both," Kelly said, and took a step away. "Meredith has done a wonderful job and she's a very sharp businesswoman."

"I was only teasing," Margee offered. "The truth is I think if tonight's any indication, give her a few years and Meredith will be able to buy and sell us all."

"Margee, if you don't mind, I'd like to speak with Kelly alone."

"Jack," Kelly admonished. "Margee and I were in the middle of a discussion."

"It's all right. We can finish it another time."

"You're sure?" Kelly asked.

"Positive. I'll see you both later. I'm going to go see if I can convince Meredith to give me a discount on a couple of things that I don't need."

"I enjoyed the conversation," Kelly told her.

"Me, too." She walked over and kissed Jack on the cheek. "See you, Callaghan. And, Kelly, if I were you, I'd keep him away from the champagne. He's in a strange mood tonight."

"She's right," Kelly said once Margee had left. "Jack, what's wrong?"

He ran his hands up and down her arms again, just to ensure himself that she was really okay. "We need to talk. There are some things I need to tell you."

With that, he led her upstairs to the apartment, where he told her the rest of what he had learned, and his suspicion that Robert Jardine might be her father, that Margee could be her sister.

"Margee?" she repeated. "But what about the fire? How did I get out of the house? Why didn't I die that night?"

"I'm guessing here, and we may never know the answer, but I'm thinking that maybe it was Evelyn who saved you that night and then she brought you to St. Ann's where she knew you'd be safe."

"It makes sense," she told him. "But why can't I remember what happened? Not even seeing that photograph in Evelyn's room brought anything back."

Sitting in the dark on the sofa in her apartment, Jack hugged her close. "You weren't quite three years old, Kelly. Your child's mind probably couldn't handle the horror of what had happened. Maybe to deal with it, you shut everything out—the good and the bad."

"But surely if Margee were my half sister I would sense it," she argued.

"Maybe not. You said you couldn't read a person's mind, but that you sensed what they were feeling. She knows you're psychic. It stands to reason that she would be guarded about what she's feeling or thinking when she's around you, wouldn't it?"

"I guess. But it just doesn't feel...right."

"Well, we'll know soon enough. I'm taking a red-eye flight to San Diego tonight and plan to see Robert Jardine tomorrow." Because he wanted to chase those shadows from her eyes, he said, "In the meantime, Ms. Santos, I don't think I got around to telling you how beautiful you look tonight."

"It's the dress and makeup," she told him, but he could see her thoughts were still on what he'd told her.

"No, it's not the dress. It's you. You're beautiful," he told her, and wondered how he could have not realized that he loved her ten years ago.

"Because it was the wrong time," she answered. "We both needed to become the people we are now. I needed to learn that the person I am deserves to be loved and that I don't need to be afraid to love." She stroked the side of his face. "I've learned that I do deserve love and that I can't be afraid of love—not if I want to be happy."

He cupped her hand with his own. "And did you learn anything else?" he asked, wanting, needing her to say the words.

"I learned that I love you."

He kissed her then, long and slow. And when he lifted his head, he said, "Say it again."

"I love you, Jack Callaghan," she whispered. "Let me show you how much."

She showed him. And when he had to leave her an hour later to head for the airport, he promised himself it would be the last time they would spend a night apart. "You sure I can't convince you to go stay at my place until I get back?"

She pushed up on her elbows. "I told you, I've got my darkroom set up now and I want to develop those pictures from the party for Meredith."

"I don't like the idea of you being here alone. I don't think it's safe."

"You know your sister is probably going to be over here at the crack of dawn, chomping at the bit to reorder stock and tally up sales and get ready for the official opening. I'll be fine."

"I'll be fine," Caroline Jardine told Jack as he sat across from her and her husband in their San Diego hotel room suite. "Robert and I have no secrets from each other."

"It's true," Robert assured him. "Now, tell me what this is about. Why did you insist on seeing me?"

"It's about Margee."

"Has something happened to Margee?" Caroline asked.

"No," Jack said quickly.

"What about Margee?" Robert asked.

Seeing no delicate way to say it, Jack just spit it out. "I know she's adopted." Ignoring Caroline's gasp, he continued, "What I don't know is why you saw the need to adopt your own child?"

"How dare you come here and make such an accusation?" Caroline Jardine huffed.

"Believe me, Mrs. Jardine. I don't like it any better than you do, but I have no choice." He withdrew the copy of Margee's original birth certificate from his coat pocket and laid it on the table between them. He nearly winced when Caroline's face paled.

"It's all right, Caroline. Jack obviously knows the truth. What I don't understand is how it concerns you," Robert told him.

"I'm dealing with a homicide that may be connected to another child who was left at St. Ann's, and I need some answers. And I need those answers fast."

"Go ahead, ask your questions," Robert told him.

Jack asked his questions and they explained about the bad patch their marriage had gone through more than thirty years ago, how Caroline's infertility had added to the strain on their relationship and Robert had had an affair. "So you adopted your own daughter?"

"Of course we adopted her. She's Robert's daughter," Caroline explained.

"She's *our* daughter," her husband corrected, and covered his wife's hand with his own. "You may not have given birth to her, but you're Margee's mother, Caroline. You have been from the moment we went to St. Ann's and the nun put her in your arms.''

It had been one of the most unpleasant things Jack had had to do—confronting these two people who were almost like family and demanding answers about their private lives. But he'd had to do it. He had to find out if Robert Jardine was Kelly's father and if Margee was a killer.

"I assure you, Jack, I strayed only once from my marriage vows. And while I regret it, I don't regret that it gave us Margee,'' Robert told him.

"And neither do I,'' Caroline added. "Do you really believe that if Robert had fathered another child that he would have walked away from her? That I would have let him walk away from her?''

"I don't know who this young woman's father is, son, but I can tell you that it's not me.''

And he believed the man. The pair loved their one child far too much not to have welcomed another. "I'm sorry I had to put you through this,'' Jack said as he stood and prepared to leave.

Robert gave him a curt nod. "I hope you find out who the young woman's father is. No one should be without family.''

Robert Jardine was right. No one should be without family. And Kelly wasn't without family. She had a grandmother—Evelyn Tompkins—and maybe it was time he went back to where it all began.

She'd missed this, Kelly admitted as the hours slipped by over the next two days and she immersed herself in her work. She'd been too busy that first day Jack was gone with Meredith to get into the darkroom. The other woman had exhausted her with all the details that needed attending to following the boutique's preview party. But when the blond dynamo had come knocking on the door that morning ready to start again, she'd drawn the line. Using the honest excuse that she needed to get the party pictures developed, she'd locked herself away in her apartment all day.

What she hadn't expected was how on edge she had been since Jack left. Nor had she been able to stop her thoughts from returning repeatedly to Sister Grace. And while it pained her to realize the nun she had loved and trusted had kept the truth from her all those years, she thought she understood why. She'd been trying to protect her, just as she had protected Lianne all those years ago from the truth about her own birth. And she'd lost her life trying to protect her, Kelly realized.

Anger pulsed through her veins as she thought of the cold-blooded woman who'd plunged that needle into the nun. Her sister. Kelly shuddered at the knowledge. Sister or not, she would keep her promise to Sister Grace. She would see the nun's killer brought to justice no matter what the consequences.

If only she could remember. Recalling how she'd felt that day when she'd touched the cold slab and felt the heat of the flames, her breath grew shallow and she dropped the canisters of film she'd retrieved from her bag. The sound echoed as they rolled across the wooden floor.

She picked up one roll and walked over to pick up the other one that had landed against the wall beneath Lianne's picture. Stooping down, she picked up the film, and as she stood, she stared at the picture. Her mother had painted this, she thought. So why couldn't she feel her? Sense her? She started to remove the picture from the wall to take it from its frame when the telephone rang.

"Hi, Jack," she said, glad to hear from him.

He laughed. "When we're married you're going to save us money on caller ID," he told her, and her heart tripped as he said the words. "Don't go all silent on me, Kelly. You *are* going to marry me."

"Where are you?" she asked, picking up noise in the background.

"I'm at the airport. It's not Margee," he told her.

Kelly sighed with relief. "I'm glad because I liked her." She paused. "Are you coming home now?"

"Not yet. I'm flying into Mississippi. Leon's picking me up at the airport and we're going to Pass Christian to see Evelyn again."

"Why? Has something happened to her?" Kelly asked.

"No. Evelyn's okay, but I don't have time to explain now. I'll be back late this evening. But if I'm not back before Meredith closes up downstairs, I want you to go home with her."

"Jack—"

"Please, Kelly. Don't argue. Just go with her. Do it for me."

"All right," she said finally.

"My flight's boarding. I've got to run. I love you."

"I love you, too," she told him. After she hung up the phone she headed back to the darkroom, where she lost herself in the magic of those moments trapped in time.

Kelly took the strips of film through the development process. Because the emulsion layer of silver halide crystals made the film light sensitive, she took care not to expose it to any light before moving it from the canisters to the development trays. She counted off the seconds needed to fix the latent image on the exposed film, then turned on the safe light. Using the low-intensity red glow of the safe light, she went to work. She picked up the plastic tongs to transfer the negatives to the negative holder first and then to the enlarger. Kelly wasn't sure how long she'd been at work when she heard a tap on the door to her darkroom.

"Kelly, it's Meredith. You in there?"

"Don't open the door," Kelly ordered.

"All right. But it's getting late and Jack said I'm supposed to take you home with me."

Kelly grimaced. "I want to finish up these pictures. You go ahead and I'll meet you later."

"I don't know," Meredith said. "Jack was real specific about not wanting you here by yourself. I'll just hang around until you're ready. Besides, I want to see the pictures. Jesus, Kelly, it's freezing in here."

"Hang on a second," she told her, and made sure she turned off the safe light and protected the film, before exiting the darkroom. One look at Meredith and it was obvious the woman was exhausted. "You look beat."

"I am," Meredith informed her, and rubbed her hands up and down her arms. "Isn't the heat working in here?"

"It is kind of cool." She adjusted the thermostat, but it didn't seem to help. So she turned on the space heater she'd found in the bathroom closet. "That should help some."

"Why don't we go on home and I'll send someone out to check the heater in the morning?" Meredith suggested.

"I really do want to finish up this last roll of film. Tell you what? Why don't you go home, get a bite to eat and come back in a couple of hours? By then I'll be finished and I'll have some proofs ready for you to look at.''

Meredith bit her lip, hesitating. "You're sure?"

"Positive. Go ahead."

Once Meredith left, Kelly returned to the darkroom, where she began studying the enlarged lighted images from the negatives that were projected on the easel. Setting the timer and f-stop to control the amount of light, she stared at the images under the lamp. She went through each negative—the ones she'd taken of Meredith, Alicia and Margee. She paused when she saw the one taken of her with Alicia. Wishing she had told the photographer to adjust the flash, she scanned the first shot in the strip of her, Meredith and Alicia. She scanned the second one he'd taken, studying the three faces. She stopped. It was easy picking Meredith out of the trio as she was in the center and her hair was down. With her and Alicia both wearing their hair up, their features were the primary focus. She shifted her gaze from one face to the other. She noted the slope of the mouths, the smiles, the noses. And were it not for her chin, she'd have been unable to tell which one was Alicia and which one was her.

"Oh, my God!"

Suddenly, Kelly froze. Her heart began to race. The phone rang twice, then stopped in the middle of the third ring. And then she smelled it—smoke.

"Son of a bitch!" Jack punched the car's accelerator, heedless of the speed limit, and cursed himself for not figuring things out sooner. "She's not answering," he told Leon.

"Try her again."

He punched out the number to Kelly's apartment again, but this time he got a busy signal. "It's busy. I'm going to try Meredith's store." But this time he got the answering machine.

Desperate, he tried his sister's cell phone.

"Hello?"

"Meredith, where's Kelly?"

"Jack? Jack is that you?" she asked as static came over the line. Cursing the wind and weak connection, he shouted and prayed she understood him.

Amid the static all he could hear her say was "What?"

Giving up, Jack zigzagged in and out of traffic, ignoring the blare of horns and the several near collisions he caused. "Try your cell phone again," he urged Leon.

Leon did. "It's dead. I forgot to charge the battery last night. I'm sorry, Jackson."

And his battery might have juice, but the weather conditions had evidently taken out a tower, so service was nonexistent. He stared over at the photo of Lianne and her daughter that his partner held. If only he'd thought sooner to check behind the picture frame. Thank God Evelyn had been lucid when he'd gone to her to ask to examine the frame where he'd found the birth certificate—a birth certificate filled out by Martin Gilbert, signed by both Lianne Tompkins and Senator Van Owen, but never filed.

"You think the old lady knew what she was talking about?" Leon asked him.

"Yeah, I do."

Evelyn had told them everything. About Lianne's affair with the senator, his wife's fury when he'd asked for a divorce, the terrible fight between the senator's wife and Kelly's mother. And the fire that was supposed to claim both their lives.

Nearing the city limits, Jack grabbed the cell phone again. The battery light flashed, indicating a low signal. Deciding not to search for Meredith, he called Alex.

"Kusak," he answered on the second ring.

"Alex, it's Jack. I don't have time to explain. Kelly's in danger. You need to get over to the apartment and call the police."

"Where's Meredith?"

"I don't know," Jack told him, and the line went dead.

Kelly fought back the terror that had bile rising in her throat as she smelled the smoke, heard the crackling of flames. She shoved open the door of the darkroom and stepped out into the apartment. The electric space heater glowed as Alicia tore pages from Sister Grace's journals and dropped them atop it. Flames leapt to life. There were small fires all over the room, she realized as Alicia doused her sofa bed with gasoline and tossed a match to it.

"We need to get out of here, Alicia," Kelly said, terrified, yet hoping to reason with the woman.

"You're not going anywhere. This time I'm going to make sure you die."

Panic made her throat tight. Kelly fought it back. "We're both going to die unless we get out of here."

"No," she told her, and the voice sounded so much like a child's. "I was there that night, you know. I was going to burn your room, too, but you locked the door."

"But you were just a child."

"I was old enough to know that you were stealing what was mine," Alicia spat out. "My mother told me how Daddy was going to leave us for you and that whore mother of yours.''

''I heard them arguing,'' Kelly said more to herself than to Alicia, remembering the sound of the woman's raised voice.

''She hit her, then Daddy came. He took my mother home and told your mother that he'd be back. But Daddy didn't know I was there, that I'd gotten out of the car. When he left, I went in and hit her with the fire poker. I always loved fire,'' she said, and Kelly could see the light of madness in her eyes. ''So I grabbed the matches by the fireplace.''

Kelly stared at the curtains now shooting up in flames. She had to get out, had to get past Alicia to the door. Don't panic, she told herself. The smoke alarm would go off and then the sprinkler would come on. It would be all right. Everything would be all right.

Only it wasn't happening. There was no scream from the smoke alarm, no water spitting out and dousing the flames. Don't panic, she told herself again. Any moment now, the alarm and water sprinkler would go off. Then someone would come. Jack would come.

''No one's going to come to save you this time. The smoke detector and sprinkler don't work. You see, I never did get around to returning the key that Peter gave me to this building when I had it listed and was looking for a tenant. Before that little bitch Meredith came alone and took over everything. So I used my key to come in here and take the battery out of the smoke alarm. Then I disconnected the sprinkler.''

Oh, God, no one was coming.

''That's right, Sarah. No one is coming to save you this time.''

Stunned that she'd known what she'd been thinking,

Kelly stared at the other woman. Alicia laughed and the sound sent a chill through Kelly's blood.

"I told you my grandmother was fey. Did you think you were the only one who could sense things?" Suddenly the smile died, turning to a look of bitter hatred. "But you even stole that from me. Mine was never as strong as yours is. Maybe once you're dead it will be."

Kelly began to cough. "Alicia, we're sisters."

"No," the other woman shouted. "I'm my daddy's girl, not you. I killed you. You should have stayed dead."

Kelly coughed again, tried to fight back the panic. Aware that Alicia could read her thoughts, she tried to blank her mind as she searched for a way to escape.

"Daddy forgave me, you know. He realized what I had done when he came back that night and found the house burning and me outside watching it. I told him that I'd killed you because you'd try to take him away from me. He promised me that I would always be his little girl and he'd never leave me. But he lied." She struck another match and tossed it into a corner, where it began to lick at the walls.

"He didn't leave you," Kelly pointed out. "He died in an accident with your mother. Remember? You told me about it."

"He died because he lied to me. All those years he paid that bastard Gilbert not to tell anyone I set the fire, and then Gilbert found out that bitch nurse of his got you out. He told Daddy you were alive and Daddy was going to leave me for you."

"No, he wasn't, Alicia. He loved you," Kelly said, and began to edge her way toward the door.

"No, he didn't. If he did, he wouldn't have written up that new will. He was going to leave you half of everything—everything that was mine! But I fixed him. He and Mother had a little accident.''

Horrified by the other woman's admission, Kelly moved a few more steps toward the door.

''Get back,'' Alicia told her. ''It's your fault he's dead. It's your fault that nun is dead, too. She said Daddy contacted her before he died. She said she had proof that he wanted you to know about him and she was going to tell you.''

''What proof?''

''I don't know. She wouldn't tell me. Just like she wouldn't tell me what name you were using. But I knew if I got rid of her, you'd come back.''

''It was you in the chapel that night. You killed her.''

''Yes,'' Alicia admitted, grinning insanely. ''You had me worried for a while that you knew it was me. That's why I found you at the party that night, and tested you. But you didn't know. You couldn't see it was me.''

No. She hadn't been able to see it was Alicia because her sister had been filled with a darkness, an emptiness of heart, of emotion, of soul. One of the crown moldings fell, slamming down on the floor and shooting flames across the wood flooring like an arrow.

In the distance, Kelly could hear the fire engine sirens. But she knew too well that the narrow streets of the French Quarter were never designed for safety and one of the greatest dangers to the old buildings was fire. They would never get here in time. ''Alicia, we have to get out of here. The whole place is going up. We'll both die.''

''I won't. I'm not afraid of fire like you are. I like the fire.''

When Alicia grabbed Lianne's watercolor and started

to toss it into the flames, Kelly charged her, tore it from the other woman's hands and stumbled toward the door.

Alicia tackled her. Kelly kicked at her, got up and started for the door again. When Alicia grabbed at her once more, Kelly swung around and hit her with the painting, using all her might. Alicia fell back into the burning window. Alicia screamed. And arms flaying, she fell out of the window onto the street below.

Horrified Kelly turned away. Sobbing, she stared at the door and the flames licking around it. Paralyzed by fear, she couldn't move. She stood there clutching the painting, tears streaming down her cheeks as she gasped for breath. Suddenly the past and present blurred.

Have to get out. Have to get out. But I'm afraid. I'm afraid. Hurry! Hurry!

"It's Nana Eve. Where are you? Unlock the door! You have to unlock the door."

"Kelly, it's Jack. Kelly, are you in there? Unlock the door, Kelly. Unlock the door."

Kelly heard Jack at the door, heard the slam of body weight against the thick wood. But it didn't give.

"Sarah, it's Nana Eve. Sarah, hang on baby. Hang on, I'll get you out."

"Kelly, hang on, baby. Hang on, I'll get you out."

Suddenly Kelly raced to the door. She screamed as she turned the locks, singeing her fingers on the hot metal. And then Jack was grabbing her, scooping her up in his arms and rushing down the stairs with her.

The cold air hit her like a slap in the face as they exited the burning building. People were all around, fire truck sirens screaming, flashing red lights everywhere.

"Where is she?" Alex demanded as he hurried up the street to where Jack stood with Kelly. "Is Meredith still inside? Jesus! Tell me where she is!"

When he started to barge past a fireman, he was blocked. "You can't go in there, fella."

"I've got to. Let me by."

"Alex! Alex, here I am," Meredith cried out, and rushed over and into Alex's open arms. "Oh, Alex. It was awful. Kelly was inside and I couldn't get there. And—"

"Thank God," Alex said, and held her close. "When I got here and saw the building in flames…I thought…" A breath shuddered through him. "God, Meredith, I thought I'd lost you."

"I'm here. But Kelly almost died and the shop's gone," she said, weeping against his chest.

"I don't give a damn about the shop. We'll build another one. I thought I'd lost you and I never told you I loved you."

"What?"

"You heard me. I love you and if you're crazy enough to still want me, we're getting married."

"Oh, Alex," Meredith cried, and threw her arms around him.

But Kelly didn't hear what followed next because the coughing started again and so did the shivering. "Hang on, baby. Hang on," Jack told her. "Where in the hell is the ambulance?"

As if in answer, the red-and-white vehicle came tearing down the street with sirens blaring and lights flashing.

"We'll take her now, sir," the paramedic told him moments later.

"Jack," she called, and began coughing again as they lifted her onto a stretcher. Despite the coughs racking her body, she reached out for him with one hand while she held on to her mother's painting with the other as they lifted her into the back of the ambulance.

He climbed in beside her and held her hand. "I'm right here, baby. I'm right here."

The paramedic put an oxygen mask on her face. She pulled it away to speak. "Jack, there's so much I need to tell you—"

He shoved the thing back on her face. "There's a lot I have to tell you, too. But we'll tell each other later. In the meantime, feel free to take a peek inside me and see how much I love you, what kind of life I have planned for us."

But she didn't have to look inside him. She had only to look inside herself now to know that she was loved for who she was. That she'd had parents who'd loved and wanted her. That she had a grandmother who'd risked her own life to save hers. That she and Jack would have a life together. That she was home and she had a family.

A home and a family. The two things she'd wanted all her life. And now they were hers.

METSY HINGLE

66926 BEHIND THE MASK   ___ $6.50 U.S. ___ $7.99 CAN.
66826 THE WAGER   ___ $5.99 U.S. ___ $6.99 CAN.

(limited quantities available)

TOTAL AMOUNT $_____
POSTAGE & HANDLING $_____
($1.00 for 1 book, 50¢ for each additional)
APPLICABLE TAXES* $_____
<u>TOTAL PAYABLE</u> $_____
(check or money order—please do not send cash)

To order, complete this form and send it, along with a check or money order for the total above, payable to MIRA Books, to: **In the U.S.:** 3010 Walden Avenue, P.O. Box 9077, Buffalo, NY 14269-9077; **In Canada:** P.O. Box 636, Fort Erie, Ontario, L2A 5X3.

Name:_____
Address:_____ City:_____
State/Prov.:_____ Zip/Postal Code:_____
Account Number (if applicable):_____
075 CSAS

*New York residents remit applicable sales taxes.
 Canadian residents remit applicable GST
 and provincial taxes.

MIRA®